THE FINEST SHORT FICTION OF A REMARKABLE DECADE AS SEEN THROUGH THE EYES OF A BRILLIANTLY GIFTED WRITER

The 1980s was one of the most remarkable decades for short stories in the entire history of science fiction. A talented new generation of writers transformed the field by combining high literary quality with highly entertaining storytelling.

In *Future on Fire*, award-winning author and critic Orson Scott Card presents a selection of incandescent visions from fifteen of the decade's most gifted writers:

Pat Cadigan	Ursula K. Le Guin	Lucius Shepard
Felix C. Gotschalk	Pat Murphy	Bruce Sterling
William Gibson	Susan Palwick	Michael Swanwick
Gregg Keizer	Rachel Pollack	Wayne Wightman
James Patrick Kelly	Kim Stanley Robinson	Connie Willis

These are not ''safe'' stories. Card has deliberately chosen stories that provoke and infuriate; that challenge our most cherished assumptions about ourselves and our future.

But *Future on Fire* is more than a collection of exceptional short fiction. In his opening essay and his critical introductions to each story in this volume, Card provides a unique and insightful perspective on this astonishing period, and on the dazzling talents who emerged from it.

Within these pages you'll discover a provocative array of possible futures. But be warned: these stories are incendiary. They will alter forever the way you view your world.

D0018500

Tor Books by Orson Scott Card

Future on
FIRE

EDITED AND INTRODUCED BY

Orson Scott
CARD

TOR

A TOM DOHERTY ASSOCIATES BOOK

FUTURE ON FIRE

Copyright © 1991 by Orson Scott Card

A Tor Book
Published by Tom Doherty Associates, Inc.
49 West 24th Street
New York, N.Y. 10010

Cover art by Ron Walotsky

ISBN: 0-812-51183-2

First printing: February 1991

Printed in the United States of America

0 9 8 7 6 5 4 3 2 1

Acknowledgments

"Rachel in Love" by Pat Murphy copyright © by Pat Murphy. First published in *Isaac Asimov's Science Fiction Magazine*. Reprinted by permission of Jean V. Naggar Literary Agency.

"Dogfight" by Michael Swanwick and William Gibson copyright © 1985 by Omni Publications International Ltd. Reprinted by arrangement with the authors.

"A Gift from the GrayLanders" by Michael Bishop copyright © 1985 by Davis Publications, Inc. Reprinted by arrangement with the author and his agent, Howard Morhaim.

"Fire Zone Emerald" by Lucius Shepard copyright © 1987 by Lucius Shepard. Reprinted by permission of the Schaffner Agency.

"Down and Out in the Year 2000" by Kim Stanley Robinson copyright © 1986 by Kim Stanley Robinson. First appeared in *Isaac Asimov's Science Fiction Magazine*. Reprinted by permission of the author.

"Angel Baby" by Rachel Pollack copyright © 1982 by Rachel Pollack. First published in *Interzone*, Summer 1982. Reprinted by permission of the author.

"The Neighbor's Wife" by Susan Palwick copyright © 1985 by Susan Palwick. Reprinted from *Amazing Stories*, May 1985, by permission of the author.

Contents

Contents

Introduction:

Science Fiction in the 1980s

IT'S 1925. YOU'RE EDITOR OF *BLUE BOOK*, AND YOU START READ-ing a manuscript just submitted by Ruffin Reddy, well known as a hack for the cheapest pulps. Obviously he is submitting a story to you so he can break into a better market—but you can't imagine why he thought *this* story would do the job.

His story is set in Germany in 1943. A really far-out yarn about how a future Germany is ruled by an insane Austrian painter who served as a non-com in the World War. This mad-man maneuvered his way into the office of chancellor during a worldwide depression, then jailed all his opponents and won the next election by arranging to have the Reichstag set ablaze and claiming the Left did it. Then he proceeded to occupy the Rhineland, forcibly unite Austria with Germany, and conquer Czechoslovakia—without Britain, France, or Russia firing a shot! The story claims that by 1943 he rules most of Europe, his Japanese allies control a vast empire in the Pacific and East Asia, and his concentration camps become death factories, slaughtering millions of Jews, gypsies, and other "undesir-ables."

Such nonsense! Nobody could believe this story! The

mature, serious leadership of Germany would never allow such an obvious madman to get control of the machinery of state. The German people would never acquiesce in genocide. And besides, this is *1925*, and it is impossible to believe that Germany, economically shattered and completely demilitarized, could ever again challenge the army of France or the British fleet.

What? Reddy claims that France will fall in a couple of *weeks*?

"We regret to inform you that your story 'Schickelgruber's Reich' does not meet our present needs." A form rejection letter, just to make sure Ruffin Reddy gets the point. But—to encourage him—you scribble a personal note underneath: "I like the way you write. Perhaps if you try a story that sticks a little closer to what is possible in the real world, our readers will find it acceptable."

Science fiction writers don't predict the future—nobody would believe our stories if we did. The real course of events is too improbable. Ronald Reagan president? An invasion of Grenada? The Party Secretary of Russia proposing serious disarmament? Capitalism in Communist China? Fax machines? Digital audio virtually replacing vinyl records? Get real. Couldn't happen.

Besides, most of us don't believe that there *is* such a thing as "the future" anyway. There are choices. There are fulcrums of history, where the will of a people—sometimes even the will of an individual—can make a difference.

Yet people can't make choices they don't see. So we show alternatives. We give our readers the experience of living in futures that are the consequence of certain choices. Choices we're making right now.

This makes science fiction potentially the realest of realistic storytelling. We don't just tell you how things *are*. We can show you how things might end up *because* of the way things are.

But is that why you read science fiction?

Partly, yes. Science fiction is not read by stupid people. It demands so much intelligent participation on the part of the reader that even the dumbest science fiction requires strenuous mental exercise. And most of that stretching arises from the fact that science fiction, by definition, takes place somewhere else. Somewhere strange. Somewhere that does not yet exist, that never has existed in this world. In order to receive a science fiction story in the first place, the reader must perform the radical act of imagining what he has never seen, mapping out an undiscovered territory from the landmarks and clues in the story. This process is so central to science fiction that those readers who are unwilling or unable to collaborate in the act of *radical imagination* do not—cannot—read it at all. Ironically, when these incapable readers discover that science fiction makes no sense to them, they usually come to the conclusion that they hate "sci-fi" because it's "too unrealistic."

So sad. Because these incapables will go through life thinking that the real world consists only of the present situation. Unable to conceive of a future different from the present, they are also generally unable to conceive of changing the present in order to control the future. And yet, poor things, they are fated to live in the future someday. Willing or not, they will be plunged into that strange and terrible land, but they will be completely unprepared because they were unable—or unwilling—to perform the act of radical imagination.

Not that science fiction readers will be prepared for exactly the future that comes. There *are* people who think they actually know the future. Like the survivalists who store up food and ammunition, plotting exactly how many of their hungry neighbors they can kill when anarchy comes. That level of fanaticism—almost a religious commitment to a dark future where they will be knights of a new feudalism—has nothing to do with science fiction.

Rather, the readers of science fiction are prepared for *many* futures. Dozens, hundreds, thousands of times they have lived through the process of apprehending a surprising new reality. No matter what the future is, they already know the process: recognize contradiction between the familiar vision of the way things are and the new order; extrapolate from the contradictions a new system of cause and effect; reconstruct a vision of the way things are that includes and accommodates the former contradictions; invent your own role in the new order; act according to your new role and new vision of reality.

Contradiction, extrapolation, reconstruction, self-invention, action—a mental system that is as familiar to science fiction readers as breathing. Who's the realist? The reader of Updike, or the reader of Asimov?

Oddly, though, the most powerful expression of this science-fictional futurethink is generally not in the novels that fill the sf/fantasy section of Waldenbooks. With rare exceptions, novels create only one new future order, and they have hundreds of pages in which to familiarize the reader with what's going on. You can slide more easily into the strange new world, because there's more time to get used to the changes.

Short stories are another matter entirely. With only five or ten thousand words to work with, the writer can't provide the reader with as much help, as many hints. Radical imagination is sharper, more startling, more painful. The result? Many readers of science fiction novels find the short stories too difficult, too challenging. Too *sudden*. Most people who consider themselves science fiction readers never read any of the science fiction magazines or anthologies.

Yet it is in the shorter lengths that each new generation of science fiction writers reinvents the field. Long before William Gibson's novel *Neuromancer* led American trend-seekers to discover the word *Cyberpunk* and twist it into nonmeaning. Cyberpunk existed, unnamed, in the short stories of Bruce Sterling, William Gibson, and Lew Shiner, and gradually reached out to embrace kindred spirits like Rudy Rucker, Pat Cadigan, and Michael Swanwick. Long before book editors felt it was safe to sink thousands of bucks into these writers' novels, magazine editors took a chance on their startling, sometimes infuriating voices. And magazine readers—the cutting edge of the science fiction audience—recognized these stories as the revolution they were meant to be.

In fact, the Cyberpunk revolution was virtually over before anybody outside the short-story audience even knew it was going on. A case might be made for the idea that as soon as a style or author or philosophy becomes familiar and safe enough for a book editor to be willing to risk serious money on it—making it a lead title, putting some effort behind it—then it is already too familiar and safe to be considered revolutionary. (There are exceptions—the late Terry Carr's Ace Specials in mid-decade; David Hartwell at Pocket, then Arbor House, now

Morrow. But risk-taking book editors are almost as rare as marsupial hippopotamuses.)

Cyberpunk got all the attention, but it wasn't the only revolution in the 1980s. Each new writer with clear vision and powerful talent is a small revolution.

Most new writers, of course, don't fit into that category. Most new writers are in the field, not because their own vision and talent drove them to tell stories, but rather because they fell in love with somebody else's vision and talent. They loved Zelazny or Asimov or Anthony or Tolkien so much that they wanted to write "just like that." The plethora of Star Trek novels are a sad testimony—imagine, people who think that Gene Roddenberry's shallow, empty characters are so intriguing that they want to write *more* of the series. Instead of radically imagining anything for themselves, they are content to tat a bit of lace onto the fringes of the shabby Star Trek tapestry.

But the Star Trek novels are just a symptom of this. To varying degrees, many other writers produce works that say more about their reading list than about their own thoughts and dreams and experiences. How many imitations of J.R.R. Tolkien, Stephen King, or—nowadays—William Gibson must they write before they become dissatisfied with repetition?

I wonder sometimes if the motivation for writers ought to be contempt, not admiration.

One writer looks at what's being published and says, "Oh, if only I could write like that! I'm going to try! Maybe someday I can do that well!"

Another looks at the same stuff and says, "Is this the best they can do? If these guys can publish, anybody *can*. *I* could!"

Shoot me for a cynic, but I think it's the second writer who's more likely to be able to perform the act of radical imagination—the second writer who will produce science fiction that lives up to what science fiction ought to be. It isn't because the second writer is negative—the act of telling stories is a positive, constructive act; even the most negative story by its very existence makes a positive statement. It's because the second writer recognizes that there is a hole in the world that only his own stories can fill.

I'm being unfair. Even the writer of the most adoring Star Trek novel still brings something of himself or herself to the work. It is impossible to tell a story without making some transformations; it is impossible to tell a story without some dependence on work that has gone before. It's a matter of degree. The same writer will seem derivative to one reader, revolutionary to another, depending on whether readers notice or care about the kind of transformations a particular writer has made.

There are great landmark books of science fiction, but even if you read all of them, you would probably not understand the field. In every decade, short fiction has led the way. It's good to remember that even some noted science fiction novelists—Isaac Asimov, for instance—did all their most important work as short fiction. Asimov's robot novels grew out of his robot stories. The Foundation series began as a series of short pieces, collected into book form only as an afterthought. And some of the most important writers in the field have never written anything significant at book length: Harlan Ellison, for instance, and Ray Bradbury.

When I speak of "shorter lengths," though, I must point out that science fiction doesn't follow the rules for other fictional forms when it comes to length. That aspect of science fiction that makes it uniquely itself—its strange milieu—takes time to create. The reader approaches a science fiction story not knowing where he is. The writer must take time to tell him. Where a writer in another genre can drop clues like "San Francisco . . . hippies . . . Hashbury" or "London . . . carriage . . . parasol" to put you in a fairly familiar time and place, the science fiction writer can't get by with such easy shorthand. There must be far more explanation about how the world of the story functions. The politics. The physics. The geology. The sociology. All might be different, and so all must have at least a few words devoted to them.

The result is that the science fiction short story almost always comes in at novelette length. A tale that minimalists could tell in two thousand words or realists in four thousand will use up seven, ten, or twelve thousand words when developed as science fiction. This is not filler, not extra verbiage. It simply takes longer to help readers orient themselves in a strange place.

Thus the science fiction short story of less than 7,500 words is a very difficult length, which requires either excellence or carelessness on the part of the writer: excellence to write with such extraordinary economy that a good science fiction story can be told so briefly; carelessness to invent such a shallow milieu or to explain a good milieu so feebly that the story, good or bad, is barely told at all.

Novelette length—7,500–17,500 words—is the optimum length for short science fiction. Anything longer and the work usually ceases to function as short fiction at all—it becomes novelistic, and must be received in a different way by the reader. Anything shorter, and it becomes very difficult to make it good as science fiction, even if it remains good as something else.

At novelette length, a writer can experiment. There's enough space to do something really fine; yet it doesn't take as much time and paper as a novel. There's not as much lost when a novelette fails as when a novel fails. Perhaps more important, it's *hard* to do something new—you're feeling your way through, exploring, discovering, building as you go. But it's not quite as hard at novelette length. A novelette can be grasped whole; it's easier to see it clearly, to understand what you're actually doing as you experiment and explore.

Also, short science fiction is extremely important to the field because most new writers first reach print in the magazines and anthologies. There's a circular reason for this. Because short fiction pays so badly and novels often pay much better, there is financial pressure for a short-fiction writer to attempt something longer. The result is often quite bad—the first novels of many fine short-story writers are pretentious, and rather embarrassing in retrospect. I am far from being the only writer to be glad that his first novel is no longer in print—and I know several others who *should* say a requiem for their first novels.

Eventually, though, most writers make the transition to longer works, and many—myself included—discover that it's very hard to go back again. The novel length gives the writer so much elbow room that it's hard to get back into short-fiction mode, with its much less sprawling exposition and fewer, more tightly-packed scenes. There's also little incentive to go back to shorter work *unless* you're consciously experimenting or have one of those rare ideas whose natural expression is at novelette length.

So magazine and anthology editors must discover new writers, bring them along, and then lose them to the book editors, so they have to go back and discover new writers all over again. The book editors, in the meantime, can do as book editors do in every other field—try to buy work that is already certifiably safe. After magazine appearances have made a new writer seem safe and familiar—or even acceptably revolutionary—it doesn't take much courage to buy their first book, especially for a couple or three thousand bucks. But short-fiction editors live on the edge all the time, trying to discern the difference between unpublishable incompetence and quirky, unusual new voices.

The good short-fiction editors *can* see the difference, at least often enough to stay in business. And it's in those quirky new voices that science fiction finds its elixir of life. For this is a field that absolutely requires strangeness, and while rigorous science fiction writers *will* continue inventing new milieus, what they *can't* keep inventing is new selves. Even as their stories (and novels) take place in new settings—sometimes with new characters—the readers begin to find the more subtle, inescapable patterns and familiarities in every writer's *oeuvre*. Even those writers who try to keep reinventing their very selves can only succeed to a superficial degree—fundamental verities remain in the unconscious, showing up in ways that the writer can't recognize because he can't conceive of a story being written any other way.

As a result, it takes infusions of new blood to keep the field growing and changing—to keep it perpetually strange. In ways they are not even aware of, new writers bring new vision. Ironically, few new writers have the experience and craft to clothe that new vision in truly fine fiction; and by the time they *have* the skill to do it, their vision usually doesn't seem all that new anymore. Only a few writers master their craft early enough in their careers to both surprise and satisfy the audience; even fewer are then able to maintain the same high level of intelligence and artistry throughout their career. Even some of the great ones stumble. They were at the forefront in the forties or fifties or sixties. Yet they are not among the best writers of today.

Who are the writers of the 1980s? Some of the grand old

names in the field were still alive in this decade, still producing strong work—but most of these had settled comfortably into rigor vivis, doing nothing to refresh and invigorate the field. They may have excellent works copyrighted within the decade—but they grew out of the sensibility of another time. They were not stories of the eighties.

Some fine writers either never wrote short fiction at all or don't write important short fiction anymore. They may be contributing, but not at lengths that can be anthologized.

And many new writers have come along whose work is so empty or derivative or clumsy or simply *young* that they have little impact on readers or other writers. They are not helping to reinvent science fiction, not yet anyway; their presence has not helped us think new thoughts because they're still busy learning the craft or rewriting the stories they admired from the decades before. Some of them will certainly become important and transformative, but their time is not yet here.

The writers of the 1980s are those who changed us all, often quite against our will. Some have become famous in the process—some of them even a little bit rich—but that's not the measure I'm using. Some of the best and most important remain fairly obscure, for the time being, but their stories live on in the memories of those lucky enough to have read them. Our world is transformed because they took their place by the communal fire and spun their yarns for whatever audience would listen.

Anyway, you can't judge a storyteller by the size of his audience. Many writers have small audiences because they're no good—but others have few readers because their vision is so strange and challenging that few readers have the wit or will to read their work. Some writers have large audiences because their stories please people who want to be tickled or touched, but never challenged; their audiences come away flattered but unfilled. Other writers have large audiences because their work is so powerful, so truthful, and so clearly presented that many people come to have their memories, their very selves, remade by a master. The size of a writer's audience tells you something about the audience. It tells you nothing about the writer.

* * *

Future on Fire is the first volume of a series that will collect, not all the "best" stories of the 1980s, but rather representative stories from all who are, in my judgment, the major short-fiction *writers* of the eighties. But that is not my only standard. The story also has to be one that I found moving, exciting, believable, clear. In other words, *good*. As any survivor of a college literature course knows quite well, there are many "major" works that are as fun to read as sociological reports on statistical surveys. These works are forced on college students the way cod liver oil used to be forced on helpless children. To my mind, fiction that tastes like medicine is no damn good. If it isn't a wonderful story *first*, who cares how "important" it is?

So in this book you will read stories by important writers, yes—but you don't have to care diddly-squat about their importance. You can read them for the power and joy of living in the worlds these writers have created. You can inhale the memories they have prepared for you, and let all their philosophical, scientific, and stylistic innovation glide right past.

By the time you're through, you'll know you were in the hands of masters, and in many cases you'll be a bit angry that you've never heard of this or that writer before. Where was this guy all my life? *This* is what I've always wished science fiction could be, without knowing that I was wishing for it. These storytellers matter, not because they fit some preconceived literary theory, but rather because when you're through reading their stories, you have been changed. These stories matter because they matter to *you*.

How do I know? I don't. All I *know*, all I can *possibly* know, is that they matter to *me*. In many cases, of course, there are other critics who agree with me. In other cases, though, I'm quite aware that I'm a voice crying in the wilderness. Nevertheless, I don't put these stories forward as a personal list—my favorite stories of the eighties. That would be one kind of anthology, but it would not be this one. Heck, I *hated* some of these stories. But I hated them for all the right reasons. They made me angry. They made me think. They made me feel. They made me remember. They *changed* me. And I dare to believe that they'll change you, too.

Who am I to decide? How dare I say which writers are

"major" and, by implication, relegate all others to secondary status? I dare it because it must be dared—by someone, at least—if only so that wiser minds can argue with my choices and, by arguing, clarify my vision. I also dare it because few other critics in this field have read as much of the short science fiction of the eighties as I have. A few best-of-the-year editors—Gardner Dozois, Art Saha, Terry Carr before he died. I don't pretend that I've read *all* the short fiction of the 1980s—but in many of the years of this decade I have read virtually everything published, and in the process I've become or remained familiar with the writers who were inventing and transforming our genre. As a critic, I've put my judgments on the line by publishing them, both in Richard E. Geis's *Science Fiction Review* and, later, my own occasional magazine *Short Form.* I've also kept up with what others were saying about them.

Some of these writers are friends of mine, but they became my friends only after I had come to admire and delight in their fiction. Most of these writers are barely acquaintances of mine; some are quite openly hostile to the kind of fiction I write and the kind of fiction I urge others to write. Some were even reluctant to let their stories be used in this anthology because we have locked horns before, on matters we both regard as important. In other words, this series is not an anthology of Uncle Orson's best buddies. This series is my honest summing-up of the decade's most important writers—whether or not I personally liked the authors or what they stand for.

It is possible that when the series is complete I will have left out one of your favorites; it is likely that I'll have included writers you never heard of. What is impossible is for you to read these volumes and remain unchanged, unmoved, uninterested. These writers have returned from the flames of the futures that live in their imaginations—come near the fire now and singe yourself.

—Orson Scott Card, January 1989

Rachel in Love
by Pat Murphy

Introduction

Most writers are pretty ordinary-looking people, not worth describing. When we look unusual it's usually on the side of gawkiness or geekishness, for ours is a profession that doesn't require us to make a strong personal impression; rather it requires us to hole up for days and weeks on end with no one but a forgiving family and a typewriter or computer for company.

But some writers do choose to present themselves with a degree of flamboyance. Some festoon themselves like cockatoos; others collect an audience by being loud, outrageous, or otherwise entertaining. Still others use their costume to declare allegiance—or at least association—with a group or movement that rejects ordinary, conventional dress.

Pat Murphy presents herself with hair cropped punkishly short, with a slender rat-tail slithering down her back. An air of cocky confidence, almost a swagger as she walks. Somehow you know at once that she'll never write a sentence like: "With heaving bosom and quavering voice she said. 'Long have I waited for you to speak of your feelings, my beloved Malcolm, so I could utter mine.' "

But her writing is passionate, and not with the angry posing we have learned to associate with the punk look. Her work is touched with neither nihilism nor rejection of society; far from being universally angry, she writes with a tough kind of compassion. The star of her stories is never herself, never the strutting writer demanding that we notice how clever and socially aware she is. Her focus is absolutely on a character in pain—in pain, but not ready to surrender.

Indeed, in one sense her fiction often follows in one of the strongest traditions in science fiction—the hero who relies on his own brains and guts to get out of his predicament. But many of these traditional "competent man" heroes are so smug you want to grab them and strangle them while shouting, "Look, Bozo, I could look just as smart as you if I had a writer making the rest of the world fit in with my plans!" Murphy's heroes arouse, not my resentment, but my sympathy, my admiration.

"Rachel in Love," though, is something extraordinary, even for a writer of such obvious talent. It won the Nebula for best novelette of 1987, but that doesn't begin to suggest what this story achieves. What "Nightfall" has been to Isaac Asimov, what "The Star" has been to Arthur C. Clark—that is what "Rachel in Love" will surely be to Pat Murphy. I suspect she'll come to curse this story in the future, as readers say to her over and over again, "Why don't you ever write anything like 'Rachel' anymore?" But she will never really regret having written it, just as you will never regret reading it. Once you have lived through this experience of losing everything and everyone you love, losing even your own body, becoming an alien creature in your own land, and yet finding new love and new hope, it will remain part of you forever.

IT IS A SUNDAY MORNING IN SUMMER AND A SMALL BROWN chimpanzee named Rachel sits on the living room floor of a remote ranch house on the edge of the Painted Desert. She is watching a Tarzan movie on television. Her hairy arms are wrapped around her knees and she rocks back and forth with suppressed excitement. She knows that her father would say that she's too old for such childish amusements—but since Aaron is still sleeping, he can't chastise her.

On the television, Tarzan has been trapped in a bamboo cage by a band of wicked Pygmies. Rachel is afraid that he won't escape in time to save Jane from the ivory smugglers who hold her captive. The movie cuts to Jane, who is tied up in the back of a jeep, and Rachel whimpers softly to herself. She knows better than to howl: she peeked into her father's bedroom earlier, and he was still in bed. Aaron doesn't like her to howl when he is sleeping.

When the movie breaks for a commercial, Rachel goes to her father's room. She is ready for breakfast and she wants him to get up. She tiptoes to the bed to see if he is awake.

His eyes are open and he is staring at nothing. His face is pale and his lips are a purplish color. Dr. Aaron Jacobs, the man Rachel calls father, is not asleep. He is dead, having died in the night of a heart attack.

When Rachel shakes him, his head rocks back and forth in time with her shaking, but his eyes do not blink and he does not breathe. She places his hand on her head, nudging him so that he will waken and stroke her. He does not move. When she leans toward him, his hand falls limply to dangle over the edge of the bed.

In the breeze from the open bedroom window, the fine wisps of gray hair that he had carefully combed over his bald spot each morning shift and flutter, exposing the naked scalp. In the other room, elephants trumpet as they stampede across the jungle to rescue Tarzan. Rachel whimpers softly, but her father does not move.

Rachel backs away from her father's body. In the living room, Tarzan is swinging across the jungle on vines, going to save Jane. Rachel ignores the television. She prowls through the house as if searching for comfort—stepping into her own small bedroom, wandering through her father's laboratory. From the cages that line the walls, white rats stare at her with hot red eyes. A rabbit hops across its cage, making a series of slow dull thumps, like a feather pillow tumbling down a flight of stairs.

She thinks that perhaps she made a mistake. Perhaps her

father is just sleeping. She returns to the bedroom, but nothing has changed. Her father lies open-eyed on the bed. For a long time, she huddles beside his body, clinging to his hand.

He is the only person she has ever known. He is her father, her teacher, her friend. She cannot leave him alone.

The afternoon sun blazes through the window, and still Aaron does not move. The room grows dark, but Rachel does not turn on the lights. She is waiting for Aaron to wake up. When the moon rises, its silver light shines through the window to cast a bright rectangle on the far wall.

Outside, somewhere in the barren rocky land surrounding the ranch house, a coyote lifts its head to the rising moon and wails, a thin sound that is as lonely as a train whistling through an abandoned station. Rachel joins in with a desolate howl of loneliness and grief. Aaron lies still and Rachel knows that he is dead.

When Rachel was younger, she had a favorite bedtime story. —Where did I come from? she would ask Aaron, using the abbreviated gestures of ASL, American Sign Language. —Tell me again.

"You're too old for bedtime stories," Aaron would say.

—Please, she'd sign. —Tell me the story.

In the end, he always relented and told her. "Once upon a time, there was a good little girl named Rachel," he said. "She was a pretty girl, with long golden hair like a princess in a fairy tale. She lived with her father and her mother and they were all very happy."

Rachel would snuggle contentedly beneath her blankets. The story, like any good fairy tale, had elements of tragedy. In the story, Rachel's father worked at a university, studying the workings of the brain and charting the electric fields that the nervous impulses of an active brain produced. But the other researchers at the university didn't understand Rachel's father; they distrusted his research and cut off his funding. (During this portion of the story, Aaron's voice took on a bitter edge.) So he left the university and took his wife and daughter to the desert, where he could work in peace.

He continued his research and determined that each individual brain produced its own unique pattern of fields, as characteristic as a fingerprint. (Rachel found this part of the story quite dull, but Aaron insisted on including it.) The shape of this "Electric Mind," as he called it, was determined by habitual patterns of thoughts and emotions. Record the Electric Mind, he postulated, and you could capture an individual's personality.

Then one sunny day, the doctor's wife and beautiful daughter went for a drive. A truck barreling down a winding cliffside road lost its brakes and met the car head-on, killing both the girl and her mother. (Rachel clung to Aaron's hand during this part of the story, frightened by the sudden evil twist of fortune.)

But though Rachel's body had died, all was not lost. In his desert lab, the doctor had recorded the electrical patterns produced by his daughter's brain. The doctor had been experimenting with the use of external magnetic fields to impose the patterns from one animal onto the brain of another. From an animal supply house, he obtained a young chimpanzee. He used a mixture of norepinephrine-based transmitter substances to boost the speed of neural processing in the chimp's brain, and then he imposed the pattern of his daughter's mind upon the brain of this young chimp, combined the two after his own fashion, saving his daughter in his own way. In the chimp's brain was all that remained of Rachel Jacobs.

The doctor named the chimp Rachel and raised her as his own daughter. Since the limitations of the chimpanzee larynx made speech very difficult, he instructed her in ASL. He taught her to read and to write. They were good friends, the best of companions.

By this point in the story, Rachel was usually asleep. But it didn't matter—she knew the ending. The doctor, whose name was Aaron Jacobs, and the chimp named Rachel lived happily ever after.

Rachel likes fairy tales and she likes happy endings. She has the mind of a teenage girl, but the innocent heart of a young chimp.

Sometimes, when Rachel looks at her gnarled brown fingers, they seem alien, wrong, out of place. She remembers having small, pale, delicate hands. Memories lie upon memories, layers upon layers, like the sedimentary rocks of the desert buttes.

Rachel remembers a blond-haired fair-skinned woman who smelled sweetly of perfume. On a Halloween long ago, this woman (who was, in these memories, Rachel's mother) painted Rachel's fingernails bright red because Rachel was dressed as a gypsy and gypsies like red. Rachel remembers the woman's hands: white hands with faintly blue veins hidden just beneath the skin, neatly clipped nails painted rose pink.

But Rachel also remembers another mother and another time. Her mother was dark and hairy and smelled sweetly of overripe fruit. She and Rachel lived in a wire cage in a room filled with chimps and she hugged Rachel to her hairy breast whenever any people came into the room. Rachel's mother groomed Rachel constantly, picking delicately through her fur in search of lice that she never found.

Memories upon memories: jumbled and confused, like random pictures clipped from magazines, a bright collage that makes no sense. Rachel remembers cages: cold wire mesh beneath her feet, the smell of fear around her. A man in a white lab coat took her from the arms of her hairy mother and pricked her with needles. She could hear her mother howling, but she could not escape from the man.

Rachel remembers a junior high school dance where she wore a new dress: she stood in a dark corner of the gym for hours, pretending to admire the crepe paper decorations because she felt too shy to search among the crowd for her friends.

She remembers when she was a young chimp: she huddled with five other adolescent chimps in the stuffy freight compartment of a train, frightened by the alien smells and sounds.

She remembers gym class: gray lockers and ugly gym suits that revealed her skinny legs. The teacher made everyone play softball, even Rachel who was unathletic and painfully shy. Rachel at bat, standing at the plate, was terrified to be the center of attention. "Easy out," said the catcher, a hard-edged girl who ran with the wrong crowd and always smelled of cigarette smoke. When Rachel swung at the ball and missed, the outfielders filled the air with malicious laughter.

Rachel's memories are as delicate and elusive as the dusty moths and butterflies that dance among the rabbit brush and sage. Memories of her girlhood never linger; they land for an instant, then take flight, leaving Rachel feeling abandoned and alone.

Rachel leaves Aaron's body where it is, but closes his eyes and pulls the sheet up over his head. She does not know what else to do. Each day she waters the garden and picks some greens for the rabbits. Each day, she cares for the animals in the lab, bringing them food and refilling their water bottles. The weather is cool, and Aaron's body does not smell too bad, though by the end of the week, a wide line of ants runs from the bed to the open window.

At the end of the first week, on a moonlit evening, Rachel decides to let the animals go free. She releases the rabbits one by one, climbing on a stepladder to reach down into the cage and lift each placid bunny out. She carries each one to the back door, holding it for a moment and stroking the soft warm fur. Then she sets the animal down and nudges it in the direction of the green grass that grows around the perimeter of the fenced garden.

The rats are more difficult to deal with. She manages to wrestle the large rat cage off the shelf, but it is heavier than she thought it would be. Though she slows its fall, it lands on the floor with a crash and the rats scurry to and fro within. She shoves the cage across the linoleum floor, sliding it down the hall, over the doorsill and onto the back patio. When she opens the cage door, rats burst out like popcorn from a popper, white in the moonlight and dashing in all directions.

Once, while Aaron was taking a nap, Rachel walked along the dirt track that led to the main highway. She hadn't planned on going far. She just wanted to see what the highway looked like, maybe hide near the mailbox and watch a car drive past. She was curious about the outside world and her fleeting fragmentary memories did not satisfy that curiosity.

She was halfway to the mailbox when Aaron came roaring up in his old jeep. "Get in the car," he shouted at her. "Right now!" Rachel had never seen him so angry. She cowered in the jeep's passenger seat, covered with dust from the road, unhappy that Aaron was so upset. He didn't speak until they got back to the ranch house, and then he spoke in a low voice, filled with bitterness and suppressed rage.

"You don't want to go out there," he said. "You wouldn't like it out there. The world is filled with petty, narrow-minded, stupid people. They wouldn't understand you. And anyone they don't understand, they want to hurt. They hurt anyone who's different. If they know that you're different, they punish you, hurt you. They'll lock you up and never let you go."

He looked straight ahead, staring through the dirty windshield. "It's not like the shows on TV, Rachel," he said in a softer tone. "It's not like the stories in books."

He looked at her then and she gestured frantically. —I'm sorry. I'm sorry.

"I can't protect you out there," he said. "I can't keep you safe."

Rachel took his hand in both of hers. He relented then, stroking her head. "Never do that again," he said. "Never."

Aaron's fear was contagious. Rachel never again walked alone the dirt track and sometimes she had dreams about bad people who wanted to lock her in a cage.

Two weeks after Aaron's death, a black-and-white police car drives slowly up to the house. When the policemen knock on the door, Rachel hides behind the couch in the living room. They knock again, try the knob, then open the door, which she had left unlocked.

Suddenly frightened, Rachel bolts from behind the couch, bounding toward the back door. Behind her, she hears one man yell, "My God! It's a gorilla!"

By the time he pulls his gun, Rachel has run out the back door and away into the hills. From the hills she watches as an ambulance drives up and two men in white take Aaron's body away. Even after the ambulance and the police car drive away, Rachel is afraid to go back to the house. Only after sunset does she return.

Just before dawn the next morning, she wakens to the sound of a truck jouncing down the dirt road. She peers out the window to see a pale green pickup. Sloppily stenciled in white on the door are the words: PRIMATE RESEARCH CENTER. Rachel hesitates as the truck pulls up in front of the house. By the time she has decided to flee, two men are getting out of the truck. One of them carries a rifle.

She runs out the back door and heads for the hills, but she is only halfway to hiding when she heard a sound like a sharp intake of breath and feels a painful jolt in her shoulder. Suddenly, her legs give way and she is tumbling backward down the sandy slope, dust coating her red-brown fur, her howl becoming a whimper, then fading to nothing at all. She falls into the blackness of sleep.

The sun is up. Rachel lies in a cage in the back of the pickup truck. She is partially conscious and she feels a tingling in her hands and feet. Nausea grips her stomach and bowels. Her body aches.

Rachel can blink, but otherwise she can't move. From where she lies, she can see only the wire mesh of the cage and the side of the truck. When she tries to turn her head, the burning in her skin intensifies. She lies still, wanting to cry out, but unable to make a sound. She can only blink slowly, trying to close out the pain. But the burning and nausea stay.

The truck jounces down a dirt road, then stops. It rocks as the men get out. The doors slam. Rachel hears the tailgate open.

A woman's voice: "Is that the animal the County Sheriff wanted us to pick up?" A woman peers into the cage. She wears a white lab coat and her brown hair is tied back in a single braid. Around her eyes, Rachel can see small wrinkles, etched by years of living in the desert. The woman doesn't look evil. Rachel hopes that the woman will save her from the men in the truck.

"Yeah. It should be knocked out for at least another half hour. Where do you want it?"

"Bring it into the lab where we had the rhesus monkeys. I'll keep it there until I have an empty cage in the breeding area."

Rachel's cage scrapes across the bed of the pickup. She feels each bump and jar as a new pain. The man swings the cage onto a cart and the woman pushes the cart down a concrete corridor. Rachel watches the walls pass just a few inches from her nose.

The lab contains rows of cages in which small animals sleepily move. In the sudden stark light of the overhead fluorescent bulbs, the eyes of white rats gleam red.

With the help of one of the men from the truck, the woman manhandles Rachel onto a lab table. The metal surface is cold and hard, painful against Rachel's skin. Rachel's body is not under her control; her limbs will not respond. She is still frozen by the tranquilizer, able to watch, but that is all. She cannot protest or plead for mercy.

Rachel watches with growing terror as the woman pulls on rubber gloves and fills a hypodermic needle with a clear solution. "Mark down that I'm giving her the standard test for tuberculosis; this eyelid should be checked before she's moved in with the others. I'll add thiabendazole to her feed for the next few days to clean out any intestinal worms. And I suppose we might as well de-flea her as well," the woman says. The man grunts in response.

Expertly, the woman closes one of Rachel's eyes. With her open eye, Rachel watches the hypodermic needle approach. She feels a sharp pain in her eyelid. In her mind, she is howling, but the only sound she can manage is a breathy sigh.

The woman sets the hypodermic aside and begins methodically spraying Rachel's fur with a cold, foul-smelling liquid. A drop strikes Rachel's eye and burns. Rachel blinks, but she cannot lift a hand to rub her eye. The woman treats Rachel with casual indifference, chatting with the man as she spreads Rachel's legs and sprays her genitals. "Looks healthy enough. Good breeding stock."

Rachel moans, but neither person notices. At last, they finish their torture, put her in a cage, and leave the room. She closes her eyes, and the darkness returns.

Rachel dreams. She is back at home in the ranch house. It is night and she is alone. Outside, coyotes yip and howl. The coyote is the voice of the desert, wailing as the wind wails when it stretches itself thin to squeeze through a crack between two boulders. The people native to this land tell tales of Coyote, a god who was a trickster, unreliable, changeable, mercurial.

Rachel is restless, anxious, unnerved by the howling of the coyotes. She is looking for Aaron. In the dream, she knows he is not dead, and she searches the house for him, wandering from his cluttered bedroom to her small room to the linoleum-tiled lab.

She is in the lab when she hears something tapping: a small dry scratching, like a wind-blown branch against the window, though no tree grows near the house and the night is still. Cautiously, she lifts the curtain to look out.

She looks into her own reflection: a pale oval face, long blonde hair. The hand that holds the curtain aside is smooth and white with carefully clipped fingernails. But something is wrong. Superimposed on the reflection is another face peering through the glass: a pair of dark brown eyes, a chimp face with red-brown hair and jug-handle ears. She sees her own reflection and she sees the outsider; the two images merge and blur. She is afraid, but she can't drop the curtain and shut the ape face out.

She is a chimp looking in through the cold, bright window-pane, she is a girl looking out; she is a girl looking in, she is an ape looking out. She is afraid and the coyotes are howling all around.

Rachel opens her eyes and blinks until the world comes into focus. The pain and tingling have retreated, but she still feels a little sick. Her left eye aches. When she rubs it, she feels a raised lump on the eyelid where the woman pricked her. She lies on the floor of a wire mesh cage. The room is hot and the air is thick with the smell of animals.

In the cage beside her is another chimp, an older animal with scruffy dark brown fur. He sits with his arms wrapped around his knees, rocking back and forth, back and forth. His head is down. As he rocks, he murmurs to himself, a mean-ingless cooing that goes on and on. On his scalp, Rachel can see a gleam of metal: a permanently implanted electrode pro-trudes from a shaven patch. Rachel makes a soft questioning sound, but the other chimp will not look up.

Rachel's own cage is just a few feet square. In one corner is a bowl of monkey pellets. A water bottle hangs on the side of the cage. Rachel ignores the food, but drinks thirstily.

Sunlight streams through the windows, sliced into small sec-tions by the wire mesh that covers the glass. She tests her cage door, rattling it gently at first, then harder. It is securely latched. The gaps in the mesh are too small to admit her hand. She can't reach out to work the latch.

The other chimp continues to rock back and forth. When Rachel rattles the mesh of her cage and howls, he lifts his head wearily and looks at her. His red-rimmed eyes are unfocused; she can't be sure he sees her.

—Hello, she gestures tentatively. —What's wrong?

He blinks at her in the dim light. —Hurt, he signs in ASL. He reaches up to touch the electrode, fingering the skin that is already raw from repeated rubbing.

—Who hurt you? she asks. He stares at her blankly and she repeats the question. —Who?

—Men, he signs.

As if on cue, there is the click of a latch and the door to the lab opens. A bearded man in a white coat steps in, followed by a clean-shaven man in a suit. The bearded man seems to be showing the other man around the lab. ''. . . only preliminary testing so far,'' the bearded man is saying. ''We've been hampered by a shortage of chimps trained in ASL.'' The two men stop in front of the old chimp's cage. ''This old fellow is from the Oregon Center. Funding for the language program was cut back and some of the animals were dispersed to other programs.'' The old chimp huddles at the back of the cage, eyeing the bearded man with suspicion.

—Hungry? the bearded man signs to the old chimp. He holds up an orange where the old chimp can see it.

—Give orange, the old chimp gestures. He holds out his hand, but comes no nearer to the wire mesh than he must to reach the orange. With the fruit in hand, he retreats to the back of his cage.

The bearded man continues, ''This project will provide us with the first solid data on neural activity during use of sign language. But we really need greater access to chimps with advanced language skills. People are so damn protective of their animals.''

''Is this one of yours?'' the clean-shaven man asks, pointing to Rachel. She cowers in the back of the cage, as far from the wire mesh as she can get.

''No, not mine. She was someone's household pet, appar-

ently. The county sheriff had us pick her up.'' The bearded
man peers into her cage. Rachel does not move; she is terrified
that he will somehow guess that she knows ASL. She stares at
his hands and thinks about those hands putting an electrode
through her skull. ''I think she'll be put in breeding stock,''
the man says as he turns away.

Rachel watches them go, wondering at what terrible people
these are. Aaron was right: they want to punish her, put an
electrode in her head.

After the men are gone, she tries to draw the old chimp into
conversation, but he will not reply. He ignores her as he eats
his orange. Then he returns to his former posture, hiding his
head and rocking himself back and forth.

Rachel, hungry despite herself, samples one of the food pellets. It has a strange medicinal taste, and she puts it back in
the bowl. She needs to pee, but there is no toilet and she
cannot escape the cage. At last unable to hold it, she pees in
one corner of the cage. The urine flows through the wire mesh
to soak the litter below, and the smell of warm piss fills her
cage. Humiliated, frightened, her head aching, her skin itchy
from the flea spray, Rachel watches as the sunlight creeps
across the room.

The day wears on. Rachel samples her food again, but rejects it, preferring hunger to the strange taste. A black man
comes and cleans the cages of the rabbits and rats. Rachel
cowers in her cage and watches him warily, afraid that he will
hurt her, too.

When night comes, she is not tired. Outside, coyotes howl.
Moonlight filters in through the high windows. She draws her
legs up toward her body, then rests with her arms wrapped
around her knees. Her father is dead, and she is a captive in a
strange place. For a time, she whimpers softly, hoping to
awaken from this nightmare and find herself at home in bed.
When she hears the click of a key in the door to the room, she
hugs herself more tightly.

A man in green coveralls pushes a cart filled with cleaning
supplies into the room. He takes a broom from the cart, and
begins sweeping the concrete floor. Over the rows of cages,
she can see the top of his head bobbing in time with his sweeping. He works slowly and methodically, bending down to sweep

carefully under each row of cages, making a neat pile of dust, dung, and food scraps in the center of the aisle.

The janitor's name is Jake. He is a middle-aged deaf man who has been employed by the Primate Research Center for the past seven years. He works night shift. The personnel director at the Primate Research Center likes Jake because he fills the federal quota for handicapped employees, and because he has not asked for a raise in five years. There have been some complaints about Jake—his work is often sloppy—but never enough to merit firing the man.

Jake is an unambitious, somewhat slow-witted man. He likes the Primate Research Center because he works alone, which allows him to drink on the job. He is an easy-going man, and he likes the animals. Sometimes, he brings treats for them. Once, a lab assistant caught him feeding an apple to a pregnant rhesus monkey. The monkey was part of an experiment on the effect of dietary restrictions on fetal brain development, and the lab assistant warned Jack that he would be fired if he was ever caught interfering with the animals again. Jake still feeds the animals, but he is more careful about when he does it, and he has never been caught again.

As Rachel watches, the old chimp gestures to Jake. —Give banana, the chimp signs. —Please banana. Jake stops sweeping for a minute and reaches down to the bottom shelf of his cleaning cart. He returns with a banana and offers it to the old chimp. The chimp accepts the banana and leans against the mesh while Jake scratches his fur.

When Jake turns back to his sweeping, he catches sight of Rachel and sees that she is watching him. Emboldened by his kindness to the old chimp, Rachel timidly gestures to him. —Help me.

Jake hesitates, then peers at her more closely. Both his eyes are shot with a fine lacework of red. His nose displays the broken blood vessels of someone who has been friends with the bottle for too many years. He needs a shave. But when he leans close, Rachel catches the scent of whiskey and tobacco. The smells remind her of Aaron and give her courage.

—Please help me, Rachel signs. —I don't belong here.

For the last hour, Jake has been drinking steadily. His view of the world is somewhat fuzzy. He stares at her blearily.

Rachel's fear that he will hurt her is replaced by the fear that he will leave her locked up and alone. Desperately she signs again. —Please please please. Help me. I don't belong here. Please help me go home.

He watches her, considering the situation. Rachel does not move. She is afraid that any movement will make him leave. With a majestic speed dictated by his inebriation, Jake leans his broom on the row of cages behind him and steps toward Rachel's cage again. —You talk? he signs.

—I talk, she signs.

—Where did you come from?

—From my father's house, she signs. —Two men came and shot me and put me here. I don't know why. I don't know why they locked me in jail.

Jake looks around, willing to be sympathetic, but puzzled by her talk of jail. —This isn't jail, he signs. —This is a place where scientists raise monkeys.

Rachel is indignant. —I am not a monkey, she signs. —I am a girl.

Jake studies her hairy body and her jug-handle ears. —You look like a monkey.

Rachel shakes her head. —No. I am a girl.

Rachel runs her hands back over her head, a very human gesture of annoyance and unhappiness. She signs sadly, —I don't belong here. Please let me out.

Jake shifts his weight from foot to foot, wondering what to do. —I can't let you out. I'll get in big trouble.

—Just for a little while? Please?

Jake glances at his cart of supplies. He has to finish off this room and two corridors of offices before he can relax for the night.

—Don't go, Rachel signs, guessing his thoughts.

—I have work to do.

She looks at the cart, then suggests eagerly, —Let me out and I'll help you work.

Jake frowns. —If I let you out, you will run away.

—No, I won't run. I will help. Please let me out.

—You promise to go back?

Rachel nods.

Warily he unlatches the cage. Rachel bounds out, grabs a whisk broom from the cart, and begins industriously sweeping bits of food and droppings from beneath the row of cages. —Come on, she signs to Jake from the end of the aisle. —I will help.

When Jake pushes the cart from the room filled with cages, Rachel follows him closely. The rubber wheels of the cleaning cart rumble softly on the linoleum floor. They pass through a metal door into a corridor where the floor is carpeted and the air smells of chalk dust and paper.

Offices let off the corridor, each one a small room furnished with a desk, bookshelves, and a blackboard. Jake shows Rachel how to empty the wastebaskets into a garbage bag. While he cleans the blackboards, she wanders from office to office, trailing the trash-filled garbage bag.

At first, Jake keeps a close eye on Rachel. But after cleaning each blackboard, he pauses to refill a cup from the whiskey bottle that he keeps wedged between the Saniflush and the window cleaner. By the time he is halfway through the second cup; he is treating her like an old friend, telling her to hurry up so that they can eat dinner.

Rachel works quickly, but she stops sometimes to gaze out the office windows. Outside, moonlight shines on a sandy plain, dotted here and there with scrubby clumps of rabbit brush.

At the end of the corridor is a larger room in which there are several desks and typewriters. In one of the wastebaskets, buried beneath memos and candybar wrappers, she finds a magazine. The title is *Love Confessions* and the cover has a picture of a man and woman kissing. Rachel studies the cover, then takes the magazine, tucking it on the bottom shelf of the cart.

Jake pours himself another cup of whiskey and pushes the cart to another hallway. Jake is working slower now, and as he works he makes humming noises, tuneless sounds that he feels only as pleasant vibrations. The last few blackboards are sloppily done, and Rachel, finished with the wastebaskets, cleans the places that Jake missed.

They eat dinner in the janitor's storeroom, a stuffy window-less room furnished with an ancient grease-stained couch, a battered black-and-white television, and shelves of cleaning supplies. From a shelf, Jake takes the paper bag that holds his lunch: a baloney sandwich, a bag of barbecued potato chips, and a box of vanilla wafers. From behind the gallon jugs of liquid cleaner, he takes a magazine. He lights a cigarette, pours himself another cup of whiskey, and settles down on the couch. After a moment's hesitation, he offers Rachel a drink, pouring a shot of whiskey into a chipped ceramic cup.

Aaron never let Rachel drink whiskey, and she samples it carefully. At first the smell makes her sneeze, but she is fascinated by the way that the drink warms her throat, and she sips some more.

As they drink, Rachel tells Jake about the men who shot her and the woman who pricked her with a needle, and he nods. —The people here are crazy, he signs.

—I know, she says, thinking of the old chimp with the electrode in his head. —You won't tell them I can talk, will you?

Jake nods. —I won't tell them anything.

—They treat me like I'm not real, Rachel signs sadly. Then she hugs her knees, frightened at the thought of being held captive by crazy people. She considers planning her escape: she is out of the cage and she is sure she could outrun Jake. As she wonders about it, she finishes her cup of whiskey. The alcohol takes the edge off her fear. She sits close beside Jake on the couch, and the smell of cigarette smoke reminds her of Aaron. For the first time since Aaron's death she feels warm and happy.

She shares Jake's cookies and potato chips and looks at the *Love Confessions* magazine that she took from the trash. The first story that she reads is about a woman named Alice. The headline reads: "I became a go-go dancer to pay off my husband's gambling debts, and now he wants me to sell my body."

Rachel sympathizes with Alice's loneliness and suffering. Alice, like Rachel, is alone and misunderstood. As Rachel slowly reads, she sips her second cup of whiskey. The story reminds her of a fairy tale; the nice man who rescues Alice from her terrible husband replaces the handsome prince who rescues the princess. Rachel glances at Jake and wonders if he will rescue her from the wicked people who locked her in the cage.

She has finished the second cup of whiskey and eaten half Jake's cookies when Jake says that she must go back to her cage. She goes reluctantly, taking the magazine with her. He promises that he will come for her again the next night, and with that she must be content. She puts the magazine in one corner of the cage and curls up to sleep.

She wakes early in the afternoon. A man in a white coat is wheeling a low cart into the lab.

Rachel's head aches with hangover and she feels sick. As she crouches in one corner of her cage, he stops the cart beside her cage and then locks the wheels. "Hold on there," he mutters to her, then slides her cage onto the cart.

The man wheels her through long corridors, where the walls are cement blocks, painted institutional green. Rachel huddles unhappily in the cage, wondering where she is going and whether Jake will ever be able to find her.

At the end of a long corridor, the man opens a thick metal door and a wave of warm air strikes Rachel. It stinks of chimpanzees, excrement, and rotting food. On either side of the corridor are metal bars and wire mesh. Behind the mesh, Rachel can see dark hairy shadows. In one cage, five adolescent chimps swing and play. In another, two females huddle together, grooming each other. The man slows as he passes a cage in which a big male is banging on the wire with his fist, making the mesh rattle and ring.

"Now, Johnson," says the man. "Cool it. Be nice. I'm bringing you a new little girlfriend."

With a series of hooks, the man links Rachel's cage with the cage next to Johnson's and opens the doors. "Go on, girl," he says. "See the nice fruit." In the cage is a bowl of sliced applies with an attendant swarm of fruit flies.

At first, Rachel will not move into the new cage. She crouches in the cage on the cart, hoping that the man will decide to take her back to the lab. She watches him get a hose and attach it to a water faucet. But she does not understand his intention until he turns the stream of water on her. A cold blast strikes her on the back and she howls, fleeing into the new cage to avoid the cold water. Then the man closes the doors, unhooks the cage, and hurries away.

The floor is bare cement. Her cage is at one end of the corridor and two walls are cement block. A door in one of the cement block walls leads to an outside run. The other two walls are wire mesh: one facing the corridor, the other, Johnson's cage.

Johnson, quiet now that the man has left, is sniffing around the door in the wire mesh wall that joins their cages. Rachel watches him anxiously. Her memories of other chimps are distant, softened by time. She remembers her mother; she vaguely remembers playing with other chimps her age. But she does not know how to react to Johnson when he stares at her with great intensity and makes a loud huffing sound. She gestures to him in ASL, but he only stares harder and huffs again. Beyond Johnson, she can see other cages and other chimps, so many that the wire mesh blurs her vision and she cannot see the other end of the corridor.

To escape Johnson's scrutiny, she ducks through the door into the outside run, a wire mesh cage on a white concrete foundation. Outside there is barren ground and rabbit brush. The afternoon sun is hot and all the other runs are deserted until Johnson appears in the run beside hers. His attention disturbs her and she goes back inside.

She retreats to the side of the cage farthest from Johnson. A crudely built wooden platform provides her with a place to sit. Wrapping her arms around her knees, she tries to relax and ignore Johnson. She dozes off for a while, but wakes to a commotion across the corridor.

In the cage across the way is a female chimp in heat. Rachel recognizes the smell from her own times in heat. Two keepers are opening the door that separates the female's cage from the adjoining cage, where a male stands, watching with great interest. Johnson is shaking the wire mesh and howling as he watches.

"Mike here is a virgin, but Susie knows what she's doing," one keeper was saying to the other. "So it should go smoothly. But keep the hose ready."

"Yeah?"

"Sometimes they fight. We only use the hose to break it up if it gets real bad. Generally, they do okay."

Mike stalks into Susie's cage. The keepers lower the cage

door, trapping both chimps in the same cage. Susie seems unalarmed. She continues eating a slice of orange while Mike sniffs at her genitals with every indication of great interest. She bends over to let Mike finger her pink bottom, the sign of estrus.

Rachel finds herself standing at the wire mesh, making low moaning noises. She can see Mike's erection, hear his grunting cries. He squats on the floor of Susie's cage, gesturing to the female. Rachel's feelings are mixed: she is fascinated, fearful, confused. She keeps thinking of the description of sex in the *Love Confessions* story: When Alice feels Danny's lips on hers, she is swept away by the passion of the moment. He takes her in his arms and her skin tingles as if she were consumed by an inner fire.

Susie bends down and Mike penetrates her with a loud grunt, thrusting violently with his hips. Susie cries out shrilly and suddenly leaps up, knocking Mike away. Rachel watches, overcome with fascination. Mike, his penis now limp, follows Susie slowly to the corner of the cage, where he begins grooming her carefully. Rachel finds that the wire mesh has cut her hands where she gripped it too tightly.

It is night, and the door at the end of the corridor creaks open. Rachel is immediately alert, peering through the wire mesh and trying to see down to the end of the corridor. She bangs on the wire mesh. As Jake comes closer, she waves a greeting.

When Jake reaches for the lever that will raise the door to Rachel's cage, Johnson charges toward him, howling and waving his arms above his head. He hammers on the wire mesh with his fists, howling and grimacing at Jake. Rachel ignores Johnson and hurries after Jake.

Again Rachel helps Jake clean. In the laboratory, she greets the old chimp, but the animal is more interested in the banana that Jake has brought than in conversation. The chimp will not reply to her questions, and after several tries, she gives up.

While Jake vacuums the carpeted corridors, Rachel empties the trash, finding a magazine called *Modern Romance* in the same wastebasket that had provided *Love Confessions*.

Later, in the Janitor's lounge, Jake smokes a cigarette, sips whiskey, and flips through one of his own magazines. Rachel reads love stories in *Modern Romance*.

Every once in a while, she looks over Jake's shoulder at grainy pictures of naked women with their legs spread wide apart. Jake looks for a long time at the picture of a blonde woman with big breasts, red fingernails, and purple-painted eyelids. The woman lies on her back and smiles as she strokes the pinkness between her legs. The picture on the next page shows her caressing her own breasts, pinching the dark nipples. The final picture shows her looking back over her shoulder. She is in the position that Susie took when she was ready to be mounted.

Rachel looks over Jake's shoulder at the magazine, but she does not ask questions. Jake's smell began to change as soon as he opened the magazine; the scent of nervous sweat mingles with the aromas of tobacco and whiskey. Rachel suspects that questions would not be welcome just now.

At Jake's insistence, she goes back to her cage before dawn.

Over the next week, she listens to the conversations of the men who come and go, bringing food and hosing out the cages. From the men's conversation, she learns that the Primate Research Center is primarily a breeding facility that supplies researchers with domestically bred apes and monkeys of several species. It also maintains its own research staff. In indifferent tones, the men talk of horrible things. The adolescent chimps at the end of the corridor are being fed a diet high in cholesterol to determine cholesterol's effects on the circulatory system. A group of pregnant females are being injected with male hormones to determine how that will affect the female offspring. A group of infants is being fed a low protein diet to determine adverse effects on their brain development.

The men look through her as if she were not real, as if she were a part of the wall, as if she were no one at all. She cannot speak to them; she cannot trust them.

Each night, Jake lets her out of her cage and she helps him clean. He brings treats: barbecued potato chips, fresh fruit, chocolate bars, and cookies. He treats her fondly, as one would treat a precocious child. And he talks to her.

At night, when she is with Jake, Rachel can almost forget

the terror of the cage, the anxiety of watching Johnson pace to and fro, the sense of unreality that accompanies the simplest act. She would be content to stay with Jake forever, eating snack food and reading confessions magazines. He seems to like her company. But each morning, Jake insists that she must go back to the cage and the terror. By the end of the first week, she has begun plotting her escape.

Whenever Jake falls asleep over his whiskey, something that happens three nights out of five, Rachel prowls the center alone, surreptitiously gathering things that she will need to survive in the desert: a plastic jug filled with water, a plastic bag of food pellets, a large beach towel that will serve as a blanket on the cool desert nights, a discarded plastic shopping bag in which she can carry the other things. Her best find is a road map on which the Primate Center is marked in red. She knows the address of Aaron's ranch and finds it on the map. She studies the roads and plots a route home. Cross country, assuming that she does not get lost, she will have to travel about fifty miles to reach the ranch. She hides these things behind one of the shelves in the janitor's storeroom.

Her plans to run away and go home are disrupted by the idea that she is in love with Jake, a notion that comes to her slowly, fed by the stories in the confessions magazines. When Jake absent-mindedly strokes her, she is filled with a strange excitement. She longs for his company and misses him on the weekends when he is away. She is happy only when she is with him, following him through the halls of the center, sniffing the aroma of tobacco and whiskey that is his own perfume. She steals a cigarette from his pack and hides it in her cage, where she can savor the smell of it at her leisure.

She loves him, but she does not know how to make him love her back. Rachel knows little about love: she remembers a high school crush where she mooned after a boy with a locker near hers, but that came to nothing. She reads the confessions magazines and Ann Landers' column in the newspaper that Jake brings with him each night, and from these sources, she learns about romance. One night, after Jake falls asleep, she types a badly punctuated, ungrammatical letter to Ann. In the letter, she explains her situation and asks for advice on how to make Jake love her. She slips the letter into a sack labeled ''Outgoing

Mail,'' and for the next week she reads Ann's column with increased interest. But her letter never appears.

Rachel searches for answers in the magazine pictures that seem to fascinate Jake. She studies the naked women, especially the big-breasted woman with the purple smudges around her eyes.

One night, in a secretary's desk, she finds a plastic case of eyeshadow. She steals it and takes it back to her cage. The next evening, as soon as the Center is quiet, she upturns her metal food dish and regards her reflection in the shiny bottom. Squatting, she balances the eye shadow case on one knee and examines its contents: a tiny makeup brush and three shades of eyes shadow—INDIAN BLUE, FOREST GREEN, and WILDLY VIOLET. Rachel chooses the shade labeled WILDLY VIOLET.

Using one finger to hold her right eye closed, she dabs her eyelid carefully with the makeup brush, leaving a gaudy orchid-colored smudge on her brown skin. She studies the smudge critically, then adds to it. Smearing the color beyond the corner of her eyelid until it disappears in her brown fur. The color gives her eye a carnival brightness, a lunatic gaiety. Working with great care, she matches the effect on the other side, then smiles at herself in the glass, blinking coquettishly.

In the other cage, Johnson bares his teeth and shakes the wire mesh. She ignores him.

When Jake comes to let her out, he frowns at her eyes.
—Did you hurt yourself? he asks.

—No, she says. Then, after a pause. —Don't you like it?

Jake squats beside her and stares at her eyes. Rachel puts a hand on his knee and her heart pounds at her own boldness.
—You are a very strange monkey, he signs.

Rachel is afraid to move. Her hand on his knee closes into a fist; her face folds in on itself, puckering around the eyes.

Then, straightening up, he signs, —I liked your eyes better before.

He likes her eyes. She nods without taking her eyes from his face. Later, she washes her face in the women's restroom, leaving dark smudges the color of bruises on a series of paper towels.

* * *

Rachel is dreaming. She is walking through the Painted Desert with her hairy brown mother, following a red rock canyon that Rachel somehow knows will lead her to the Primate Research Center. Her mother is lagging behind: she does not want to go to the center; she is afraid. In the shadow of a rock outcropping, Rachel stops to explain to her mother that they must go to the center because Jake is at the center.

Rachel's mother does not understand sign language. She watches Rachel with mournful eyes, then scrambles up the canyon wall, leaving Rachel behind. Rachel climbs after her mother, pulling herself over the edge in time to see the other chimp loping away across the wind-blown red cinder-rock and sand.

Rachel bounds after her mother, and as she runs she howls like an abandoned infant chimp, wailing her distress. The figure of her mother wavers in the distance, shimmering in the heat that rises from the sand. The figure changes. Running away across the red sands is a pale blonde woman wearing a purple sweatsuit and jogging shoes, the sweet-smelling mother that Rachel remembers. The woman looks back and smiles at Rachel. ''Don't howl like an ape, daughter,'' she calls. ''Say Mama.''

Rachel runs silently, dream running that takes her nowhere. The sand burns her feet and the sun beats down on her head. The blonde woman vanishes in the distance, and Rachel is alone. She collapses on the sand, whimpering because she is alone and afraid.

She feels the gentle touch of fingers grooming her fur, and for a moment, still half asleep, she believes that her hairy mother has returned to her. She opens her eyes and looks into a pair of dark brown eyes, separated from her by wire mesh. Johnson. He has reached through a gap in the fence to groom her. As he sorts through her fur, he makes soft cooing sounds, gentle comforting noises.

Still half asleep, she gazes at him and wonders why she was so fearful. He does not seem so bad. He grooms her for a time, and then sits nearby, watching her through the mesh. She brings a slice of apple from her dish of food and offers it to him. With her free hand, she makes the sign for apple. When he takes it, she signs again: apple. He is not a particularly quick student, but she has time and many slices of apple.

All Rachel's preparations are done, but she cannot bring herself to leave the center. Leaving the center means leaving Jake, leaving potato chips and whiskey, leaving security. To Rachel, the thought of love is always accompanied by the warm taste of whiskey and potato chips.

Some nights, after Jake is asleep, she goes to the big glass doors that lead to the outside. She opens the doors and stands on the steps, looking down into the desert. Sometimes a jackrabbit sits on its haunches in the rectangles of light that shine through the glass doors. Sometimes she sees kangaroo rats, hopping through the moonlight like rubber balls bounding on hard pavement. Once, a coyote trots by, casting a contemptuous glance in her direction.

The desert is a lonely place. Empty. Cold. She thinks of Jake snoring softly in the janitor's lounge. And always she closes the door and returns to him.

Rachel leads a double life: janitor's assistant by night, prisoner and teacher by day. She spends her afternoons drowsing in the sun and teaching Johnson new signs.

On a warm afternoon, Rachel sits in the outside run, basking in the sunlight. Johnson is inside, and the other chimps are quiet. She can almost imagine she is back at her father's ranch, sitting in her own yard. She naps and dreams of Jake.

She dreams that she is sitting in his lap on the battered old couch. Her hand on his chest: a smooth pale hand with red-painted fingernails. When she looks at the dark screen of the television set, she can see her reflection. She is a thin teenager with blonde hair and blue eyes. She is naked.

Jake is looking at her and smiling. He runs a hand down her back and she closes her eyes in ecstasy.

But something changes when she closes her eyes. Jake is grooming her as her mother used to groom her, sorting through her hair in search of fleas. She opens her eyes and sees Johnson, his diligent fingers searching through her fur, his intent brown eyes watching her. The reflection on the television screen shows two chimps, tangled in each others' arms.

Rachel wakes to find she is in heat for the first time since she came to the center. The skin surrounding her genitals is swollen and pink.

For the rest of the day, she is restless, pacing to and fro in her cage. On his side of the wire mesh wall, Johnson is equally restless, following her when she goes outside, sniffing long and hard at the edge of the barrier that separates him from her.

That night, Rachel goes eagerly to help Jake clean. She follows him closely, never letting him get far from her. When he is sweeping, she trots after him with the dustpan and he almost trips over her twice. She keeps waiting for him to notice her condition, but he seems oblivious.

As she works, she sips from a cup of whiskey. Excited, she drinks more than usual, finishing two full cups. The liquor leaves her a little disoriented, and she sways as she follows Jake to the janitor's lounge. She curls up close behind him on the couch. He relaxes with his arms resting on the back of the couch, his legs stretching out before him. She moves so that she presses against him.

He stretches, yawns, and rubs the back of his neck as if trying to rub away stiffness. Rachel reaches around behind him and begins to gently rub his neck, reveling in the feel of his skin, his hair against the backs of her hands. The thoughts that hop and skip through her mind are confusing. Sometimes it seems that the hair that tickles her hands is Johnson's; sometimes, she knows it is Jake's. And sometimes it doesn't seem to matter. Are they really so different? They are not so different.

She rubs his neck, not knowing what to do next. In the confessions magazine, this is where the man crushes the woman in his arms. Rachel climbs into Jack's lap and hugs him, waiting for him to crush her in his arms. He blinks at her sleepily. Half asleep, he strokes her, and his moving hand brushes near her genitals. She presses herself against him, making a soft sound in her throat. She rubs her hip against his crotch, aware now of a slight change in his smell, in the tempo of his breathing. He blinks at her again, a little more awake now. She bares her teeth in a smile and tilts her head back to lick his neck. She can feel his hands on her shoulders, pushing her away, and she knows what he wants. She slides from his lap and turns, presenting him with her pink genitals, ready to be mounted, ready to have him penetrate her. She moans in anticipation, a low inviting sound.

He does not come to her. She looks over her shoulder and he is still sitting on the couch, watching her through half-closed eyes. He reaches over and picks up a magazine filled with pictures of naked women. His other hand drops to his crotch and he is lost in his own world.

Rachel howls like an infant who has lost his mother, but he does not look up. He is staring at the picture of the blonde woman.

Rachel runs down dark corridors to her cage, the only home she has. When she reaches her corridor, she is breathing hard and making small lonely whimpering noises. In the dimly lit corridor, she hesitates for a moment, staring into Johnson's cage. The male chimp is asleep. She remembers the touch of his hands when he groomed her.

From the corridor, she lifts the gate that leads into Johnson's cage and enters. He wakes at the sound of the door and sniffs the air. When he sees Rachel, he stalks toward her, sniffing eagerly. She let him finger her genitals, sniff deeply of her scent. His penis is erect and he grunts in excitement. She turns and presents herself to him and he mounts her, thrusting deep inside. As he penetrates, she thinks, for a moment, of Jake and the thin blonde teenage girl named Rachel, but then the moment passes. Almost against her will she cries out, a shrill exclamation of welcoming and loss.

After he withdraws his penis, Johnson grooms her gently, sniffing her genitals and softly stroking her fur. She is sleepy and content, but she knows she cannot delay.

Johnson is reluctant to leave his cage, but Rachel takes him by the hand and leads him to the janitor's lounge. His presence gives her courage. She listens at the door and hears Jake's soft breathing. Leaving Johnson in the hall, she slips into the room. Jake is lying on the couch, the magazine draped over his legs. Rachel takes the equipment that she has gathered and stands for a moment, staring at the sleeping man. His baseball cap hangs on the arm of a broken chair, and she takes that to remember him by.

Rachel leads Johnson through the empty halls. A kangaroo rat, collecting seeds in the dried grass near the glass doors, looks up curiously as Rachel leads Johnson down the steps. Rachel carries the plastic shopping bag slung over her shoulder. Somewhere in the distance, a coyote howls, a long yapping wail. His cry is joined by others, a chorus in the moonlight.

Rachel takes Johnson by the hand and leads him into the desert.

A cocktail waitress, driving from her job in Flagstaff to her home in Winslow, sees two apes dart across the road, hurrying away from the bright beams of her headlights. After wrestling with her conscience (she does not want to be accused of drinking on the job), she notifies the county sheriff.

A local newspaper reporter, an eager young man fresh out of journalism school, picks up the story from the police report and interviews the waitress. Flattered by his enthusiasm for her story and delighted to find a receptive ear, she tells him the details that she failed to mention to the police; one of the apes was wearing a baseball cap and carrying what looked like a shopping bag.

The reporter writes up a quick humorous story for the morning edition, and begins researching a feature article to be run later in the week. He knows that the newspaper, eager for news in a slow season, will play a human-interest story up big—kind of *Lassie, Come Home* with chimps.

Just before dawn, a light rain begins to fall, the first rain of spring. Rachel searches for shelter and finds a small cave formed by three tumbled boulders. It will keep off the rain and hide them from casual observers. She shares her food and water with Johnson. He has followed her closely all night, seemingly intimidated by the darkness and the howling of distant coyotes. She feels protective toward him. At the same time, having him with her gives her courage. He knows only a few gestures in ASL, but he does not need to speak. His presence is comfort enough.

Johnson curls up in the back of the cave and falls asleep quickly. Rachel sits in the opening and watches dawnlight wash the stars from the sky. The rain rattles against the sand, a comforting sound. She thinks about Jake. The baseball cap on her head still smells of his cigarettes, but she does not miss him. Not really. She fingers the cap and wonders why she thought she loved Jake.

The rain lets up. The clouds rise like fairy castles in the distance and the rising sun tints them pink and gold and gives them flaming red banners. Rachel remembers when she was young and Aaron read her the story of Pinocchio, the little puppet who wanted to be a real boy. At the end of his adventures, Pinocchio, who has been brave and kind, gets his wish. He becomes a real boy.

Rachel had cried at the end of the story and when Aaron asked why, she had rubbed her eyes on the backs of her hairy hands. —I want to be a real girl, she signed to him. —A real girl.

"You are a real girl," Aaron had told her, but somehow she had never believed him.

The sun rises higher and illuminates the broken rock turrets of the desert. There is a magic in this barren land of unassuming grandeur. Some cultures send their young people to the desert to seek visions and guidance, searching for true thinking spawned by the openness of the place, the loneliness, the beauty of emptiness.

Rachel drowses in the warm sun and dreams a vision that has the clarity of truth. In the dream, her father comes to her. "Rachel," he says to her, "it doesn't matter what anyone thinks of you. You're my daughter."

—I want to be a real girl, she signs.

"You *are* real," her father says. "And you don't need some two-bit drunken janitor to prove it to you." She knows she is dreaming, but she also knows that her father speaks the truth. She is warm and happy and she doesn't need Jake at all. The sunlight warms her and a lizard watches her from a rock, scurrying for cover when she moves. She picks up a bit of loose rock that lies on the floor of the cave. Idly, she scratches on the dark red sandstone wall of the cave. A lopsided heart shape. Within it, awkwardly printed: Rachel and Johnson. Between them, a plus sign. She goes over the letters again and again, leaving scores of fine lines on the smooth rock surface. Then, late in the morning, soothed by the warmth of the day, she sleeps.

* * *

Shortly after dark, an elderly rancher in a pickup truck spots two apes in a remote corner of his ranch. They run away and lose him in the rocks, but not until he has a good look at them. He calls the police, the newspaper, and the Primate Center.

The reporter arrives first thing the next morning, interviews the rancher, and follows the men from the Primate Center as they search for evidence of the chimps. They find monkey shit near the cave, confirming that the runaways were indeed nearby. The news reporter, an eager and curious young man, squirms on his belly into the cave and finds the names scratched on the cave wall. He peers at it. He might have dismissed them as the idle scratchings of kids, except that the names match the names of the missing chimps. "Hey," he called to his photographer. "Take a look at this."

The next morning's newspaper displays Rachel's crudely scratched letters. In a brief interview, the rancher mentioned that the chimps were carrying bags. "Looked like supplies," he said. "They looked like they were in for a long haul."

On the third day, Rachel's water runs out. She heads toward a small town, marked on the map. They reach it in the early morning—thirst forces them to travel by day. Beside an isolated ranch house, she finds a faucet. She is filling her bottle when Johnson grunts in alarm.

A dark-haired woman watches from the porch of the house. She does not move toward the apes, and Rachel continues filling the bottle. "It's all right, Rachel," the woman, who has been following the story in the papers, calls out. "Drink all you want."

Startled, but still suspicious, Rachel caps the bottle and, keeping her eyes on the woman, drinks from the faucet. The woman steps back into the house. Rachel motions Johnson to do the same, signaling for him to hurry and drink. She turns off the faucet when he is done.

They are turning to go when the woman emerges from the house carrying a plate of tortillas and a bowl of apples. She sets them on the edge of the porch and says, "These are for you."

The woman watches through the window as Rachel packs

the food into her bag. Rachel puts away the last apple and gestures her thanks to the woman. When the woman fails to respond to the sign language, Rachel picks up a stick and writes in the sand of the yard. "THANK YOU," Rachel scratches, then waves good-bye and sets out across the desert. She is puzzled, but happy.

The next morning's newspaper includes an interview with the dark-haired woman. She describes how Rachel turned on the faucet and turned it off when she was through, how the chimp packed the apples neatly in her bag and wrote in the dirt with a stick.

The reporter also interviews the director of the Primate Research Center. "These are animals," the director explains angrily. "But people want to treat them like they're small hairy people." He describes the Center as "primarily a breeding center with some facilities for medical research." The reporter asks some pointed questions about their acquisition of Rachel.

But the biggest story is an investigative piece. The reporter reveals that he has tracked down Aaron Jacobs' lawyer and learned that Jacobs left a will. In this will, he bequeathed all his possessions—including his house and surrounding land—to "Rachel, the chimp I acknowledge as my daughter."

The reporter makes friends with one of the young women in the typing pool at the research center, and she tells him the office scuttlebutt: people suspect that the chimps may have been released by a deaf and drunken janitor, who was subsequently fired for negligence. The reporter, accompanied by a friend who can communicate in sign language, finds Jake in his apartment in downtown Flagstaff.

Jake, who has been drinking steadily since he was fired, feels betrayed by Rachel, by the Primate Center, by the world. He complains at length about Rachel: They had been friends, and then she took his baseball cap and ran away. He just didn't understand why she had run away like that.

"You mean she could talk?" the reporter asks through his interpreter.

—Of course she can talk, Jake signs impatiently. —She is a smart monkey.

The headlines read: "Intelligent chimp inherits fortune!" Of course, Aaron's bequest isn't really a fortune and she isn't just a chimp, but close enough. Animal rights activists rise up in Rachel's defense. The case is discussed on the national news. Ann Landers reports receiving a letter from a chimp named Rachel; she had thought it was a hoax perpetrated by the boys at Yale. The American Civil Liberties Union assigns a lawyer to the case.

By day, Rachel and Johnson sleep in whatever hiding places they can find: a cave; a shelter built for range cattle; the shell of an abandoned car, rusted from long years in a desert gully. Sometimes Rachel dreams of jungle darkness, and the coyotes in the distance become a part of her dreams, their howling becomes the cries of her fellow apes.

The desert and the journey have changed her. She is wiser, having passed through the white-hot love of adolescence and emerged on the other side. She dreams, one day, of the ranch house. In the dream, she has long blonde hair and pale white skin. Her eyes are red from crying and she wanders the house restlessly, searching for something that she has lost. When she hears coyotes howling, she looks through a window at the darkness outside. The face that looks in at her has jug-handle ears and shaggy hair. When she sees the face, she cries out in recognition and opens the window to let herself in.

By night, they travel. The rocks and sands are cool beneath Rachel's feet as she walks toward her ranch. On television, scientists and politicians discuss the ramifications of her case, describe the technology uncovered by investigation of Aaron Jacobs' files. Their debates do not affect her steady progress toward her ranch or the stars that sprinkle the sky above her.

It is night when Rachel and Johnson approach the ranch-house. Rachel sniffs the wind and smells automobile exhaust and strange humans. From the hills, she can see a small camp beside a white van marked with the name of a local television station. She hesitates, considering returning to the safety of the desert. Then she takes Johnson by the hand and starts down the hill. Rachel is going home.

Dogfight

by Michael Swanwick and William Gibson

Introduction

It happens that the first work of William Gibson's that I read was Neuromancer, *his first and, so far, most successful novel. It was compulsively readable, and it achieved what so few science fiction novels ever do: a detailed near-future that is different from the present reality and yet is connected to it. The style and plot were reminiscent of the hard-boiled detective tradition, which I enjoy, but it was the mastery of milieu that made* Neuromancer *such an extraordinary book.*

But it left a sort of bitter aftertaste in my mouth. It appeared to me to be a hopeless, despairing vision, which seemed to honor suicide and self-destruction in a world where almost no one ever created anything. It was morally confusing to me; I wasn't sure if Gibson meant me to adopt the hip but cynical attitude of the hero, or stand ironically aside and reject the moral stance of all the characters. I finally came to the conclusion that Gibson was a writer I should admire, while rejecting his moral worldview.

Then, a while later, I attended a convention in Washington, D.C., where Michael Swanwick was reading a new story. I attended in large part because I had such respect for his first novel, In the Drift. *Artistically less successful than Gibson's, it was still a remarkable debut—and I was more sympathetic to the way Swanwick seemed to view the world.*

Swanwick comes across exactly as a writer should—a little tweedy, a little seedy, and bright as hell. He started to introduce the story. It was called "Dogfight," and it was a collaboration between Swanwick and Gibson.

My heart sank. It was too late to get up and walk out. I was sitting in the front row—hard to be subtle from that position. It wasn't because of my partial dislike for Gibson's work that I wanted to leave. It was the word collaboration. While there are some inspired collaborations in the history of science fiction—Kornbluth and Pohl, Niven and Pournelle—most collaborations end up being neither fish nor fowl. The presence of two names under the title usually makes me want to save a story until I have more time—for instance, during the last ten years of my retirement, when I'm bedridden and have read everything else ever published.

But within paragraphs my fears were gone; within a few pages I knew this story was on its way to being a masterwork. Here was the same level of detailed milieu creation that had made Neuromancer such astonishingly good science fiction. Here also was the same iron-hard attention to fully-rounded character that had made me have such high hopes for Michael Swanwick's future work. I have a weak spot for stories about games that consume the lives of their players, but "Dogfight" kept insisting on being much, much more than that.

As Swanwick neared the end of the story, however, I began to feel an old familiar dread. They were going to go for the easy, cop-out, ain't-life-a-bitch ending that has long been the mark of fashionably angst-ridden adolescent writers. The child's version of tragedy. Romeo and Juliet, where everybody dies because the author felt like it, instead of Lear, where the tragedy arises inevitably out of the characters.

But no. Not at all. "Dogfight" ended as well as it had begun. And in my delight—and relief—I concluded that Swanwick had been a very good collaborator for Gibson. I was absolutely certain that Gibson had wanted the nihilistic ending, and Swanwick, with his unerring sense for character, had insisted on the far more truthful (and difficult) ending that the story achieved.

I went up to Swanwick and, as I enthused about the story, I

mentioned my relief at the ending. As I remember the conversation, Swanwick confirmed that I was half right. They had wanted to follow different paths at the end, and they were pretty much the two alternatives I had assumed.

But, said Swanwick, it was Gibson who insisted on the good ending, the one you're about to read. Insisted until Swanwick saw the light and agreed. Go figure.

It was almost certain that, along with Lucius Shepard, William Gibson will be one of my two least controversial choices as "most important short-fiction writers of the 1980s." Though many of us discovered him through his novel, Neuromancer, *his marvelously rich milieu creation was already fully developed in the short stories that had been appearing since the beginning of the decade. He remains, with Bruce Sterling and Lew Shiner, one of the three pillars of the Cyberpunk movement that will certainly be the most-remembered phenomenon of the eighties; and it's Gibson's work, his style, his milieu that most people think of when they think of Cyberpunk. Indeed, most imitators of and hangers-on to the Cyberpunk movement think that by aping Gibson's work they have thus written "Cyberpunk," completely missing the point that what Gibson wrote was one example of a methodology that still remains completely beyond most of these imitators' abilities or ambitions.*

Michael Swanwick came late to the Cyberpunk movement, but he came the right way. He never ceased being himself; he never, as far as I can tell, imitated anybody. What he did was bring a new rigor to the invention of his fiction, which did not detract from what he already did well. His fame has not yet blossomed as Gibson's has (a statement that is equally true of all other writers of the eighties), but when he and Gibson wrote this story, they were not unequally yoked together. They plowed a straight furrow; they wrote a story that both can be proud of throughout what will surely be long and remarkable careers.

H‍E MEANT TO KEEP ON GOING, RIGHT DOWN TO FLORIDA. Work passage on a gunrunner, maybe wind up conscripted into some rat-ass rebel army down in the war zone. Or maybe, with that ticket good as long as he didn't stop riding, he'd just never get off—Greyhound's Flying Dutchman. He grinned at his faint reflection in cold, greasy glass, while the downtown lights of Norfolk slid past, the bus swaying on tired shocks as the driver slung it around a final corner. They shuddered to a halt in the terminal lot, concrete lit gray and harsh like a prison exercise yard. But Deke was watching himself starve, maybe in some snowstorm out of Oswego, with his cheek pressed up against that same bus window, and seeing his remains swept out at the next stop by a muttering old man in faded coveralls. One way or the other, he decided, it didn't mean shit to him. Except his legs seemed to have died already. And the driver called a twenty-minute stopover—Tidewater Station, Virginia. It was an old cinder-block building with two entrances to each rest room, holdover from the previous century.

Legs like wood, he made a halfhearted attempt at ghosting the notions counter, but the black girl behind it was alert, guarding the sparse contents of the old glass case as though her ass depended on it. *Probably does*, Deke thought, turning away. Opposite the washrooms, an open doorway offered GAMES, the word flickered feebly in biofluorescent plastic. He could see a crowd of the local kickers clustered around a pool table. Aimless, his boredom following him like a cloud, he stuck his head in. And saw a biplane, wings no longer than his thumb, blossom bright-orange flame. Corkscrewing, trailing smoke, it vanished the instant it struck the green-felt field of the table.

"Tha's right, Tiny," a kicker bellowed, "you *take* that sumbitch!"

"Hey," Deke said. "What's going on?"

The nearest kicker was a bean pole with a black mesh Peterbilt cap. "Tiny's defending the Max," he said, not taking his eyes from the table.

"Oh, yeah? What's that?" But even as he asked, he saw it: a blue enamel medal shaped like the Maltese cross, the slogan *Pour le Mérite* divided among its arms.

The Blue Max rested on the edge of the table, directly before a vast and perfectly immobile bulk wedged into a fragile-looking chrome tube chair. The man's khaki workshirt would have hung on Deke like the folds of a sail, but it bulged across that bloated torso so tautly that the tiny buttons threatened to tear away at any instant. Deke thought of Southern troopers he'd seen on his way down; of what weird, gut-heavy endotype balanced on gangly legs that looked like they'd been borrowed from some other body. Tiny might look like that if he stood, but on a larger scale—a forty-inch jeans inseam that would need a woven-steel waistband to support all those pounds of swollen gut. If Tiny were ever to stand at all—for now Deke saw that that shiny frame was actually a wheelchair. There was something disturbingly childlike about the man's face, an appalling suggestion of youth and even beauty in features buried in fold and jowl. Embarrassed, Deke looked away. The other man, the one standing across the table from Tiny, had bushy sideburns and a thin mouth. He seemed to be trying to push something with his eyes, wrinkles of concentration spreading from the corners. . . .

"You dumbshit or what?" The man with the Peterbilt cap turned, catching Deke's Indo proleboy denims, the brass chains at his wrists, for the first time. "Why don't you get your ass lost, fucker. Nobody wants your kind in here." He turned back to the dogfight.

Bets were being made, being covered. The kickers were producing the hard stuff, the old stuff, liberty-headed dollars and Roosevelt dimes from the stamp-and-coin stores, while more cautious betters slapped down antique paper dollars laminated in clear plastic. Through the haze came a trio of red planes, flying in formation. Fokker D VIIs. The room fell silent. The Fokkers banked majestically under the solar orb of a two-hundred-watt bulb.

The blue Spad dove out of nowhere. Two more plunged from the shadowy ceiling, following closely. The kickers swore, and one chuckled. The formation broke wildly. One Fokker dove almost to the felt, without losing the Spad on its tail. Furiously, it zigged and zagged across the green flatlands but to no avail. At last it pulled up, the enemy hard after it, too steeply—and stalled, too low to pull out in time.

A stack of silver dimes was scooped up.

The Fokkers were outnumbered now. One had two Spads on

its tail. A needle-spray of tracers tore past its cockpit. The Fokker slip-turned right, banked into an Immelmann, and was behind one of its pursuers. It fired, and the biplane fell, tumbling.

"Way to go, Tiny!" The kickers closed in around the table.

Deke was frozen with wonder. It felt like being born all over again.

Frank's Truck Stop was two miles out of town on the Commercial Vehicles Only route. Deke had tagged it, out of idle habit, from the bus on the way in. Now he walked back between the traffic and the concrete crash-guards. Articulated trucks went slamming past, big eight-segmented jobs, the wash of air each time threatening to blast him over. CVO stops were easy makes. When he sauntered into Frank's, there was nobody to doubt that he'd come in off a big rig, and he was able to browse the gift shop as slowly as he liked. The wire rack with the projective wetware wafers was located between a stack of Korean cowboy shirts and a display for Fuzz Buster mudguards. A pair of Oriental dragons twisted in the air over the rack, either fighting or fucking, he couldn't tell which. The game he wanted was there: a wafer labeled SPADS&FOKKERS. It took him three seconds to boost it and less time to slide the magnet—which the cops in DC hadn't even bothered to confiscate—across the universal security strip.

On the way out, he lifted two programming units and a little Batang facilitator-remote that looked like an antique hearing aid.

He chose a highstack at random and fed the rental agent the line he'd used since his welfare rights were yanked. Nobody ever checked up; the state just counted occupied rooms and paid.

The cubicle smelled faintly of urine, and someone had scrawled Hard Anarchy Liberation Front slogans across the walls. Deke kicked the trash out of a corner, sat down, back to the wall, and ripped open the wafer pack.

There was a folded instruction sheet with diagrams of loops, rolls and Immelmanns, a tube of saline paste, and a computer list of operational specs. And the wafer itself, white plastic with a blue biplane and logo on one side, red on the other. He turned it over and over in his hand: SPADS&FOKKERS, FOKKERS&SPADS. Red and blue. He fitted the Batang behind his ear, after coating the inductor surface with paste, jacked its fiberoptic ribbon into the programmer, and plugged the programmer into the wall current. Then he slid the wafer into the programmer. It was a cheap set, Indonesian, and the base of his skull buzzed uncomfortably as the program ran. But when it was done, a sky-blue Spad darted restlessly through the air a few inches from his face. It almost glowed, it was so real. It had the strange inner life that fanatically detailed museum-grade models often have, but it took all of his concentration to keep it in existence. If his attention wavered at all, it lost focus, fuzzing into a pathetic blur.

He practiced until the battery in the earset died, then slumped against the wall and fell asleep. He dreamed of flying, in a universe that consisted entirely of white clouds and blue sky, with no up and down, and never a green field to crash into.

He woke to a rancid smell of frying krill-cakes and winced with hunger. No cash, either. Well, there were plenty of student types in the stack. Bound to be one who'd like to score a programming unit. He hit the hall with the boosted spare. Not far down was a door with a poster on it: THERE'S A HELL OF A GOOD UNIVERSE NEXT DOOR. Under that was a starscape with a cluster of multicolored pills, torn from an ad for some pharmaceutical company, pasted over an inspirational shot of the "space colony" that had been under construction since before he was born. LET'S GO, the poster said, beneath the collaged hypnotics.

He knocked. The door opened, security slides stopping it at a two-inch slice of girl-face. "Yeah?"

"You're going to think this is stolen." He passed the programmer from hand to hand. "I mean because it's new, a virtual cherry, and the bar code's still on it. But listen, I'm not gonna argue the point. No. I'm gonna let you have it for only like half of what you'd pay anywhere else."

"Hey, wow, *really*, no kidding?" The visible fraction of

mouth twisted into a strange smile. She extended her hand, palm up, a loose fist. Level with his chin. "Lookahere!"

There was a hole in her hand, a black tunnel that ran right up her arm. Two small, red lights. Rat's eyes. They scurried toward him—growing, gleaming. Something gray streaked forward and leaped for his face.

He screamed, throwing his hands up to ward it off. Legs twisting, he fell, the programmer shattered under him.

Silicate shards skittered as he thrashed, clutching his head. Where it hurt, it hurt—it hurt very badly indeed.

"Oh my God!" Slides unsnapped, and the girl was hovering over him. "Here, listen, come on." She dangled a blue hand towel. "Grab onto this and I'll pull you up."

He looked at her through a wash of tears. Student. That fed look, the oversized sweatshirt, teeth so straight and white they could be used as a credit reference. A thin gold chain around one ankle (fuzzed, he saw with baby-fine hair). Choppy Japanese haircut. Money. "That sucker was gonna be my dinner," he said ruefully. He took hold of the towel and let her pull him up.

She smiled but skittishly backed away from him. "Let me make it up to you," she said. "You want some food? It was only a projection, okay?"

He followed her in, wary as an animal entering a trap.

"Holy shit," Deke said, "this is *real cheese* . . ." He was sitting on a gutsprung sofa, wedged between a four-foot teddy bear and a loose stack of floppies. The room was ankle deep in books and clothes and papers. But the food she magicked up . . . Gouda cheese and tinned beef and honest-to-God greenhouse wheat wafers . . . was straight out of the Arabian Nights.

"Hey," she said. "We know how to treat a proleboy right, huh?" Her name was Nance Bettendorf. She was seventeen. Both her parents had jobs—greedy buggers—and she was an engineering major at William and Mary. She got top marks except in English. "I guess you must really have a thing about rats. You got some kind of phobia about rats?"

He glanced sidelong at her bed. You couldn't see it, really, it was just a swell in the ground cover. "It's not like that. It just reminded me of something else, is all."

"Like what?" She squatted in front of him, the big shirt riding high up one smooth thigh.

"Well . . . did you ever see the—" his voice involuntarily rose and rushed past the words—"*Washington Monument?* Like at night? It's got these two little . . . red lights on top, aviation markers or something, and I, and I . . ." He started to shake.

"You're afraid of the Washington Monument?" Nance whooped and rolled over with laughter, long tanned legs kicking. She was wearing crimson bikini panties.

"I would rather die than look at it again," he said levelly.

She stopped laughing then, sat up, studied his face. White, even teeth worried at her lower lip, like she was dragging up something she didn't want to think about. At last she ventured, "Brainlock?"

"Yeah," he said bitterly. "They told me I'd never go back to DC. And then the fuckers laughed."

"What did they get you for?"

"I'm a thief." He wasn't about to tell her that the actual charge was career shoplifting.

"Lotta old *computer* hacks spent their lives programming machines. And you know what? The human brain is not a goddamn bit like a machine, no way. They just don't program the same." Deke knew this shrill desperate rap, this long, circular jive that the lonely string out to the rare listener; knew it from a hundred cold and empty nights spent in the company of strangers. Nance was lost in it, and Deke, nodding and yawning, wondered if he'd even be able to stay awake when they finally hit that bed of hers.

"I built that projection I hit you with myself," she said, hugging her knees up beneath her chin. "It's for muggers, you know? I just happened to have it on me, and I threw it at you 'cause I thought it was so funny, you trying to sell me that shit little Indojavanese programmer." She hunched forward and held out her hand again. "Look here." Deke cringed. "No, no, it's okay, I swear it, this is different." She opened her hand.

A single, blue flame danced there, perfect and everchanging. "Look at that," she marveled. "Just look. I programmed that. It's not some diddly little seven-image job either. It's a continuous two-hour look, seven thousand two hundred seconds, never the same twice, each instant as individual as a fucking snowflake!''

The flame's core was glacial crystal, shards and facets flashing up, twisting and gone, leaving behind near-subliminal images so bright and sharp that they cut the eye. Deke winced. People mostly. Pretty little naked people, fucking. ''How the hell did you do that?''

She rose, bare feet slipping on slick magazines, and melodramatically swept folds of loose printout from a raw plywood shelf. He saw a neat row of small consoles, austere and expensive looking. Custom work. ''This is the real stuff I got here. Image facilitator. Here's my fast-wipe module. This is a brain-map one-to-one function analyzer.'' She sang off the names like a litany. ''Quantum flicker stabilizer. Program splicer. An image assembler . . .''

''You need all that to make one little flame?''

''You betcha. This is all state of the art, professional projective wetware gear. It's years ahead of anything you've seen.''

''Hey,'' he said. ''you know anything about SPADS&-FOKKERS?''

She laughed. And then, because he sensed the time was right, he reached to take her hand.

''Don't you touch me, motherfuck, don't you *ever touch me*!'' Nance screamed, and her hand slammed against the wall as she recoiled, white and shaking with terror.

''Okay!'' He threw up his hands. ''Okay! I'm nowhere near you. Okay?''

She cowered from him. Her eyes were round and unblinking; tears built up at the corners, rolled down ashen cheeks. Finally, she shook her head. ''Hey. Deke. Sorry. I should've told you.''

''Told me what?'' But he had a creepy feeling . . . already knew. The way she clutched her head. The weakly spasmodic way her hands opened and closed. ''You got a brainlock, too.''

''Yeah.'' She closed her eyes. ''It's a chastity lock. My asshole parents paid for it. So I can't stand to have anybody touch me or even stand too close.'' Eyes opened in blind hate. ''I didn't even *do* anything. Not a fucking thing. But they've both got jobs and they're so horny for me to have a career that they can't piss straight. They're afraid I'd neglect my studies if I got, you know, involved in sex and stuff. The day the brainlock comes off I am going to fuck the vilest, greasiest, hairiest . . ."

She was clutching her head again. Deke jumped up and rummaged through the medicine cabinet. He found a jar of B-complex vitamins, pocketed a few against need, and brought two to Nance, with a glass of water. "Here." He was careful to keep his distance. "This'll take the edge off."

"Yeah, yeah," she said. Then, almost to herself. "You must really think I'm a jerk."

The games room in the Greyhound station was almost empty. A lone, long-jawed fourteen-year-old was bent over a console, maneuvering rainbow fleets of submarines in the murky grind of the North Atlantic.

Deke sauntered in, wearing his new kicker drag, and leaned against a cinder-block wall made smooth by countless coats of green enamel. He'd washed the dye from his proleboy butch, boosted jeans and T-shirt from the Goodwill, and found a pair of stompers in the sauna locker of a highstack with cut-rate security.

"Seen Tiny around, friend?"

The subs darted like neon guppies. "Depends on who's asking."

Deke touched the remote behind his left ear. The Spad snaprolled over the console, swift and delicate as a dragonfly. It was beautiful; so perfect, so *true* it made the room seem an illusion. He buzzed the grid, millimeters from the glass, taking advantage of the programmed ground effect.

The kid didn't even bother to look up. "Jackman's," he said. "Down Richmond Road, over by the surplus."

Deke let the Spad fade in mid-climb.

Jackman's took up most of the third floor of an old brick building. Deke found Best Buy War Surplus first, then a broken neon sign over an unlit lobby. The sidewalk out front was littered with another kind of surplus—damaged vets, some of them dating back to Indochina. Old men who'd left their eyes under Asian suns squatted beside twitching boys who'd inhaled mycotoxins in Chile. Deke was glad to have the battered elevator doors sigh shut behind him.

A dusty Dr. Pepper clock at the far side of the long, spectral room told him it was a quarter to eight. Jackman's had been embalmed twenty years before he was born, sealed away behind a yellowish film of nicotine, of polish and hair oil. Directly beneath the clock, the flat eyes of somebody's grandpappy's prize buck regarded Deke from a framed, blown-up snapshot gone the slick sepia of cockroach wings. There was the click and whisper of pool, the squeak of a workboot twisting on linoleum as a player leaned in for a shot. Somewhere high above the green-shaped lamps hung a string of crepe-paper Christmas bells faded to dead rose. Deke looked from one cluttered wall to the next. No facilitator.

"Bring one in, should we need it," someone said. He turned, meeting the mild eyes of a bald man with steel-rimmed glasses. "My name's Cline, Bobby Earl. You don't look like you shoot pool, mister." But there was nothing threatening in Bobby Earl's voice or stance. He pinched the steel frames from his nose and polished the thick lenses with a fold of tissue. He reminded Deke of a shop instructor who'd patiently tried to teach him retrograde biochip installation. "I'm a gambler," he said, smiling. His teeth were white plastic. "I know I don't much look it."

"I'm looking for Tiny," Deke said.

"Well," replacing the glasses, "you're not going to find him. He's gone up to Bethesda to let the VA clean his plumbing for him. He wouldn't fly against you anyhow."

"Why not?"

"Well, because you're not on the circuit or I'd know your face. You any good?" When Deke nodded, Bobby Earl called down the length of Jackman's, "Yo, Clarence! You bring out that facilitator. We got us a flyboy."

Twenty minutes later, having lost his remote and what cash he had left, Deke was striding past the broken soldiers of Best Buy.

"Now you let me tell you, boy," Bobby Earl had said in a fatherly tone as, hand on shoulder, he led Deke back to the elevator. "You're not going to win against a combat vet—you listening to me? I'm not even especially good, just an old grunt who was on hype fifteen, maybe twenty times. Ol' Tiny, he was a *pilot*. Spent his entire enlistment hyped to the gills. He's got membrane attenuation real bad . . . you ain't never going to beat him.''

It was a cool night. But Deke burned with anger and humiliation.

"Jesus, that's crude," Nance said as the Spad strafed mounds of pink underwear. Deke, hunched up on the couch, yanked her flashy little Braun remote from behind his ear.

"Now don't you get on my case too, Miss rich-bitch gonna-have-a-job—"

"Hey, lighten up! It's nothing to do with you—it's just *tech*. That's a really primitive wafer you got there. I mean, on the street maybe it's fine. But compared to the work I do at school, it's—hey. You ought to let me rewrite it for you.''

"Say what?"

"Lemme beef it up. These suckers are all written in hexadecimal, see, cause the industry programmers are all washed-out computer hacks. That's how they think. But let me take it to the reader–analyzer at the department, run a few changes on it, translate it into a modern wetlanguage. Edit out all the redundant intermediaries. That'll goose up your reaction time, cut the feedback loop in half. So you'll fly faster and better. Turn you into a real pro, Ace!" She took a hit off her bong, then doubled over laughing and choking.

"Is that legit?" Deke asked dubiously.

"Hey, why do you think people buy gold-wire remotes? For the prestige? Shit. Conductivity's better, cuts a few nanoseconds off the reaction time. And reaction time is the name of the game, kiddo.''

"No," Deke said. "If it were that easy, people'd already have it. Tiny Montgomery would have it. He'd have the best."

"Don't you ever *listen*?" Nance set down the bong; brown water slopped onto the floor. "The stuff I'm working with is three years ahead of anything you'll find on the street.''

"No shit," Deke said after a long pause. "I mean, you can do that?"

It was like graduating from a Model T to a ninety-three Lotus. The Spad handled like a dream, responsive to Deke's slightest thought. For weeks he played the arcades, with not a

nibble. He flew against the local teens and by ones and threes
shot down their planes. He took chances, played flash. And
the planes tumbled . . .

Until one day Deke was tucking his seed money away, and
a lanky black straightened up from the wall. He eyed the laminateds in Deke's hand and grinned. A ruby tooth gleamed.
"You know," the man said, "I *heard* there was a casper who
could fly, going up against the kiddies."

"Jesus," Deke said, spreading Danish butter on a kelp stick.
"I wiped the *floor* with those spades. They were good, too."

"That's nice, honey," Nance mumbled. She was working
on her finals project, sweating data into a machine.

"You know, I think what's happening is I got real talent for
this kind of shit. You know? I mean, the program gives me an
edge, but I got the stuff to take advantage of it. I'm really
getting a rep out there, you know?" Impulsively, he snapped
on the radio. Scratchy Dixieland brass blared.

"Hey," Nance said. "Do you *mind?*"

"No, I'm just—" He fiddled with the knobs, came up with
some slow, romantic bullshit. "There. Come on; stand up.
Let's dance."

"Hey, you know I can't—"

"Sure you can, sugarcakes." He threw her the huge teddy
bear and snatched up a patchwork cotton dress from the floor.
He held it by the waist and sleeve, tucking the collar under his
chin. It smelled of patchouli, more faintly of sweat, "See, I
stand over here, you stand over there. We dance. Get it?"

Blinking softly, Nance stood and clutched the bear tightly.
They danced then, slowly, staring into each other's eyes. After
a while, she began to cry. But still, she was smiling.

Deke was daydreaming, imagining he was Tiny Montgomery wired into his jumpjet. Imagined the machine responding
to his slightest neural twitch, reflexes cranked *way* up, hype
flowing steadily into his veins.

Nance's floor became jungle, her bed a plateau in the An-
dean foothills, and Deke flew his Spad at forced speed, as if
it were a full-wired interactive combat machine. Computerized
hypos fed a slow trickle of high-performance enhancement me-

lange into his bloodstream. Sensors were wired directly into his skull—pulling a supersonic snapturn in the green-blue bowl of sky over Bolivian rain forest. Tiny would have *felt* the airflow over control surfaces.

Below, grunts hacked through the jungle with hype-pumps strapped above elbows to give them that little extra death-dance fury in combat, a shot of liquid hell in a blue plastic vial. Maybe they got ten minutes worth in a week. But coming in at treetop level, reflexes cranked to the max, flying so low the ground troops never spotted you until you were on them, phosgene agents released, away and gone before they could draw a bead . . . it took a constant trickle of hype just to maintain. And the direct neuron interface with the jumpjet was a two-way street. The onboard computers monitored biochemistry and decided when to open the sluice gates and give the human component a killer jolt of combat edge.

Dosages like that ate you up. Ate you good and slow and constant, etching the brain surfaces, eroding away the brain-cell membranes. If you weren't yanked from the air promptly enough, you ended up with brain-cell attenuation—with reflexes too fast for your body to handle and your fight-or-flight reflexes fucked real good . . . .

"I aced it, proleboy!"

"Hah?" Deke looked up, startled, as Nance slammed in, tossing books and bag onto the nearest heap.

"My finals project—I got exempted from exams. The prof said he'd never seen anything like it. Uh, hey, dim the lights, wouldja? The colors are weird on my eyes."

He obliged. "So show me. Show me this wunnerful thing."

"Yeah, okay." She snatched up his remote, kicked clear standing space atop the bed, and struck a pose. A spark flared into flame in her hand. It spread in a quicksilver line up her arm, around her neck, and it was a snake, with triangular head and flickering tongue. Molten colors, oranges and reds. It slithered between her breasts. "I call it a firesnake," she said proudly.

Deke leaned close, and she jerked back.

"Sorry. It's like your flame, huh? I mean, I can see these tiny little fuckers in it."

"Sort of." The firesnake flowed down her stomach. "Next

month I'm going to splice two hundred separate flame programs together with meld justification in between to get the visuals. Then I'll tap the mind's body image to make it self-orienting. So it can crawl all over your body without your having to mind it. You could wear it dancing.''

"Maybe I'm dumb. But if you haven't done the work yet, how come I can see it?''

Nance giggled. "That's the best part—half the work isn't done yet. Didn't have the time to assemble the pieces into a unified program. Turn on that radio, huh? I want to dance.'' She kicked off her shoes. Deke tuned in something gutsy. Then, at Nance's urging, turned it down, almost to a whisper.

"I scored two hits of hype, see.'' She was bouncing on the bed, weaving her hands like a Balinese dancer. "Ever try the stuff? In-credible. Gives you like absolute concentration. Look here.'' She stood *en pointe*. "Never done that before.''

"Hype,'' Deke said. "Last person I heard of got caught with that shit got three years in the infantry. How'd you score it?''

"Cut a deal with a vet who was in grad school. She bombed out last month. Stuff gives me perfect visualization. I can hold the projection with my eyes shut. It was a snap assembling the program in my head.''

"On just two hits, huh?''

"One hit. I'm saving the other. Teach was so impressed he's sponsoring me for a job interview. A recruiter from I. G. Feuchtwaren hits campus in two weeks. That cap is gonna sell him the program *and* me. I'm gonna cut out of school two years early, straight into industry, do not pass jail, do not pay two hundred dollars.''

The snake curled into a flaming tiara. It gave Deke a funny-creepy feeling to think of Nance walking out of his life.

"I'm a witch,'' Nance sang, "a wetware witch.'' She shucked her shirt over her head and sent it flying. Her fine, high breasts moved freely, gracefully, as she danced. "I'm gonna make it''—now she was singing a current pop hit—"to the . . . top!'' Her nipples were small and pink and aroused. The firesnake licked at them and whipped away.

"Hey, Nance,'' Deke said uncomfortably. "Calm down a little, huh?''

"I'm celebrating!" She hooked a thumb into her shiny gold panties. Fire swirled around hand and crotch. "I'm the virgin goddess, baby, and I have the pow-er!" Singing again.

Deke looked away. "Gotta go now," he mumbled. Gotta go home and jerk off. He wondered where she'd hidden that second hit. Could be anywhere.

There was a protocol to the circuit, a tacit order of deference and precedence as elaborate as that of a Mandarin court. It didn't matter that Deke was hot, that his rep was spreading like wildfire. Even a name flyboy couldn't challenge who he wished. He had to climb the ranks. But if you flew every night. If you were always available to anybody's challenge. And if you were good . . . well, it was possible to climb fast.

Deke was one plane up. It was tournament fighting, three planes against three. Not many spectators, a dozen maybe, but it was a good fight, and they were noisy. Deke was immersed in the manic calm of combat when he realized suddenly that they had fallen silent. Saw the kickers stir and exchange glances. Eyes flicked past him. He heard the elevator doors close. Coolly, he disposed of the second of his opponent's planes, then risked a quick glance over his shoulder.

Tiny Montgomery had just entered Jackman's. The wheelchair whispered across browning linoleum, guided by tiny twitches of one imperfectly paralyzed hand. His expression was stern, blank, calm.

In that instant, Deke lost two planes. One to deresolution—gone to blur and canceled out by the facilitator—and the other because his opponent was a real fighter. Guy did a barrel role, killing speed and slipping to the side, and strafed Deke's bi-plane as it shot past. It went down in flames. Their last two planes shared altitude and speed, and as they turned, trying for position, they naturally fell into a circling pattern.

The kicker made room as Tiny wheeled up against the table. Bobby Earl Cline trailed after him, lanky and casual. Deke and his opponent traded glances and pulled their machines back from the pool table so they could hear the man out. Tiny smiled. His features were small, clustered in the center of his pale, doughy face. One finger twitched slightly on the chrome handrest. "I heard about you." He looked straight at Deke.

His voice was soft and shockingly sweet, a baby-girl little voice. "I heard you're good."

Deke nodded slowly. The smile left Tiny's face. His soft, fleshy lips relaxed into a natural pout, as if he were waiting for a kiss. His small, bright eyes studied Deke without malice. "Let's see what you can do, then."

Deke lost himself in the cool game of war. And when the enemy went down in smoke and flame, to explode and vanish against the table, Tiny wordlessly turned his chair, wheeled it into the elevator, and was gone.

As Deke was gathering up his winnings, Bobby Earl eased up to him and said, "The man wants to play you."

"Yeah?" Deke was nowhere near high enough on the circuit to challenge Tiny. "What's the scam?"

"Man who was coming up from Atlanta tomorrow canceled. Ol' Tiny, he was spoiling to go up against somebody new. So it looks like you get your shot at the Max."

"Tomorrow? Wednesday? Doesn't give me much prep time."

Bobby Earl smiled gently. "I don't think that makes no nevermind."

"How's that, Mr. Cline?"

"Boy, you just ain't got the *moves*, you follow me? Ain't got no surprises. You fly just like some kinda beginner, only faster and slicker. You follow what I'm trying to say?"

"I'm not sure I do. You want to put a little action on that?"

"Tell you truthful," Cline said. "I been hoping on that." He drew a small black notebook from his pocket and licked a pencil stub. "Give you five to one. They's nobody gonna give no fairer odds than that."

He looked at Deke almost sadly. "But Tiny, he's just naturally better'n you, and that's all she wrote, boy. He lives for that goddamned game, ain't *got* nothing else. Can't get out of that goddamned chair. You think you can best a man who's fighting for his life, you are just lying to yourself."

Norman Rockwell's portrait of the colonel regarded Deke dispassionately from the Kentucky Fried across Richmond Road from the coffee bar. Deke held his cup with hands that were cold and trembling. His skull bummed with fatigue. Cline was right, he told the colonel. I can go up against Tiny, but I can't win. The colonel stared back, gaze calm and level and not particularly kindly, taking in the coffee bar and Best Buy and all his drag-ass kingdom of Richmond Road. Waiting for Deke to admit to the terrible thing he had to do.

"The bitch is planning to leave me *any*way," Deke said aloud. Which made the black countergirl look at him funny, then quickly away.

"Daddy called!" Nance danced into the apartment, slamming the door behind her. "And you know what? He says if I can get this job and hold it for six months, he'll have the brainlock reversed. Can you *believe* it? Deke?" She hesitated. "You okay?"

Deke stood. Now that the moment was on him, he felt unreal, like he was in a movie or something. "How come you never came home last night?" Nance asked.

The skin on his face was unnaturally taut, a parchment mask. "Where'd you stash the hype, Nance? I need it."

"Deke," she said, trying a tentative smile that instantly vanished. "Deke, that's mine. My hit. I need it. For my interview."

He smiled scornfully. "You got money. You can always score another cap."

"Not by Friday! Listen. Deke, this is really important. My whole life is riding on this interview. I need that cap. It's all I got!"

"Baby, you got the fucking world! Take a look around you— six ounces of blond Lebanese hash! Little anchovy fish in tins. Unlimited medical coverage, if you need it." She was backing away from him, stumbling against the static waves of unwashed bedding and wrinkled glossy magazines that crested at the foot of her bed. "Me, I never had a glimmer of any of this. Never had the kind of edge it takes to get along. Well, this one time I am gonna. There is a match in two hours that I am going to fucking well win. Do you hear me?" He was working himself into a rage, and that was good. He needed it for what he had to do.

Nance flung up an arm, palm open, but he was ready for that and slapped her hand aside, never even catching a glimpse of the dark tunnel, let alone those little red eyes. They were both falling, and he was on top of her, her breath hot and rapid in his face. "Deke! Deke! I *need* that hit. Deke, my *interview*, it's the only . . . I gotta . . . gotta . . ." She twisted her face away, crying into the wall. "Please God, please don't . . ."

"Where did you stash it?"

Pinned against the bed under his body, Nance began to spasm, her entire body convulsing in pain and fear.

"Where is it?"

Her face was bloodless, gray corpse flesh, and horror burned in her eyes. Her lips squirmed. It was too late to stop now; he'd crossed over the line. Deke felt revolted and nauseated, all the more so because on some unexpected and unwelcome level, he was *enjoying* this.

"Where is it, Nance?" And slowly, very gently, he began to stroke her face.

Deke summoned Jackman's elevator with a finger that moved as fast and straight as a hornet and landed daintily as a butterfly on the call button. He was full of bouncy energy, and it was all under control. On the way up, he whipped off his shades and chuckled at his reflection in the finger-smudged chrome. The blacks of his eyes were like pinpricks, all but invisible, and still the world was neon bright.

Tiny was waiting. The cripple's mouth turned up at the corners into a sweet smile as he took in Deke's irises, the exaggerated calm of his notions, the unsuccessful attempt to mime an undrugged clumsiness. "Well," he said, in that girlish voice, "looks like I have a treat in store for me."

The Max was draped over one tube of the wheelchair. Deke took up position and bowed, not quite mockingly. "Let's fly." As challenger, he flew defense. He materialized his planes at a conservative altitude, high enough to dive, low enough to have warning when Tiny attacked. He waited.

The crowd tipped him. A fatboy with brilliantined hair looked startled, a hollow-eyed cracker started to smile. Murmurs rose. Eyes shifted slow motion in heads frozen by hyped-up reaction time. Took maybe three nanoseconds to pinpoint the source of attack. Deke whipped his head up, and—

Sonofabitch, he was *blind*! The Fokkers were diving straight from the two-hundred-watt bulb, and Tiny had suckered him into staring right at it. His vision whited out. Deke squeezed lids tight over welling tears and frantically held visualization. He split his flight, curved two biplanes right, one left. Immediately twisting each a half-turn, then back again. He had to dodge randomly—he couldn't tell where the hostile warbirds were.

Tiny chuckled. Deke could hear him through the sounds of the crowd, the cheering and cursing and slapping down of coins that seemed to syncopate independent of the ebb and flow of the duel.

When his vision returned an instant later, a Spad was in flames and falling. Fokkers tailed his surviving planes, one on one and two on the other. Three seconds into the game, and he was down one.

Dodging to keep Tiny from pinning tracers on him, he looped the single-pursued plane about and drove the other toward the blind spot between Tiny and the light bulb.

Tiny's expression went very calm. The faintest shadow of disappointment—of contempt, even—was swallowed up by tranquility. He tracked the planes blandly, waiting for Deke to make his turn.

Then, just short of the blind spot, Deke shoved his Spad into a dive, the Fokkers overshooting and banking wildly to either side, twisting around to regain position.

The Spad swooped down on the third Fokker, pulled into position by Deke's other plane. Fire strafed wings and crimson fuselage. For an instant nothing happened, and Deke thought he had a fluke miss. Then the little red mother veered left and went down, trailing black, oily smoke.

Tiny frowned, small lines of displeasure marring the perfection of his mouth. Deke smiled. One even, and Tiny held position.

Both Spads were tailed closely. Deke swung them wide, and then pulled them together from opposite sides of the table. He drove them straight for each other, neutralizing Tiny's advantage . . . neither could fire without endangering his own planes. Deke cranked his machines up to top speed, slamming them at each other's noses.

An instant before they crashed, Deke sent the planes over

and under one another, opening fire on the Fokkers and twisting away. Tiny was ready. Fire filled the air. Then one blue and one red plane soared free, heading in opposite directions. Behind them, two biplanes tangled in midair. Wings touched, slewed about, and the planes crumpled. They fell together, almost straight down, to the green felt below.

Ten seconds in and four planes down. A black vet pursed his lips and blew softly. Someone else shook his head in disbelief.

Tiny was sitting straight and a little forward in his wheelchair, eyes intense and unblinking, soft hands plucking feebly at the grips. None of that amused and detached bullshit now; his attention was riveted on the game. The kickers, the table, Jackman's itself, might not exist at all for him. Bobby Earl Cline laid a hand on his shoulder; Tiny didn't notice. The planes were at opposite ends of the room, laboriously gaining altitude. Deke jammed his against the ceiling, dim through the smoky haze. He spared Tiny a quick glance, and their eyes locked. Cold against cold. "Let's see your best," Deke muttered through clenched teeth.

They drove their planes together.

The hype was peaking now, and Deke could see Tiny's tracers crawling through the air between the planes. He had to put his Spad into the line of fire to get off a fair burst, then twist and band so the Fokker's bullets would slip by his undercarriage. Tiny was every bit as hot, dodging Deke's fire and passing so close to the Spad their landing gears almost tangled as they passed.

Deke was looping his Spad in a punishingly tight turn when the hallucinations hit. The felt writhed and twisted—became the green hell of Bolivian rain forest that Tiny had flown combat over. The walls receded to gray infinity, and he felt the metal confinement of a cybernetic jumpjet close in around him.

But Deke had done his homework. He was expecting the hallucinations and knew he could deal with them. The military would never pass on a drug that couldn't be fought through. Spad and Fokker looped into another pass. He could read the tensions in Tiny Montgomery's face, the echoes of combat in deep jungle sky. They drove their planes together, feeling the torqued tensions that fed straight from instrumentation to hindbrain, the adrenaline pumps kicking in behind the armpits, the cold, fast freedom of airflow over jet-skin mingling with the smells of hot metal and fear sweat. Tracers tore past his face, and he pulled back, seeing the Spad zoom by the Fokker again, both untouched. The kickers were just going ape, waving hats and stomping feet, acting like God's own fools. Deke locked glances with Tiny again.

Malice rose up in him, and though his nerve was taut as the carbon-crystal whiskers that kept the jumpjets from falling apart in superman turns over the Andes, he counterfeited a casual smile and winked. Jerking his head slightly to one side, as if to say, "Lookahere."

Tiny glanced to the side.

It was only for a fraction of a second, but that was enough. Deke pulled as fast and tight an Immelmann—right on the edge of theoretical tolerance—as he had ever been seen on the circuit, and he was hanging on Tiny's tail.

Let's see you get out of this one, sucker.

Tiny rammed his plane straight down at the green, and Deke followed after. He held his fire. He had Tiny where he wanted him.

Running. Just like he'd been on his every combat mission. High on exhilaration and hype, maybe, but running scared. They were down to the felt now, flying treetop level. Break, Deke thought, and jacked up the speed. Peripherally, he could see Bobby Earl Cline, and there was a funny look on the man's face. A pleading kind of look. Tiny's composure was shot; his face was twisted and tormented.

Now Tiny panicked and dove his plane in among the crowd. The biplanes looped and twisted between the kickers. Some jerked back involuntarily, and others laughingly swatted at them with their hands. But there was a hot glint of terror in Tiny's eyes that spoke of an eternity of fear and confinement, two edges sawing away at each other endlessly. . . .

The fear was death in the air, the confinement a locking away in metal, first of the aircraft, then of the chair. Deke could read it all in his face: Combat was the only out Tiny had had, and he'd taken it every chance he got. Until some anonymous *nationalista* with an antique SAM tore him out of that blue/green Bolivian sky and slammed him straight down to

Richmond Road and Jackman's and the smiling killer boy he faced this one last time across the faded cloth.

Deke rocked up on his toes, face burning with that million-dollar smile that was the trademark of the drug that had already fried Tiny before anyone ever bothered to blow him out of the sky in a hot tangle of metal and mangled flesh. It all came together then. He saw that flying was all that held Tiny together. That daily brush of fingertips against death, and then rising up from the metal coffin, alive again. He'd been holding back collapse by sheer force of will. Break that willpower, and mortality would come pouring out and drown him. Tiny would lean over and throw up in his own lap.

And Deke drove it home. . . .

There was a moment of stunned silence as Tiny's last plane vanished in a flash of light. "I did it," Deke whispered. Then, louder, "Son of a bitch, I did it!"

Across the table from him, Tiny twisted in his chair, arms jerking spastically; his head lolled on one shoulder. Behind him, Bobby Earl Cline stared straight at Deke, his eyes hot coals.

The gambler snatched up the Max and wrapped its ribbon around a stack of laminateds. Without warning, he flung the bundle at Deke's face. Effortlessly, casually, Deke plucked it from the air.

For an instant, then, it looked like the gambler would come at him, right across the pool table. He was stopped by a tug on his sleeve. "Bobby Earl," Tiny whispered, his voice choking with humiliation, "you gotta get me . . . out of here. . . ."

Stiffly, angrily, Cline wheeled his friend around, and then away, into shadow.

Deke threw back his head and laughed. By God, he felt good! He stuffed the Max into a shirt pocket, where it hung cold and heavy. The money he crammed into his jeans. Man, he had to jump with it, his triumph leaping up through him like a wild thing, fine and strong as the flanks of a buck in the deep woods he'd seen from a Greyhound once, and for this one moment it seemed that everything was worth it somehow, all the pain and misery he'd gone through to finally win.

But Jackman's was silent. Nobody cheered. Nobody crowded

around to congratulate him. He sobered, and silent, hostile faces swam into focus. Not one of these kickers was on his side. They radiated contempt, even hatred. For an interminably drawn-out moment the air trembled with potential violence . . . and then someone turned to the side, hawked up phlegm, and spat on the floor. The crowd broke up, muttering, one by one drifting into the darkness.

Deke didn't move. A muscle in one leg began to twitch, harbinger of the coming hype crash. The top of his head felt numb, and there was an awful taste in his mouth. For a second he had to hang onto the table with both hands to keep from falling down forever, into the living shadow beneath him, as he hung impaled by the prize buck's dead eyes in the photo under the Dr. Pepper clock.

A little adrenaline would pull him out of this. He needed to celebrate. To get drunk or stoned and talk it up, going over the victory time and again, contradicting himself, making up details, laughing and bragging. A starry old night like this called for big talk.

But standing there with all of Jackman's silent and vast and empty around him, he realized suddenly that he had nobody left to tell it to.

Nobody at all.

A Gift from the GrayLanders
by Michael Bishop

Introduction

I first met Michael Bishop by mail. I had read some of his fiction and admired it; I had also read a couple of installments of his column in Thrust *magazine. He seemed intelligent and humane, and his fiction was interesting, though sometimes overliterary for my tastes.*

He wrote to tell me that he had reviewed my first novel in a guest review column he had written for Fantasy & Science Fiction. *He wanted to apologize for having criticized the fact that the cover of my novel called me a "Hugo Award winner," when in fact I had never won a Hugo. He realized now that it was unfair to criticize a writer for what the publisher puts on the cover—writers have no control over that. As a bit of poetic justice, he said, he had just received copies of his new book; on the cover, the publisher had called him a "Nebula Award winner," which at the time was not yet true.*

All this was pleasant enough—writing that letter showed that Bishop had the sort of conscience Abraham Lincoln was famous for. He wasn't content to say, "Oh, well, it's just a review." I have since learned that Bishop's fastidiousness about ethical detail is rare almost to the point of uniqueness in our rather murky literary community. In retrospect I realize that I certainly don't measure up; there are quite a few who wouldn't dream of trying.

But it wasn't this event that made Michael Bishop one of the most important people in the science fiction field to me, personally. It was the review he wrote of my first novel.

Let's put it kindly. He hated it.

But he hated it intelligently. He had understood what I was trying to do with the book and explained exactly why I failed. I have read rave reviews of books of mine that left me in despair—if even my aficionados don't get what I'm doing, what hope do I have? But in panning my book, Michael Bishop gave me an insight that made it possible for my second novel to be a quantum leap ahead of my first. Bishop does not read without understanding; he does not criticize without teaching.

He not only helped me in my fiction, he also set a standard for one thing that good criticism must achieve. It must illuminate, not smear; it must build, not destroy.

In years since then, Mike and I have become friends—after a fashion. We don't always agree—far from it. He and I have been in conflict more than once over critical matters—once in print, more often in private letters. But our critical discussions are not as important to me as what he has given to me as a writer of fiction. Despite all our dissimilarities, one thing Bishop and I have in common is a refusal to deny the spiritual and religious side of human life. From his seventies masterwork "Death and Designation among the Asadi" to his triumphant novel Ancient of Days *in the eighties, he has not been afraid to invite us to understand and sympathize with characters who are part of a religious community or who struggle with questions of faith. In a field that rarely touches religion except to ridicule it, this makes Bishop a rare bird indeed.*

But this is only a small part of his accomplishment. Bishop's pattern is to take small characters—quiet people, unnoticed people—and make them so important to us that we take them completely into our hearts, weeping for their pain, rejoicing in their accomplishments. The standard technique in our romantic genre is to make characters important by inflating them—giving them worlds to save. The standard literary technique, which has seduced almost as many, is to make characters im-

portant by burdening them with the unbearable weight of obvious symbolism. Bishop rarely uses either method. Instead he makes our experience of his characters' inner life so real, so complete, so powerful, that they become important to us out of love.

"The Gift of the Graylanders" is a sad and beautiful story about the end of the world. Normally the phrase "end of the world" suggests universal cataclysm. Bishop reminds us that each of us lives in a world completely different from all others, because it is filtered through our own needs and perceptions and memories. The "end of the world" is a private experience for each of us, and even a holocaust does not make us identical. I love this story for the same reason that I love Mike Bishop—because he has the truth in him.

IN THE HOUSE WHERE MOMMY TOOK HIM SEVERAL MONTHS after she and Daddy stopped living together, Cory had a cot downstairs. The house belong to Mommy's sister and her sister's husband Martin, a pair of unhappy people who already had four kids of their own. Aunt Clara's kids had real bedrooms upstairs, but Mommy told Cory that he was lucky to have a place to sleep at all and that anyway a basement was certainly a lot better than a hot-air grate on a Denver street or a dirty stable like the one that the Baby Jesus had been born in.

Cory hated the way the basement looked and smelled. It had walls like concrete slabs on the graves in cemeteries. Looking at them, you could almost see those kinds of slabs turned on their ends and pushed up against one another to make this small square prison underground. The slabs oozed wetness. You could make a handprint on the walls just by holding your palm to the concrete. When you took your hand away, it smelled gray. Cory knew that dead people smelled gray too, especially when they had been dead a long time—like the people who were only bones and whom he had seen grinning out of magazine photographs without any lips or eyeballs or hair. Cory

sometimes lay down on his cot wondering if maybe an army
of those gray-smelling skeletons clustered on the other side of
the basement walls, working with oddly silent picks and shovels to break through the concrete and carry him away to the
GrayLands where their deadness made them live.

Maybe, though, the gray-smelling creatures beyond the
basement walls were not really skeletons. Maybe they were
Clay People. On his cousins' black-and-white TV set, Cory
had seen an old movie serial about a strange planet. Some of
the planet's people lived underground, and they could step into
or out of the walls of rock that tied together a maze of tunnels
beneath the planet's surface. They moved through dirt and rock
the way that a little boy like Cory could move through water
in summer or loose snow in winter. The brave, blond hero of
the serial called these creatures the Clay People, a name that
fit them almost perfectly, because they looked like monsters
slapped together out of wet mud and then put out into the sun
to dry. Every time they came limping into view with that tinny
movie-serial music rum-tum-tumping away in the background,
they gave Cory a bad case of the shivers.

Later, lying on his cot, he would think about them trying to
come through the oozy walls to take him away from that motel
in Ratón, New Mexico. For a long time that day, Daddy had
hidden in the room with the vending machines. Going in there
for a Coke, Cory had at first thought that Daddy was a monster. His screams had brought Mommy running and also the
motel manager and a security guard; and the "kidnap plot"—
as Mommy had called it later—had ended in an embarrassing
way for Daddy, Daddy hightailing it out of Ratón in his beat-
up Impala like a drug dealer making a getaway in a TV cop
show. But what if the Clay People were better kidnappers than
Daddy? What if they came through the walls and grabbed him
before he could awake and scream for help? They would surely
take him back through the clammy grayness to a place where
dirt would fill his mouth and stop his ears and press against
his eyeballs, and he would be as good as dead with them forever and ever.

So Cory hated the basement. Because his cousins disliked
the windowless damp of the place as much as he did, they
seldom came downstairs to bother him. Although that was okay

when he wanted to be by himself, he never really wanted to be
by himself *in the basement*. Smelling its mustiness, touching
its greasy walls, feeling like a bad guy in solitary, Cory could
not help but imagine unnamable danger and deadness surrounding him. Skeletons. Clay People. Monsters from the
earthen dark. It was okay to be alone on a mountain trail or
even in a classroom at school, but to be alone in this basement
was to be punished for not having a daddy who came home
every evening the way that daddies were supposed to. Daddy
himself, who had once tried to kidnap Cory, would have never
made him spend his nights in this kind of prison. Or, if for
some reason Daddy could not have prevented the arrangement,
he would have stayed downstairs with Cory to protect him from
the creatures burrowing toward him from the GrayLands.

"Cory, there's *nothing* down here to be afraid of," Mommy
said. "And you don't want your mother to share your bedroom
with you, do you? A big seven-year-old like you?"

"No," he admitted. "I want my daddy."

"Your daddy can't protect you. He can't or won't provide
for you. That's why we had to leave him. He only tried to grab
you back, Cory, to hurt me. Don't you understand?"

Daddy hurt Mommy? Cory shook his head.

"I'm sorry it's a basement," Mommy said. "I'm sorry it's
not a chalet with a big picture window overlooking a mountain
pass, but things just haven't been going that way for us lately."

Cory rolled over on his cot so that the tip of his nose brushed
the slablike wall.

"Tell me what you're afraid of," Mommy said. "If you tell
me, maybe we can handle it together—whatever it is."

After some more coaxing, but without turning back to face
her, Cory began to talk about the skeletons and the Clay People
from the GrayLands beyond the sweating concrete.

"The GrayLands?" Mommy said. "There aren't any
GrayLands, Cory. There may be skeletons, but they don't get
up and walk. They certainly don't use picks and shovels to dig
their way into basements. And the Clay People, well, they're
just television monsters, make-believe, nothing at all for a big
boy like you to worry about in real life."

"I want to sleep on the couch upstairs."

"You can't, Cory. You've got your own bathroom down here,

and when you wake up and have to use it, well, you don't disturb Uncle Martin or Aunt Clara or any of the kids. We've been through all this before, haven't we? You know how important it is that Marty gets his sleep. He has to get up at four in order to make his shift at the fire station.''

"I won't use the bathroom upstairs. I won't even drink nothin' before I go to bed.''

"Cory, hush.''

The boy rolled over and pulled himself up onto his elbows so that he could look right into Mommy's eyes. "I'm scared of the GrayLands. I'm scared of the gray-smellin' monsters that're gonna come pushin' through the walls from over there.''

Playfully, Mommy mussed his hair. "You're impossible, you know that? Really impossible.''

It was as if she could not wholeheartedly believe in his fear. In fact, she seemed to think that he had mentioned the GrayLands and the monsters who would come forth from them only as a boy's cute way of prompting adult sympathy. He did not like the basement (Mommy was willing to concede that point), but this business of a nearby subterranean country of death and its weird gray-smelling inhabitants was only so much childish malarky. The boy missed his father, and Mommy could not assume Daddy's role as protector—as bad as Clinton himself had been at it—because in a young boy's eyes a woman was not a man. And so she mussed his hair again and abandoned him to his delusive demons.

Cory never again spoke to anyone of the GrayLands. But each night, hating the wet clayey smell of the basement and its gummy linoleum floor and the foil-wrapped heating ducts bracketed to the ceiling and the naked light bulb hanging like a tiny dried gourd from a bracket near the unfinished stairs, he would huddle under the blankets on his cot and talk to the queer creatures tunneling stealthily toward him from the GrayLands—the Clay People, or Earth Zombies, or Bone Puppets, that only he of all the members of this mixed-up household actually believed in.

"Stay where you are,'' Cory would whisper at the wall. "Don't come over here. Stay where you are.''

The monsters—whatever they were—obeyed. They did not

break through the concrete to grab him. Of course, maybe the concrete was too thick and hard to let them reach him without a lot more work. They could still be going at it, picking away. The Clay People on that movie planet had been able to walk through earth without even using tools to clear a path for themselves, but maybe Earth's earth was packed tighter. Maybe good old-fashioned Colorado concrete could hold off such single-minded creatures for months. Cory hoped that it could. For safety's sake, he would keep talking to them, begging them to stay put, pleading with them not to undermine the foundations of his uncle's house with their secret digging.

Summer came, and they still had not reached him. The walls still stood against them, smooth to the touch here, rough there. Some of the scratches in the ever-glistening grayness were like unreadable foreign writing. These scratches troubled Cory. He wondered if they had always been there. Maybe the tunneling creatures had scribbled them on the concrete from the other side, not quite getting the tips of their strange writing instruments to push through the walls but by great effort and persistence just managing to press marks into the outer surface where a real human being like him could see them. The boy traced these marks with his finger. He tried to spell them out. But he had gone through only his first year in school, and the task of decipherment was not one he could accomplish without help. Unfortunately, he could not apply for help without breaking the promise that he had made to himself never to speak of the GrayLanders to anyone in Aunt Clara's family. If Mommy could muster no belief in them, how could he hope to convince his hard-headed cousins, who liked him best when he was either running errands for them or hiding from them in the doubtful sanctuary of the basement?

Then Cory realized that maybe he was having so much trouble reading the GrayLanders' damp scratches not because he was slow or the scratches stood for characters in a foreign tongue, but because his tormentors' painstaking method of pressing them outward onto the visible portions of the walls made the characters arrive there *backwards*. Cory was proud of himself for figuring this out. He filched a pocket mirror from the handbag of the oldest girl and brought it down the creaking stairs to test his theory.

This girl, fifteen-year-old Gina Lynn, caught him holding the mirror against one of the rougher sections of wall, squinting back and forth between the concrete and the oval glass. Meanwhile, with the nub of a broken pencil, he was struggling to copy the reversed scratches onto a tatter of paper bag. Cory did not hear Gina Lynn come down the stairs because he was concentrating so hard on this work. He was also beginning to understand that his wonderful theory was not really proving out. The mysterious calligraphy of the GrayLanders continued to make no sense.

"You're just about the weirdest little twerp I've ever seen," Gina Lynn said matter-of-factly. "Give me back my mirror."

Startled and then shamefaced, Cory turned around. He yielded the mirror. Gina Lynn asked him no questions, knowing from past experience that he would respond with monosyllables if at all, but began to bruit it around the house that he could read the marks in concrete the way that some people could read cloud formations or chicken entrails. Uncle Martin, who was home for a long weekend, thought this discovery about his sister-in-law's son hilarious. He called Cory into the living room to rag him about taking the mirror but especially about holding it up to the shallow striations in the otherwise blank gray face of a basement wall.

"Out with it," he said. "What'd that stupid wall tell you? No secrets, now. I want me a tip straight from the Cee-ment itself. What's a rock-solid investment for a fella like Uncle Marty with only so much cash to spare?"

Cory could feel his face burning.

"Come on, cuz. This is a relative talkin', kid. Let me in— let us *all* in—on what's going down, basement-wise."

"Who's gonna take the World Series this year?" twelve-year-old David promptly asked.

"Is Hank Danforth gonna ask Gina Lynn to his pool party?" Faye, disturbingly precocious for nine, wondered aloud.

("Shut up," Gina Lynn cautioned her.)

And thirteen-year old Deborah said, "Is war gonna break out? Ask your stupid wall if the Russians're gonna bomb us."

"Maybe the wall was askin' him for some cold cream," Uncle Martin said. "You know, to put on its wrinkles." All four of Uncle Martin's bratty kids laughed. "You were just writin' down the brand, weren't you Cory? Don't wanna bring home the wrong brand of cold cream to smear on your favorite wall. After all, you're the fella who's gotta face the damn thing every morning, aren't you?''

"Silica Lotion," Gina Lynn said. "Oil of Grah-velle."

Mommy had a job as a cash-register clerk somewhere. She was not at home. Cory fixed his eyes on Uncle Martin's belt buckle, a miniature brass racing car, and waited for their silly game to end. When it did, without his once having opened his mouth to reply to their jackass taunts, he strode with wounded dignity back down to the corner of the basement sheltering his cot. Alone again, he peered for a time at the marks that Gina Lynn's mirror had not enabled him to read. The scratches began to terrify him. They coded a language that he had not yet learned. They probably contained taunts—threats, in fact—crueler and much more dangerous than any that his uncle and cousins had just shied off him for sport.

Two days later, in Uncle Martin's detached garage, Cory found a gallon of yellow paint that Aunt Clara had bought nearly three summers ago to take care of the house's peeling shutters. He also found a brush and an aerosol can of black enamel that David had recently used to touch up the frame on his ten-speed. These items the boy carried downstairs to his private sanctuary.

Stripped to his Jockey briefs, he began to slap runny gouts of latex brilliance all over the disturbing hieroglyphs. At first, he hid a few of them behind the dripping image of a huge lopsided egg yolk. Then swinging his arm in everwidening arcs, he expanded this clownish shape into the brim of a festive straw sombrero. The sombrero rim grew to be gong-sized, and the gong ballooned to the dimensions of one of those giant yellow teacups whirling around and around in a local amusement park. Finally, though, Cory had his circle as big as a small sun, a ball of good cheer radiating into the basement as if the very paint itself had caught fire.

He outlined the sun with the black spray paint and added flares and fiery peninsulas that cried out for yet more yellow. Then he painted smaller lamps on other portions of this wall and on the other walls too, and squat tropical birds with combs and wattles, and pineapples as big as the lamps, and a long yellow beach under the glowering sun. His arms ran yellow, as did his pipe-cleaner thighs, as did his caved-in belly and chest, while his face seemed to reflect back the brightness of the obliterated gray that he strove to cover over permanently. If he had to live and sleep in this dank hole in the ground, let it be a happy hole in the ground. Let the light of artificial suns, two-dimensional lamps, and crudely drafted fruits and cockatoos spill into his basement through the pores of the very cement.

Let there be light.

Let there be light to hold the GrayLanders at bay. For Cory believed that the work he had done, the symbols he had splashed up around his cot like a fence of sunlight, would keep the creatures beyond the subterranean walls from bursting through them to steal him away from Mommy and the real world of automobiles and mountains and football stadiums—the real world in which she was trying to make a place for both of them. Maybe he was safer now.

But while Cory was admiring what he had done, David came down the steps to ask him to go to the store. His older cousin saw him three-quarters naked and striped like an aborigine in the midst of a yellow-gray jungle unlike any terrain that David had expected to find only a floor below the family's TV room.

"Holy shit," he said and backed away up the steps as if Cory might be planning to slit his throat on the spot.

A moment or two later, Uncle Martin came storming down the steps in a pair of rope-soled boots that made the whole unfinished structure tremble like a medieval assault tower in an old Tyrone Power movie. He could not believe what Cory had done. He bruised the boy's arm and upper chest shaking him this way and that to demonstrate his disbelief and his unhappiness. He threw Cory onto his cot with such force that it collapsed under the blow and dumped the boy sidelong so that his head struck a section of painted concrete. Yellow paint smudged the whorl pattern of hair on Cory's crown, and a trickle of red worked through the smudge to enrage Uncle Martin even further.

"This is *my* house!" he shouted, slapping Cory again. "No one gave you permission to do this!"

Aunt Clara's pant-suited legs appeared halfway up the trembling stairs. More of her came into view as she descended. When Uncle Martin drew back his forearm to administer another crackling wallop, she cried, "Marty, don't! Something's happenin' on the news. You like the news. Come see what's goin' on. Try to relax. I'll take care of this. Come watch the news."

Uncle Martin's forearm halted inches from Cory's eyes. "Ain't nobody gonna take care of this, Clara!" he shouted. "We'll jes' leave our little Piggaso down here to moon over his shitty goddamn yellow masterpieces! Forever, maybe!" He thrust Cory into the wall to punctuate this last threat, kicked the crumpled cot, and pounded back up the steps, pulling Aunt Clara along with him. Then the door slammed. Soon after, the naked light bulb near the staircase went out; and the boy knew that one of his cousins, at Uncle Martin's bidding, had flipped the circuit breaker controlling the power supply to the basement.

But for a narrow line of light beneath the door at the top of the steps, Cory crouched beside his cot in utter darkness. Then someone—maybe Uncle Martin himself—put something— probably a rolled-up towel—along the base of the door; and the not quite utter darkness of his prison took on a thoroughness that made the boy think that someone—possibly a GrayLander—had stuck an altogether painless needle into his eyeballs and injected them with ink. He still had eyeballs, of course, but they had gone solid back on him, like licorice jawbreakers or moist ripe olives. With such eyes, he could "see" only darkness.

What about the fat yellow sun that he had painted? What about the beach, the pineapples, the sunlamps, and the cockatoos? He put his hands on the damp slabs of the basement walls and felt each invisible figure for reassurance. Was the dampness only the sweat of soil-backed concrete, or was it instead an indication of undried paint? Cory could not tell. When he sniffed his hands, they gave off the familiar odor of grayness—but even bright yellow pigment could acquire that smell when, like a glaze of fragile perfume, it was applied to an upright slab of earthen gray. The boy wiped his hands on his chest. Was he wiping off a smear of latex sunshine or the clammy perspiration of underground cement? Because he would never be able to tell, he gave up trying.

Then he heard a pounding overhead and knew that Mommy had come home from work. She and Uncle Martin were just beyond the door at the top of the stairs, arguing.

"For Chrissake, Marty, you can't keep him locked up in the basement—no matter what he's done!"

"Watch me, Claudia! Jes' you watch me!"

"I'm going down there to see him! I'm his mother, and I've got a right to see him! Or else he's gonna come up here to see us!"

"What he's gonna do, woman, is stew in the dumb-fuckin' Piggaso mess he's made!"

"He hasn't even had his dinner!"

"Who says he deserves any?"

"He's my son, and I'm going to let him out!"

Then Cory's darkness was riven by the kind of noise that a big dog makes when it slams its body into a fence slat, and Mommy was screaming, and Aunt Clara was cursing both Mommy and Uncle Martin, and the staircase scaffolding was doing the shimmy-shimmy in its jerrybuilt moorings. Crash followed crash, and curses curses, and soon all the upper portions of the house seemed to be waltzing to the time-keeping of slaps and the breakage of dinnerware or random pieces of bric-a-brac. Cory waited for the rumpus to end, fully expecting Mommy to triumph and the door to open and the darkness to give way to a liberating spill of wattage that would light up the big yellow sun and all the other happy symbols that he had painted. Instead, when the noise ceased and the house stopped quaking, the darkness kept going, and so did the silence, and the only reasons that Cory could think of were that Mommy and her brother-in-law had killed each other or that Mommy had finally agreed with Uncle Marty that Cory really did deserve to sit alone in the dark for trying to beautify the dumb-ass basement walls.

Whatever had happened upstairs, the door did not open, and the ink in his eyeballs got thicker and thicker, and he came to realize that he would have to endure both the dark and the steady approach of the GrayLanders—Clay People, Earth Zombies, Bone Puppets—as either a premeditated punishment or a spooky sort of accident. (Maybe a burglar had broken in during the argument and stabbed everybody to death before Mommy could tell him that her son was locked in the basement. Maybe Mommy had purposely said nothing to the bad guy about him, for fear that the bad guy would get worried and come downstairs to knife Cory, too.) Anyway, he was trapped, with no lights and nothing to eat and streaks of yellow paint all over his invisible body and only a tiny bathroom and trickles of rusty tap water for any kind of comfort at all.

Cory crept up the rickety stairs, putting a splinter into one palm when he gripped the guard rail too hard. At the top, he beat on the door in rapid tattoos that echoed on his side like the clatter of a fight with bamboo staves at the bottom of an empty swimming pool. "Let me out!" he shouted. "Let me out of here!" Which was not dignified, he knew, but which was necessary, here at the beginning of his confinement, as a test of Uncle Martin's will to hold him. If noise would make his uncle nervous, if pleading would make the man relent, the boy knew that he had to try such tactics, for Mommy's sake as well as his. But it was no use, and finally he sat down and bit at the splinter in his palm until he had its tip between his baby teeth and managed to pull it free of the punctured flesh sheathing it.

Darkness swallows time. Cory decided that darkness swallows time when he had been alone in the black basement so long that he could not remember being anywhere else even a quarter of the time that he had spent hunched on his cot waiting for the darkness to end. He could not tell whether time was stretching out like a pull of saltwater taffy or drawing up like a spider when you hold a match over its body. Time was not something that happened in the dark at all. The dark had swallowed it. It was trying to digest time somewhere deep in its bowels, but when time emerged again, Cory felt sure that it would be a foul thing, physically altered and hence bad-smelling—gray-smelling, probably—and unwelcome. He almost hoped that the dark would swallow him, too, so that he would not have to confront the stench of time when, altered in this bad but inevitable way, it came oozing into the world again.

Once, he thought he heard sirens. Maybe Uncle Martin had gone to a fire somewhere.

Later, though, he was more concerned that the GrayLanders were getting closer to breaking through the basement's outer wall than that some poor stranger's house had caught fire. He put his hands on the upright slab next to him. He did this to hold the slab in place, to prop it up against the gritty Gray-Landers straining their molecules through the earth—straining them the way that Aunt Clara strained orange juice on Saturday mornings—to scratch backward messages into the cement in a language so alien that not even a mirror could translate it for Cory. No longer able to *see* these messages, then, he began to *feel* the striations embodying them. Maybe the Bone Puppets, the Earth Zombies, the Clay People, or whatever they were, preferred to contact living human beings with *feel*able rather than *see*able symbols.

Like Braille, sort of.

Didn't that make sense? It was smart to think that monsters living underground, in everlasting subterranean dark, would be blind, wasn't it? Cory's first-grade teacher had taught them about moles, which could only see a little, and had even shown them a film about cave animals that had no eyes at all because, in their always-dark environments, they had *revolved* that way. Well, the GrayLanders were probably like those cave animals, eyeless, blind, totally and permanently blind, because by choice and biological development they made their home in darkness. Which was why they would write backwards on the walls in symbols that you had to feel and then turn around in your head to get the meaning of.

Cory worked hard to let the alien Braille of the GrayLanders talk to him through his fingertips. Probably, their messages would let him know what sort of horrible things they planned to do to him when they at last got through the concrete. Probably, the symbols were warnings. Warnings meant to terrify. A really smart kid would leave them be, but because he had been locked into a place that he could not escape without the aid of the adults upstairs—grownups a kid would ordinarily expect to make some responsible decisions for him and maybe for themselves too—Cory had to struggle to parse the queer dents and knobbles on his own. Alone, in the dark, it was better to know than not to know, even if what you learned made your gut turn over and the hair in the small of your back prickle. So far, though, he was learning nothing. All their stupid tactile messages made no sense, either forwards at the tips of his fingers or backwards or sideways or upside-down in the ever-turning but ever-slipping vise of his mind.

"You're blind and you can't even write blind-writing!" Cory shouted. He pounded on the sweaty slab beside his cot as centuries ago he had pounded on the door at the top of the staircase. Thwap! thwap! thwap! and not even the satisfaction of an echo. Bruised fists and a bit lip, only.

Cory forced the bent legs on his cot back under the canvas contraption, but pinched the web between his thumb and forefinger. He lay down on his cot nursing the pinch and staring through ink-filled eyes at the heavy nothing pressing down on him like the bleak air pressure of a tomb. With a bleak black here and a bleak black there (he crooned to himself), here a black, there a black, everywhere a bleak black, Uncle Marty had a tomb, ee-ai, ee-ai-oh. The melody of this nursery song kept running in his head in almost exactly the way that the darkness kept restating itself all around him. They were both inescapable, and pretty soon they got mixed up in Cory's mind as if they were mirror-image phenomena that he could not quite see straight and hence could not distinguish between or make any useful sense of.

Upstairs, as faint as the buzzing of a single summer mosquito, sirens again.

And then, somehow, the sun that Cory had painted on the wall—the humongous yellow orb with hair-curler geysers and flares around its circumference—lit up like a flashbulb as big as a Mobile Oil sign. But unlike any kind of flashbulb, Cory's sun did not go out again. Instead, in the bargain-basement catacombs of his aunt and uncle's house, it continued incandescently to glow. Everything in the basement was radiated by its light. Cory had to lift one paint-smeared forearm to shield his eyes from the fierce intensity of its unbearable glowing. The images of sunlamps on this and other walls, and of birds of paradise, and of bananas, pineapples, and papayas—*all* these clumsy two-dimensional images began to burn. They did so with a ferociousness only a little less daunting than that of

Cory's big latex sun. It seemed to the boy that God Himself had switched the power back on. For some private reason, though, He had chosen not to use the orthodox avenue of the wiring already in place.

No, instead He had moved to endow with blinding brightness the symbols of life and sunshine that *Cory* had splashed on the walls. If Mommy would not help him, God would. If his aunt, uncle, and four bratty cousins would not release him to daylight, well, God would bring a gift of greatly multiplied daylight right down into the basement to him. Although grateful for this divine favor, the boy helplessly turned aside from the gift. It was too grand, too searing, and that for a brief instant he had actually been able to see the bone inside the forearm shielding his eyes fretted Cory in a way that his gratitude was unable to wipe from his memory.

And then, almost as if he had dreamed the divine gift, darkness reasserted itself, like a television screen shrinking down to one flickering central spot and going black right in the middle of a program that he had waited all day to see.

Ee-ai, ee-ai-oh.

Cory sat still on his cot. *Something* had happened. For an instant or two, the ink had been squeezed out of his eyeballs, and a liquid like lighter fluid had been poured into them. Then the liquid had ignited, and burned, and used itself up, whereupon the ink had come flooding back. Or something like that. Cory was still seeing fuzzy haloes of light on the congealed blackness of the ink. Fireflies. Glowing amoebas. Migrating match flames. Crimson minnows. They swam and they swam, and no one gave a damn about the boy in the basement.

And then it seemed to him that overhead a whirlwind had struck the neighborhood. The darkness roared, and the staircase began doing the shimmy-shimmy again. But this time the shaking got so violent that the steps and guard rails—a tiny din within the great bombast of the Rocky Mountain hurricane raging above him—broke loose of the scaffolding and like the bars of a big wooden xylophone tumbled into and percussed down upon one another with the discordant music of catastrophe, plink! plunk! crash! ka-BOOM-bah! clatter-clatter!

It would have been funny, sort of, except that the roaring and the quaking and the amplified sighing of whatever was going on upstairs—*what* stairs!—in the real world, the terrifying playground of wild beasts and grownups, would not stop. Cory feared that his head might soon explode with the noise. In fact, he began to think that the noise was *inside* his skull, a balloon of sound inflating toward a ka-BOOM! that would decorate the gray-smelling walls with glistening oysterlike bits of his brain. Gray on gray.

The endless roaring swallowed time. Cory began to forget that the world had not always entertained such noise. It seemed a kind of constant, like air. He wondered if maybe the GrayLanders were the culprits, howling from all the topless basements in his aunt and uncle's neighborhood that they had succeeded in breaking into from their earthen grottos. If so, they would soon be here too, and time would both begin again and stop forever when they opened the sky for him with their grating godforsaken howls.

Maybe air was not a constant. Cory was suddenly having trouble breathing. Also, the clammy walls had begun to hiss, as if the ooze invisibly streaking them had heated to a temperature enabling them to steam. Gasping, he got down off the cot and crawled along the floor to the niche where an old-timey water heater, unemployed since the final days of the Eisenhower administration, squatted like the sawed-off fuselage of a rocket. Cory could not see it now, of course, but he remembered what it looked like. The metal wrapping the cylinder scalded his naked shoulder as he crawled past the antique.

Still gasping, bewildered by the difficulty of refilling his lungs, the boy slumped behind the old heater and turned his face toward an aperture in the concrete wall—an accident of pouring—through which a faint breath of warm rather than desert-hot air blew. He twisted his itching, inflamed body around so that he could thrust his entire head into this anomalous vent. The lip of concrete at its bottom sliced into his neck, but he ignored the minor discomfort to gulp the air leaking through. A gift from the GrayLanders? Maybe. Cory refused to question it, he just gulped and gulped, meanwhile praying that the noise would die down and the heat ease off and his oxygen supply return to normal.

In this unlikely posture, the boy fell asleep. Or, at least, consciousness left him.

* * *

When Cory awoke, his ears were buzzing, but the whirlwind had ceased. He pulled his head out of the rough spout in the concrete and found that he could comfortably breathe. He crawled out from behind the old gas water heater. An eerie kind of darkness held the day, but he could see again, as if through blowing smoke or murky water. Parts of the basement ceiling had fallen in, but all the walls were standing, and on them, as dim as the markings on the bottom of a scummy swimming pool, wavered the childish symbols that he had brushed and spray-painted onto the cement. Soot and grime dusted his handiwork, giving a disheartening dinginess to the latex yellow that a while ago—an hour, a day, a millennium—had shouted God's glory at him. Soot and dust drifted around the dry sump of the basement like airborne chaff in the granary of a farm in western Kansas.

He looked up. The staircase had collapsed, and the door that he had pounded on, well, that door no longer occupied the doorjamb framing an empty portal at the top of the fallen stairs. In fact, the doorjamb was gone. Where it should have stood, a refrigerator slouched, its hind rollers hanging off the edge of the oddly canted floor. How it had wound up in that place, in that position, Cory could not clearly say, but because the walls of the upper portions of the house had evaporated, along with the ceiling, the furniture, and its human occupants, he did not spend much time worrying about the recent adventures of the parboiled refrigerator. High above the ruins of the house, the sky looked like a crazy-quilt marbling of curdled mayonnaise and cold cocoa and dissolving cotton candy and burnt tomato paste. Yucky-weird, all of it.

Just as gut-flopping as the sky, everything stank and distant moans overlay the ticks of scalded metal or occasionally pierced the soft static of down-sifting black snow. Although summer, this snow was slanting out of the nightmare sky. Appropriately, it was nightmare snow, flakes like tarnished-silver cinders, as acrid as gunpowder, each cinder the size of a weightless nickel, quarter, or fifty-cent piece. Right now, the boy was sheltered from their fall by a swag-bellied warp of ceiling, but he had made up his mind to climb out of the basement and to go walking bareheaded through the evil ebony storm.

Bareheaded, barechested, and barefoot.

Before the GrayLanders came.

Which they surely would, now that the grownups, by flattening everything, had made their tunneling task so much the easier. One of the outer basement walls had already begun to crumble. It would be a relaxing breaststroke for the Clay People, Earth Zombies, or Bone Puppets to come weaving their cold molecules through that airy stuff. And they had to be on their way.

Cory got out of the basement. It took a while, but by mounting the staircase rubble and leaping for the edge of the floor near the teetering refrigerator and pulling himself up to chin height and painstakingly boosting one leg over, he was finally able to stand on the tilting floor. Then, propellering his arms to maintain his balance, he watched with astonished sidelong glances as his Aunt Clara's big Amana toppled from its perch and dropped like a bomb into the staircase ruins below it. A geyser of dust rose to meet the down-whirling cinders.

But he kept from falling, and looked around, and saw that no longer did the tall buildings of Denver, whose tops it had once been easy to see from his aunt and uncle's neighborhood, command the landscape, which had been horribly transfigured. Debris and charred dead people and blasted trees and melted automobiles lay about the boy in every direction, and the mountains to the west, although still there, were veiled by the photogenic-negative snowfall, polarized phosphor dots of lilting deadliness.

Cory pulled his vision back from the mountains. "Mommy!" he cried. "Mommy!" Because he had no reasonable hope of an answer in this unrecognizable place, he started walking. Some of the burnt lumps in the rubble were probably all that remained of certain people he had known, but he had no wish to kneel beside them to check out this nauseating hunch. Instead, he walked. And it was like walking through a dump the dimensions of . . . well, of Denver itself. Maybe it was even bigger than that. The ubiquitous black snow and the yucky-weird sky suggested as much.

And then he saw his first GrayLander. The sight made him halt, clench his fists, and let go of a harsh yelping scream that scalded his throat the way that the down-whirling cinders had

begun to burn his skin. The GrayLander paid him no mind,
and although he wanted to scream again, he could not force
his blistered voicebox to do as he bid it. For which reason,
frozen to the plane of crazed asphalt over which he had been
picking his way, Cory simply gaped.

Well over six feet tall, the GrayLander was almost as naked
as he. The boy could not tell if it were Clay Person, Earth
Zombie, or Bone Puppet—it seemed to be a little of all three,
if not actually a hybrid of other ugly gray-smelling ogres of
which he had never even dreamed. The GrayLander's ungainly
head looked like a great boiled cauliflower, or maybe a deflated
basketball smeared with some kind of milky paste. If the creature had eyes, Cory could not see them, for its brow, an almost
iridescent purple ridge in the surrounding milkiness, over-
lapped the sockets where most earth-born animals would have
eyes. The creature's heavy lips, each of which reminded Cory
of albino versions of the leeches that sometimes attacked people in television horror movies, were moving, ever moving,
like greasy toy-tank treads that have slipped off their grooves.
Maybe it had heard the boy approach—the huge, stunned creature—for it turned toward him and pushed an alien noise from
between its alien lips.

"Haowah meh," it said. "Haowah meh."

When it turned, the purple-gray skin on its breasts, belly,
and thighs slumped like hotel draperies accidentally tilted off
their ends. Cory took a careful step back. One of the monster's
arms showed more bone below the elbow than flesh, as did its
leg below the knee on the same side. Pale lips still moving,
the GrayLander extended its other arm toward the boy, the arm
that might almost have been mistaken for a man's, and opened
its blackened paw to reveal a tiny glistening spheroid. The
monster shoved this object at Cory, as if urging him either to
contemplate it at length or to take it as a memento of their
meeting.

Squinting at the object in the unceasing rain of cinders, Cory
understood that it was an eyeball. The GrayLander, blind,
wanted him to have its eyeball. Just as he had suspected, the
GrayLanders whom he had been waiting to come after him
were sightless. They had eyes, apparently, but years of living
in the dark, ignoring the realms of light just above their heads,

had robbed their optical equipment of the ability to see. What, then, could be more useless than the gift of a GrayLander's eyeball? Cory was outraged. The whirlwind had finally freed this stupid creature—and all its equally ugly relatives wandering like a benumbed zombies across the blasted landscape—from its subterranean darkness, and it was trying to give him something that had never been of the least value to itself or to any of its kind.

"Haoweh meh," it said again.

The boy's anger overcame his fear. He jumped forward, snatched the eye from the monster's paw, and flung it off the hideous body of the GrayLander so that it bounced back at him like the tiny red ball connected to a bolo paddle by a rubber tether.

Then, knowing nothing at all about where he was going or what he would do when he got there, Cory began to run. The dump that Denver and its suburbs had become seemed too big to escape easily, but he had to try, and he had to try in spite of the fact that as he ran many of the yucky GrayLanders loitering bewilderedly in the rubble called to him to stop—to stop and help them, to stop and share both their pain and their bewilderment. Cory would not stop. He was angry with the blind monsters. They were people in disguise, people just like his dead mommy, his dead aunt and uncle, and his dead cousins. He was angry with them because they had fooled him. All along, he had been living among the GrayLanders and they had never once—until now—stepped forward to let him know that, under their skins, they and their human counterparts were absolutely identical.

Fire Zone Emerald
by Lucius Shepard

Introduction

Lucius Shepard brought the third world to science fiction.

Ever since it began as a publishing category in the United States, American science fiction has been astonishingly chauvinistic. The overwhelming majority of the old pulp space operas had Americans in every good-guy role. Bad humans and bad aliens (good aliens were rare) all acted like Nazis or Communists—and all were certainly foreign.

In the "Golden Age," dominated by the twin influences of editor John W. Campbell and author Robert A. Heinlein, scientific and technological accuracy replaced sheer adventure as the determinant of what made science fiction valid. But the American sensibility only narrowed. The "competent man" who starred in most Astounding stories (and virtually every story by Robert Heinlein) was invariably the great-grandson of the Connecticut Yankee. He always saw the world through the eyes of a cheerful, skeptical, individualistic New Englander who could make or fix anything once he set his mind to it.

As the authors of the forties and fifties created their collective version of the future, the dominant vision was of an outer space run by Yankees. And when America put its boys into space and onto the moon, they did their best to live up to the image science fiction had created. Of course we had to be first on the moon! Everybody knew Americans belonged there!

That bright-eyed American image was shattered during the New Wave of the 1960s, echoing the attitudes of the American Left during the Vietnam War. Yet still, to an astonishing degree, American writers still peopled even their ugly futures with Yankee heroes. The difference was that now the bad guys were Americans, too.

Even with Bruce Sterling's call for diamond-hard science fiction that recognized the existence of a wider world, most Cyberpunks still persisted in dealing only with those parts of the third world that had been most Americanized—most technologized, urbanized, skyscrapered, wired, incorporated and bureaucratized.

Lucius Shepard didn't experience America the way most American writers do. He didn't begin his fiction career knowing only the landscape of the American popular writer: the mythos of the whitewashed American farmhouse or the reality of Old McDonald's suburbia. Nor was he limited to the landscape of the American academic-literary writer, whose world generally includes only the university and Manhattan Island. The writers of the American South found a way to diverge from these patterns, only to fall into ruts of their own. Their awareness stopped long before they reached the Rio Grande. Shepard's didn't.

Shepard has spent many years of his life living among the poor on an island off the Honduran Coast. He was a journalist, but did not function as most American journalists do, hanging around the cities, clinging to the American amenities that in most third-world countries are found only among the urban rich. He lived among the Honduran people, and lived as they lived, until he became so much a part of their lives that they stopped seeing him as particularly foreign, but rather regarded him as something of a neighbor, even a friend.

He learned to see Americans as others see us. He saw the picture that we present, particularly in Latin America, where we are represented almost exclusively by gawking tourists who don't speak the language, journalists who clearly despise and avoid the common people, and, most loathsomely, the white men who come there to do business—which invariably means extracting great profit from the poverty of desperately underpaid workers.

Shepard knows that this vision is not accurate—that most of the folk of Latin America would probably not resent, envy, and despise most of the folk of the United States. The trouble is, the common people never get to know each other. And while the view of America that Shepard's Honduran neighbors have is not accurate, it is true. That is, as long as the U.S. officially treats Latin America as colonies over which we may exercise ultimate authority without any responsibility for the consequences of our self-centered decisions, then the people of those nations are not wrong to regard us as a nation of tourists, who come to stare and be amused; journalists, who come to take pictures of the sort of scenes that Latin Americans are least proud of, in order to shame these proud people before the rest of the world; and businessmen, who come to steal. Since that is what the U.S. sends to them, that is what we truly are to them.

In Central America and the Caribbean, there is one more kind of American they know very well: Soldiers. Marines. To them, behind all the tourists and journalists and businessmen, there is the iron fist that makes sure these banana and sugar and coffee "republics" don't make too much trouble. Oh, pardon me—my mistake—the soldiers go to help keep these little nations safe from Communism! Or anyway, that's the latest reason given.

Most Americans have forgotten—or never knew—that our soldiers used to go in at the behest of the United Fruit Company or Texaco or the dictator who guaranteed American interests. When we have sent troops there in the past, it has cost us almost nothing. We hardly noticed. But the citizens of these countries are well aware that American intervention has almost always cost them dearly, both in freedom and in economic well-being. They have groaned under the dictators who killed their children with the guns we sold them, who tortured them in prisons built with the few profits we allowed to stay in their country. To us, these things were unnoticeably minor; to them, they were devastating, unforgettable.

Like the American Navy boys who, playing tourist in Ha-

vana, pissed at the base of the statue of Martí and climbed up
and sat on his head. They were drunk. They were having fun.
It never occurred to them that to proud Cubans—which is all
Cubans—they were desecrating the honor of the man who was
their George Washington, their Patrick Henry, their Thomas
Jefferson. The Cuban police were able to protect the sailors so
they could get back to their ship without being torn apart by
the humiliated, outraged crowd that had witnessed their act.
The American ambassador tried to make amends. He laid a
wreath at the statue of Martí. To the Cubans, this gesture could
only seem offensivly patronizing, for the sailors remained un-
punished.

The punishment finally came, vicariously, at the Bay of Pigs.

Lucius Shepard has written many kinds of stories: the delicate fantasy of "The Man Who Painted the Dragon Griaule,"
still my favorite of his works; comedy; horror; and strange
stories that fit no category. But the stories that first attracted
wide attention, that seared the conscience of his readers, were
the tales set in a future Central American war. Most readers
responded primarily to the echoes of Vietnam or the implied
political statements about Nicaragua and the contras—most
read these tales, in other words, as American stories.

But unconsciously, like it or not, we received another message as well. We began to see Hondurans and Salvadorans and
Nicaraguans, not as a backdrop, but in the foreground. We
began to see them as they see themselves, with the nobility and
honor and pride that sustains them; we began to understand
them without requiring them to resemble us. Lucius Shepard
introduced us to the real aliens—the rest of humanity, which
does not speak our language or share our values, which does
not respect our naive faith that technological superiority will
save us. They are more likely to pray for rescue to a Virgin or
saint whose image is but thinly laid over the terrible, powerful
gods of the Mayas and Aztecs or of the Guinea coast. Shepard's
stories tell us that their prayers are as likely to be answered as
our own.

Shepard's stories show us what only Cortés among the con-
querors clearly understood—that these people are too powerful
and beautiful to be converted or destroyed. They will absorb
many blows, but each would-be conqueror will either go away,

leaving them unchanged, or live among them, until their grand-
children or great-grandchildren are absorbed. We've been at
the Caribbean conquest business for only a century. It took the
Spanish three hundred years to learn their lesson. Maybe we'll
be quicker.

"**A**IN'T IT WEIRD, SOLDIER BOY?" SAID THE VOICE IN
Quinn's ear. "There you are, strollin' along in that little ol'
green suit of armor, feelin' all cool and killproof . . . and
wham! You're down and hurtin' bad. Gotta admit, though, them
suits do a job. Can't recall nobody steppin' onna mine and
comin' through it as good as you."

Quinn shook his head to clear the cobwebs. His helmet rattled, which was not good news. He doubted any of the connections to the computer in his backpack were still intact. But
at least he could move his legs, and that was very good news,
indeed. The guy talking had a crazed lilt to his voice, and
Quinn thought it would be best to take cover. He tried the
computer; nothing worked except for map holography. The visor display showed him to be a blinking red dot in the midst
of a contoured green glow: eleven miles inside Guatemala from
its border with Belize; in the heart of the Peten Rain Forest;
on the eastern edge of Fire Zone Emerald.

"Y'hear me, soldier boy?"

Quinn sat up, wincing as pain shot through his legs. He felt
no fear, no panic. Though he had just turned twenty-one, this
was his second tour in Guatemala, and he was accustomed to
being in tight spots. Besides, there were a lot worse places he
might have been stranded. Up until two years before, Emerald
has been a staging area for Cuban and guerrilla troops; but
following the construction of a string of Allied artillery bases
to the west, the enemy had moved their encampments north
and—except for recon patrols such as Quinn's—the fire zone
had been abandoned.

"No point in playin' possum, man. Me and the boys'll be

there in ten–fifteen minutes, and you gonna have to talk to us then.''

Ten minutes. Shit! Maybe, Quinn thought, if he talked to the guy, that would slow him down. "Who are you people?" he asked.

"Name's Mathis. Special Forces, formerly attached to the First Infantry.'' A chuckle. "But you might say we seen the light and opted outta the service. How 'bout you, man? You gotta name?''

"Quinn. Edward Quinn.'' He flipped up his visor; heat boiled into the combat suit, overwhelming the cooling system. The suit was scorched and shredded from the knees down; plastic armor glinted in the rips. He looked around for his gun. The cable that had connected it to the computer had been severed, probably by shrapnel from the mine, and the gun was not to be seen. "You run across the rest of my patrol?''

A static-filled silence. " 'Fraid I got bad tidin's, Quinn Edward. 'Pears like guerrillas took out your buddies.''

Despite the interference, Quinn heard the lie in the voice. He scoped out the terrain. Saw that he was sitting in a cathedral-like glade: vaults of leaves pillared by the tapering trunks of ceibas and giant figs. The ground was carpeted with ferns; a thick green shade seemed to be welling from the tips of the fronds. Here and there, shafts of golden light penetrated the canopy, and these were so complexly figured with dust motes that they appeared to contain flaws and fracture planes, like artifacts of crystal snapped off in mid-air. On three sides, the glade gave out into dense jungle; but to the east lay a body of murky green water, with a forested island standing about a hundred feet out. If he could find his gun, the island might be defensible. Then a few days' rest and he'd be ready for a hike.

"Them boys wasn't no friends of yours,'' said Mathis. "You hit that mine, and they let you lie like meat on the street.''

That much Quinn believed. The others had been too wasted on the martial arts ampules to be trustworthy. Chances were they simply hadn't wanted the hassle of carrying him.

"They deserved what they got,'' Mathis went on. "But you, now . . . boy with your luck. Might just be a place for you in the light.''

"What's that mean?'' Quinn fumbled a dispenser from his

hip pouch and ejected two ampules—a pair of silver bullets—into his palm. Two, he figured, should get him walking.

"The light's holy here, man. You sit under them beams shinin' through the canopy, let 'em soak into you, and they'll stir the truth from your mind." Mathis said all this in dead-earnest, and Quinn, unable to mask his amusement, said, "Oh, yeah?"

"You remind me of my ol' lieutenant," said Mathis. "Man used to tell me I's crazy, and I'd say to him, 'I ain't ordinary crazy, sir. I'm crazy-gone-to-Jesus.' And I'd 'splain to him what I knew from the light, that we's s'posed to build the kingdom here. Place where a man could live pure. No machines, no pollution." He grunted as if tickled by something. "That's how you be livin' if you can cut it. You gonna learn to hunt with knives, track tapir by the smell. Hear what weather's comin' by listenin' to the cry of a bird."

"How 'bout the lieutenant?" Quinn asked. "He learn all that?"

"Y'know how it is with lieutenants, man. Sometimes they just don't work out."

Quinn popped an ampule under his nose and inhaled. Waited for the drugs to kick in. The ampules were the Army's way of insuring that the high incidence of poor battlefield performance during the Vietnam War would not be repeated: each contained a mist of pseudo-endorphins and RNA derivatives that elevated the user's determination and physical potentials to heroic levels for thirty minutes or thereabouts. But Quinn preferred not to rely on them, because of their destructive side-effects. Printed on the dispenser was a warning against abuse, one that Mathis—judging by his rap—had ignored. Quinn had heard similar raps from guys whose personalities had been eroded, replaced in part by the generic mystic-warrior personality supplied by the drugs.

" 'Course," said Mathis, breaking the silence, "it ain't only the light. It's the Queen. She's one with the light."

"The Queen?" Quinn's senses had sharpened. He could see the spidery shapes of monkeys high in the canopy and could hear a hundred new sounds. He spotted the green plastic stock of his gun protruding from beneath a fern not twenty feet away; he came to his feet, refusing to admit to his pain, and went over to it. Both upper and lower barrels were plugged with dirt.

" 'Member them Cuban 'speriments where they was linkin' up animals and psychics with computer implants? Usin' 'em for spies?"

"That was just bullshit!" Quinn set off toward the water. He felt disdain for Mathis and recognized that to be a sign of too many ampules.

"It ain't no bullshit. The Queen was one of them psychics. She's linked up with this little ol' tiger cat. What the Indians call a *tigrillo*. We ain't never seen her, but we seen the cat. And once we got tuned to her, we could feel her mind workin' on us. But at first she can slip them thoughts inside your head without you ever knowin'. Twist you 'round her finger, she can."

"If she's that powerful," said Quinn, smug with the force of his superior logic, "then why's she hidin' from you?"

"She ain't hidin'. We gotta prove ourselves to her. Keep the jungle pure, free of evildoers. Then she'll come to us."

Quinn popped the second ampule. "Evildoers? Like my patrol, huh? That why you wasted my patrol?"

"Whoo-ee!" said Mathis after a pause. "I can't slide nothin' by you, can I, Quinn Edward?"

Quinn's laughter was rich and nutsy: a two-ampule laugh. "Naw," he said, mocking Mathis' cornpone accent. "Don't reckon you can." He flipped down his visor and waded into the water, barely conscious of the pain in his legs.

"Your buddies wasn't shit for soldiers," said Mathis. "Good thing they come along, though. We was runnin' low on ampules." He made a frustrated noise. "Hey, man. This armor ain't nothin' like the old gear . . . all this computer bullshit. I can't get nothin' crankin' 'cept the radio. Tell me how you work these here guns."

"Just aim and pull." Quinn was waist-deep in water, perhaps a quarter of the way to the island, which from that perspective—with its three towering vine-enlaced trees—looked like the overgrown hulk of an old sailing ship anchored in a placid stretch of jade.

"Don't kid a kidder," said Mathis. "I tried that."

"You'll figure it out," Quinn said. "Smart peckerwood like you."

"Man, you gotta attitude problem, don'tcha? But I 'spect the Queen'll straighten you out."

"Right! The Invisible Woman!"

"You'll see her soon enough, man. Ain't gonna be too long 'fore she comes to me."

"To *you*?" Quinn snickered. "That mean you're the king?"

"Maybe." Mathis pitched his voice low and menacing. "Don't go thinkin' I'm just country pie, Quinn Edward. I been up here most of two years, and I got this place down. I can tell when a fly takes a shit! Far as you concerned, I'm lord of the fuckin' jungle."

Quinn bit back a sarcastic response. He should be suckering this guy, determining his strength. Given that Mathis had been on recon prior to deserting, he'd probably started with around fifteen men. "You guys taken many casualties?" he asked after slogging another few steps.

"Why you wanna know that? You a man with a plan? Listen up, Quinn Edward. If you figgerin' on takin' us out, 'member them fancy guns didn't help your buddies, and they ain't gonna help you. Even if you could take us out, you'd still have to deal with the Queen. Just 'cause she lives out on the island don't mean she ain't keepin' her eye on the shore. You might not believe it, man, but right now, right this second, she's all 'round you."

"What island?" The trees ahead suddenly seemed haunted-looking.

"Little island out there on the lake. You can see it if you lift your head."

"Can't move my head," said Quinn. "My neck's fucked up."

"Well, you gonna see it soon enough. And once you healed, you take my advice and stay the hell off it. The Queen don't look kindly on trespassers."

On reaching the island, Quinn located a firing position from which he could survey the shore: a weedy patch behind a fallen tree trunk hemmed in by bushes. If Mathis was as expert in jungle survival as he claimed, he'd have no trouble in discovering where

Quinn had gone; and there was no way to tell how strong an influence his imaginary Queen exerted, no way to be sure whether the restriction against trespassing had the severity of a taboo or was merely something frowned on. Not wanting to take chances, Quinn spent a frantic few minutes cleaning the lower barrel of his gun, which fired miniature fragmentation grenades.

"Now where'd you get to, Quinn Edward?" said Mathis with mock concern. "Where *did* you get to?"

Quinn scanned the shore. Dark avenues led away between the trees, and staring along them, his nerves were keyed by every twitching leaf, every shift of light and shadow. Clouds slid across the sun, muting its glare to a shimmering platinum gray; a palpable vibration underscored the stillness. He tried to think of something pleasant to make the waiting easier, but nothing pleasant occurred to him. He wetted his lips and swallowed. His cooling system set up a whine.

Movement at the margin of the jungle, a shadow resolving into a man wearing olive-drab fatigues and carrying a rifle with a skeleton stock . . . likely an old AR-18. He waded into the lake, and as he closed on the island, Quinn trained his scope on him and saw that he had black shoulder-length hair framing a haggard face; a ragged beard bibbed his chest and dangling from a thong below the beard was a triangular piece of mirror. Quinn held his fire, waiting for the rest to emerge. But no one else broke cover, and he realized that Mathis was testing him, was willing to sacrifice a pawn to check out his weaponry.

"Keep back!" he shouted. But the man kept plodding forward, heaving against the drag of the water. Quinn marveled at the hold Mathis must have over him: he *had* to know he was going to die. Maybe he was too whacked out on ampules to give a shit, or maybe Mathis' Queen somehow embodied the promise of a swell afterlife for those who died in battle. Quinn didn't want to kill him, but there was no choice, no point in delaying the inevitable.

He aimed, froze a moment at the sight of the man's fear-widened eyes; then he squeezed the trigger.

The hiss of the round blended into the explosion, and the man vanished inside a fireball and geysering water. Monkeys screamed; birds wheeled up from the shoreline trees. A veil of oily smoke drifted across the lake, and within seconds a pair of legs floated to the surface, leaking red. Quinn felt queasy and sick at heart.

"Man, they doin' wonders with ordinance nowadays," said Mathis.

Infuriated, Quinn fired a spread of three rounds into the jungle.

"Not even close, Quinn Edward."

"You're a real regular army asshole, aren't you?" said Quinn. "Lettin' some poor fucker draw fire."

"You got me wrong, man! I sent that ol' boy out 'cause I loved him. He been with me almost four years, but his mind was goin', reflexes goin'. You done him a favor, Quinn Edward. Reduced his confusion to zero"—Mathis' tone waxed evangelic—"and let him shine forevermore!"

Quinn had a mental image of Mathis, bearded and haggard like the guy he'd shot, but taller, rawboned: a gaunt rack of a man with rotting teeth and blown-away pupils. Being able to fit even an imaginary face to his target tuned his rage higher, and he fired again.

"Awright, man!" Mathis' voice was burred with anger; the cadences of his speech built into a rant. "You want bang-bang, you got it. But you stay out there, the Queen'll do the job for me. She don't like nobody creepin' 'round her in the dark. Makes her crazy. You go on, man! Stay there! She peel you down to meat and sauce!"

His laughter went high into a register that Quinn's speakers distorted, translating it as a hiccuping squeal, and he continued to rave. However, Quinn was no longer listening. His attention was fixed on the dead man's legs spinning past on the current. A lace of blood eeled from the severed waist. The separate strands looked to be spelling out characters in some oriental script; but before Quinn could try to decipher them, they lost coherence and were whirled away by the jade green medium into which—staring with fierce concentration, giddy with drugs and fatigue—he, too, felt he was dissolving.

At twilight, when streamers of mist unfurled across the water, Quinn stood down from his watch and went to find a secure place in which to pass the night: considering Mathis' leeriness about his Queen's nocturnal temper, he doubted there would be any trouble before morning. He beat his way through the brush and came to an enormous ceiba tree whose trunk split into two main branchings; the split formed a wide crotch that would support him comfortably. He popped an ampule to stave off pain, climbed up and settled himself.

Darkness fell; the mist closed in, blanketing moon and stars. Quinn stared out into pitch-black nothing, too exhausted to think, too buzzed to sleep. Finally, hoping to stimulate thought, he did another ampule. After it had taken effect, he could make out some of the surrounding foliage—vague scrolled shapes that each had their own special shine—and he could hear a thousand plops and rustles that blended into a scratchy percussion, its rhythms providing accents for a pulse that seemed to be coming up from the roots of the island. But there were no crunchings in the brush, no footsteps.

No sign of the Queen.

What a strange fantasy, he thought, for Mathis to have created. He wondered how Mathis saw her. Blond, with a ragged Tarzan-movie skirt? A black woman with a necklace of bones? He remembered driving down to see his old girlfriend at college and being struck by a print hung on her dorm room wall. It had shown a night jungle, a tiger prowling through fleshy vegetation, and—off to the side—a mysterious-looking woman standing naked in moonshadow. That would be his image of the Queen. It seemed to him that the woman's eyes had been glowing . . . But maybe he was remembering it wrong, maybe it had been the tiger's eyes. He had liked the print, had peered at the artist's signature and tried to pronounce the name. "Roo-see-aw," he'd said, and his girl had given a haughty sniff and said, "Roo-sō. It's Roo-sō." Her attitude had made clear what he had suspected: that he had lost her. She had experienced a new world, one that had set its hooks in her; she had outgrown their little North Dakota farming town, and she had outgrown him as well. What the war had done to him was similar, only the world he had outgrown was a much wider place: he'd learned that he just wasn't cut out for peace and quiet anymore.

Frogs chirred, crickets sizzled, and he was reminded of the hollow near his father's house where he had used to go after chores to be alone, to plan a life of spectacular adventures. Like the island, it had been a diminutive jungle—secure, yet

not insulated from the wild—and recognizing the kinship between the two places caused him to relax. Soon he nodded out
into a dream, one in which he was twelve years old again,
fiddling with the busted tractor his father had given him to
repair. He'd never been able to repair it, but in the dream he
worked a gruesome miracle. Wherever he touched the metal,
blood beaded on the flaking rust; blood surged rich and dark
through the fuel line; and when he laid his hands on the corroded pistons, steam seared forth and he saw that the rust had
been transformed into red meat, that his hands had left scorched
prints. Then that meat-engine shuddered to life and lumbered
off across the fields on wheels of black bone, ploughing raw
gashes in the earth, sowing seeds that overnight grew into fiery
stalks yielding fruit that exploded on contact with the air.

It was such an odd dream, forged from the materials of his
childhood yet embodying an alien sensibility, that he came
awake, possessed by the notion that it had been no dream but
a sending. For an instant he thought he saw a lithe shadow at
the foot of the tree. The harder he stared at it, though, the less
substantial it became, and he decided it must have been a hal-
lucination. But after the shadow had melted away, a wave of
languor washed over him, sweeping him down into uncon-
sciousness, manifesting so suddenly, so irresistibly, that it
seemed no less a sending than the dream.

At first light, Quinn popped an ampule and went to inspect
the island, stepping cautiously through the gray mist that still
merged jungle and water and sky, pushing through dripping
thickets and spiderwebs diamonded with dew. He was certain
that Mathis would launch an attack today. Since he had survived a night with the Queen, it might be concluded that she
favored him, that he now posed a threat to Mathis' union with
her . . . and Mathis wouldn't be able to tolerate that. The best
course, Quinn figured, would be to rile Mathis up, to make
him react out of anger and to take advantage of that reaction.

The island proved to be about a hundred and twenty feet
long, perhaps a third of that across at the widest, and—except
for a rocky point at the north end and a clearing some thirty
feet south of the ceiba tree—was choked with vegetation. Vines
hung in graceful loops like flourishes depended from illumi-

nated letters; ferns clotted the narrow aisles between the bushes; epiphytes bloomed in the crooks of branches, punctuating the grayness with points of crimson and purple. The far side of the island was banked higher than a man could easily reach; but to be safe, Quinn mined the lowest sections with frags. In places where the brush was relatively sparse, he set flares head-high, connecting them to trip-wires that he rigged with vines. Then he walked back and forth among the traps, memorizing their locations.

By the time he had done, the sun had started to burn off the mist, creating pockets of clarity in the gray, and, as he headed back to his firing position, it was then he saw the tiger cat. Crouched in the weeds, lapping at the water. It wasn't much bigger than a housecat, with the delicate build and wedge-shaped head of an Abyssinian, and fine black stripes patterning its tawny fur. Quinn had seen such animals before while on patrol, but the way this one looked, so bright and articulated in contrast to the dull vegetable greens, framed by the eddying mist, it seemed a gateway had been opened onto a more vital world, and he was for the moment too entranced by the sight to consider what it meant. The cat finished its drink, turned to Quinn and studied him; then it snarled, wheeled about and sprang off into the brush.

The instant it vanished, Quinn became troubled by a number of things. How he'd chosen the island as a fortress; how he'd gone straight to the best firing position; how he'd been anticipating Mathis. All this could be chalked up to common sense and good soldiering . . . yet he had been so assured, so definite. The assurance could be an effect of the ampules; but then Mathis had said the Queen could slip thoughts into your head without you knowing. Until you became attuned to her, that is. Quinn tasted the flavors of his thoughts, searching for evidence of tampering. He knew he was being ridiculous, but panic flared in him nonetheless and he popped an ampule to pull himself together. Okay, he told himself. Let's see what the hell's going on.

For the next half hour he combed the island, prying into thickets, peering at treetops. He found no trace of the Queen, nor did he spot the cat again. But if she could control his mind, she might be guiding him away from her traces. She might be following him, manipulating him like a puppet. He spun around, hoping to catch her unawares. Nothing. Only bushes threaded with mist, trembling in the breeze. He let out a cracked laugh. Christ, he was an idiot! Just because the cat lived on the island didn't mean the Queen was real; in fact, the cat might be the core of Mathis' fantasy. It might have inhabited the lakeshore, and when Mathis and his men had arrived, it had fled out here to be shut of them . . . or maybe even this thought had been slipped into his head. Quinn was amazed by the subtlety of the delusion, at the elusiveness with which it defied both validation and debunking.

Something crunched in the brush.

Convinced that the noise signaled an actual presence, he swung his gun to cover the bushes. His trigger-finger tensed, but after a moment he relaxed. It was the isolation, the general weirdness, that was doing him in. Not some bullshit mystery woman. His job was to kill Mathis, and he'd better get to it. And if the Queen *were* real, well, then she did favor him and he might have help. He popped an ampule and laughed as it kicked in. Oh, yeah! With modern chemistry and the Invisible Woman on his side, he'd go through Mathis like a rat through cheese. Like fire through a slum. The drugs—or perhaps it was the pour of a mind more supple than his own—added a lyric coloration to his thoughts, and he saw himself moving with splendid athleticism into an exotic future wherein he killed the king and wed the shadow and ruled in Hell forever.

Quinn was low on frags, so he sat down behind the fallen tree trunk and cleaned the upper barrel of his gun: it fired caseless .22 caliber ammunition. Set on automatic, it could chew a man in half; but wanting to conserve bullets, he set it to fire single shots. When the sun had cleared the treeline, he began calling to Mathis on his radio. There was no response at first, but finally a gassed, irascible voice answered, saying, "Where the fuck you at, Quinn Edward?"

"The island." Quinn injected a wealth of good cheer into his next words. "Hey, you were right about the Queen!"

"What you talkin' 'bout?"

"She's beautiful! Most beautiful woman I've ever seen."

"You seen her?" Mathis sounded anxious. "Bullshit!"

Quinn thought about the Rousseau print. "She got dark,

satiny skin and black hair down to her ass. And the whites of her eyes, it looks like they're glowin' they're so bright. And her tits, man. They ain't too big, but the way they wobble around"—he let out a lewd cackle—"it makes you wanna get down and frolic with them puppies."

"Bullshit!" Mathis repeated, his voice tight.

"Unh-uh," said Quinn. "It's true. See, the Queen's lonely, man. She thought she was gonna have to settle for one of you lovelies, but now she's found somebody who's not so fucked up."

Bullets tore through the bushes on his right.

"Not even close," said Quinn. More fire; splinters flew from the tree trunk. "Tell me, Mathis." He supressed a giggle. "How long's it been since you had any pussy?" Several guns began to chatter, and he caught sight of a muzzle flash; he pinpointed it with his own fire.

"You son of a bitch!" Mathis screamed.

"Did I get one?" Quinn asked blithely. "What's the matter, man? Wasn't he ripe for the light?"

A hail of fire swept the island. The cap-pistol sounds, the volley of hits on the trunk, the bullets zipping through the leaves, all this enraged Quinn, touched a spark to the violent potential induced by the drugs. But he restrained himself from returning the fire, wanting to keep his position hidden. And then, partly because it was another way of ragging Mathis, but also because he felt a twinge of alarm, he shouted, "Watch out! You'll hit the Queen!"

The firing broke off. "Quinn Edward!" Mathis called.

Quinn kept silent, examining that twinge of alarm, trying to determine if there had been something un-Quinnlike about it.

"Quinn Edward!"

"Yeah, what?"

"It's time," said Mathis, hoarse with anger. "Queen's tellin' me it's time for me to prove myself. I'm comin' at you, man!"

Studying the patterns of blue-green scale flecking the tree trunk, Quinn seemed to see the army of his victims—grim, desanguinated men—and he felt a powerful revulsion at what he had become. But when he answered, his mood swung to the opposite pole. "I'm waitin', asshole!"

"Y'know," said Mathis, suddenly breezy. "I got a feelin' it's gonna come down to you and me, man. 'Cause that's how she wants it. And can't nobody beat me one-on-one in my own backyard." His breath came as a guttural hiss, and Quinn realized that this sort of breathing was typical of someone who had been overdoing the ampules. "I'm gonna overwhelm you, Quinn Edward," Mathis went on. "Gonna be like them ol' Jap movies. Little men with guns actin' all brave and shit 'til they see somethin' big and hairy comin' at 'em, munchin' treetops and spittin' fire. Then off they run, yellin', 'Tokyo is doomed!' "

For thirty or forty minutes, Mathis kept up a line of chatter, holding forth on subjects as varied as the Cuban space station and Miami's chances in the AL East. He launched into a polemic condemning the new statutes protecting the rights of prostitutes ("Part of the kick's bein' able to bounce 'em 'round a little, y'know."), then made a case for Antarctica being the site of the original Garden of Eden, and then proposed the theory that every President of the United States had been a member of a secret homosexual society ("Half them First Ladies wasn't nothin' but guys in dresses."). Quinn didn't let himself be drawn into conversation, knowing that Mathis was trying to distract him; but he listened because he was beginning to have a sense of Mathis' character, to understand how he might attack.

Back in Lardcan, Tennessee or wherever, Mathis had likely been a charismatic figure, glib and expansive, smarter than his friends and willing to lead them from the rear into fights and petty crimes. In some ways he was a lot like the kid Quinn had been, only Quinn's escapades had been pranks, whereas he believed Mathis had been capable of consequential misdeeds. He could picture him lounging around a gas station, sucking down brews and plotting meanness. The hillbilly con-artist out to sucker the Yankee: that would be how he saw himself in relation to Quinn. Sooner or later he would resort to tricks. That was cool with Quinn; he could handle tricks. But he wasn't going to underestimate Mathis. No way. Mathis had to have a lot on the ball to survive the jungle for two years, to rule a troop of crazed Green Berets. Quinn just hoped Mathis would underestimate him.

The sun swelled into an explosive glare that whitened the sky and made the green of the jungle seem a livid, overripe color. Quinn popped ampules and waited. The inside of his head came to feel heavy with violent urges, as if his thoughts were congealing into a lump of mental plastique. Around noon, somebody began to lay down covering fire, spraying bullets back and forth along the bank. Quinn found he could time these sweeps, and after one such had passed him by, he looked out from behind the tree trunk. Four bearded, long-haired men were crossing the lake from different directions. Plunging through the water, lifting their knees high. Before ducking back, Quinn shot the two on the left. Saw them spun around, their rifles flung away. He timed a second sweep, then picked off the two on the right; he was certain he had killed one, but the other might only have been wounded. The gunfire homed in on him, trimming the bushes overhead. Twigs pinwheeled; cut leaves sailed like paper planes. A centipede had ridden one of the leaves down and was still crawling along its fluted edge. Quinn didn't like its hairy mandibles, its devil's face. Didn't like the fact it had survived while men had not. He let it crawl in front of his gun and blew it up into a fountain of dirt and grass.

The firing stopped.

Branches ticking the trunk; water slopping against the bank; drips. Quinn lay motionless, listening. No unnatural noises. But where were those drips coming from? The bullets hadn't splashed up much water. Apprehensions spidered his backbone. He peeked up over the top of the tree trunk . . . and cried out in shock. A man was standing in the water about four feet away, blocking the line of fire from the shore. With the mud freckling his cheeks, strands of bottomweed ribboning his dripping hair, he might have been the wild mad king of the lake. Skull-face; staring eyes; survival knife dangling loosely in his hand. He blinked at Quinn. Swayed, righted himself, blinked again. His fatigues were plastered to his ribs, and a big bloodstain mapped the hollow of his stomach. Fresh blood pumped from the hole Quinn had punched. The man's cheeks bulged: it looked as if he wanted to speak but was afraid more would come out than just words.

"Jesus . . . shit," he said sluggishly. His eyes half-rolled back, his knees buckled. Then he straightened, glancing around as if walking somewhere unfamiliar. He appeared to notice

Quinn, frowned and staggered forward, swinging the knife in a lazy arc.

Quinn got off a round before the man reached him. The bullet seemed to paste a red star under the man's eye, stamping his features with a rapt expression. He fell atop Quinn, atop the gun, which—jammed to automatic—kept firing. Lengths of wet hair hung across Quinn's faceplate, striping his view of branches and sky; the body jolted with the bullets tunneling through.

Two explosions nearby.

Quinn pushed the body away, belly-crawled into the brush and popped an ampule. He heard a *thock* followed by a bubbling scream: somebody had tripped a flare. He did a count and came up with nine dead . . . plus the guy laying down covering fire. Mathis, no doubt. It would be nice if that were all of them, but Quinn knew better. Somebody else was out there. He felt him the way a flower feels the sun—autonomic reactions waking, primitive senses coming alert.

He inched deeper into the brush. The drugs burned bright inside him; he had the idea they were forming a manlike shape of glittering particles, an inner man of furious principle. Mats of blight-dappled leaves pressed against his faceplate, then slid away with underwater slowness. It seemed he was burrowing through a mosaic of muted colors and coarse textures into which even the concept of separateness had been subsumed, and so it was that he almost failed to notice the boot: a rotting brown boot with vines for laces. Visible behind a spray of leaves about six feet off. The boot shifted, and Quinn saw an olive-drab trouserleg tucked into it.

His gun was wedged beneath him, and he was certain the man would move before he could ease it out. But apparently the man was playing bird dog, his senses straining for a clue to Quinn's whereabouts. Quinn lined the barrel up with the man's calf just above the boottop. Checked to make sure it was set on automatic. Then he fired, swinging the barrel back and forth an inch to both sides of his center mark.

Blood erupted from the calf, and a hoarse yell was drawn out of Quinn by the terrible hammering of the gun. The man fell screaming. Quinn tracked fire across the ground, and the screams were cut short.

The boot was still standing behind the spray of leaves, now sprouting a tattered stump and a shard of bone.

Quinn lowered his head, resting his faceplate in the dirt. It was as if all his rectitude had been spat out through the gun. He lay thoughtless, drained of emotion. Time seemed to collapse around him, burying him beneath a ton of decaying seconds. After a while a beetle crawled onto the faceplate, walking upside-down; it stopped at eye-level, tapped its mandibles on the plastic and froze. Staring at its grotesque underparts, Quinn had a glimpse into the nature of his own monstrosity: a tiny armored creature chemically programmed to a life of stalking and biting, and between violences, lapsing into a stunned torpor.

"Quinn Edward?" Mathis whispered.

Quinn lifted his head; the beetle dropped off the faceplate and scurried for cover.

"You got 'em all, didn'tcha?"

Quinn wormed out from under the brush, got to his feet and headed back to the fallen tree trunk.

"Tonight, Quinn Edward. You gonna see my knife flash . . . and then fare-thee-well." Mathis laughed softly. "It's me she wants, man. She just told me so. Told me I can't lose tonight."

Late afternoon, and Quinn went about disposing of the dead. It wasn't something he would ordinarily have done, yet he felt compelled to be rid of them. He was too weary to puzzle over the compulsion and merely did as it directed, pushing the corpses into the lake. The man who had tripped the flare was lying in some ferns, his face seared down to sinew and laceworks of cartilage; ants were stitching patterns across the blood-slick bone of the skull. Having to touch the body made Quinn's flesh nettle cold, and bile flooded his throat.

That finished, he sat in the clearing south of the ceiba and popped an ampule. The rays of sunlight slanting through the canopy were as sharply defined as lasers, showing greenish-gold against the backdrop of leaves. Sitting beneath them, he felt guided by no visionary purpose; he was, however, gaining a clearer impression of the Queen. He couldn't point to a single thought out of the hundreds that cropped up and say, that one, that's hers. But as if she were filtering his perceptions, he was coming to know her from everything he experienced. It seemed the island had been steeped in her, its mists and midnights modified by her presence, refined to express her moods; even its overgrown terrain seemed to reflect her nature: shy, secretive, yet full of gentle stirrings. Seductive. He understood now that the process of becoming attuned to her was a process of seduction, one you couldn't resist because you, too, were being steeped in her. You were forced into a lover's involvement with her, and she was a woman worth loving. Beautiful . . . and strong. She'd needed that strength in order to survive, and that was why she couldn't help him against Mathis. The life she offered was free from the terrors of war, but demanded vigilance and fortitude. Though she favored him—he was sure of that—his strength would have to be proved. Of course Mathis had twisted all this into a bizarre religion . . .

Christ!

Quinn sat up straight. Jesus fucking Christ! He was really losing it. Mooning around like some kid fantasizing about a movie star. He'd better get his ass in gear, because Mathis would be coming soon. Tonight. It was interesting how Mathis—knowing his best hope of taking Quinn would be at night—had used his delusion to overcome his fear of the dark, convincing himself that the Queen had told him he would win . . . or maybe she *had* told him.

Fuck that, Quinn told himself. He wasn't that far gone.

A gust of wind roused a chorus of whispery vowels from the leaves. Quinn flipped his visor. It was hot, cloudless, but he could smell rain and the promise of a chill on the wind. He did an ampule. The drugs withdrew the baffles that had been damping the core of his anger. Confidence was a voltage surging through him, keying new increments of strength. He smiled, thinking about the fight to come, and even that smile was an expression of furious strength, a thing of bulked muscle fibers and trembling nerves. He was at the center of strength, in touch with every rustle, his sensitivity fueled by the light-stained brilliance of the leaves. Gazing at the leaves, at their infinite shades of green, he remembered a line of a poem he'd read once: "*. . . green flesh, green hair, and eyes of coldest silver . . .*" Was that how the Queen would be? If she were real? Transformed into a creature of pure poetry by the unearthly radiance of Fire Zone Emerald. Were they all acting out a mythic drama distilled from the mundane interactions of love and war, performing it in the flawed heart of an immense green jewel whose reality could only be glimpsed by those blind enough to see beyond the chaos of the leaves into its precise facets and fractures? Quinn chuckled at the wasted profundity of his thought and pictured Mathis dead, himself the king of that dead man's illusion, robed in ferns and wearing a leafy crown.

High above, two wild parrots were flying complicated loops and arcs, avoiding the hanging columns of light as if they were solid.

Just before dusk, a rain squall swept in, lasting only a few minutes but soaking the island. Quinn used it for cover, moving about and rigging more flares. He considered taking a stand on the rocky point at the north end: it commanded a view of both shores, and he might get lucky and spot Mathis as he crossed. But it was risky—Mathis might stop *him*—and he decided his best bet would be to hide, to outwait Mathis. Waiting wasn't Mathis' style. Quinn went back to the ceiba tree and climbed past the crotch to a limb directly beneath an opening in the canopy, shielded by fans of leaves. He switched his gun to its high explosive setting. Popped an ampule. And waited.

The clouds passed away south, and in the half-light the bushes below seemed to assume topiary shapes. After fifteen minutes, Quinn did another ampule. Violet auras faded in around ferns, pools of shadow quivered, and creepers looked to be slithering like snakes along the branches. A mystic star rose in the west, shining alone above the last pink band of sunset. Quinn stared at it until he thought he understood its sparkling message.

The night that descended was similar to the one in the Rousseau print, with a yellow globe moon carving geometries of shadow and light from the foliage. A night for tigers, mysterious ladies, and dark designs. Barnacled to his branch, Quinn felt that the moonlight was lacquering his combat gear, giving it the semblance of ebony armor with gilt filigree, enforcing upon him the image of a knight about to do battle for his lady. He supposed it was possible that such might actually be the case. It was true that his perception of the Queen was growing stronger and more particularized; he even thought he could tell where she was hiding: the rocky point. But he doubted he could trust the perception . . . and besides, the battle itself, not its motive, was the significant thing. To reach that peak moment when perfection drew blood, when you muscled confusion aside and—as large as a constellation with the act, as full of stars and blackness and primitive meaning—you were able to look down onto the world and know you had outperformed the ordinary. Nothing, neither an illusory motive or the illusion of a real motive, could add importance to that.

Shortly after dark, Mathis began to chatter again, regaling Quinn with anecdote and opinion, and by the satisfaction in his voice, Quinn knew he had reached the island. Twenty minutes passed, each of them ebbing away, leaking out of Quinn's store of time like blood dripping from an old wound. Then a burst of white incandescence to the south, throwing vines and bushes into skeletal silhouette . . . and with it a scream. Quinn smiled. The scream had been a dandy imitation of pain, but he wasn't buying it. He eased a flare from his hip pouch. It wouldn't take long for Mathis to give this up.

The white fire died, muffled by the rain-soaked foliage, and finally Mathis said, "You a cautious fella, Quinn Edward."

Quinn popped two ampules.

"I doubt you can keep it up, though," Mathis went on. "I mean, sooner or later you gotta throw caution to the winds."

Quinn barely heard him. He felt he was soaring, that the island was soaring, arrowing through a void whose sole feature it was and approaching the moment for which he had been waiting: a moment of brilliant violence to illuminate the flaws at the heart of the stone, to reveal the shadow play. The first burn of the drugs subsided, and he fixed his eyes on the shadows south of the ceiba tree.

Tension began to creep into Mathis' voice, and Quinn was not surprised when—perhaps five minutes later—he heard the stutter of AR-18: Mathis firing at some movement in the brush. He caught sight of a muzzle flash, lifted his gun. But the next instant he was struck by an overpowering sense of the Queen, one that shocked him with its suddenness.

She was in pain. Wounded by Mathis' fire.

In his mind's eye, Quinn saw a female figure slumped against a boulder, holding her lower leg. The wound wasn't serious, but he could tell she wanted the battle to end before worse could happen.

He was mesmerized by her pervasiveness—it seemed if he were to flip up his visor, he would breathe her in—and by what appeared to be a new specificity of knowledge about her. Bits of memory were surfacing in his thoughts; though he didn't quite believe it, he could have sworn they were hers: a shanty with a tin roof amid fields of tilled red dirt; someone walking on a beach; a shady place overhung by a branch dripping with orchids, with insects scuttling in and out of the blooms, mining some vein of sweetness. That last memory was associated with the idea that it was a place where she went to daydream, and Quinn felt an intimate resonance with her, with the fact that she—like him—relied on that kind of retreat.

Confused, afraid for her yet half-convinced that he had slipped over the edge of sanity, he detonated his flare, aiming it at the opening in the canopy. An umbrella of white light bloomed overhead. He tracked his gun across eerily lit bushes and . . . there! Standing in the clearing to the south, a man wearing combat gear. Before the man could move, Quinn blew him up into marbled smoke and flame. Then, his mind ablaze with victory, he began to shinny down the branch. But as he descended, he realized that something was wrong. The man had just stood there, made no attempt to duck or hide. And his gun. It had been like Quinn's own, not an AR-18.

He had shot a dummy or a man already dead!

Bullets pounded his back, not penetrating but knocking him out of the tree. Arms flailing, he fell into a bush. Branches tore the gun from his grasp. The armor deadened the impact, but he was dazed, his head throbbing. He clawed free of the bush just as Mathis' helmeted shadow—looking huge in the dying light of the flare—crashed through the brush and drove a rifle stock into his faceplate. The plastic didn't shatter, webbing over with cracks; but by the time Quinn had recovered, Mathis was straddling him, knees pinning his shoulders.

"How 'bout that?" said Mathis, breathing hard.

A knife glinted in his hand, arced downward and thudded into Quinn's neck, deflected by the armor. Quinn heaved, but Mathis forced him back and this time punched at the faceplate with the hilt of the knife. Punched again, and again. Bits of plastic sprayed Quinn's face, and the faceplate was now so thoroughly cracked, it was like looking up through a crust of glittering rime. It wouldn't take many more blows. Desperate, Quinn managed to roll Mathis onto his side and they grappled silently. His teeth bit down on a sharp plastic chip and he tasted blood. Still grappling, they struggled to their knees, then to their feet. Their helmets slammed together. The impact came as a hollow click over Quinn's radio, and that click seemed to switch on a part of his mind that was as distant as a flare, calm and observing; he pictured the two of them to be black giants with whirling galaxies for hearts and stars articulating their joints, doing battle over the female half of everything. Seeing it that way gave him renewed strength. He wrangled Mathis off-balance, and they reeled clumsily through the brush. They fetched up against the trunk of the ceiba tree, and for a few seconds they were frozen like wrestlers muscling for an advantage. Sweat poured down Quinn's face; his arms quivered. Then Mathis tried to butt his faceplate, to finish the job he had begun with the hilt of the knife. Quinn ducked, slipped his hold, planted a shoulder in Mathis' stomach and drove him backward. Mathis twisted as he fell, and Quinn turned him onto his stomach. He wrenched Mathis' knife-arm behind his back, pried the knife loose. Probed with the blade, searching for a seam between the plates of neck armor. Then he pressed it in just deep enough to prick the skin. Mathis went limp. Silent.

"Where's all the folksy chit-chat, man?" said Quinn, excited.

Mathis maintained his silent immobility, and Quinn wondered if he had snapped, gone catatonic. Maybe he wouldn't have to kill him. The light from the flare had faded, and the moon-dappled darkness that had filled in reminded Quinn of the patterns of blight on the island leaves: an infection at whose heart they were clamped together like chitinous bugs.

"Bitch!" said Mathis, suddenly straining against Quinn's hold. "You lied, goddamn you!"

"Shut up," said Quinn, annoyed.

"Fuckin' bitch!" Mathis bellowed. "You tricked me!"

"I said to shut up!" Quinn gave him a little jab, but Mathis began to thrash wildly, nearly impaling himself, shouting, "Bitch!"

"Shut the fuck up!" said Quinn, growing angrier but also trying to avoid stabbing Mathis, beginning to feel helpless, to feel that he would have to stab him, that it was all beyond his control.

"I'll kill you bitch!" screamed Mathis. "I'll . . ."

"Stop it!" Quinn shouted, not sure to whom he was crying out. Inside his chest, a fuming cell of anger was ready to explode.

Mathis writhed and kicked. "I'll cut out your fuckin' . . ."

Poisonous burst of rage. Mandibles snipping shut, Quinn shoved the knife home. Blood guttered in Mathis' throat. One gauntleted hand scrabbled in the dirt, but that was all reflexes.

Quinn sat up feeling sluggish. There was no glory. It had been a contest essentially decided by a gross stupidity: Mathis' momentary forgetfulness about the armor. But how could he have forgotten? He'd seen what little effects bullets had. Quinn took off his helmet and sucked in hits of the humid air. Watched a slice of moonlight jiggle on Mathis' faceplate. Then a blast of static from his helmet radio, a voice saying, ". . . you copy?"

"Ain't no friendlies in Emerald," said another radio voice. "Musta been beaners sent up that flare. It's a trap."

"Yeah, but I got a reading like infantry gear back there. We should do a sweep over that lake."

Chopper pilots, Quinn realized. But he stared at the helmet with the mute awe of a savage, as if they had been alien voices speaking from a stone. He picked up the helmet, unsure what to say.

Please, no . . .

The words had been audible, and he realized that she had made him hear them in the sighing of the breeze.

Static fizzling. ". . . get the hell outta here."

The first pilot again. "Do you copy? I repeat, do you copy?"

What, Quinn thought, if this had all been the Queen's way of getting rid of Mathis, even down to that last flash of anger, and now, now that he had done the job, wouldn't she get rid of him?

Please, stay . . .

Quinn imagined himself back in Dakota, years spent watching cattle die, reading mail order catalogues, drinking and drinking, comparing the Queen to the dowdy farmgirl he'd have married, and one night getting a little too morbidly weary of that nothing life and driving out onto the flats and riding the forty-five caliber express to nowhere. But at least that was proven, whereas this . . .

Please . . .

A wave of her emotion swept over him, seeding him with her loneliness and longing. He was truly beginning to know her now, to sense the precise configurations of her moods, the stoicism underlying her strength, the . . .

"Fuck it!" said one of the pilots.

The static from Quinn's radio smoothed to a hiss, and the night closed down around him. His feeling of isolation nailed him to the spot. Wind seethed in the massy crown of the ceiba, and he thought he heard again the whispered word *Please*. An icy fluid mounted in his spine. To shore up his confidence, he popped an ampule, and soon the isolation no longer troubled him, but rather seemed to fit about him like a cloak. This was the path he had been meant to take, the way of courage and character. He got to his feet, unsteady on his injured legs, and eased past Mathis, slipping between two bushes. Ahead of him, the night looked to be a floating puzzle of shadow and golden light: no matter how careful he was, he'd never be able to locate all his mines and flares.

But she would guide him.

Or would she? Hadn't she tricked Mathis? Lied to him?

More wind poured through the leaves of the ceiba tree, gusting its word of entreaty, and intimations of pleasure, of sweet green mornings and soft nights, eddied up in the torrent of her thoughts. She surrounded him, undeniable, as real as perfume, as certain as the ground beneath his feet.

For a moment he was assailed by a new doubt. God, he said to himself. Please don't let me be crazy. Not just ordinary crazy.

Please . . .

Then, suffering mutinies of the heart at every step, repelling them with a warrior's conviction, he moved through the darkness at the center of the island toward the rocky point, where— her tiger crouched by her feet, a ripe jungle moon hanging above like the emblem of her mystique—either love or fate might be waiting.

Down and Out in the Year 2000
by Kim Stanley Robinson

Introduction

Kim Stanley Robinson even looks like a writing professor. He fairly oozes education. He gazes at you through soft and thoughtful eyes that have been hooded by years of meditation and contemplation—or of wearing glasses. But, unlike most college writing teachers, Robinson actually knows how to teach writing. Many former students attest it; the fact that Campbell Award winner Karen Joy Fowler was one of his students proves it.

Telling you that Robinson is a professor, though, might lead you to certain expectations. Some will be correct: his writing is full of symbol and allusion; the pacing of his stories is often slow; some of his stories are virtually essays, leading to the apprehension of an idea rather than the release of causal tension.

But he will also surprise you. His stories do not take place in some academic never-never land, full of mid-life crises and blocked writers and contempt for the bourgeoisie. On the contrary, he deals with immediate experience, not by describing it, but by making you experience it. Some of his finest works have evoked his beloved sport of mountain climbing with the sort of breathtaking reality that Melville brought to whaling. And his work shows a constant awareness of the wider political, economic, and cultural worlds of his characters.

Many science fiction writers who have literary pretensions quickly abandon the very things that make science fiction worth doing—the creation of strange milieus, the intensity of romantic characterization, the primacy of event over character. Robinson seems to move in the other direction—he is a literary writer who is gradually bringing more and more of science fiction to his work. The result is that as I have tracked Robinson's work over time, I have been delighted with the way he constantly broadens the appeal of his work, never losing the intelligence, sensibility, and awareness of literary tradition that have been with him from the start.

"Down and Out in the Year 2000" seems at first to be extrapolative satire: if we keep on the way we're going, look at the mess we're going to get into. It can also be read as analogue, asserting that we're already doing, subtly, what goes on in the story's future. But such decoding, I think, misses the most fundamental aspect of all of Robinson's work: the deep humaneness of the man. When you live in his world, when you see events through his eyes, you soon realize the deep admiration he had for those who have the strength to remain civilized when there is no longer profit in it—and the compassion he also has for those too weak.

IT WAS GOING TO BE HOT AGAIN. SUMMER IN WASHINGTON, D.C.—Leroy Robinson woke and rolled on his mattress, broke into a sweat. That kind of a day. He got up and kneeled over the other mattress in the small room. Debra shifted as he shaded her from the sun angling in the open window. The corners of her mouth were caked white and her forehead was still hot and dry, but her breathing was regular and she appeared to be sleeping well. Quietly Leroy slipped on his jeans and walked down the hall to the bathroom. Locked. He waited; Ramon came out wet and groggy. "Morning, Robbie." Into the bathroom, where he hung his pants on the hook and did his morning ritual. One bloodshot eye, staring back at him from the splinter of mirror still in the frame. The dirt around the toilet base. The shower curtain blotched with black algae, as if it had a fatal disease. That kind of morning.

Out of the shower he dried off with his jeans and started to sweat again. Back in his room Debra was still sleeping. Worried, he watched her for a while, then filled his pockets and went into the hall to put on sneakers and tank-top. Debra slept light these days, and the strangest things would rouse her. He jogged down the four flights of stairs to the street, and sweating freely stepped out into the steamy air.

He walked down 16th Street, with its curious alternation of condo fortresses and abandoned buildings, to the Mall. There, big khaki tanks dominated the broad field of dirt and trash and tents and the odd patch of grass. Most of the protesters were still asleep in their scattered tent villages, but there was an active crowd around the Washington Monument, and Leroy walked on over, ignoring the soldiers by the tanks.

The crowd surrounded a slingshot as tall as a man, made of a forked tree branch. Inner tubes formed the sling, and the base was buried in the ground. Excited protesters placed balloons filled with red paint into the sling, and fired them up at the monument. If a balloon hit above the red that already covered the tower, splashing clean white—a rare event, as the monument was pure red up a good third of it—the protesters cheered crazily. Leroy watched them as they danced around the sling after a successful shot. He approached some of the calmer seated spectators.

"Want to buy a joint?"

"How much?"

"Five dollars."

"Too much, man! You must be kidding! How about a dollar?"

Leroy walked on.

"Hey, wait! One joint, then. Five dollars . . . shit."

"Going rate, man."

The protester pushed long blond hair out of his eyes and pulled a five from a thick clip of bills. Leroy got the battered

Marlboro box from his pocket and took the smallest joint from it. "Here you go. Have fun. Why don't you fire one of them paint bombs at those tanks, huh?"

The kids on the ground laughed. "We will when you get them stoned!"

He walked on. Only five joints left. It took him less than an hour to sell them. That meant thirty dollars, but that was it. Nothing left to sell. As he left the Mall he looked back at the monument; under its wash of paint it looked like a bone sticking out of raw flesh.

Anxious about coming to the end of his supply, Leroy hoofed it up to Dupont Circle and sat on the perimeter bench in the shade of one of the big trees, footsore and hot. In the muggy air it was hard to catch his breath. He ran the water from the drinking fountain over his hands until someone got in line for a drink. He crossed the circle, giving a wide berth to a bunch of lawyers in long-sleeved shirts and loosened ties, lunching on wine and cheese under the watchful eye of their bodyguard. On the other side of the park Delmont Briggs sat by his cup, almost asleep, his sign propped on his lap. The wasted man. Delmont's sign—and a little side business—provided him with just enough money to get by on the street. The sign, a battered square of cardboard, said PLEASE HELP—HUNGRY. People still looked through Delmont like he wasn't there, but every once in a while it got to somebody. Leroy shook his head distastefully at the idea.

"Delmont, you know any weed I can buy? I need a finger baggie for twenty."

"Not so easy to do, Robbie." Delmont hemmed and hawed and they dickered for a while, then he sent Leroy over to Jim Johnson, who made the sale under a cheery exchange of the day's news, over by the chess tables. After that Leroy bought a pack of cigarettes in a liquor store, and went up to the little triangular park between 17th, S, and New Hampshire, where no police or strangers ever came. They called it Fish Park for the incongruous cement whale sitting by one of the trash cans. He sat down on the long broken bench, among his acquaintances who were hanging out there, and fended them off while he carefully emptied the Marlboros, cut some tobacco into the weed, and refilled the cigarette papers with the new mix. With their ends twisted he had a dozen more joints. They smoked one and he sold two more for a dollar each before he got out of the park.

But he was still anxious, and since it was the hottest part of the day and few people were about, he decided to visit his plants. He knew it would be at least a week till harvest, but he wanted to see them. Anyway it was about watering day.

East between 16th and 15th he hit no-man's-land. The mixed neighborhood of fortress apartments and burned-out hulks gave way to a block or two of entirely abandoned buildings. Here the police had been at work, and looters had finished the job. The buildings were battered and burnt out, their ground floors blasted wide open, some of them collapsed entirely, into heaps of rubble. No one walked the broken sidewalk; sirens a few blocks off, and the distant hum of traffic, were the only signs that the whole city wasn't just like this. Little jumps in the corner of his eye were no more than that; nothing there when he looked directly. The first time, Leroy had found walking down the abandoned street nerve-racking; now he was reassured by the silence, the stillness, the no-man's-land smell of torn asphalt and wet charcoal, the wavering streetscape empty under a sour milk sky.

His first building was a corner brownstone, blackened on the street sides, all its windows and doors gone, but otherwise sound. He walked past it without stopping, turned and surveyed the neighborhood. No movement anywhere. He stepped up the steps and through the doorway, being careful to make no footprints in the mud behind the doorjamb. Another glance outside, then up the broken stairs to the second floor. The second floor was a jumble of beams and busted furniture, and Leroy waited a minute to let his sight adjust to the gloom. The staircase to the third floor had collapsed, which was the reason he had chosen this building, no easy way up. But he had a route worked out, and with a leap he grabbed a beam hanging from the stairwell and hoisted himself onto it. Some crawling up the beam and he could swing onto the third floor, and from there a careful walk up gapped stairs brought him to the fourth floor.

The room surrounding the stairwell was dim, and he had jammed the door to the next room, so that he had to crawl through a hole in the wall to get through. Then he was there.

Sweating profusely, he blinked in the sudden sunlight, and stepped to his plants, all lined out in plastic pots on the far wall. Eleven medium-sized female marijuana plants, their splayed green leaves drooping for lack of water. He took the rain funnel from one of the gallon jugs and watered the plants. The buds were just longer than his thumbnail; if he could wait another week or two at least, they would be the size of his thumb or more, and worth fifty bucks apiece. He twisted off some water leaves and put them in a baggie.

He found a patch of shade and sat with the plants for a while, watched them soak up the water. Wonderful green they had, lighter than most leaves in D.C. Little red threads in the buds. The white sky lowered over the big break in the roof, huffing little gasps of muggy air onto them all.

His next spot was several blocks north, on the roof of a burned-out hulk that had no interior floors left. Access was by way of a tree growing next to the wall. Climbing it was a challenge, but he had a route here he took, and he liked the way leaves concealed him even from passersbys directly beneath him once he got above the lowest branches.

The plants here were younger—in fact one had sprouted seeds since he last saw them, and he pulled the plant out and put it in the baggie. After watering them and adjusting the aluminum foil rain funnels on the jug tops, he climbed down the tree and walked back down 14th.

He stopped to rest in Charlie's Baseball Club. Charlie sponsored a city team with the profits from his bar, and old members of the team welcomed Leroy, who hadn't been by in a while. Leroy had played left field and batted fifth a year or two before, until his job with the park service had been cut. After that he had had to pawn his glove and cleats, and he had missed Charlie's minimal membership charge three seasons running, and so he had quit. And then it had been too painful to go by the club, and drink with the guys and look at all the trophies on the wall, a couple of which he had helped to win. But on this day he enjoyed the fan blowing, and the dark, and the fries that Charlie and Fisher shared with him.

Break over, he went to the spot closest to home, where the new plants were struggling through the soil, on the top floor of an empty stone husk on 16th and Caroline. The first floor was a drinking place for derelicts, and old Thunderbird and whiskey bottles, half still in bags, littered the dark room, which smelled of alcohol, urine, and rotting wood. All the better: few people would be foolish enough to enter such an obviously dangerous hole. And the stairs were as near gone as made no difference. He climbed over the holes to the second floor, turned and climbed to the third.

The baby plants were fine, bursting out of the soil and up to the sun, the two leaves covered by four, up into four again. . . . He watered them and headed home.

On the way he stopped at the little market that the Vietnamese family ran, and bought three cans of soup, a box of crackers and some Coke. "Twenty-two oh five tonight, Robbie," old Huang said with a four-toothed grin.

The neighbors were out on the sidewalk, the women sitting on the stoop, the men kicking a soccer ball about aimlessly as they watched Sam sand down an old table, the kids running around. Too hot to stay inside this evening, although it wasn't much better on the street. Leroy helloed through them and walked up the flights of stairs slowly, feeling the day's travels in his feet and legs.

In his room Debra was awake, and sitting up against her pillows. "I'm hungry, Leroy." She looked hot, bored; he shuddered to think of her day.

"That's a good sign, that means you're feeling better. I've got some soup here should be real good for you." He touched her cheek, smiling.

"It's too hot for soup."

"Yeah, that's true, but we'll let it cool down after it cooks, it'll still taste good." He sat on the floor and turned on the hot plate, poured water from the plastic jug into the pot, opened the can of soup, mixed it in. While they were spooning it out Rochelle Jackson knocked on the door and came in.

"Feeling better, I see." Rochelle had been a nurse before

her hospital closed, and Leroy had enlisted her help when Debra fell sick. "We'll have to take your temperature later."

Leroy wolfed down crackers while he watched Rochelle fuss over Debra. Eventually she took a temperature and Leroy walked her out.

"It's still pretty high, Leroy."

"What's she *got*?" he asked, as he always did. Frustration . . .

"I don't know any more than yesterday. Some kind of flu I guess."

"Would a flu hang on this long?"

"Some of them do. Just keep her sleeping and drinking as much as you can, and feed her when she's hungry. —Don't be scared, Leroy."

"I can't help it! I'm afraid she'll get sicker. . . . And there ain't nothing I can do!"

"Yeah, I know. Just keep her fed. You're doing just what I would do."

After cleaning up he left Debra to sleep and went back down to the street, to join the men on the picnic tables and benches in the park tucked into the intersection. This was the "living room" on summer evenings, and all the regulars were there in their usual spots, sitting on tables or bench backs. "Hey there, Robbie! What's happening?"

"Not much, not much. No man, don't kick that soccer ball at me, I can't kick no soccer ball tonight."

"You been walking the streets, hey?"

"How else we going to find her to bring her home to you?"

"Hey lookee here, Ghost is bringing out his TV."

"It's Tuesday night at the movies, y'all!" Ghost called out as he approached and plunked a little hologram TV and a Honda generator on the picnic table. They laughed and watched Ghost's pale skin glow in the dusk as he hooked the system up.

"Where'd you get this one, Ghost? You been sniffing around the funeral parlors again?"

"You bet I have!' Ghost grinned. "This one's picture is all fucked up, but it still works—I think—"

He turned the set on and blurry three-dee figures swam into shape in a cube above the box—all in dark shades of blue.

"Man, we *must* have the blues tonight," Ramon remarked. "Look at that!"

"They all look like Ghost," said Leroy.

"Hey, it works, don't it?" Ghost said. Hoots of derision. "And dig the sound! The sound works—"

"Turn it up then."

"It's up all the way."

"What's this?" Leroy laughed. "We got to watch frozen midgets whispering, is that it Ghost? What do midgets say on a cold night?"

"Who the fuck is this?" said Ramon.

Johnnie said, "That be Sam Spade, the greatest computer spy in the world."

"How come he live in that shack, then?" Ramon asked.

"That's to show it's a tough scuffle making it as a computer spy, real tough."

"How come he got four million dollars' worth of computers right there in the shack, then?" Ramon asked, and the others commenced giggling, Leroy loudest of all. Johnnie and Ramon could be killer sometimes. A bottle of rum started around, and Steve broke in to bounce the soccer ball on the TV, smashing the blue figures repeatedly.

"Watch out now, Sam about to go plug his brains in to try and find out who he is."

"And then he gonna be told of some stolen *wetware* he got to find."

"I got some wetware myself, only I call it a shirt."

Steve dropped the ball and kicked it against the side of the picnic table, and a few of the watchers joined in a game of pepper. Some men in a stopped van shouted a conversation with the guys on the corner. Those watching the show leaned forward. "Where's he gonna go?" said Ramon. "Hong Kong? Monaco? He gonna take the bus on over to Monaco?"

Johnnie shook his head. "Rio, man. Fucking Rio de Janeiro."

Sure enough, Sam was off to Rio. Ghost choked out an objection: "Johnnie—ha!—you must have seen this one before."

Johnnie shook his head, though he winked at Leroy. "No man, that's just where all the good stolen wetware ends up."

A series of commercials interrupted their fun: deodorant,

burglarkillers, cars. The men in the van drove off. Then the show was back, in Rio, and Johnnie said, "He's about to meet a slinky Afro-Asian spy."

When Sam was approached by a beautiful black Asian woman the men couldn't stand it. "Y'all *have* seen this one before!" Ghost cried.

Johnnie sputtered over the bottle, struggled to swallow. "No way! Experience counts, man, that's all."

"And Johnnie has watched one hell of a lot of Sam Spade," Ramon added.

Leroy said, "I wonder why they're always Afro-Asian."

Steve burst in, laughed. "So they can fuck all of us at once, man!" He dribbled on the image, changed the channel. *"—army command in Los Angeles reports that the rioting killed at least—"* He punched the channel again. "What else we got here—man!—what's *this*?"

"Cyborgs Versus Androids," Johnnie said after a quick glance at the blue shadows. "Lots of fighting."

"Yeah!" Steve exclaimed. Distracted, some of the watchers wandered off. "I'm a cyborg myself, see, I got these false teeth!"

"Shit."

Leroy went for a walk around the block with Ramon, who was feeling good. "Sometimes I feel so good, Robbie! So strong! I walk around this city and say, the city is falling apart, it can't last much longer like this. And here I am like some kind of animal, you know, living day to day by my wits and figuring out all the little ways to get by . . . you know there are people living up in Rock Creek Park like Indians or something, hunting and fishing and all. And it's just the same in here, you know. The buildings don't make it no different. Just hunting and scrapping to get by, and man I feel so *alive*—" he waved the rum bottle at the sky.

Leroy signed. "Yeah." Still, Ramon was one of the biggest fences in the area. It was really a steady job. For the rest. . . . They finished their walk, and Leroy went back up to his room. Debra was sleeping fitfully. He went to the bathroom, soaked his shirt in the sink, wrung it out. In the room it was stifling, and not even a waft of a breeze came in the window. Lying on his mattress sweating, figuring out how long he could make their money last, it took him a long time to fall asleep.

The next day he returned to Charlie's Baseball Club to see if Charlie could give him any piecework, as he had one or two times in the past. But Charlie only said no, very shortly, and he and everyone else in the bar looked at him oddly, so that Leroy felt uncomfortable enough to leave without a drink. After that he returned to the Mall, where the protesters were facing the troops ranked in front of the Capitol, dancing and jeering and throwing stuff. With all the police out it took him a good part of the afternoon to sell all the joints left, and when he had he walked back up 17th Street feeling tired and worried. Perhaps another purchase from Delmont could string them along a few more days. . . .

At 17th and Q a tall skinny kid ran out into the street and tried to open the door of a car stopped for a red light. But it was a protected car despite its cheap look, and the kid shrieked as the handle shocked him. He was still stuck by the hand to it when the car roared off, so that he was launched through the air and rolled over the asphalt. Cars drove on by. A crowd gathered around the bleeding kid. Leroy walked on, his jaw clenched. At least the kid would live. He had seen bodyguards gun thieves down in the street, kill them dead and walk away.

Passing Fish Park he saw a man sitting on a corner bench looking around. The guy was white, young; his hair was blond and short, he wore wire-rimmed glasses, his clothes were casual but new, like the protesters' down on the Mall. He had money. Leroy snarled at the sharp-faced stranger, approached him.

"What you doing here?"

"Sitting!" The man was startled, nervous. "Just sitting in a park!"

"This ain't no *park*, man. This is our front yard. You see any front yard to these apartment buildings here? No. This here is our front yard, and we don't like people just coming into it and sitting down anywhere!"

The man stood and walked away, looked back once, his

expression angry and frightened. The other man sitting on the park benches looked at Leroy curiously.

Two days later he was nearly out of money. He walked over to Connecticut Avenue, where his old friend Victor played harmonica for coins, when he couldn't find other work. Today he was there, belting out "Amazing Grace." He cut it off when he saw Leroy. "Robbie! What's happening?"

"Not much. You?"

Victor gestured at his empty hat, on the sidewalk before him. "You see it. Don't even have seed coin for the cap, man."

"So you ain't been getting any gardening work lately?"

"No, no. Not lately. I do all right here, though. People still pay for music, man, some of them. Music's the angle." He looked at Leroy, face twisted up against the sun. They had worked together for the park service, in times past. Every morning through the summers they had gone out and run the truck down the streets, stopping at every tree to hoist each other up in slings. The one hoisted had to stand out from trunk or branches like an acrobat, moving around to cut off every branch below twelve feet, and it took careful handling of the chain saw to avoid chopping into legs and such. Those were good times. But now the park service was gone, and Victor gazed at Leroy with a stoic squint, sitting behind an empty hat.

"Do you ever look up at the trees anymore, Robbie?"

"Not much."

"I do. They're growing wild, man! Growing like fucking weeds! Every summer they go like crazy. Pretty soon people are gonna have to drive their cars through the branches. The streets'll be tunnels. And with half the buildings in this area falling down . . . I like the idea that the forest is taking this city back again. Running over it like kudzu, till maybe it just be forest again at last."

That evening Leroy and Debra ate tortillas and refries, purchased with the last of their money. Debra had a restless night, and her temperature stayed high. Rochelle's forehead wrinkled as she watched her.

Leroy decided he would have to harvest a couple of the

biggest plants prematurely. He could dry them over the hot plate and be in business by the following day.

The next afternoon he walked east into no-man's-land, right at twilight. Big thunderheads loomed to the east, lit by the sun, but it had not rained that day and the muggy heat was like an invisible blanket, choking each breath with moisture. Leroy came to his abandoned building, looked around. Again the complete stillness of an empty city. He recalled Ramon's tales of the people who lived forever in the no-man's-land, channeling rain into basement pools, growing vegetables in empty lots, and existing entirely on their own with no need for money. . . .

He entered the building, ascended the stairs, climbed the beam, struggled sweating up to the fourth floor and through the hole into his room.

The plants were gone.

"Wha . . ." He kneeled, feeling like he had been punched in the stomach. The plastic pots were knocked over, and fans of soil lay spread over the old wood flooring.

Sick with anxiety he hurried downstairs and jogged north to his second hideaway. Sweat spilled into his eye and it stung fiercely. He lost his breath and had to walk. Climbing the tree was a struggle.

The second crop was gone too.

Now he was stunned, shocked almost beyond thought. Someone must have followed him. . . . It was nearly dark, and the mottled sky lowered over him, empty but somehow, now watchful. He descended the tree and ran south again, catching his breath in a sort of sobbing. It was dark by the time he reached 16th and Caroline, and he made his way up the busted stairs using a cigarette for illumination. Once on the fourth floor the lighter revealed broken pots, dirt strewn everywhere, the young plants gone. That small they hadn't been worth anything. Even the aluminum foil rain funnels on his plastic jugs had been ripped up and thrown around.

He sat down, soaking wet with sweat, and leaned back against the scored, moldy wall. Leaned his head back and looked up at the orange-white clouds, lit by the city.

After a while he stumbled downstairs to the first floor and stood on the filthy concrete, among the shadows and the discarded bottles. He went and picked up a whiskey bottle, sniffed it. Going from bottle to bottle he poured whatever drops remained in them into the whiskey bottle. When he was done he had a finger or so of liquor, which he downed in one long pull. He coughed. Threw the bottle against the wall. Picked up each bottle and threw it against the wall. Then he went outside and sat on the curb, and watched the traffic pass by.

He decided that some of his old teammates from Charlie's Baseball Club must have followed him around and discovered his spots, which would explain why they had looked at him so funny the other day. He went over to check it out immediately. But when he got there he found the place closed, shut down, a big new padlock on the door.

"What happened?" he asked one of the men hanging out on the corner, someone from this year's team.

"They busted Charlie this morning. Got him for selling speed, first thing this morning. Now the club be gone for good, and the team too."

When he got back to the apartment building it was late, after midnight. He went to Rochelle's door and tapped lightly.

"Who is it?"

"Leroy." Rochelle opened the door and looked out. Leroy explained what had happened. "Can I borrow a can of soup for Debra for tonight? I'll get it back to you."

"Okay. But I want one back soon, you hear?"

Back in his room Debra was awake. "Where you been, Leroy?" she asked weakly. "I was worried about you."

He sat down at the hot plate, exhausted.

"I'm hungry."

"That's a good sign. Some cream of mushroom soup, coming right up." He began to cook, feeling dizzy and sick. When Debra finished eating he had to force the remaining soup down him.

Clearly, he realized, someone he knew had ripped him off— one of his neighbors, or a park acquaintance. They must have guessed his source of weed, then followed him as he made his rounds. Someone he knew. One of his friends.

* * *

Early the next day he fished a newspaper out of a trashcan and looked through the short column of want ads for dishwashing work and the like. There was a busboy job at the Dupont Hotel and he walked over and asked about it. The man turned him away after a single look: "Sorry, man, we looking for people who can walk out into the restaurant, you know." Staring in one of the big silvered windows as he walked up New Hampshire, Leroy saw what the man saw: his hair spiked out everywhere as if he would be a Rasta in five or ten years, his clothes were torn and dirty, his eyes wild. . . . With a deep stab of fear he realized he was too poor to be able to get any job—beyond the point where he could turn it around.

He walked the shimmery black streets, checking phone booths for change. He walked down to M Street and over to 12th, stopping in at all the grills and little Asian restaurants, he went up to Pill Park and tried to get some of his old buddies to front him, he kept looking in pay phones and puzzling through blown scraps of newspaper, desperately hoping that one of them might list a job for him . . . and with each footsore step the fear spiked up in him like the pain lancing up his legs, until it soared into a thoughtless panic. Around noon he got so shaky and sick-feeling he had to stop, and despite his fear he slept flat on his back in Dupont Circle park through the hottest hours of the day.

In the late afternoon he picked it up again, wandering almost aimlessly. He stuck his fingers in every phone booth for blocks around, but other fingers had been there before his. The change boxes of the old farecard machines in the Metro would have yielded more, but with the subway system closed, all those holes into the earth were gated off, and slowly filing with trash. Nothing but big trash pits.

Back at Dupont Circle he tried a pay phone coin return and got a dime. "Yeah," he said aloud; that got him over a dollar. He looked up and saw that a man had stopped to watch him: one of the fucking lawyers, in loosened tie and long-sleeved shirt and slacks and leather shoes, staring at him open-mouthed as his group and his bodyguard crossed the street, Leroy held up the coin between thumb and forefinger and glared at the man, trying to impress on him the reality of a dime.

* * *

He stopped at the Vietnamese market. "Huang, can I buy some soup from you and pay you tomorrow?"

The old man shook his head sadly. "I can't do that, Robbie. I do that even once, and"—he wiggled his hands—"the whole house come down. You know that."

"Yeah. Listen, what can I get for—" he pulled the day's change from his pocket and counted it again. "A dollar ten."

Huang shrugged. "Candy bar? No?" He studied Leroy. "Potatoes. Here two potatoes from the back. Dollar ten."

"I didn't think you had any potatoes."

"Keep them for family, you see. But I sell these to you."

"Thanks, Huang." Leroy took the potatoes and left. There was a trash dumpster behind the store; he considered it, opened it, looked in. There was a half-eaten hot dog—but the stench overwhelmed him, and he remembered the poisonous taste of the discarded liquor he had punished himself with. He let the lid of the dumpster slam down and went home.

After the potatoes were boiled and mashed and Debra was fed, he went to the bathroom and showered until someone hammered on the door. Back in his room he still felt hot, and he had trouble catching his breath. Debra rolled from side to side, moaning. Sometimes he was sure she was getting sicker, and at the thought his fear spiked up and through him again, he got so scared he couldn't breathe at all. . . . "I'm hungry, Leroy. Can't I have nothing more to eat?"

"Tomorrow, Deb, tomorrow. We ain't got nothing now."

She fell into an uneasy sleep. Leroy sat on his mattress and stared out the window. White-orange clouds sat overhead, unmoving. He felt a bit dizzy, even feverish, as if he was coming down with whatever Debra had. He remembered how poor he had felt even back when he had had his crops to sell, when each month ended with such a desperate push to make rent. But now . . . He sat and watched the shadowy figure of Debra, the walls, the hotplate and utensils in the corner, the clouds out the window. Nothing changed. It was only an hour or two before dawn when he fell asleep, still sitting against the wall.

* * *

Next day he battled fever to seek out potato money from the pay phones and the gutters, but he only had thirty-five cents when he had to quit. He drank as much water as he could hold, slept in the park, and then went to see Victor.

"Vic, let me borrow your harmonica tonight."

Victor's face squinted with distress. "I can't, Robbie. I need it myself. You know—" pleading with him to understand.

"I know," Leroy said, staring off into space. He tried to think. The two friends looked at each other.

"Hey, man, you can use my kazoo."

"What?"

"Yeah, man, I got a good kazoo here, I mean a big metal one with a good buzz to it. It sounds kind of like a harmonica, and it's easier to play it. You just hum notes." Leroy tried it. "No, hum, man. Hum in it."

Leroy tried again, and the kazoo buzzed a long crazy note.

"See? Hum a tune, now."

Leroy hummed around for a bit.

"And then you can practice on my harmonica till you get good on it, and get your own. You ain't going to make anything with a harmonica till you can play it, anyway."

"But this—" Leroy said, looking at the kazoo.

Victor shrugged. "Worth a try."

Leroy nodded. "Yeah." He clapped Victor on the shoulder, squeezed it. Pointed at Victor's sign, which said *Help a musician!* "You think that helps?"

Victor shrugged. "Yeah."

"Okay. I'm going to get far enough away so's I don't cut into your business."

"You do that. Come back and tell me how you do."

"I will."

So Leroy walked south to Connecticut and M, where the sidewalks were wide and there were lots of banks and restaurants. It was just after sunset, the heat as oppressive as at midday. He had a piece of cardboard taken from a trashcan, and now he tore it straight, took his ballpoint from his pocket and copied Delmont's message. PLEASE HELP—HUNGRY. He had always admired its economy, how it cut right to the main point.

But when he got to what appeared to be a good corner, he

couldn't make himself sit down. He stood there, started to leave, returned. He pounded his fist against his thigh, stared about wildly, walked to the curb and sat on it to think things over.

Finally he stepped to a bank pillar mid-sidewalk and leaned back against it. He put the sign against the pillar face-out, and put his old baseball cap upside-down on the ground in front of him. Put his thirty-five cents in it as seed money. He took the kazoo from his pocket, fingered it. "Goddamn it," he said at the sidewalk between clenched teeth, "If you're going to make me live this way, you're going to have to pay for it." And he started to play.

He blew so hard that the kazoo squealed, and his face puffed up till it hurt. "Columbia, the Gem of the Ocean," blasted into all the passing faces, louder and louder—

When he had blown his fury out he stopped to consider it. He wasn't going to make any money that way. The loose-ties and the career women in dresses and running shoes were staring at him and moving out toward the curb as they passed, huddling closer together in their little flocks as their bodyguards got between him and them. No money in that.

He took a deep breath, started again. "Swing Low, Sweet Chariot." It really was like singing. And what a song. How you could put your heart into that one, your whole body. Just like singing.

One of the flocks had paused off to the side; they had a red light to wait for. It was as he had observed with Delmont: the lawyers looked right through beggars, they didn't want to think about them. He played louder, and one young man glanced over briefly. Sharp face, wire-rims—with a start Leroy recognized the man as the one he had harassed out of Fish Park a couple days before. The guy wouldn't look at Leroy directly, and so he didn't recognize him back. Maybe he wouldn't have anyway. But he was hearing the kazoo. He turned to his companions, student types gathered to the lawyer flock for the temporary protection of the bodyguard. He said something to them—"I love street music," or something like that—and took a dollar from his pocket. He hurried over and put the folded bill in Leroy's baseball cap, without looking up at Leroy. The *Walk* light came on, they all scurried away. Leroy played on.

That night after feeding Debra her potato, and eating two himself, he washed the pot in the bathroom sink, and then took a can of mushroom soup up to Rochelle, who gave him a big smile.

Walking down the stairs he beeped the kazoo, listening to the stairwell's echoes. Ramon passed him and grinned. "Just call you Robinson Caruso." he said, and cackled.

"Yeah."

Leroy returned to his room. He and Debra talked for a while, and then she fell into a half-sleep, and fretted as if in a dream.

"No, that's all right," Leroy said softly. He was sitting on his mattress, leaning back against the wall. The cardboard sign was face down on the floor. The kazoo was in his mouth, and it half buzzed with his words. "We'll be all right. I'll get some seeds from Delmont, and take the pots to new hideouts, better ones." It occurred to him that rent would be due in a couple of weeks; he banished the thought. "Maybe start some gardens in no-man's-land. And I'll practice on Vic's harmonica, and buy one from the pawn shop later." He took the kazoo from his mouth, stared at it. "It's strange what will make money."

He kneeled at the window, stuck his head out, hummed through the kazoo. Tune after tune buzzed the still, hot air. From the floor below Ramon stuck his head out his window to object: "Hey, Robinson Caruso! Ha! Ha! Shut the fuck up, I'm trying to sleep!" But Leroy only played quieter. "Columbia, the Gem of the Ocean"—

Angel Baby
by Rachel Pollack

Introduction

I read "Angel Baby" in the first Interzone *anthology.* Interzone, *Britain's one remaining professional science fiction magazine, serves in the eighties the role that Harlan Ellison's* Dangerous Visions *anthology performed for the sixties—it publishes writers whose works are so bizzarre or painful that it is inconceivable they could be published anywhere else. I knew nothing of the magazine except its name, however, when I picked up the hardcover American edition of the first anthology. It was not an evening of light reading.*

But it was an evening of enlightenment, and Pollack's story was one of the most dazzling. For a moment I thought this was just another Rosemary's Baby *inversion of the story of the birth of Christ, but I quickly learned otherwise. There is an angry intelligence at work here that, like a river in flood, resists the well-channeled ways, cutting its own channel through the fictional terrain.*

Beyond what you read in this story I know nothing whatever about Rachel Pollack. This story is enough for me to know she belongs in this anthology—she is one of the writers of the 1980s.

THE ANGEL CAME AT ME IN THE IBM PARKING LOT, THE huge double football field of concrete behind the long grey factory. Like I did every day in summer I'd gone there to pick up my mother's car. Every afternoon she would drive to work, and an hour or two later, after I'd cleaned up my dinner, I could go get the car and visit my friends or go to the shopping centers or the movies. At a quarter to twelve Mrs. Jacobi, who lived across the street and worked a couple of departments down from my mother, would take Mom home, telling the same old pumpkin jokes year after year. My mother could have gone to work with Mrs. Jacobi too, and saved me the twenty-minute walk to the parking lot down by the river, but my mother claimed Mrs. Jacobi sometimes came late and it made her nervous that her work record should depend on someone else.

The angel came over the river away from the mountains. I remember thinking, crazylike, that it must have come from one of the Catskill hotels, one of the resorts where rich people went to get away from the city.

I saw the eyes first. I don't know how, but I did. You'd think I'd see the wings before anything, but no, I looked up, I don't know why, it wasn't like anything called me or anything, I just looked up with the car keys in my hand, and I saw—they looked like small shiny bits of metal floating towards me. I stared at them. I didn't feel faint or nauseous, just weird, like my skin or something was sliding off into those horrible cold eyes.

Then I saw the wings. I guess he was coming straight toward me, because I first saw a wavy line of white, dipping down in the center, then coming up again. I squinted and shook my head, and then he must have shifted, because suddenly the wings filled the whole sky, like a long white cloud pointed at both ends, and narrow in the middle. Very slowly it moved, up and down, up and down. Christ, how slowly those wings beat, they took over my breath, forcing my lungs to open and close so slow that my chest burned. They made me want to cover myself, like *I* was somehow naked, and not him.

I managed to look around in the parking lot, and I saw, I guess maybe five or six or seven people, walking to their cars and looking tired, like they'd worked overtime and hadn't finished whatever they had to do. A couple were running and checking the big clock over the door, some guy with a big black leather briefcase. And none of them saw. I didn't cry out, I didn't even think of it. My eyes went back to the angel.

The wings looked like they could cover the whole parking lot, like they'd sweep the cars right off the concrete and just smash the whole row of trees separating the front and back lots. And in between, the legs sticking out, the arms hanging down, his hard naked body.

He was very thin, kind of stretched out, I even thought I could see his ribs. His skin shone. Not much, not as much as the wings. It made me think of the radium watch my father had had when I was a little kid and he let me take it in the closet and shut the door so I could see it glow. The angel's skin shone a lot like that, except it wasn't green but white, like watery milk, so that for a moment I thought of an old movie I'd seen on TV, where they've got this radioactive milk and the scientists are trying to find it and they keep showing it moving around until it ends up on someone's table, pale and glowing. But of course I only thought that for a moment. Later, when I tried to remember his skin, I thought of the way snow looks under a full moon. Even now, I sometimes can't stand to look at snow at night, and I won't even let Jimmy out of the house after dark in winter.

I don't think I realized the angel was coming for me until the last moment. He just came closer and closer, getting larger, and in a funny way *smaller*, as I could see he wasn't really so big, his body no longer, I mean no taller than Bobby Beauhawk, the basketball player who kept breaking things in my bio class. (I wrote 'longer' because once my mother took me on a vacation, she said we could both use a rest, but she meant me, and we went to Florida and I saw this alligator lying in the mud, and I started to scream because it was just as long, exactly as long as the angel.) The wings weren't short, they could have stretched over two or three cars easy, but nothing like as long as I thought when I saw them far away.

I never saw—his thing. I know that sounds really crazy, but I just didn't see it. I have some picture of it in my head as bright red and pointy, so maybe I saw it unconsciously or something, but I don't remember anything about it. Even as I realized he was coming right at me and I should run or something, I went back to looking at his eyes. I felt like I could look inside them, not into his head, but into all the things he'd seen, his own world. I saw it like a place where the sky filled up with lightning all the time, where nothing ever stayed in one piece, where the ground kept melting and turning into water, or even huge fires that jumped up——Except it always stayed cold. Cold like you can't possibly imagine, like no one ever even thought of heat, even knew what it was.

One of the wings knocked me to the ground—I screamed, afraid I'd hit my head—and then his long fingers started fumbling at my clothes, stiff and clumsy like he didn't know what he was doing. I thought of Mary Tunache, who made out with that exchange student and later told us all he didn't even know how to get her bra off.

He didn't mean to knock me over, not like he wanted to force me or anything like that, he just couldn't use his hands very well, our world was too clumsy for him. I know that, because once he'd got my clothes off he just started stroking me, long strokes with his fingers all spread out, like the way my piano teacher used to hold her hands over the keys before she began. At first his fingers seemed horribly cold, and it wasn't until I saw the lines of blood down my breasts and stomach that I realized they weren't fingers at all, but claws, long and thin, a pale gold that picked up reddish highlights from the sun, like my friend Marie's hair that everyone envies so much.

The claws just touched my skin but they reached into me too, and they stirred up something all the way down. I started making noises, they sounded like animal imitations, but they weren't. I was talking his language, his people's talk, nor talk but shrieks and whistles that didn't mean anything like our words do, they just said everything they needed to say. Everything.

I want to get this right, put it down just like it happened, but I can't. It's not fair. I know what to say, but I don't know the words. Whatever I saw makes it something else. How can I use human words to describe angel language? If I could only speak that again I wouldn't have to describe.

The funny thing was, nobody heard me, the one or two people I could see in the lot didn't even turn, some woman walked past only an aisle away, in the middle of my screams I could hear the click of her heels. But she didn't hear me, she couldn't even see the angel spread over me, with his wings curving over the tops of the cars.

Reading this it strikes me how crazy it sounds. If no one else saw it, then it didn't happen, right? Well, I think that no matter how crazy a person is, he's got to know, secretly anyway, when he's made something up. Maybe that's what makes them unhappy and violent, because inside they know it's not true, yet outside they can't get away from it.

But the angel was real all the way down, so much that for weeks afterward my mother and my friends looked and sounded fake to me, like people on television saying words that someone else has written and no one cares about.

I don't really know when the angel . . . entered me. I know he did because later when I checked I wasn't a virgin anymore, but I don't remember. It doesn't matter. Can you understand? What really counted was speaking the angel's language.

I don't even know when it ended. Suddenly I was lying alone, between my mother's car and some Cadillac, my body all scratched, as much by the pebbles under me as by the claws, and in the sky I could see the angel, his back and legs incredibly bright, getting larger and larger until they covered the whole sun and sky. And then they were gone.

I grabbed up my clothes, found the car keys on the ground, and scrambled inside. I lay there on the back seat, still not excited or frightened or happy or sad, or anything like that. What the angel did, what he showed me, made me, you can't find any feelings to go with it. I've got a kind of thing about feelings. I think they make up a sort of language we use, just like words, to tell ourselves what's happened to us. They explain things. Happiness says, this was a good experience, you enjoyed it, sadness says, this one was crummy, you didn't like it.

But the angel didn't need any explanations. I'd spoken his language. If I could have I would have given up feelings, and words, forever. But you try to do that without the angel's language and you just become fake.

But that came later. Lying there on the back seat I tried to hold on to what the angel had given me. I tried making those sounds again, only they came out stupid so I stopped right away. I tried to remember the things I'd seen in his eyes and that came a little clearer, except it was only a memory.

One thing real remained. The angel's message. His promise. The angel wanted a child. No, the angel never wanted anything. He was going to have a child. And he'd chosen me as the mother. That's not right either. He didn't choose, didn't find me worthy or anything like that. In the angel's world nothing gets chosen or picked out. You'd think I would wonder why he picked me. But I'd seen that world, I'd talked it, and I knew you didn't need any reason for anything.

I was going to have the angel's child. Except I couldn't do it right away. My human body couldn't hold his angel seed. It wouldn't burn up or anything, the two things just wouldn't fit together. So the first time he came just to prepare me. What he did would change me, not all at once, but slowly, over years until I was ready for him. The only thing I had to do was allow it to work. That meant no husband or lovers, no human disturbing that slow movement all the way through me. Lying there in the car I had to laugh a little. It reminded me of my mother telling me that "virginity still matters. No man wants soiled goods, no matter what he says."

Well, the angel had certainly soiled me, and whatever any man might want I was going to make sure that dirt soiled me all the way down. The angel had promised me a child and I planned to get it.

The strange thing was, I knew that wanting the angel's child already cut me off from him. Wanting things, that's what makes us people and not angels. But I couldn't help it.

I lay there for a while, breathing the hot stuffy air of the car but not wanting to open the windows, watching the sky darken. Finally I heard a couple of men laughing and hid on the floor while I pulled my clothes on. When they'd gone I got up and drove home.

For the next few days I tried, like I said, not to feel anything. I thought it would help me hold on to the angel language. But that was gone. Finished. The angel had dropped me back in the human world and I had to teach myself all over how to work in it. Besides, I could see my mother was getting suspicious.

At first her job and the summer heat kept her so wrapped

up she didn't notice anything. I was really glad of that. I'd
spent hours scrubbing the blood stains off my clothes and the
back seat of the car. But the next evening, when I called my
mother after she'd driven to work, she just went on about the
heat and the men in her department wanting a young secretary
with big tits instead of someone who could type and cared
about her work, and how I shouldn't forget to water the lawn
before it got dark.

For a few days it went like that, but then she started to ask
did I feel okay, why didn't I go visit my friends or go to a
movie, get away from the heat. I didn't say anything, just made
a face and moved away when she tried to touch me. One day
she told me of a dance the Lutheran Center was giving at
Speckled Lake, and all my friends were going, why didn't I
go, maybe I'd meet someone there, if I sat at home every night
I'd just get depressed.

I could see her watching me closely, and it took me a minute
to realize the test she'd set up. She didn't care about the dance,
well, she did, but more, she wanted to see how I'd react to her
interfering. Almost too late I shouted, "You called all my
friends? Jesus, how could you do that? Didn't I tell you I hate
it when you butt in like that?" She had to fight not to smirk
as she apologized and went on to say, even so, maybe I should
go to the dance anyway, now that the damage was done, no
sense in my denying myself.

The funny thing was, she was playing a part just as much
as I was. It made me wonder how much she knew. For just a
second the crazy idea hit me that an angel (or the angel, maybe
there was only one, except it made no difference how many
there were, they were all the same), maybe the angel had come
to her, to everybody, and everyone kept it hidden, thinking no
one would understand, so that if I told the truth, everyone else
would want to.

But no, I could see in my mother's face, and later, in other
people's faces when I looked at them in the street, she'd never
seen those eyes. I could tell by looking at hers. You could go
a certain way into them and then they stopped.

Later, after my mother had apologized again, I lay up in my
room with the fan on, and thought about my feelings, like
anger or sadness, and how they only described things, but how,

without the angel talk, I couldn't do anything else. It's all fake, I thought, no matter which way I go. If I acted like other people, that wasn't real, but if I tried not to, if I tried to act like the angel, that made me even more fake. The best I could do, I decided, was act like ordinary people but at least remember the truth. I got up and went to the mirror and looked at my eyes. I thought they looked different than they used to, but how could I tell without seeing them from before at the same time, I thought they went all the way down, but I could only see them in the glass which made everything flat and dull. If only I could really look in my own eyes. The angel can, I thought. He can look at himself from the outside and in at the same time.

The next day I went into town, to Woolworth's, and bought a diary, one of those blue plastic things with thick gold-edged paper and a lock on the cover. If I couldn't act like the angel, I thought, I should at least write it all down so I wouldn't forget. I planned to write something every day, all my thoughts and feelings, even if I had to use human language, so when the angel came back I'd have stayed close to him.

The first couple of days I must have filled up half the book. I imagined ending up with a whole stock of diaries and giving them to the angel or maybe saving them for the baby. But then my daily writing started getting shorter. I found myself trying to think of things to say, or writing about my mother or people I saw or something like that, just to fill up the pages. So I told myself I didn't need to write every day, I would just put things in when they came to me, like if I remembered something about the wings or the claws then I could put it down with the date.

For a few weeks I kept doing it, then I just sort of forgot. I've still got it. I read it recently, while Jimmy was out playing with his toy cars. I thought I'd hate it, thought it would sound stupid. But it said so much, so many beautiful things, almost like some little piece of angel language translated into English. Why didn't I keep doing it, I thought, and began to cry, angry at the same time, because tears, and even anger had nothing to do with it, they pushed aside the angel voice, leaving nothing but human talk in its place.

Around the time I got the diary I also made the claw. I got

some clay (at first I thought of papier mâché, but decided I wanted something better and besides, I couldn't remember how to make papier mâché) and spent hours bending, twisting, pinching, sometimes screaming and throwing it at the wall (I waited till my mother went to work) because I couldn't get it right.

Finally I told myself I'd never get it right, and settled for a version that didn't try to look just like it, but instead gave me a kind of memory of it. I'd bought a little book on clay which told me how to bake it, and then I painted it, gold with a bit of red glitter, but afterwards I was sorry because the paint took away from the memory. It looked too fake. I thought of using turpentine but decided I'd better leave it alone.

I kept the claw in my drawer, underneath my underwear. Sometimes, sitting in school, or watching television, I imagined the claw inside my clothes, touching me, and I'd get so excited I couldn't stand it. I'd feel like I could burn right through my skin. One time Mrs. Becker called on me in English class, to say what some character in Shakespeare said to his mother or something, and I just stammered at her, my mouth half hanging open, while everybody tried not to laugh, whispering things back and forth, until finally Mrs. Becker called on Chris Bloom, who always knew everything.

Other times, if my mother or the kids at school were bothering me, I would go home and take out the claw and hold it against me or make it stroke my body, just like his had done, sometimes hard enough to make blood come out. Or else I would just put it next to me while I slept.

My mother kept after me a lot. She wanted me to date more, to go to dances, have lots of boy friends, she wanted all the girls to envy me, and she was scared they pitied me instead. She couldn't stand that.

The funny thing was, I didn't really mind dating. I thought at first that I could never do it again because I had to keep myself clean for the angel, for the baby. And I thought that all the boys would look so clumsy and stupid and thick, their voices all hard and ugly. I thought any time they'd ask me I'd want to laugh or gag. But then I discovered they didn't touch each other at all, boys and the angel. They had nothing to do with each other, despite my being in the middle, like a kind of bridge connecting them. I saw it almost as two different mes, the one that belonged to the angel, and the one that went to the movies with Billy Glaston or Jeffrey Sterner.

But if I didn't mind dating, I didn't care either. I made no effort, and like my mother told me, the bees'll fly around a pot of warm honey, not a glass of cold water. It wasn't like I dressed sloppy or didn't use makeup, that would have made more trouble than it was worth, it was just that I paid no special attention to what boys said, and didn't try to laugh in a nice way, or give boys any special looks, things like that.

But I got dates anyway, sometimes with boys too ugly or dumb or just clumsy to try for the popular girls, boys who automatically looked for someone in their range. I didn't care. If someone asked me to the movies and I wanted to see the picture I went. I knew I couldn't let any boys do anything with me, so what difference did it made who took me? Only, I avoided the really ugly boys, not for myself, but so people wouldn't make fun of me.

One boy got to me, at least a little. His name was Jim Kinney, though around that time he told everyone to call him James, figuring it sounded more adult or intellectual or something. Jim—James—knew more about computers than half of IBM. In fact, when he was just a junior in high school he got permission to use the big computers down in the factory and wrote some program or other that IBM bought for a huge pile of money. He planned to use some of it, he said, to publish a book of his poetry. Poetry and science, Jim said, were "two horses pulling the same chariot." He often talked like that. He even showed me some of his poems. He didn't write about nature or love or stuff like that. Jim wrote about truth and knowledge and God, though he said he didn't mean God like in the church.

What he did mean was what got me excited about him. When I read his poems carefully, getting around the fancy words, like "the sheer blank wall of mortal ignorance", I saw he was writing about the difference between human talk and angel language. He knows, I thought, and got goosepimples, almost like when I could feel the angel claw under my clothes.

But how could an angel visit him? Did they visit boys? The thought upset me the same time it excited me. Maybe a woman angel needed a human man to make her pregnant. Maybe he was also waiting. Out of breath I looked up at him. And saw it wasn't true. He should have been looking at my face, my eyes, testing me the way I would have done him. Instead, he was reading his own poem over my shoulder. "Should I explain it to you?" he said, when he should have waited for me to say something. I could see he really cared about the human words, whatever he pretended.

That day I gave him back his poems and told him I didn't feel well, and ran home. (Later he told me he thought his poems had made me sick, and we both laughed.) But over the next few days I kept thinking about him.

I'm not sure what made Jim interested in me. He wasn't ugly, and he sure wasn't stupid, he could even play sports pretty good, and for a while he had a car, but it broke down. You'd think he could have gotten any girl he wanted, and wouldn't look at someone like me who never made an effort. But maybe the other girls found him too weird, writing poetry and playing tricks with computers. Too smart. Anyway, his car was already gone by the time he started taking me out.

Once Jim and I got started my mother just bounced off the walls with happiness. Not only was I acting more normal, but I was doing it with someone who had "rich" written all over him.

Myself, I didn't really know why I was doing it. I liked being with Jim, I liked when he called me, when he helped me with my homework, or when we went to the movies (which he called "cinema"), but it still confused me when I thought about the angel. One night Jim and I had gone to a carnival and got home late. I said goodnight to him, and then to my mother (she always waited up for me), and went upstairs laughing at the way some boy had looked so sick coming off the snap-the-whip.

I opened the drawer with my nightgown in it. And then suddenly I started to cry. I'd forgotten the angel. A whole night had gone by and I hadn't thought about him at all. I pushed aside my clothes and grabbed the claw, but then I just threw it down again.

I sat down on the bed and rubbed the tears away, feeling my eye makeup smear. Did I still care? Did I still believe? I opened my diary and stared at the last date. Two years ago. For two whole years I'd had nothing to say. I knew I didn't really stop believing. I couldn't. But I wondered—now that years had gone by, did it still mean anything? Anything more than Jim's poems? Maybe the angel had lied to me and would never come back. Or maybe it had meant what it said, but had forgotten as soon as it left me. Maybe only humans remembered things. How could memory exist in a sky full of fire?

The whole time Jim and I had gone around together I hadn't let him touch me. Well, sometimes we'd hold hands and he'd put an arm around me, but whenever he moved in for something more, even just a kiss, I pushed him away. I had to make up a whole story about how my mother hadn't kissed my father until they were almost engaged, and I really wanted to act different than that but I couldn't help it. I could tell a couple of times Jim was fed up and didn't want to see me any more, but I guess he liked me, or liked having a girlfriend, because he always came back.

But now I thought, if the angel's not coming back, why should I keep so clean for him? I decided the next time Jim tried to kiss me I would let him. The strange thing was, the next night he tried again—we'd gone to the movies and Howard Johnson's, and Jim stopped to show me some craters on the moon on the way home, though we both knew he didn't care about them any more than me—and still I pushed him away. I couldn't make myself do it.

Jim shrugged. "I'm sorry," he said in a voice that really meant "Screw you." He started walking away from me but I called him. In fact, I called him in a really strange voice, like I'd taken charge, which surprised me as much as him. He came back and held my shoulders and for a moment we looked at each other—not for any real reason, I think, but just because people in the movies always look at each other before they kiss. Part of me wanted to stop, to shove him really hard and run away, but I wouldn't let that happen. I made myself stand there, and when his mouth, already half open, came down towards mine I closed my eyes and kissed him.

I never felt such pain in my life. Like some burning knife coming right up my insides all the way to my face. I screamed, and then I did shove Jim, so hard he fell right on his backside.

For a moment he lay there, all bent over, holding his stomach with his face all screwed up and wet with tears or sweat, and I knew the pain had hit him too. He kind of gagged and got to his feet. "You're sick," he said, "you're really, really sick." He had to keep himself from running as he got away from me.

I walked home slowly, making dumb whimpering noises. Inside I became like two people, one of them miserable that Jim had run off and now no one wanted me, and scared because he was right and they'd lock me up screaming in a strait-jacket—and the other shaking with joy because the angel was real, the fire had come because his power had worked its way deep inside me and any day now the angel would come back and give me its baby. And I knew, too, that the first me, the unhappy one, was a fake, built up out of years of acting normal to satisfy my mother and the kids and teachers at school. I'd almost let it take over, convince me the real one had never existed. But the angel had saved me.

Graduation came soon after, saving me from my mother as well, and her constant asking what had happened with me and "James." I'd applied to college, mostly because everyone else did, and when the fall came I went off to Albany State. I didn't stay long. The stuff there didn't mean anything more than the stuff in high school. Maybe the other kids got something out of it. But I was waiting for the angel to come back.

I moved down to New York. No reason really. I got a job in the city tax department, sorting forms, making spot checks on people's income tax returns, things like that, and I found an apartment in Queens, one of those streets with six-story apartment houses where rich people used to live. (My building had a big lobby with even a picture made of tiles on the floor, but the tiles were too faded or broken for me to make it out. The elevator never worked.) And I waited.

Months went by, almost two years really. I'm not sure what I did all that time, how I managed to use up the days. I watched TV, read the paper, sometimes went to people's houses, or movies, or even parties. It didn't make any difference. Now and then one of the men, one of the shy or ugly ones, asked me out, or even made a pass. I never got nasty or aggressive, but none of them ever tried anything again.

Then one weekend I went for a walk in Greenwich Village.
I'd taken to walking a lot, all around, though mostly Manhattan. I liked looking at the buildings, sometimes staring up just
like a tourist. I liked the way they were so big, so heavy. That
day in the Village, they were having one of those sidewalk art
shows, with the painters standing alongside trying to look relaxed while they watched everybody passing by. I thought of
Jim and his poems.

Then, on Bleecker Street, I came to an exhibit of photos.
Most of them showed buildings or people bent over in funny
ways, or tricks, like a cat jumping out of someone's chest, but
one of them—I almost didn't see it, or maybe I saw it subconsciously, because I walked right past it at first, then stopped
just like a hand had grabbed my shoulders and turned me
around. The picture wasn't large, 8 ″ by 11 ″ I later found out.
It showed nothing but light. Wavy sheets of light with slivers
of dark buried inside them.

I just about grabbed the woman standing beside the photos.
"That picture," I said. "Did you take that?"

"No," she said, frightened I was going to attack her, or the
exhibit. "No, they're all by different people. I'm just taking a
turn—"

"How much is it?"

"Fifty dollars."

I checked my wallet though I knew I'd only brought fifteen.
"Shit," I said, then I did grab her jacket. "I'm going home to
get some more money. Don't sell that picture to anyone else.
Do you understand?" She nodded, her mouth hanging open.

I had to meet the person who'd taken the picture, but first I
had to get the thing itself. I couldn't stand the idea of someone
else buying it. Someone who didn't know. It would have taken
too long to go home, but I knew someone who lived pretty
close, on East 6th Street. I pushed through the crowds, begging
God to make Joan be at home. She was, and loaned me the
money. I think she was scared not to.

When I got back the photo was still there, but the woman
had put a little sign next to it saying "Sold." I must have
scared her too. I gave her the money and stood shifting from
one leg to the other while she carefully wrapped it for me.

"Listen," I said to her once I had it in my hand, "the person who took this, where can I find her?"

She looked scared, her eyes moving away from me to see who might help her if I got really crazy. "How do you know it's a woman?" she said.

"Please," I told her. "You've got to help me."

"Well," she said, "I guess it's okay." She gave me a name and an address near Wall Street. I nearly knocked over some people looking for a cab. The building turned out to be an old office building reaching some twenty stories above the dirty luncheonettes and cheap clothing stores. I stood there staring at it, thinking the goddamn woman had lied to me, until I looked in the lobby and saw the doorman sitting on a wooden stool and reading the *Post*. Then I realized it must be one of those places where they'd converted some of the empty offices into apartments.

The doorman didn't wear a uniform or anything like that, just jeans and a dirty sweater, but he still wouldn't let me up until he'd checked with the woman. I didn't know what I'd do if she didn't answer. I had planned to sit by her door if she wasn't there but the doorman wouldn't let me do that, I knew, and I didn't want to have to stand on the street.

She was there. When the doorman asked who I was I told him, "Just say I want to ask about her picture. Her photo." He made a face and repeated it. It seemed like a whole minute before the scratchy voice said to come up.

When I got off the elevator she was already standing in the faded yellow hall, looking a little sick in the fluorescent light. She was tall, much taller than me, with a wide face and straight dull brown hair that didn't help it any. I only noticed these things, and her loose blue cotton dress and white plastic sandals, because it's the kind of thing my mother used to point out. But really I watched the way her hands jumped about looking for a relaxed way to hold themselves, while her eyes, looking very glary behind blue-tinted glasses, jumped onto the package I held. "You said photo," she said. "Just one? Which one do you mean? Where did you get it?"

I tore off the wrapping and held it up. Her breath sounded like something jumping down her throat. "Where did you get this?" I said. "Tell me what it is."

She started telling me all sorts of things, about light, and filters, and double exposures, all sorts of things, talking very fast, like she didn't want me to interrupt. But I said nothing, just held the photo, refusing to give it up to her hands that kept clutching at it like she didn't even know they were doing it. And she wouldn't look at me, not for more than a second, except she kept doing that, looking at me, then jumping her eyes away again. And suddenly she stopped all the stuff she was saying, because she knew, and I knew, she could have taken that picture with a snapshot camera, with an old Brownie like the one my mother kept in her bedroom because my father had used it as a kid.

I said, "It's him, isn't it? It's him."

And suddenly she started saying how she shouldn't have sold it, she never meant to sell it, she still kept the negative, she just needed money so bad, she never thought anyone would *know*.

I don't know who grabbed who first, but somehow we were holding each other and kissing, and couldn't stop, and crying. And the fire didn't hurt, or not so much as that other time, with Jim. It hurt, it hurt her too, she made a kind of choked sound, but it hurt more like lowering yourself into a hot bath where it comes up first around your legs and then your groin and finally your breasts. And then the fire is gone because you've made it all the way in, and it feels so good, so strong, stronger than anything, with the sweat pouring off your face and the steam beating the breath out of you.

Her name was Jo, short for Josephine I thought, but she said no, it was always Jo, and we sort of moved in together, even though we both kept our own places. You'd think I would have worried about us being, you know, both girls, but that never bothered either of us, it was the angel that brought us together, not anything else. When I touched her, her breasts or below, it felt really nice, very soft and warm, but also I saw it as somewhere the angel had touched. Sometimes one of us would make claws with our hands and run it down the other's stomach, but we always stopped that right away, like it embarrassed us. I never showed her the claw I'd made.

The really strange thing was, neither of us ever talked about it. We just kept copies of the photo up in each of our apartments, facing the bed in mine, over the refrigerator in hers because even though she wasn't fat she said the kitchen was her favorite room, and sometimes we'd sit or lie together, staring at it, even make love after looking at it. But we could never make ourselves talk.

We wanted to. At least I did. Sometimes, usually at breakfast for some reason, like the morning gave me a new start, I would try to think of how to begin, and Jo would also look like she wanted to say something. Then one of us would talk about the weather or the brand of orange juice or someone at work, and that was it for another day. I never even found out when the angel had come to her or where.

Maybe if we could have talked about the angel we would have stayed together longer. I don't know. In everything else we were so different. Jo was very artsy. She did television things, not programs or stories, just pictures of her moving very slowly or even standing completely still, all wrapped up in aluminum foil. She did it herself of course, she'd gotten her own camera, and then she sent tapes to art galleries, where I guess they showed them instead of pictures. And she used to wear those old saggy dresses she got in some filthy shop on St. Mark's Place, not just because they were cheap, I offered to give her money for real clothes, but because she liked them.

Her friends were artsy too, doing things like writing stories that made no sense, and they had to publish them themselves on really cheap paper because no regular magazine wanted to buy them. Her friends all thought of me as weird or funny or something, because I worked in an office and didn't wear torn clothes, and they didn't understand how Jo and I had gotten together. But that didn't matter. I knew that Jo didn't care about her "friends" any more than I cared about mine. It was just a game she was playing while she waited for the angel to come back.

For the first few months we were very careful with each other, very polite, except when we looked at the picture or made love. But after a while, we started to fight. About clothes, or where to go to eat, or people we knew, never anything that mattered. Because only the angel mattered. And we didn't talk about that.

So we started fighting, and then making excuses not to see

each other, and finally one night I went to her place after work and let myself in with the key, and there over the refrigerator door was a note saying she'd gone to San Francisco for some "video festival" and didn't know when she was coming back. She'd taken the picture.

I got angry. I called up her friends and asked for her address but they said she didn't have one yet and of course she'd send it to me. I got really depressed too, thinking of how to kill myself without any pain. Yet at the same time I knew it didn't matter. I still had my copy of her picture. That's what really counted.

I don't mean my anger or depression were nothing or they went away just like that. As far as I can tell it hit me as hard as anyone else who'd gotten dumped like that, and it lasted almost longer than the actual time we'd spent together. The thing is, for other people those sorts of feelings are all they've got. But I was waiting for the angel, and anything else just got added on top of that.

The experience with Jo did have one big effect on me. I didn't want to be alone any more. Like when I decided I couldn't give up feelings if I couldn't keep the angel language, now I knew I wanted people, lovers, at least if the angel wasn't coming back. I didn't forget my promise and keeping myself clean. I just figured that if I didn't really care, if I remembered I was only doing it "until," then it wouldn't change anything.

So I began to date, not just to pass the time or see a movie, but for the person. The first time some guy tried to kiss me, a divorced guy named Bobby, I didn't know what to do. Would the pain hit me? Maybe it went all right with Jo only because the angel had also come to her. But no. Being with Jo had already changed me. I could kiss or let someone touch me— or more—and nothing happened. I mean no pain.

One thing—I made sure not to get pregnant. I used a dia-phragm but I also took the pill, secretly, so people wouldn't know I did both and once some guy discovered my pills and he called me sick, like Jim had done, and said I should see a shrink. I told him to go to hell and it was worth any trouble not to get anything of *his* growing inside me.

Sometimes I wondered, what if the angel came back and the

pills made it so I couldn't get pregnant with him either? But I didn't think a bunch of pills could stop the angel.

I didn't really live with anybody, though I sort of went steady a few times, once with another girl, a typist from work named Karen. Karen worried a lot about people at work or her family finding out about us. Once we went away to a hotel for the weekend and she brought along her cousin who lived with a guy, so we could make it look like two normal couples, even registering that way, then sneaking into the right rooms when no one was looking. I didn't really mind, though it bothered me that I had to watch the way I looked at her in restaurants or places like that. I knew how to hide things myself.

One guy even wanted to marry me. His name was Allen and I met him in my cousin Jack's house. He'd spent some years in the navy which was why he'd never gotten married, he said. He liked to show slides of all the countries he'd visited, and sometimes he imitated the funny way the people talked. He said it amazed him how many languages there were. Without thinking I said, "They're all just human languages." He looked at me funny and asked what I meant. I told him nothing.

When Allen said we should get married I didn't know what to do. I really like him a lot, he was the only person I knew who enjoyed walking around the city as much as me, he could even show me things I'd missed. And I was sick of my crummy apartment.

But I didn't know what marriage would mean. Did it count in some way that dating and sex didn't? Allen wanted to get married in a church. His brother Michael was a minister and Allen liked to joke about Mike needing the business. Would that mean more than marriage by a judge? I didn't think so. Marriage was still something two humans did, whatever the church said. Why should the angel care about marriage any more than he cared about two people riding the subway together? Nothing humans did meant anything. Or maybe the other way around. Everything humans did had to mean something because humans couldn't stand it otherwise. Only the angel did things that didn't mean something else, something explained in words or feelings.

Still, when Allen insisted I give him an answer I said no. He got really angry, said I had to tell him why. Give him a reason. I told him I didn't have one and that was the truth. Refusing to marry Allen was the closest I ever came to angel talk, because after I'd gone through everything in my mind, I ended up saying no, for no reason at all.

Of course Allen didn't understand that. He'd go back and forth between begging me and screaming at me, sometimes calling me up late at night and just about biting through the phone. He got my mother on his side and the two of them went after me so much I sometimes thought of going to San Francisco like Jo and leaving a note on the refrigerator. Later, when I got pregnant, Allen figured I'd said no because I was already screwing someone else, and he sent letters to everyone calling me a prostitute in about six or seven languages. "Prostitute" was the one word he'd learned in all the countries he'd visited.

The angel came on Saturday morning when I couldn't sleep. Sometimes I wonder, if I'd stayed in bed would the angel have broken through the window, or would he have flown right past the house, and I'd never have seen him again? But the rash had stopped me from sleeping, and maybe the angel made the rash in some way.

The thing was, the night before the angel came, I'd spotted some funny red bumps all over my stomach and backside. They didn't itch, but I still spread Calordryl all over, and I guess I didn't wait long enough for it to dry because the sheets got all sticky. That, and thinking about Allen, woke me really early. When I couldn't get back to sleep I decided to go for a walk. It was late May and sunny, very pretty with all the trees full of leaves, especially a few blocks away where the houses got much fancier, with regular lawns, almost like Long Island.

That's where the angel came for me, right in front of a gray brick split-level with a Cadillac in the driveway and probably another one in the garage. Maybe the angel liked Cadillacs. I didn't see it coming at all this time. I was looking at some flowers with really pretty colors and little colored rocks spread all through them.

Suddenly I turned—maybe I heard the wings—and saw him, almost right up against me, his blank eyes, the huge wings, one of them almost brushing the house's picture window. His mouth hung open, really wide, but I didn't hear anything. I didn't see any teeth, only a long tongue that kept flicking back and forth. Then he pushed me to the ground.

I had trouble getting off my clothes. I was only wearing a light jacket, but his claws kept getting in the way until I almost shouted at him to let me do it. Then I lay back, trying to stare in his eyes, see his world again, while I waited for his claws to stroke me, for my voice to explode in his sounds, his perfect language.

Instead, he just shoved himself at me, pushing me into the wet dirt, his wings thumping the lawn and the street, his tongue slapping my cheek, my neck, my forehead, burning the skin. I wanted to scream, or cry, or beg, but I couldn't. I wouldn't. If he wouldn't let me speak angel language, I wasn't going to give him the satisfaction of hearing anything human coming out of me.

At the same time I thought, it's my fault, I betrayed him. I ruined myself. I became too human. But now, I wonder, maybe it just happened that way and would have been the same if I'd never gone with Allen or Jo or anyone.

I didn't watch him leave. I just lay there on the ground, curled up and hitting the grass with my fist. Finally, I got scared someone would see me, naked and crazy like that, and lock me up. I got my clothes and ran home.

Five times the next week I almost tore up the picture, the one Jo had left. Ten times in the next month I almost tried to call Jo herself and ask if the angel had come back to her too. I ended up doing nothing. What difference could any of it make now that the angel had come back and shut me out?

When I found out I was pregnant I didn't know what to do. I almost went for an abortion. I didn't know if I could, if whatever they did would work any better than the pills had. I was wild. I walked up and down the streets in midtown, waving my arms in a pouring rain and stopping every now and then to make a noise like a roar or a shriek. I couldn't figure out if I was afraid or angry or thrilled, but all the choices sounded pretty rotten, all of them feelings, talk. I wanted to see the angel world and all I could see was my goddamn belly getting bigger and bigger.

One thing I knew. I didn't want any doctor to deliver the baby. I wanted to do it myself. I'd never even seen a baby being born, outside of the movies they showed the girls in high school, and of course they only showed ordinary babies. This one I didn't even know how long it would take, the regular nine months, or ten, or six, or what. But I just decided if the angel was using a human woman then probably it wouldn't run that different from a regular birth. And I didn't want any doctors near me.

So I read books and took courses and did exercises, and when I figured the time was getting close I rented a house by a lake—it was someone's summer house but they had it insulated for winter too—and stocked it with lots of food and any medicine I could get without a prescription. Then I set everything up—I'd gotten some books on midwifing so I knew pretty much what I needed. And I waited.

It was horrible. The pain filled the whole room, it rolled off the walls at me, it went on for hours and hours so that I thought the kid must have braced itself inside and would never come out. I was scared I was going to die. The angel was killing me because I'd betrayed it. If only I could phone a hospital, tell them I needed a caesarean. But I'd torn out the wires in case I'd get scared and want an ambulance, and now, when I really needed one, I couldn't call anywhere. I wondered if I could somehow drive my car, at least down to the snowmobile center down the road. But when I tried to walk I couldn't even get out of bed.

It went on for so long I started seeing things. I imagined myself outside, with snow all around, and the angel circling way over my head.

When the baby did come out it came so quickly I didn't know it had happened. I went on pushing, with the kid lying there on the soaking wet sheets. When I realized I'd done it I lay back, shaking so much the whole bed made this awful squeaking noise. Probably it had squeaked like that for hours, and I was cursing and crying so much I never noticed. I picked up the kid and cut the cord and cleaned him off as best as I could. I had to get rid of the afterbirth and get him breathing and everything, and I knew I better do it all at once, because if I stopped I'd just fall asleep. At last I held him up so I could look at him.

A haze or something must have covered my eyes because it

took awhile before I could actually see him, what he really
looked like. When I did see I just stared at him. Wings grew
on his back, small, dirty white, not feathers but sort of rough,
almost like cheap leather, the kind you get on pocketbooks
bought at one of those downtown discount stores. For the first
time I realized the angel's wings were like that, leather and not
feathers at all. Even while I stared at him his sad little wings
fluttered a couple of times and then came right off. They fell
on my leg. I screamed and knocked them onto the floor. When
I looked for them a couple of days later they were gone. Crum-
bled right into dust, maybe.

His hands did the same thing. I don't mean they fell off, but
they changed, from claws to ordinary baby hands, the hard
curved claw fingers shrinking to stubby human ones.

There's nothing left, I thought. All that pain for nothing.
But I was wrong. He had his father's eyes, cold, very hard,
and empty. Even now you can see it, not all the time, but
sometimes he'll put down his truck or his cap gun, or else he'll
just stand there when some other kid throws the ball to him.
Then you can see that metal coldness take over his eyes, and
you know he's looking right past you, into a world of lightning,
and fire that jumps into the sky, a world where the sounds say
everything, and not just words.

He's going to find it hard, much harder than I ever did. I
only saw it, only spoke to it once. But he's got to look at that
world all the time. And live in this one.

The Neighbor's Wife
by Susan Palwick

Introduction

This introduction is longer than the story. It could hardly be otherwise, since the story is only a few lines of verse.

Verse? Then it's a poem, not a story!

That attitude reflects one of the sad failures of twentieth-century English-language literature. Because of the triumph of lyric over narrative verse, we honestly think that a poem is somehow the opposite *of a story, that if something is a poem it cannot be a story.*

Today I sat in conversation with a screenwriting professor at a major university, discussing the problems that English majors have when they attempt to write screenplays. "They come into class with long screenplays full of pretty language with lots of feelings and symbols in which nothing happens," *he said. "They don't understand that films require* stories; *that other stuff is for poems."*

I couldn't argue with his point—that writing for the screen still demands what the academic-literary community has long since abandoned: the tale. But it made me sad that he simply took it for granted that it was all right for poems to have no story content at all—for them to be "pretty language with lots of feelings and symbols." Most of us do these days.

Most, but not all. Judson Jerome, a fine poet and a longtime poetry columnist for Writer's Digest, has made it his personal crusade in recent years to get poets to stop writing self-indulgent sniveling (my term—he is much less impolite about it) and start using the techniques of verse to tell more powerful, memorable, and beautiful stories than can possibly be told in prose. There is a reason why the great stories of the ancient world were all in verse—and it isn't just because verse is easier to memorize. Or rather, the reasons that verse is easier to memorize are also the reasons why storytellers used to use verse: because the verse sets up an incantatory rhythm in the mind; because the music becomes part of the experience and memory of the story; because a story in verse feels more important than one in prose; and because all of this carries the story to the center of the listener's mind.

The listener, not the reader. Even if you read silently to yourself—even if you don't move your lips—verse demands to be heard. You play it out with a voice inside your head; the storyteller is more immediately present in a story told in verse than in a story told in prose.

Some of us use verse in disguise. I do it often, ever since my days as a playwright. I had come to love the way Shakespeare would lapse into rhymed verse to give a sense of closure and completion to a play or scene; in my fiction, I often write closures in highly rhythmic verse. Though the lines are run in like prose, in order not to call attention to the structure, the effect is there. Verse works—and it works better in stories than it does in the rhapsodic or symbolic lyrics we now call "poetry."

Years ago, in graduate school, I fell in love with Spenser, and so admired The Faerie Queene that I resolved to duplicate, not Spenser's subject or style, but his technique. I set out to write a verse hero-poem in the American frontier vernacular. The result was a fragment called "Prentice Alvin and the No-Good Plow." I felt that the story, the pseudo-vernacular narrative voice, and the verse all succeeded in doing what I wanted. But I lost faith in the verse—I eventually abandoned it, saving only the story and the voice for the novels that make up my Tales of Alvin Maker series.

Others have had more courage. Frederick Turner's The New World *is a full-length epic poem in contemporary vernacular English; it is also a fine science fiction novel. In a world where talentless writers serve up warmed-over Joyce and Faulkner and call what results "experimental," I must pronounce Turner's work truly experimental, for he is doing what few others even realize is worth attempting. And, unlike the excesses of Joyce and Faulkner, Turner's experiment works. His accomplishment teaches us a way to write better and clearer and more powerful stories.*

Judson Jerome has also written several stories in verse. One, I heard him read at a writers conference in Cape Cod. It was the tale of a man whose job was to give tuberculosis tests to monkeys just shipped to a lab for medical experiments. On a Friday night, a monkey tests positive. The people who normally destroy the monkeys with tuberculosis have already gone home, so the tester and his co-worker set out to kill the diseased monkey themselves. The story is one of the most haunting, terrible, glorious literary experiences I've ever had. Even as I was remade by the story itself, the exploitative writer inside my head was saying, "Ah! So that is possible! So that's what verse can do with a tale!"

Since then, I have heard Jerome read a marvelous science fiction short story called "Jaguars." I asked him to let me submit it to the science fiction magazines. He readily agreed, in part because he expected it to have no chance of publication elsewhere. After all, he has a devil of a time getting "poetry" magazines to publish anything as long as narrative poems have to be; that the story is also science fiction *is the kiss of death. I assured him that things were different in the field of science fiction.*

And things are *different, though perhaps not yet different enough. Gardner Dozois, for instance, agreed with me that "Jaguars" was a fine story, well worth publishing. But he could not, in the real world, justify devoting that many pages of* Asimov's *to a poem. The readers would not stand for it. And he's right. American readers simply are not trained to read poems any longer than a few lines—it's daring when a magazine publishes a poem that takes up more than a page.*

Yet, even if length keeps "Jaguars" out of the magazines

(watch for it in a forthcoming original anthology), the science fiction editors are *open to poems that tell stories—or, as I prefer to think of it, stories told in verse. Indeed, the very concept of ''science fiction poetry'' almost demands an abandonment of lyric and a turn to either discursive poetry—not often seen since Pope—or narrative poetry, like Susan Palwick's ''The Neighbor's Wife.''*

This story is deceptively short. Like the stable in C. S. Lewis's Narnia, it is much larger on the inside than it is on the outside. With astonishing economy, Palwick implies a whole community, full of varied characters who are bound together by one thing: their loyalty to one of their own, who has found a way to assuage his grief and loss. If I had dared to tackle such a provocative story, I would have taken three hundred pages to do it, and yet I could have accomplished no more than Palwick achieves in these few lines. Like a spider's web, which is most visible at the center, where the strands are close-strung, you'll find that this story hangs on threads that connect in all directions, reaching much farther than you notice at first glance, implying and containing a novel's worth of story in a few perfectly chosen words.

It's short. You can read it many times.

I met Susan Palwick at the Sycamore Hill Writers Workshop. I was appalled, having already found such depth and brilliance and understanding in her poem, to discover that she was a mere child. Well, she was barely in her twenties, anyway, so young and frail-looking that it makes a man feel protective despite his best efforts to overcome his biological imperatives. But we all quickly learned that Palwick doesn't need protection. Young as she is, she held her own with as powerful a group of egos as you are likely to find in the absence of Donald Trump, Edward Koch, and Lee Iacocca.

Best of all, she has barely begun to write. We have fifty or sixty years of Susan Palwick's stories ahead of us—that's good news, and not just for science fiction.

It sprouts wings every few weeks
but as yet has flown no further
than the woodpile in the yard
where we found it six months ago.

Colin Wilcox thought it was his wife
returned as an angel. It still wore
its headset then, lying trapped
in a crushed metal basket; Colin freed it,

muttering something about harps and haloes,
and the rest of us stayed quiet. Colin carried it
into the house and for three weeks nursed it
in his bed, on the side unwarmed since Marella,

the old Marella, had her heart attack.
When it could walk on six legs Colin taught
it to fry bacon, weed the garden, milk
the goats, which cower at its touch.

"Reminding her what she forgot in Heaven,"
he tells us, but she has not remembered speech,
this new Marella who is purple and croaks
like bullfrogs on the hottest summer nights,

who surely came from somewhere, if not from God.
Lately it uses those stubby wings to carry
the heaviest logs from the woodpile. For Colin's sake
no one has tried to frighten it away.

I Am the Burning Bush
by Gregg Keizer

Introduction

The first writing class I ever taught was for the evening school at the University of Utah. It was billed as a science fiction writing course, and each semester I got an array of talented, hardworking students. It was a good class. Most made progress, and some produced truly remarkable work. Unfortunately, I could only teach them as much about the writing process as I understood at the time. In years since, I have learned a great deal more, and nowadays I'm able to help my students make far more progress; back then, however, if it wasn't the blind leading the blind, then it was the blind being led by a guy with a squint.

Into this exuberant but confusing environment came Gregg Keizer, a junior high school English teacher who thought he might be a writer. From his first story it was clear that I had little to teach him. He already knew how. He had mastered the skillful use of point of view, so that his work felt professional; just as important, his stories were infused with strangeness and pain, so that reading them was never comfortable, but always memorable.

I remember making a foolish bet about one story he turned

in. *"If you haven't sold this within a year, I'll run naked through the halls of Orson Spencer Hall"* (the building where the class met). Well, I have since learned never to underestimate the ability of editors to resist a startling new voice. It took more than a year. Gregg reminded me of the bet and offered to get his camera to record my streak. I told him to go to hell. Instead, he sent the story to Ellen Datlow, the new fiction editor at Omni. Bingo. *"I Am the Burning Bush"* at last found its way into print.

Like many new writers, he just had to wait until an editor came along who was in sympathy with the stories he had to tell. Some writers wait for many painful years; some give up and stop trying. Gregg was lucky to find a sympathetic editor fairly early. But when he did, luck had nothing to do with the fact that his stories were full of searing light.

So why haven't you heard more about him? Because it's a fact of life in the field of science fiction that it usually takes a certain volume of work before you get widely noticed. Your short fiction also has to appear in the magazines than other writers read the most—which in those days meant Asimov's and F&SF—but not Omni, where Gregg's strongest work appeared. And it helps if you put out a novel or two.

Gregg's career did not follow the necessary track. After an initial spate of sales, to Omni and elsewhere, Gregg began to work on a novel. It was tough going—it's a wrenching transition for most short story writers. At the same time, he was starting a new job as a book editor at Compute! Books (one more statistic in the American education system's effort to drive out its finest teachers). He became so thoroughly and successfully involved in his job, eventually becoming editor of Compute! Magazine, and the birth of his and Lori's daughter Emily gave him such wonderful and time-consuming distractions at home, that his vacation from fiction stretched to months, then to years.

His last completed story, which he brought to the Sycamore Hill Writers Workshop, was a devastating look at a future South Africa. He had been drawn to explore the contradictory Boer culture in part because of his own Dutch ancestry; the story had the kind of agonizing involvement that comes when a writer feels he is telling about *"us,"* not *"them,"* The workshop par-

ticipants were unanimous in the belief that even without revision it was a powerful work; with revision, it would deserve, perhaps even win, awards. But that story remained unrevised and unsubmitted through the long years of his self-imposed exile from science fiction.

The exile is over. Recently I had the pleasure of buying Keizer's first new story in years, also set within a future Boer culture, for my Eutopia *anthology. He still has the vision and the fire. If anything, his craft is better than ever, despite—or perhaps because of—the long hiatus.*

However, I feel obliged, because of my personal standard of unrelenting honesty, to tell you one terrible secret about Gregg Keizer. When he plays Trivial Pursuit, and another person is struggling to think of an answer, Gregg has no mercy. With unrestrained glee he chirrups, "I know I know!"—a locution he no doubt picked up from some obnoxious seventh-grade intellectual he once taught. This would be tolerable if he had the good grace to lose, so we could taunt him in return. But he does not lose, and so it is not tolerable. I felt I had to tell you this, so you would not think too well of him.

I AM THE DEADMAN.

I could feel the texture of the rope as it dug into the flesh around my neck. It was not the first time that I had died for lifers, but it was not the best time, either. It was to be a simple death, only a hanging. Nothing spectacular.

They think I do not feel the pain, but I do. The pain is always the same, like a white-hot needle through my lips. It was the same now, even though it had been over a year since I'd last died in front of them. For a year I had experienced the private deaths, dying only for myself, loathing the memories of their lifer touches. But something had driven me back to them again. I remembered now that it wasn't the pain. Perhaps it was the way their eyes went wide when I walked into a room. Or maybe it was only their money.

For a moment, as I saw my feet arc in the air, seemingly

reaching for the knotted rope, I forgot that I would be alive again. I tried to scream but couldn't get anything past the hemp that clamped my throat.

Thankfully, blissfully, I blacked out.

I opened my eyes, and everything was blurred, as if I were drunk on alcohol and reeling around the room. I realized that I still twirled on the end of the rope. It was only uncomfortable now. Someone handed me a knife; I reached up and cut myself down. I landed on the thick carpet that seemed to live under everything here.

The twisting colors, red to green to rusted scrap in a browning field, swept through me, and I knew now why I couldn't stop dying in front of them. I could feel. I could smell the sweat of my body. I touched my neck gently, slowly, marveling at the feelings as my fingertips brushed the skin. I was surprised I'd been able to stay away for a whole year and knew I'd never be able to again.

My mind seemed to freeze the scene around me in split-second frames. I felt warm and relaxed, as if I'd just had an excellent brandy or had finished making love. Every particle of my body sparkled inside, knowing that it was alive, unmarked, and whole. The sensations I had felt during my private deaths paled in my memory.

I even felt a pinch of kindness toward the lifers around me, another symptom of resurrection. I stroked my wrist, my thigh, knowing, without looking, where they were. I could now hear the whispers of the lifers. Before I had had to read their lips. I was alive, sensitive again. Except for my eyes, the disease overpowers all my sensory organs when I am between deaths. Only death restores my senses to me. It even enhances them.

I knew the satiated feeling in my belly would soon be replaced by nausea. I would want to vomit, but I would only be able to spit into my hand and wipe my hand on my tunic. Then I would not even feel the spittle. I would slip into the deprivation I felt between deaths. But that time was hours away, and I could *feel* again, more than I have ever felt when I've died alone, for myself. I inhaled deeply and looked up.

The lifers around me applauded softly as I took the rope from around my neck and threw it on the floor in front of me. The semicircle that pinned me in the corner was front-ranked with women, some of them daring to touch the edges of my clothing. One of them, sloppily made up and wearing clothes too cheap for this party, went so far as to stroke the skin of my neck. Still feeling confused from the resurrection, I said nothing to her. I only wondered how she had managed to get in. Like the rest of the lifers around me, she had the shiny-eyed look of a fingertoucher and whispered in that familiar hoarse croak that the drug creates. The hostess, her dress adorned with tiny jewels, pushed her way through the crowd and clutched my arm tightly.

"Wasn't that the best?" she yelled above her guests' voices. I looked at her. I felt her fingers knead my arm, and I almost pushed her away. But she had paid for it, all of it.

"I've heard of better deaths," said a man who'd made his way over to me. He had his arms crossed over his chest, and I could see his eyes glittering from fingertouch. The lifers had become silent, waiting for me to respond. I turned my back on him and faced the hostess again.

"You invite critics?" I asked her.

"I apologize for him," she said. "You can see he has pressed too much fingertouch." She looked at me. "He'll be asked to leave in a few minutes." I could hear some of the lifers mutter in agreement.

Silently the lifers came to me, one by one, and kissed the hand I held out to them. Their lips rasped against my knuckles, and one woman's tongue wetted a finger. Some of them do that, hoping it will increase the chance of infection. They all looked at me expectantly, with that lifer expression of mingled excitement and awe. But I couldn't speak. I couldn't say it. The woman standing next to me squeezed my arm, but I kept silent. She finally tired of waiting.

"I have shown you," she said, using the words I should have used. "Follow me."

The lifers started whispering again, and the hostess relaxed, her hand curled loosely around my arm.

"That's Crandel, of the department stores," she whispered to me, pointing to a man walking toward us. "I was so lucky to get him to come tonight. Talk to him for me." Then she left me, her body moving fluidly around the room, touching every-one with a press of fingertouch, saying good-bye.

"I enjoyed it very much. I have wanted to meet you for some time," Crandel said, standing in front of me. I noticed that his blue eyes were not lit by fingertouch.

"Thank you," I said, delighting in the sound of his voice, yet wanting to be left alone with my reborn senses. I looked up, but the hostess was busy chatting on the opposite side of the room.

"I got my license only yesterday," he said. "I was lucky to get in tonight. What's it like anyway?"

I remembered the colors, the freeze-framing, the touch of a finger on skin, and the warmth. "It's like eating too many sweets." I always give frivolous answers, but they never notice.

"I've done everything else, I guess. They say it feels delicious. Better than fingertouch." He paused, his eyes looking at my hand. I knew he wanted to touch me again, but I could permit it only once. "You were captain on the ship," he said.

They all think I was the captain. "No. Weapons officer," I said, my words quick. He shrugged, as if it didn't matter.

"What are my chances of infection?" he asked, trying to disguise his feelings.

"Same as everyone else's," I said, looking for the hostess again.

"Is there no way to increase the chance?" he began. They all come to that question before long. He looked hungrily at my face.

"No," I said, my reborn senses allowing me to feel contempt. It tasted like tainted meat in my mouth.

I watched him press a pinch of fingertouch into the skin around his lips. His eyes—lifer eyes now—gleamed.

"Since the ice is broken, who wants to go first?" the hostess called from across the room, loudly enough so that even those in the back could hear.

"Excuse me," Crandel said softly, pulling away. I thought someone had called to him, but he walked to the window. Glancing back, he bowed slightly, then opened the window wide.

"I wish you a good death," he said. "Wish me the same." I could have mouthed the words I've heard so many lifers speak.

He climbed onto the sill, shoving the curtains aside with one hand and using the other to grip the frame. Then he stepped over the edge and was gone. I thought I could hear a scream as he fell to the ground fifty floors below, but I wasn't really sure.

I made my way to another corner, away from the lifers who were perfunctorily killing themselves. The hostess tried to touch me again, but I pulled away from her. I found a drink on a table and sipped its sourness while I watched them commit suicide one by one. They weren't very creative; I've died so many times, in almost every way. They were lifers, registered suicides, approved by the government. They knew what they were doing. They lusted for immortality through their death and hoped they would acquire the disease that raged within me and made me a DeadMan. They wanted to die and resurrect, to be like me.

Suddenly a woman was by my elbow. She held a thin knife in her hand and looked at it intently.

"Are you going to do it here?" I asked. She nodded, still looking at the knife. "Why do it by me?"

"Why not?" she replied.

"Why do it anyway?" I watched her and sipped my drink.

She smiled and opened her mouth as if to answer me. Instead, she brought the knife to her throat and slit it. The blood spattered my tunic, and she thumped to the floor.

I turned from her and concentrated on my body's putting itself together again. The scenes of violence in the room swept before me. I could still feel the sparkle of my resurrection, although not as strongly.

They call us deaders. DeadMen, undead, vampires, regeneratives, regens, and other names I like even less. My body cannot die. It displays the symptoms, but its cells regenerate almost as quickly as they are destroyed. I am, in effect, immortal. I can die and resurrect within minutes. I have died three hundred seventy-three times for them, including the hanging tonight. I have died thousands of times more for myself, but I do not tally those deaths.

The parasitic disease that I and my five shipmates brought back from that hell world mutated somehow when we came home and made us DeadMen. The parasite keeps its host alive, not letting us truly die. Only when it is busy regenerating cells does it release its grip on our senses. We found that out on the return trip, the first time one of us tried to kill himself. We can infect others, but only rarely and only immediately after death—our own temporary deaths and the lifers' usually permanent ones. The meds have no cure. Lifers swarm around us, touching us, hoping to catch the disease and live forever. They know little of what they desire. They do not realize what they must relinquish if they do succeed in catching the disease and becoming immortal. Their sensations will wither, as mine did. They are so eager to discard them in exchange for immortality. Perhaps that is why they are so distasteful to me.

Barely one out of a hundred becomes immortal. And the immortals we create cannot infect others. The infection mutates again in its second generation. Only the crew of the *Acheron*, the six DeadMen, can bestow immortality.

And only through death can we feel and taste and smell. And only in front of lifers can we feel more than a semblance of the sensations we once had.

"Your death was exquisite," a voice whispered beside me. "How do you do it?" I looked down. It was a girl, perhaps seventeen or so, with a bowl of fingertouch powder in her hands. Her eyes reflected every light in the room.

"How do you come to life again?" she asked, a bit more loudly now. "My name is Lynx. What is yours?"

"DeadMan," I answered, smiling at her. I shook my head when she lifted the bowl a little. I stay away from fingertouch. It's a lifer drug. It's not for DeadMen.

"No, no, no, I mean your real name, the one that your friends call you, the one—"

"I don't give my name to lifers," I said.

"How do you do it?" she asked again.

"It just works," I said. I thought she would be satisfied with that.

"You don't know how you—"

"You ask too many questions, lifer."

She seemed confused and weaved slowly in place. I thought she was going to fall, but she steadied herself by putting a hand on my arm. Carefully I lifted it off and let it drop to her side. She hadn't paid for me, and so I didn't have to let her touch me.

"Are you going to kill yourself, too?" I asked.

She giggled, looking up at me with reflecting eyes. "I don't think I can. I've got the papers and everything, but I don't know whether I can go through with it." She paused for a moment, dipped a finger into the powder, and pressed it against her forehead. I watched her rub the fingertouch deep into her pores. She reached out and stroked my arm and my wrist. I glanced at her hand, and she pulled it away. My skin was cold where she had touched it. "I mean, it's pretty permanent, isn't it?"

"For you it most probably is," I said.

I picked up another drink, stepping over the bodies that patterned the floor. There was only a handful of lifers still alive in the room, but most were trying to kill themselves. The more zoned ones were having trouble holding the knives and blasters or finding the windows. I leaned against a wall, wondering whether any here would become infected and live forever.

A man stumbled and fell on an upturned blade held by a corpse. I smiled at myself. Stupid, one-death-is-all-you've-got lifers.

I was playing with my newest pinner in the game room when the call buzzed for me. I ignored it and finished the round before shutting off the machine. Its silvered surface darkened as the call buzzed again. Perhaps it was a client. I let it buzz anyway.

The pinner's power cord was badly frayed, but I pulled hard on it, jerking it out of the socket. I plugged another game into it, switched it on, and ran up a good score. The buzzing didn't stop.

I couldn't concentrate on the game. So I went to my window and looked out over the city. I'd broken the railing long ago and had never replaced it. I grasped the window frame. Crandel's eyes gleamed in my memory. I wanted to feel the dim sparkle of a private death, but I'd promised myself I'd have only one each day. The residue of the death I'd had two hours before lingered, but it was fading. I could hear, but I could not feel my fingers.

I must have been standing there for a long time before I heard the door open behind me. I had never had a lifer in my house before. I found out that they are not in the habit of knocking before entering.

"Bin?" she asked. It was the girl from the party—Lynx was her name.

I nodded, wondering who had told her my name. It couldn't have been the hostess from the night before. She had drowned herself in the bath.

"Can I come in?" The open door was already a bright square of light behind her.

I stepped back as she closed the door, wondering whether she would leap for me and try to clasp her body around mine in order to increase her chance of contamination. Twice lifers had tried that, but I sidestepped them both. Her eyes weren't shiny with fingertouch, yet I didn't think she was perfectly straight, either.

"I've got a license to kill myself," she declared, grinning.

"So?"

"I'd like you to help me. I can't do it myself." She touched the top button of her tunic, playing with it for a moment.

She stood still while I laughed. I turned my back on her and walked to the bar. I fixed a drink, not bothering to offer her one.

"Get out of here, lifer," I hissed. "You haven't got enough to pay me."

"Yes, I do; yes, I do. Here. See?" She held a fistful of crumpled bills toward me. They were all hundred-credit notes.

"Not enough, lifer. I kill only myself. Get one of your friends to do it for you." I began laughing at her again.

"Don't do that," she begged. I couldn't stop. "I said, don't do that," she repeated, pulling a needle gun out of another pocket.

I glanced at the gun. "What are you going to do? Kill me? Even the quickest poison won't work, lifer."

She let the gun drop to her side. The credit notes fluttered to the floor, but she made no move to pick them up.

"Please help me, Mr. Bin. You're the only one I know who can help me." She licked her lips, and I thought I saw a tear in the corner of one eye, but, then, it could've been the start of a fingertouch zone.

I shook my head slowly, waiting for the one question that

lifers always ask. Perhaps she truly could not kill herself, but I doubted it. She was only more brazen in her desire to increase the possibility of contamination, believing that the touch of my hands as I killed her would give her a greater chance of immortality. Idly I wondered whether killing a lifer *would* increase the chance of the disease's leaping from me, but I let the thought fade. The image of putting my hands on lifer skin sickened me.

It has always amazed me how eager lifers are to die. "Get out, Lynx."

She turned and went to the door, her arms limp and her walk almost a shuffle. She had one hand on the door handle when she looked back at me.

"I have always admired you, DeadMan. Ever since I can remember, I've worshiped you. How you come back after each death. How you die with such grace, such calm."

"It won't work, lifer," I said. "You'll have to do it yourself. You can't pay me enough to make me help you die."

The door slammed as she left. I spent the next half-hour picking up the credit notes, counting and shuffling them into neat piles. In my opinion, whatever a man finds in his own house is his.

This party was even more opulent than the one the night before. It had to be, because it was Hansa's party.

I looked into her eyes as she held my hands in hers. She smiled slyly, gripping my fingers hard in greeting. I had had a private death before coming, and its sensations dully remained. I glanced away from her gaze and started counting eyes around the room. People always paid attention to what Hansa did, and there were almost as many looking at her as there were watching me. I shrugged to myself. Did it matter what a lifer thought of me? Hansa pointed out the city councilman and the area's fingertouch pusher, making sure I knew who they were. They were to have the best possible view when I died, she told me.

Fingertouch was drifting around the room, as if it were ash left on the ground after a fire. I actually saw one man, already zoned into oblivion, throw a small bowl of the stuff into the air and watch it float to the carpet. The press of people around Hansa and me was too thick to get through, and so I had to wait until a waiter went by with a tray of touch and a single glass on it. Hansa had remembered my eccentric taste for alcohol.

I could feel her thigh press against mine as she talked to some of her guests. I let her do what she wanted. It was her party, and she had paid me enough to keep me quiet for the night. I looked at her again and noticed the scars around her neck where she had once tied a rope around it. That was the only time she had tried to kill herself, as far as I knew. Hansa threw parties for the lifers, but she didn't take the final step with them at night's end. Perhaps that was one of the reasons why I was glad whenever she hired me.

I turned to look at the crowd again and saw Lynx, that little bitch. She was on the other side of the room, and so I couldn't see whether her eyes were glossy or not, but I knew she had been watching me. I saw her turn her head quickly when I spotted her. I rubbed the palms of my hands down the sides of my pants. Somehow she made me nervous.

The fingertouch pusher stood in front of me, blocking my view of Lynx. "How can I be a DeadMan?" he asked. "I heard I can be one if I die right. I'll pay you whatever you want."

His forehead was gray from the overdose of fingertouch he had pressed into his skin. He wouldn't die tonight; he was too zoned to do anything lethal to himself.

"Leave me alone," I said.

"But Hansa said you'd talk to me."

"Hansa was wrong. No lifer can be a DeadMan." Suddenly I wished it were true. Hansa wasn't paying me enough for this.

After a half-hour of small talk with her guests, Hansa got them to clear a circle for me. The ones in front pressed a final bit of fingertouch into their skin. I smiled to them all, knowing that three-quarters of them were having a hard time focusing on me. I had counted on that when I had planned my deaths for this party. I had an attention-getter to lead things off.

I sat in the cleared spot, the legs of the lifers encircling me. I pulled out a small glass bottle from my tunic pocket, took out the stopper and poured the liquid over my head and shoulders. The fumes were overpowering and smelled somewhat sweet. I looked at the legs around me through a shimmering wave of fumes. Then I pulled out the match.

I always seem to hesitate before I go through with it, wondering why I cannot be satisfied with my private deaths. This time was not unlike any other. Perhaps it was in my mind, the certainty that I felt more, tasted more, when I died in front of them. We had spoken of it, Kiel, Sarreen, Fede, Langley, Tonner, and I, when we discovered the extent of the damage to our senses caused by the disease. They all felt more, too, in front of the lifers. The meds could not find a reason, but it was true. So we died for them in order to feel more and feel it longer.

I held the small piece of wood that I had found in an antiques store and studied it for several minutes, taking in the colors of the wood and the blue tip. Then the hesitation passed, and I could only hope that the thing would light when I struck it.

It did. I heard myself screaming as the gasoline caught and I burst into flame.

My God, I hadn't known it would be like this. Stop it, please, stop it. Not my eyes, no, no, not my eyes. Oh, God damn it, it's gotten into my eyes.

But the sense of being alive in every cell, every particle, was the same as always when I awoke. I saw the brilliant colors with eyes that were untouched and watched the room flicker, frame by frozen frame. I was sure at that instant that the lifers expected something like this when they killed themselves. But most would never see and feel this. Most would never resurrect, as I did.

I died for them twice more that night, killing myself again before the nausea came. After each death, lifers kissed my hand, said their words, and then some killed themselves. Their numbers diminished, but it was a large party. Each time I awoke was better than the last. The rust in front of my eyes got more detailed after each death. The lifers became quieter each time I awoke from the dead. By the end of the third death, the ones still left stood four meters from me. They looked at me, of course. They never stop doing that. But they would not talk to me or touch the charred fragments of my clothing. They touched their faces with the gray dust from the bowls that still circulated around the room. Not even Hansa dared stand next to me after I died that third time.

"Good work, DeadMan," someone giggled from a corner. Everyone in the room turned to see who it was. Lynx stepped through the small assemblage and came toward me. She had a blaster in her hand, which she pointed at me. An uncontrollable chill swept up my back.

"Won't you talk to me?" she asked, moving the dark end of the blaster in a small circle, its circumference my skull. Hansa made a movement forward, and Lynx edged the blaster to let her know she could swing it fast enough. Hansa backed away.

I had been silent the whole time, watching Lynx and the weapon she held. If she pulled the trigger, it would be an inconvenience to me, nothing more. But she had no right to threaten me, much less kill me. Only a DeadMan may kill a DeadMan.

"Now we'll talk, DeadMan," she said quietly, her fingers tracing the curves of her breasts as she stared at me.

"No deals," I said.

"I haven't even asked you anything yet." She seemed to be pouting. The expression made her hideous. Her fingers still played with the fabric of her blouse.

"You're going to ask me if I'll help you walk off the window ledge, or if I'll light the match for you. I told you before, no deals with lifers. I kill only myself."

"What have you got against me?" She let the mouth of the blaster droop, and I stepped forward. She flicked it back up and melted a hole in the floor a few centimeters from my feet. I stopped. Her voice was so casual that she might have been holding a drink in her hand. "I can't do it by myself. I need someone to guide me through. You've been there before; you can show me. I want to do it while I'm young. I don't want to live forever in an old body." She looked up expectantly. They all believe *they* will be the one to steal the disease and resurrect after their suicide. "Not one of us," she said, moving the blaster slightly to indicate the lifers in the room, "has been there before. They can't help me. You can."

I looked at her, letting rage build up.

"You have no right to touch me!" I bellowed the words,

and the crowd backed away. Lynx stood her ground. She looked at me with surprise, as if she didn't know what she had done. "None of you can touch me. You want to die? Here, let me show you how to do it, lifer!"

I went right up to her, grabbing the end of the blaster, as if I were going to twist it toward her. I could hear the other lifers in the room screaming when I brought the mouth of the weapon to Lynx's face. I thought she'd let go then, thinking I meant to kill her. But she couldn't let go of her life—or else she knew I didn't mean to go through with it.

She was faster than I was. Why should I have learned to be clever in a struggle? She moved her wrist back, then twisted it around, using my movements to strengthen her own, and pointed the blaster at my belly. I still held on to the weapon, but I couldn't help looking down at the point where the blaster's mouth disappeared into the flesh of my abdomen.

I felt no nervousness, no last hesitation in my mind, as I watched her finger tighten on the trigger. She was going to kill me.

There was no pain, perhaps because the blaster was so quick in its destruction. Neither was there the unique pleasure that I was used to experiencing when I resurrected. I saw no sweeping range of impossible colors, nor did I watch the room freeze itself into individual frames. I didn't even feel the warming in my belly. I had my senses still, but they were bland. Was this what the lifers hunted for?

Lynx was sitting on the floor in front of me, cradling the blaster in her hands, hugging it. She was crooning to herself in a voice too low for me to hear the words. The room was still full of Hansa's guests, but they were pressed back near the walls, as far away from Lynx as they could get.

The interruption had not quieted the hatred in me. I felt it in the slamming of my pulse in my throat. I walked to her and stood over her. She looked up, but her eyes were vacant. Had she had time to press herself with fingertouch? Had I been dead that long this time?

"You killed me, lifer," I whispered so that only she could hear me. She didn't look up. I grabbed her by the throat and pulled her to her feet. My fingers were creating white patterns in her skin.

"Look at me." I paused. "How will you pay me? You owe me for one death." I tightened my grip, then loosened it so that she could answer. "How will you pay me? I don't die cheaply, lifer."

"Kill me," she spat, "and we're even."

"No deal. I want my fee. I want money for my death."

"I don't have any. You can check with the banks. Ask Hansa. She knows. Ask her. Go ahead. I'm tapped, not a credit."

"You worthless little bitch!" I shouted. The lifers moved even closer to the walls. "You killed me and you can't pay?" I strengthened my grip on her neck, watching her mouth flutter as she tried to draw air into her lungs. "You won't pay? You want to die? Feel it then, lifer, feel it." My voice was out of control now, loud enough to frighten even Hansa. I saw her from the corner of my eye, and she was white-faced. No one was pressing fingertouch anymore. No one had to. I was giving them a zone they hadn't experienced before.

I pressed both hands around Lynx's neck and squeezed until her tongue began to inch out of her mouth. Her face was turning colors. First red, then rust, then an indigo that reminded me of ink. I shook her the way a dog shakes a piece of meat.

"How does it feel, lifer? Good? Let me know when you see the pretty colors, lifer."

Then I saw her smile. Through the grotesqueness of her mottled skin, even through her thrusting tongue, I could see her smile. She was getting what she wanted. I was giving it to her. She wanted to die, and I was doing all the work.

I let my hands fall from her neck, dropping her to the carpet. I could hear her body hit the floor and her gasping breath as if from a long distance. I stood still and stared at her for a long time. Then I looked at the lifers in the room and at Hansa. Some were dipping into the gray bowls and pressing fingertouch into their cheeks and foreheads. Hansa's face had resumed its normal color. She wasn't even looking at me. She was talking to three of her guests, gesturing widely as she made her point or finished her witticism.

Lynx was crumpled on the carpet, her face pale but her breathing almost normal. She had torn her high-necked blouse away from her throat, and it hung around her waist. She was sobbing.

"Almost, lifer," I whispered. "You almost made me do it."

She looked up at me. "Why did you stop? You goddamned DeadMan, why did you stop when it was so close?"

I wanted to ask her whether she had seen the merest of shifting colors, the briefest freeze-framing of the room. But I couldn't overcome my disgust.

"Because I hate you, lifer. I hate you." I knew it was true as I said it. I knew that I depended on them for the feel of skin on skin, the taste of sweetmeats, the sound of the wind through my clothes.

But I felt contaminated, soiled by the girl's obscene use of me. Perhaps I had always known that the lifers consumed me, as they consumed their gray drug, but I had refused to acknowledge it. Lynx's use of my death, once so exquisite, had made me see the lifers for what they were.

They used me as I used them. But I could still feel without them, while they could not live forever without the DeadMan and his disease. *I* was more necessary.

"I hate you all," I said. I wanted to shout it, but my control had returned and a DeadMan doesn't shout to lifers. He talks. They listen. I turned and strode out of the room. I didn't even stop to collect my fee from Hansa. She would send it to me.

The night air was clean and smelled of a storm coming over the mountains. I pulled a silvered flask from my tunic pocket and drank deeply of the burning liquor. I heard a scream in the distance. It seemed to be coming from the other side of the towering building, where Hansa's apartment was. Perhaps they were already throwing themselves from her windows.

When the scream ended, I knew how to get back at them. The silence told me how.

The lifers wanted to die; I would make them live, as *I* lived. Maybe I could nail every window shut. Maybe I could dull every knife in the city. Maybe I could buy all the rope and matches in all the shops.

I've died nearly four hundred times for them. I will save four hundred of them to get even. Or maybe save one, four hundred times. I could follow Lynx, protect her from herself.

Every time she'd try to plunge a blade into herself or fuse her body with a blaster, I would be there. I would stop her.

I will miss the shifting colors and the feeling of warmth in my belly I get from dying in front of them. I will not quit dying; I don't think I could do that. But I will stop dying for them. I know I can do it this time. I have the image of Lynx's smile to keep me away from that kind of death forever.

I drank the last drop from the flask and put it back in my pocket. I thought I heard another scream from around the corner of the building. I hurried back inside and began to take the stairs two at a time.

Pretty Boy Crossover
by Pat Cadigan

Introduction

Pat Cadigan, now of Kansas City, Missouri, has been so closely identified with the Cyberpunk movement that when she gave birth to "Bobzilla, scourge of the Midwest," she was quickly dubbed "Cybermom." It's a delightfully appropriate sobriquet for her, since her punkish, counter-culture heroes live in a world that is constantly evaluated by an author who wants her children to become a little better than they are. The world of her stories is often—usually—dark and forbidding, and her characters tend to be people that I wouldn't want to invite over for Sunday dinner. Yet each time I read one of her tales, I find a powerful kinship with these lost-and-found-again souls. She refuses to allow aliens to remain completely alien.

I came to know Cadigan when we served together on the Nebula Jury a few years ago. Her letters were full of wit and intelligence; it was impossible not to like her at once. "Pretty Boy Crossover" was published in a January issue of F&SF. I knew at once that this tale of identity at risk was one of those emotional, unforgettable stories that inevitably winds up on award ballots. I told her so. When she expressed some skepticism, I made some outlandish wager with her. Fortunately, I won. *I think my victory required her to eat some inedible substance. In the interest of keeping her healthy to write many more stories—and to continue civilizing Bobzilla—I released her from the obligation. Such are the sacrifices we make for literature.*

Writers often find strange training grounds in which to practice and develop the craft of writing. I was an editor for a religious magazine. Gene Wolfe edited trade journals. Many, many writers wrote pornography until they learned enough craft to graduate to truly sophisticated literature—like science fiction.

Pat Cadigan writes greeting cards for Hallmark.

So if you someday get a Valentine that sears your fingers, don't sue Hallmark. Just lick the scars and think of Cadigan.

First you see video. Then you wear video.
Then you eat video. Then you *be* video.

—*The Gospel According to Visual Mark*

Watch or Be Watched.

—*Pretty Boy Credo*

"WHO MADE YOU?"

"You mean recently?"

Mohawk on the door smiles and takes his picture. "You in. But only you, okay? Don't try to get no friends in, hear that?"

"I hear. And I ain't no fool. I got no friends."

Mohawk leers, leaning forward. "Pretty Boy like you, no friends?'

"Not in this world." He pushes past the Mohawk, ignoring the kissy-kissy sounds. He would like to crack the bridge of Mohawk's nose and shove bone splinters into his brain but he is lately making more effort to control his temper and besides, he's not sure if any of that bone splinters in the brain stuff is really true. He's a Pretty Boy, all of sixteen years old, and tonight could be his last chance.

The club is Noise. Can't sneak into the bathroom for quiet, the Noise is piped in there, too. Want to get away from Noise? Why? No reason. But this Pretty Boy has learned to think between the beats. Like walking between the raindrops to stay dry, but he can do it. This Pretty Boy thinks things all the time—*all* the time. Subversive (and, he thinks so much that he knows that word *subversive*, sixteen, Pretty, or not). He thinks things like *how many Einsteins have died of hunger and thirst under a hot African sun* and *why can't you remember being born* and *why is music common to every culture* and especially *how much was there going on that he didn't know about and how could he find out about it.*

And this is all the time, one thing after another running in his head, you can see by his eyes. It's for def not much like a Pretty Boy but it's one reason why they want him. That he *is* a Pretty Boy is another and one reason why they're halfway home getting him.

He knows all about them. Everybody knows about them and everybody wants them to pause, look twice, and cough up a card that says, Yes, we see possibilities, please come to the following address during regular business hours on the next regular business day for regular further review. Everyone wants it but this Pretty Boy, who once got five cards in a night and tore them all up. But here he is, still a Pretty Boy. He thinks enough to know this is a failing in himself that he likes being Pretty and chased and that is how they could end up getting him after all and that's b-b-b-bad. When he thinks about it, he thinks it with the stutter. B-b-b-bad. B-b-b-bad for him because he doesn't God help him want it, no, no, n-n-n-no. Which may make him the strangest Pretty Boy still live tonight and every night.

Still live and standing in the club where only the Prettiest Pretty Boys can get in any more. Pretty Girls are too easy, they've got to be better than Pretty and besides, Pretty Boys like to be Pretty all alone, no help thank you so much. This Pretty Boy doesn't mind Pretty Girls or any other kind of girls. Lately, though he has begun to wonder how much longer it will be for him. Two years? Possibly a little longer? By three it will be for def over and the Mohawk on the door will as soon spit in his face as leer in it.

If they don't get to him.

And if they *do* get to him, then it's never over and he can be wherever he chooses to be and wherever that is will be the center of the universe. They promise it, unlimited access in your free hours and endless hot season, endless youth. Pretty Boy Heaven, and to get there, they say, you don't even really have to die.

He looks up the dj's roost, far above the bobbing, boogieing crowd on the dance floor. They still call them djs even though they aren't discs any more, they're chips and there's more than just sound on a lot of them. The great hyper-program, he's been told, the ultimate of ultimates, a short walk from there to the fourth dimension. He suspects this stuff comes from low-steppers shilling for them, hoping they'll get auditioned if they do a good enough shuck job. Nobody knows what it's really like except the ones who are there and you can't trust them, he figures. Because maybe they *aren't*, any more. Not really.

The dj sees his Pretty upturned face, recognizes him even though it's been a while since he's come back here. Part of it was wanting to stay away from them and part of it was that the thug on the door might not let him in. And then, of course, he *had* to come, to see if he could get in, to see if anyone still wanted him. What was the point of Pretty if there was nobody to care and watch and pursue? Even now, he is almost sure he can feel the room rearranging itself around his presence in it and the dj confirms this is true by holding up a chip and pointing it to the left.

They are squatting on the make-believe stairs by the screen, reminding him of pigeons plotting to take over the world. He doesn't look too long, doesn't want to give them the idea he'd like to talk. But as he turns away, one, the younger man, starts to get up. The older man and the woman pull him back.

He pretends a big interest in the figures lining the nearest wall. Some are Pretty, some are female, some are undecided, some are very bizarre, or wealthy, or just charity cases. They all notice him and adjust themselves for his perusal.

Then one end of the room lights up with color and new

noise. Bodies dance and stumble back from the screen where images are forming to rough music.

It's Bobby, he realizes.

A moment later, there Bobby's face on the screen; sixteen feet high, even Prettier than he'd been when he was loose among the mortals. The sight of Bobby's Pretty-Pretty face fills him with anger and dismay and a feeling of loss so great he would strike anyone who spoke Bobby's name without his permission.

Bobby's lovely slate-gray eyes scan the room. They've told him senses are heightened after you make the change and go over but he's not so sure how that's supposed to work. Bobby looks kind of blind up there on the screen. A few people wave at Bobby—the dorks they let in so the rest can have someone to be hip in front of—but Bobby's eyes move slowly back and forth, back and forth, and then stop, looking right at him.

"Ah . . ." Bobby whispers it, long and drawn out. "Aaaaaahhhh."

He lifts his chin belligerently and stares back at Bobby.

"You don't have to die any more," Bobby says silkily. Music bounces under his words. "It's beautiful in here. The dreams can be as real as you want them to be. And if you want to be, you can be with me."

He knows the commercial is not aimed only at him but it doesn't matter. This is *Bobby*. Bobby's voice seems to be pouring over him, caressing him, and it feels too much like a taunt. The night before Bobby went over, he tried to talk him out of it, knowing it wouldn't work. If they'd actually refused him, Bobby would have killed himself, like Franco had.

But now Bobby would live forever and ever, if you believed what they said. The music comes up louder but Bobby's eyes are still on him. He sees Bobby mouth his name.

"Can you really see me, Bobby?" he says. His voice doesn't make it over the music but if Bobby's senses are so heightened, maybe he hears it anyway. If he does, he doesn't choose to answer. The music is a bumped-up remix of a song Bobby used to party-till-he-puked to. The giant Bobby-face fades away to be replaced with a whole Bobby, somewhat larger than life, dancing better than the old Bobby ever could, whirling along changing scenes of streets, rooftops and beaches. The locales are nothing special but Bobby never did have all that much imagination, never wanted to go to Mars or even to the South Pole, always just to the hottest club. Always he liked being the exotic in plain surroundings and he still likes it. He always loved to get the looks. To be watched, worshipped, pursued. Yeah. He can see this is Bobby-heaven. The whole world will be giving him the looks now.

The background on the screen goes from street to the inside of a club; *this* club, only larger, better, with an even hipper crowd, and Bobby shaking it with them. Half the real crowd is forgetting to dance now because they're watching Bobby, hoping he's put some of them into his video. Yeah, that's the dream, get yourself remixed in the extended dance version.

His own attention drifts to the fake stairs that don't lead anywhere. They're still perched on them, the only people who are watching *him* instead of Bobby. The woman, looking overaged in a purple plastic sacsuit, is fingering a card.

He looks up at Bobby again. Bobby is dancing in place and looking back at him, or so it seems. Bobby's lips move soundlessly but so precisely he can read the words: *This can be you. Never get old, never get tired, it's never last call, nothing happens unless you want it to and it could be you. You. You.* Bobby's hands point to him on the beat. *You. You. You.*

Bobby. Can you really see me?

Bobby suddenly breaks into laughter and turns away, shaking it some more.

He sees the Mohawk from the door pushing his way through the crowd, the real crowd, and he gets anxious. The Mohawk goes straight for the stairs, where they make room for him, rubbing the bristly red strip of hair running down the center of his head as though they were greeting a favored pet. The Mohawk looks as satisfied as a professional glutton after a food-race victory. He wonders what they promised the Mohawk for letting him in. Maybe some kind of limited contract. Maybe even a try-out.

Now they are all watching him together. Defiantly, he touches a tall girl dancing nearby and joins her rhythm. She smiles down at him, moving between him and them purely by chance but it endears her to him anyway. She is wearing a flap of translucent rag over secondskins, like an old-time showgirl.

Over six feet tall, not beautiful with that nose, not even pretty, but they let her in so she could be tall. She probably doesn't know that; she probably doesn't know anything that goes on and never really will. For that reason, he can forgive her the hard-tech orange hair.

A Rude Boy brushes against him in the course of a dervish turn, asking acknowledgment by ignoring him. Rude Boys haven't changed in more decades than anyone's kept track of, as though it were the same little group of leathered and chained troopers buggering their way down the years. The Rude Boy isn't dancing with anyone. Rude Boys never do. But this one could be handy, in case of an emergency.

The girl is dancing hard, smiling at him. He smiles back, moving slightly to her right, watching Bobby possibly watching him. He still can't tell if Bobby really sees anything. The scene behind Bobby is still a double of the club, getting hipper and hipper if that's possible. The music keeps snapping back to its first peak passage. Then Bobby gestures like God and he sees *himself*. He is dancing next to Bobby, Prettier than he ever could be, just the way they promise. Bobby doesn't look at the phantom but at him where he really is, lips moving again. *If you want to be, you can be with me. And so can she.*

His tall partner appears next to the phantom of himself. She is also much improved, though still not Pretty, or even pretty. The real girl turns and sees herself and there's no mistaking the delight in her face. Queen of the Hop for a minute or two. Then Bobby sends her image away so that it's just the two of them, two Pretty Boys dancing the night away, private party, stranger go find your own good time. How it used to be sometimes in real life, between just the two of them. He remembers hard.

"B-b-b-bobby!" he yells, the old stutter reappearing. Bobby's image seems to give a jump, as though he finally heard. He forgets everything, the girl, the Rude Boy, the Mohawk, them on the stairs, and plunges through the crowd toward the screen. People fall away from him as though they were re-enacting the Red Sea. He dives for the screen, for Bobby, not caring how it must look to anyone. What would they know about it, any of them. He can't remember in his whole sixteen years ever hearing one person say, *I love my friend.* Not Bobby, not even himself.

He fetches up against the screen like a slap and hangs there, face pressed to the glass. He can't see it now but on the screen Bobby would seem to be looking down at him. Bobby never stops dancing.

The Mohawk comes and peels him off. The others swarm up and take him away. The tall girl watches all this with the expression of a woman who lives upstairs from Cinderella and wears the same shoe size. She stares longingly at the screen. Bobby waves bye-bye and turns away.

"Of course, the process isn't reversible," says the older man. The steely hair has a careful blue tint; he has sense enough to stay out of hip clothes.

They have laid him out on a lounger with a tray of refreshments right by him. Probably slap his hand if he reaches for any, he thinks.

"Once you've distilled something to pure information, it just can't be reconstituted in a less efficient form," the woman explains, smiling. There's no warmth to her. *A less efficient form.* If that's what she really thinks, he knows he should be plenty scared of these people. Did she say things like that to Bobby? And did it make him even *more* eager?

"There may be no more exalted a form of existence than to live as sentient information," she goes on. "Though a lot more research must be done before we can offer conversion on a larger scale."

"Yeah?" he says. "Do they know that, Bobby and the rest?"

"Oh, there's nothing to worry about," says the younger man. He looks as though he's still getting over the pain of having outgrown his boogie shoes. "The system's quite perfected. What Grethe means is we want to research more applications for this new form of existence."

"Why not go over yourselves and do that, if it's so *exalted*."

"There are certain things that need to be done on this side," the woman says bitchily. "Just because—"

"Grethe." The older man shakes his head. She pats her slicked-back hair as though to soothe herself and moves away.

"We have other plans for Bobby when he gets tired of being

featured in clubs," the older man says. "Even now, we're educating him, adding more data to his basic information configuration—"

"That would mean he ain't really *Bobby* any more, then, huh?"

The man laughs. "Of course he's Bobby. Do you change into someone else every time you learn something new?"

"Can you prove I *don't*?"

The man eyes him warily. "Look. You *saw* him. Was that Bobby?"

"I saw a video of Bobby dancing on a giant screen."

"That *is* Bobby and it will remain Bobby no matter what, whether he's poured into a video screen in a dot pattern or transmitted the length of the universe."

"That what you got in mind for him? Send a message to nowhere and the message is him?"

"We could. But we're not going to. We're introducing him to the concept of higher dimensions. The way he is now, he could possibly break out of the three-dimensional level of existence, pioneer a whole new plane of reality."

"Yeah? And how do you think you're gonna get Bobby to do *that*?"

"We convince him it's entertaining."

He laughs. "That's a good one. Yeah. Entertainment. You get to a higher level of existence and you'll open a club there that only the hippest can get into. It figures."

The older man's face gets hard. "That's what all you Pretty Boys are crazy for, isn't it? Entertainment?"

He looks around. The room must have been a dressing room or something back in the days when bands had been live. Somewhere overhead he can hear the faint noise of the club but he can't tell if Bobby's still on. "You call this entertainment?"

"I'm tired of this little prick," the woman chimes in. "He's thrown away opportunities other people would kill for—"

He makes a rude noise. "Yeah, we'd all kill to be someone's data chip. You think I really believe Bobby's real just because I can see him on a *screen*?"

The older man turns to the younger one. "Phone up and have them pipe Bobby down here." Then he swings the lounger around so it faces a nice modern screen implanted in a shored-up cement-block wall.

"Bobby will join us shortly. Then he can tell you whether he's real or not himself. How will that be for you?"

He stares hard at the screen, ignoring the man, waiting for Bobby's image to appear. As though they really bothered to communicate regularly with Bobby this way. Feed in that kind of data and memory and Bobby'll believe it. He shifts uncomfortably, suddenly wondering how far he could get if he moved fast enough.

"My *boy*," says Bobby's sweet voice from the speaker on either side of the screen and he forces himself to keep looking as Bobby fades in, presenting himself on the same kind of lounger and looking mildly exerted, as though he's just come off the dance floor for real. "Saw you shakin' it upstairs awhile ago. You haven't been here for such a long time. What's the story?"

He opens his mouth but there's no sound. Bobby looks at him with boundless patience and indulgence. So Pretty, hair the perfect shade now and not a bit dry from the dyes and lighteners, skin flawless and shining like a healthy angel. Overnight angel, just like the old song.

"My *boy*," says Bobby. "Are you struck, like, shy or *dead?*"

He closes his mouth, takes one breath. "I don't like it, Bobby. I don't like it this way."

"Of course not, lover. You're the Watcher, not the Watchee, that's why. Get yourself picked up for a season or two and your disposition will *change*."

"You really like it, Bobby, being a blip on a chip?"

"Blip on a chip, your ass. I'm a universe now. I'm, like, *everything*. And, hey, dig—I'm on every channel." Bobby laughed. "I'm happy I'm sad!"

"S-A-D," comes in the older man. "Self-Aware-Data."

"Ooo-eee," he says. "Too clever for me. Can I get out of here now?"

"What's your hurry?" Bobby pouts. "Just because I went over you don't love me anymore?"

"You always were screwed up about that, Bobby. Do you know the difference between being loved and being watched?"

"Sophisticated boy," Bobby says. "So wise, so learned. So fully packed. On this side, there is no difference. Maybe there never was. If you love me, you watch me. If you don't look, you don't care and if you don't care I don't matter. If I don't matter, I don't exist. Right?"

He shakes his head.

"No, my boy, I *am* right." Bobby laughs. "You believe I'm right, because if you *didn't*, you wouldn't come shaking your Pretty Boy ass in a place like *this*, now, would you? You *like* to be watched, get seen. You see me, I see you. Life goes on."

He looks up at the older man, needing relief from Bobby's pure Prettiness. "How does he see me?"

"Sensors in the equipment. Technical stuff, nothing you care about."

He sighs. He should be upstairs or across town, shaking it with everyone else, living Pretty for as long as he could. Maybe in another few months, this way would begin to look good to him. By then they might be off Pretty Boys and looking for some other type and there he'd be, out in the cold-cold, sliding down the other side of his peak and no one would *want* him. Shut out of something going on that he might want to know about after all. Can he face it? He glances at the younger man. All grown up and no place to glow. Yeah, but can *he* face it?

He doesn't know. Used to be there wasn't much of a choice and now that there is, it only seems to make it worse. Bobby's image looks like it's studying him for some kind of sign, Pretty eyes bright, hopeful.

The older man leans down and speaks low into his ear. "We need to get you before you're twenty-five, before the brain stops growing. A mind taken from a still-growing brain will blossom and adapt. Some of Bobby's predecessors have made marvelous adaptation to their new medium. Pure video: there's a staff that does nothing all day but watch and interpret their symbols for breakthroughs in thought. And we'll be taking Pretty Boys for as long as they're publicly sought-after. It's the most efficient way to find the best performers, go for the ones everyone wants to see or be. The top of the trend is closest to heaven. And even if you never make a breakthrough, you'll still be entertainment. Not such a bad way to live for a Pretty Boy. Never have to age, to be sick, to lose touch. You spent

most of your life young, why learn how to be old? Why learn
how to live without all the things you have now—''

He puts his hands over his ears. The older man is still talking
and Bobby is saying something and the younger man and the
woman come over to try to do something about him. Refreshments are falling off the tray. He struggles out of the lounger
and makes for the door.

''Hey, my *boy*,'' Bobby calls after him. ''Gimme a minute
here, gimme what the problem is.''

He doesn't answer. What can you tell someone made of pure
information anyway?

There's a new guy on the front door, bigger and meaner
than His Mohawkness but he's only there to keep people out,
not to keep anyone *in*. You want to jump ship, go to, you poor
un-hip asshole. Even if you are a Pretty Boy. He reads it in the
guy's face as he passes from noise into the three A.M. quiet of
the street.

Buffalo Gals,
Won't You Come Out Tonight
by Ursula K. Le Guin

Introduction

Ursula K. Le Guin, more than any other science fiction writer, has won the respect of America's academic-literary establishment. There is no evidence, however, that she wooed them anymore than she tried to win our *favor in the sixties and seventies, when she swept the Hugos and Nebulas with* The Left Hand of Darkness *and* The Dispossessed *and various pieces of short fiction. Le Guin simply writes what she believes in and cares about, and does it in the way that seems most appropriate to her. Then she offers it, and lets us sort ourselves into communities as we respond.*

She is never ashamed of the audience that loves her work. Not for her the Margaret Atwood pose of horror, denying that her work is something as hideous as science fiction. Le Guin declares that she is, at times, a science fiction writer. At other times, she is not.

Along the way, she keeps redefining what science fiction is. She is one of a small group of science fiction writers who achieved great success early, but refused to keep writing the same kind of story that had won such acclaim. Like Samuel R. Delany and Roger Zelazny, she has willingly moved away from safe ground, from stories she already knew *how to write, and has dared to create stories that she* didn't *know how to write until she wrote them.*

As a result, her fiction is always surprising and new. Sometimes, too, it is disappointing, especially to readers who want the next story to give them exactly the same feeling they got from "The Ones Who Walk Away from Omelas." Such readers don't understand that to get the same feeling they got from "Omelas," they should re-read "Omelas." No writer has a duty to write the same story twice. Indeed, self-derivative writing becomes, in the long run, self-destructive writing. Imitation of past triumphs rarely leads to future triumphs. A string of sequels may make for good marketing, but does anyone voluntarily read Tom Sawyer, Detective? *Le Guin has never made the mistake of writing* The Right Hand of Darkness *or* The Repossessed.

Instead, she has found entirely new ways to tell stories. "Buffalo Gals" is comic, as the title suggests; it is also brooding, dangerous, sad. It is about death and loss; it is about community and belonging. It is told in a plain, folk-tale-ish voice; it is a baffling labyrinth of fact and illusion. The subject is defiantly real, while "objective reality" seems shadowy and thin. Twenty years after her first awards, Le Guin won the 1988 Hugo for this story—which is so different from her early work that if the same name were not under the title, it would be hard to guess the same author wrote them.

And yet it is *the same author, and while all the obvious aspects of her writing have developed and changed over the years, the inner core has not. Her work is still literary yet blessed with largeness of vision; she still makes romantic connection with the soul. And, as always, she writes not to be admired, but to transform us.*

I

"You FELL OUT OF THE SKY," THE COYOTE SAID.

Still curled up tight, lying on her side, her back pressed against the overhanging rock, the child watched the coyote with

one eye. Over the other eye she kept her hand cupped, its back
on the dirt.

"There was a burned place in the sky, up there alongside
the rimrock, and then you fell out of it," the coyote repeated,
patiently as if the news was getting a bit stale. "Are you hurt?"

She was all right. She was in the plane with Mr. Michaels,
and the motor was so loud she couldn't understand what he
said even when he shouted, and the way the wind rocked the
wings was making her feel sick, but it was all right. They were
flying to Canyonville. In the plane.

She looked. The coyote was still sitting there. It yawned. It
was a big one, in good condition, its coat silvery and thick.
The dark tear-line from its long yellow eye was as clearly
marked as a tabby cat's.

She sat up, slowly, still holding her right hand pressed to
her right eye.

"Did you lose an eye?" the coyote asked, interested.

"I don't know," the child said. She caught her breath and
shivered. "I'm cold."

"I'll help you look for it," the coyote said. "Come on! If
you move around you won't have to shiver. The sun's up."

Cold lonely brightness lay across the falling land, a hundred
miles of sagebrush. The coyote was trotting busily around,
nosing under clumps of rabbit-brush and cheatgrass, pawing at
a rock. "Aren't you going to look?" it said, suddenly sitting
down on its haunches and abandoning the search. "I knew a
trick once where I could throw my eyes way up into a tree and
see everything from up there, and then whistle, and they'd come
back into my head. But that goddam bluejay stole them, and
when I whistled nothing came. I had to stick lumps of pine
pitch into my head so I could see anything. You could try that.
But you've got one eye that's OK, what do you need two for?
Are you coming, or are you dying there?"

The child crouched, shivering.

"Well, come if you want to," said the coyote, yawned again,
snapped at a flea, stood up, turned, and trotted away among
the sparse clumps of rabbit-brush and sage, along the long
slope that stretched on down and down into the plain streaked
across by long shadows of sagebrush. The slender, grey-yellow

animal was hard to keep in sight, vanishing as the child watched.

She struggled to her feet, and without a word, though she kept saying in her mind, "Wait, please wait," she hobbled after the coyote. She could not see it. She kept her hand pressed over the right eyesocket. Seeing with one eye there was no depth; it was like a huge, flat picture. The coyote suddenly sat in the middle of the picture, looking back at her, its mouth open, its eyes narrowed, grinning. Her legs began to steady and her head did not pound so hard, though the deep, black ache was always there. She had nearly caught up to the coyote when it trotted off again. This time she spoke. "Please wait!" she said.

"OK," said the coyote, but it trotted right on. She followed, walking downhill into the flat picture that at each step was deep.

Each step was different underfoot; each sage bush was different, and all the same. Following the coyote she came out from the shadow of the rimrock cliffs, and the sun at eyelevel dazzled her left eye. Its bright warmth soaked into her muscles and bones at once. The air, that all night had been so hard to breathe, came sweet and easy.

The sage bushes were pulling in their shadows and the sun was hot on the child's back when she followed the coyote along the rim of a gully. After a while the coyote slanted down the undercut slope and the child scrambled after, through scrub willows to the thin creek in its wide sandbed. Both drank.

The coyote crossed the creek, not with a careless charge and splashing like a dog, but singlefoot and quiet like a cat; always it carried its tail low. The child hesitated, knowing that wet shoes make blistered feet, and then waded across in as few steps as possible. Her right arm ached with the effort of holding her hand up over her eye. "I need a bandage," she said to the coyote. It cocked its head and said nothing. It stretched out its forelegs and lay watching the water, resting but alert. The child sat down nearby on the hot sand and tried to move her right hand. It was glued to the skin around her eye by dried blood. At the little tearing-away pain, she whimpered; though it was a small pain it frightened her. The coyote came over close and poked its long snout into her face. Its strong, sharp smell was in her nostrils. It began to lick the awful, aching blindness, cleaning and cleaning with its curled, precise, strong, wet tongue, until the child was able to cry a little with relief, being comforted. Her head was bent close to the grey-yellow ribs, and she saw the hard nipples, the whitish belly-fur. She put her arm around the she-coyote, stroking the harsh coat over back and ribs.

"OK," the coyote said, "let's go!" And set off without a backward glance. The child scrambled to her feet and followed. "Where are we going?" she said, and the coyote, trotting on down along the creek, answered, "On down along the creek . . ."

There must have been a while she was asleep while she walked, because she felt like she was waking up, but she was walking along, only in a different place. She didn't know how she knew it was different. They were still following the creek, though the gully was flattened out to nothing much, and there was still sagebrush range as far as the eye could see. The eye— the good one—felt rested. The other one still ached, but not so sharply, and there was no use thinking about it. But where was the coyote?

She stopped. The pit of cold into which the plane had fallen re-opened and she fell. She stood falling, a thin whimper making itself in her throat.

"Over here!"

The child turned. She saw a coyote gnawing at the half-dried-up carcass of a crow, black feathers sticking to the black lips and narrow jaw.

She saw a tawny-skinned woman kneeling by a campfire, sprinkling something into a conical pot. She heard the water boiling in the pot, though it was propped between rocks, off the fire. The woman's hair was yellow and grey, bound back with a string. Her feet were bare. The upturned soles looked as dark and hard as shoe soles, but the arch of the foot was high, and the toes made two neat curving rows. She wore blue-jeans and an old white shirt. She looked over at the girl. "Come on, eat crow!" she said. The child slowly came toward the woman and the fire, and squatted down. She had stopped falling and felt very light and empty; and her tongue was like a piece of wood stuck in her mouth.

Coyote was now blowing into the pot or basket or whatever it was. She reached into it with two fingers, and pulled her hand away shaking it and shouting, "Ow! Shit! Why don't I ever have any spoons?" She broke off a dead twig of sagebrush, dipped it into the pot, and licked it. "Oh, boy," she said. "Come on!"

The child moved a little closer, broke off a twig, dipped. Lumpy pinkish mush clung to the twig. She licked. The taste was rich and delicate.

"What is it?" she asked after a long time of dipping and licking.

"Food. Dried salmon mush," Coyote said. "It's cooling down." She stuck two fingers into the mush again, this time getting a good load, which she ate very neatly. The child, when she tried, got mush all over her chin. It was like chopsticks, it took practice. She practiced. They ate turn and turn until nothing was left in the pot but three rocks. The child did not ask why there were rocks in the mushpot. They licked the rocks clean. Coyote licked out the inside of the pot-basket, rinsed it once in the creek, and put it onto her head. It fit nicely, making a conical hat. She pulled off her bluejeans. "Piss on the fire!" she cried, and did so, standing straddling it. "Ah, steam between the legs!" she said. The child, embarrassed, thought she was supposed to do the same thing, but did not want to, and did not. Bareassed, Coyote danced around the dampened fire, kicking her long thin legs out and singing,

"Buffalo gals, won't you come out tonight,
Come out tonight, come out tonight,
Buffalo gals, won't you come out tonight,
And dance by the light of the moon?"

She pulled her jeans back on. The child was burying the remains of the fire in creek-sand, heaping it over, seriously, wanting to do right. Coyote watched her.

"Is that you?" she said. "A Buffalo Gal? What happened to the rest of you?"

"The rest of me?" The child looked at herself, alarmed.

"All your people."

"Oh. Well, Mom took Bobbie, he's my little brother, away with Uncle Norm. He isn't really my uncle, or anything. So Mr. Michaels was going there anyway so he was going to fly me over to my real father, in Canyonville. Linda, my stepmother, you know, she said it was OK for the summer anyhow if I was there, and then we could see. But the plane."

In the silence the girl's face became dark red, then greyish white. Coyote watched, fascinated. "Oh," the girl said, "Oh—Oh—Mr. Michaels—he must be—Did the—"

"Come on!" said Coyote, and set off walking.

The child cried, "I ought to go back—"

"What for?" said Coyote. She stopped to look round at the child, then went on faster. "Come on, Gal!" She said it as a name; maybe it was the child's name, Myra, as spoken by Coyote. The child, confused and despairing, protested again, but followed her. "Where are we going? Where *are* we?"

"This is my country," Coyote answered, with dignity, making a long, slow gesture all round the vast horizon. "I made it. Every goddam sage bush."

And they went on. Coyote's gait was easy, even a little shambling, but she covered the ground; the child struggled not to drop behind. Shadows were beginning to pull themselves out again from under the rocks and shrubs. Leaving the creek, they went up a long, low, uneven slope that ended away off against the sky in rimrock. Dark trees stood one here, another way over there; what people called a juniper forest, a desert forest, one with a lot more between the trees than trees. Each juniper they passed smelled sharply, cat-pee smell the kids at school called it, but the child liked it; it seemed to go into her mind and wake her up. She picked off a juniper berry and held it in her mouth, but after a while spat it out. The aching was coming back in huge black waves, and she kept stumbling. She found that she was sitting down on the ground. When she tried to get up her legs shook and would not go under her. She felt foolish and frightened, and began to cry.

"We're home!" Coyote called from way on up the hill.

The child looked with her one weeping eye, and saw sagebrush, juniper, cheatgrass, rimrock. She heard a coyote yip far off in the dry twilight.

She saw a little town up under the rimrock, board houses, shacks, all unpainted. She heard Coyote call again, "Come on, pup! Come on, Gal, we're home!" She could not get up, so she tried to go on all fours, the long way up the slope to the houses under the rimrock. Long before she got there, several people came to meet her. They were all children, she thought at first, and then began to understand that most of them were grown people, but all were very short; thcy wcre broad-bodied, fat, with fine, delicate hands and feet. Their eyes were bright. Some of the women helped her stand up and walk, coaxing her, "It isn't much farther, you're doing fine." In the late dusk lights shone yellow-bright through doorways and through unchinked cracks between boards. Woodsmoke hung sweet in the quiet air. The short people talked and laughed all the time, softly. "Where's she going to stay?"—"Put her in with Robin, they're all asleep already!"—"Oh, she can stay with us."

The child asked hoarsely, "Where's Coyote?"

"Out hunting," the short people said.

A deeper voice spoke: "Somebody new has come into town?"

"Yes, a new person," one of the short men answered.

Among these people the deep-voiced man bulked impressive; he was broad and tall, with powerful hands, a big head, a short neck. They made way for him respectfully. He moved very quietly, respectful of them also. His eyes when he stared down at the child were amazing. When he blinked, it was like the passing of a hand before a candle flame.

"It's only an owlet," he said. "What have you let happen to your eye, new person?"

"I was—We were flying—"

"You're too young to fly," the big man said in his deep, soft voice. "Who brought you here?"

"Coyote."

And one of the short people confirmed: "She came here with Coyote, Young Owl."

"Then maybe she should stay in Coyote's house tonight," the big man said.

"It's all bones and lonely in there," said a short woman with fat cheeks and a striped shirt. "She can come with us."

That seemed to decide it. The fat-cheeked woman patted the child's arm and took her past several shacks and shanties to a low, windowless house. The doorway was so low even the child had to duck down to enter. There were a lot of people inside, some already there and some crowding in after the fat-cheeked woman. Several babies were fast asleep in cradle-boxes in corners. There was a good fire, and a good smell, like toasted sesame seeds. The child was given food, and ate a little, but her head swam and the blackness in her right eye kept coming across her left eye so she could not see at all for a while. Nobody asked her name or told her what to call them. She heard the children call the fat-cheeked woman Chipmunk. She got up courage finally to say, "Is there somewhere I can go to sleep, Mrs. Chipmunk?"

"Sure, come on," one of the daughters said, "in here," and took the child into a back room, not completely partitioned off from the crowded front room, but dark and uncrowded. Big shelves with mattresses and blankets lined the walls. "Crawl in!" said Chipmunk's daughter, patting the child's arm in the comforting way they had. The child climbed onto a shelf, under a blanket. She laid down her head. She thought, "I didn't brush my teeth."

II

She woke; she slept again. In Chipmunk's sleeping room it was always stuffy, warm, and half-dark, day and night. People came in and slept and got up and left, night and day. She dozed and slept, got down to drink from the bucket and dipper in the front room, and went back to sleep and doze.

She was sitting up on the shelf, her feet dangling, not feeling bad any more, but dreamy, weak. She felt in her jeans pockets. In the left front one was a pocket comb and a bubblegum wrapper, in the right front, two dollar bills and a quarter and a dime.

Chipmunk and another woman, a very pretty dark-eyed plump one, came in. "So you woke up for your dance!" Chipmunk greeted her, laughing, and sat down by her with an arm around her.

"Jay's giving you a dance," the dark woman said. "He's going to make you all right. Let's get you all ready!"

There was a spring up under the rimrock, that flattened out into a pool with slimy, reedy shores. A flock of noisy children splashing in it ran off and left the child and the two women to bathe. The water was warm on the surface, cold down on the feet and legs. All naked, the two soft-voiced laughing women, their round bellies and breasts, broad hips and buttocks gleaming warm in the late afternoon light, sluiced the child down, washed and stroked her limbs and hands and hair, cleaned around the cheekbone and eyebrow of her right eye with infinite softness, admired her, sudsed her, rinsed her, splashed her out of the water, dried her off, dried each other off, got dressed, dressed her, braided her hair, braided each other's hair, tied feathers on the braid-ends, admired her and each other again, and brought her back down into the little straggling town and to a kind of playing field or dirt parking lot in among the houses. There were no streets, just paths and dirt, no lawns and gardens, just sagebrush and dirt. Quite a few people were gathering or wandering around the open place, looking dressed up, wearing colorful shirts, print dresses, strings of beads, earrings. "Hey there, Chipmunk, Whitefoot!" they greeted the women.

A man in new jeans, with a bright blue velveteen vest over a clean, faded blue workshirt, came forward to meet them, very handsome, tense, and important. "All right, Gal!" he said in a harsh, loud voice, which startled among all these soft-speaking people. "We're going to get that eye fixed right up tonight! You just sit down here and don't worry about a thing." He took her wrist, gently despite his bossy, brassy manner, and led her to a woven mat that lay on the dirt near the middle of the open place. There, feeling very foolish, she had to sit down, and was told to stay still. She soon got over feeling that everybody was looking at her, since nobody paid her more attention than a checking glance or, from Chipmunk or Whitefoot and their families, a reassuring wink. Every now and then Jay rushed over to her and said something like, "Going to be as good as new!" and went off again to organize people, waving his long blue arms and shouting.

Coming up the hill to the open place, a lean, loose, tawny

figure—and the child started to jump up, remembered she was to sit still, and sat still, calling out softly, "Coyote! Coyote!"

Coyote came lounging by. She grinned. She stood looking down at the child. "Don't let that Bluejay fuck you up, Gal," she said, and lounged on.

The child's gaze followed her, yearning.

People were sitting down now over on one side of the open place, making an uneven half-circle that kept getting added to at the ends until there was nearly a circle of people sitting on the dirt around the child, ten or fifteen paces from her. All the people wore the kind of clothes the child was used to, jeans and jeans jackets, shirts, vests, cotton dresses, but they were all barefoot; and she thought they were more beautiful than the people she knew, each in a different way, as if each one had invented beauty. Yet some of them were also very strange: thin black shining people with whispery voices, a long-legged woman with eyes like jewels. The big man called Young Owl was there, sleepy-looking and dignified, like Judge McCown who owned a sixty-thousand-acre ranch; and beside him was a woman the child thought might be his sister, for like him she had a hook nose and big, strong hands; but she was lean and dark, and there was a crazy look in her fierce eyes. Yellow eyes, but round, not long and slanted like Coyote's. There was Coyote sitting yawning, scratching her armpit, bored. Now somebody was entering the circle: a man, wearing only a kind of kilt and a cloak painted or beaded with diamond shapes, dancing to the rhythm of the rattle he carried and shook with a buzzing fast beat. His limbs and body were thick yet supple, his movements smooth and pouring. The child kept her gaze on him as he danced past her, around her, past again. The rattle in his hand shook almost too fast to see, in the other hand was something thin and sharp. People were singing around the circle now, a few notes repeated in time to the rattle, soft and tuneless. It was exciting and boring, strange and familiar. The Rattler wove his dancing closer and closer to her, darting at her. The first time she flinched away, frightened by the lunging movement and by his flat, cold face with narrow eyes, but after that she sat still, knowing her part. The dancing went on, the singing went on, till they carried her past boredom into a floating that could go on forever.

Jay had come strutting into the circle, and was standing beside her. He couldn't sing, but he called out, "Hey! Hey! Hey! Hey!" in his big, harsh voice, and everybody answered from all round, and the echo came down from the rimrock on the second beat. Jay was holding up a stick with a ball on it in one hand, and something like a marble in the other. The stick was a pipe: he got smoke into his mouth from it and blew it in four directions and up and down and then over the marble, a puff each time. Then the rattle stopped suddenly, and everything was silent for several breaths. Jay squatted down and looked intently into the child's face, his head cocked to one side. He reached forward, muttering something in time to the rattle and the singing that had started up again louder than before; he touched the child's right eye in the black center of the pain. She flinched and endured. His touch was not gentle. She saw the marble, a dull yellow ball like beeswax, in his hand; then she shut her seeing eye and set her teeth.

"There!" Jay shouted. "Open up. Come on! Let's see!"

Her jaw clenched like a vise, she opened both eyes. The lid of the right one stuck and dragged with such a searing white pain that she nearly threw up as she sat there in the middle of everybody watching.

"Hey, can you see? How's it work? It looks great!" Jay was shaking her arm, railing at her. "How's it feel? Is it working?"

What she saw was confused, hazy, yellowish. She began to discover, as everybody came crowding around peering at her, smiling, stroking and patting her arms and shoulders, that if she shut the hurting eye and looked with the other, everything was clear and flat; if she used them both, things were blurry and yellowish, but deep.

There, right close, was Coyote's long nose and narrow eyes and grin. "What is it, Jay?" she was asking, peering at the new eye. "One of mine you stole that time?"

"It's pine pitch," Jay shouted furiously. "You think I'd use some stupid secondhand coyote eye? I'm a doctor!"

"Ooooh, ooooh, a doctor," Coyote said. "Boy, that is one ugly eye. Why didn't you ask Rabbit for a rabbit-dropping? That eye looks like shit." She put her lean face yet closer, till the child thought she was going to kiss her; instead, the thin, firm tongue once more licked accurate across the pain, cooling, clearing. When the child opened both eyes again the world looked pretty good.

"It works fine," she said.

"Hey!" Jay yelled. "She says it works fine! It works fine, she says so! I told you! What'd I tell you?" He went off waving his arms and yelling. Coyote had disappeared. Everybody was wandering off.

The child stood up, stiff from long sitting. It was nearly dark; only the long west held a great depth of pale radiance. Eastward the plains ran down into the night.

Lights were on in some of the shanties. Off at the edge of town somebody was playing a creaky fiddle, a lonesome chirping tune.

A person came beside her and spoke quietly: "Where will you stay?"

"I don't know," the child said. She was feeling extremely hungry. "Can I stay with Coyote?"

"She isn't home much," the soft-voiced woman said. "You were staying with Chipmunk, weren't you? Or there's Rabbit, or Jackrabbit, they have families . . ."

"Do you have a family?" the girl asked, looking at the delicate, soft-eyed woman.

"Two fawns," the woman answered, smiling. "But I just came into town for the dance."

"I'd really like to stay with Coyote," the child said after a little pause, timid, but obstinate.

"OK, that's fine. Her house is over here." Doe walked along beside the child to a ramshackle cabin on the high edge of town. No light shone from inside. A lot of junk was scattered around the front. There was no step up to the half-open door. Over the door a battered pine board, nailed up crooked, said BIDE-A-WEE.

"Hey, Coyote? Visitors," Doe said. Nothing happened.

Doe pushed the door farther open and peered in. "She's out hunting, I guess. I better be getting back to the fawns. You going to be OK? Anybody else here will give you something to eat—you know . . . OK?"

"Yeah. I'm fine. Thank you," the child said.

She watched Doe walk away through the clear twilight, a

severely elegant walk, small steps; like a woman in high heels, quick, precise, very light.

Inside Bide-A-Wee it was too dark to see anything and so cluttered that she fell over something at every step. She could not figure out where or how to light a fire. There was something that felt like a bed, but when she lay down on it, it felt more like a dirty-clothes pile, and smelt like one. Things bit her legs, arms, neck, and back. She was terribly hungry. By smell she found her way to what had to be a dead fish hanging from the ceiling in one corner. By feel she broke off a greasy flake and tasted it. It was smoked dried salmon. She ate one succulent piece after another until she was satisfied, and licked her fingers clean. Near the open door starlight shone on water in a pot of some kind; the child smelled it cautiously, tasted it cautiously, and drank just enough to quench her thirst, for it tasted of mud and was warm and stale. Then she went back to the bed of dirty clothes and fleas, and lay down. She could have gone to Chipmunk's house, or other friendly households; she thought of that as she lay forlorn in Coyote's dirty bed. But she did not go. She slapped at fleas until she fell asleep.

Along in the deep night somebody said, "Move over, pup," and was warm beside her.

Breakfast, eaten sitting in the sun in the doorway, was dried-salmon-powder mush. Coyote hunted, mornings and evenings, but what they ate was not fresh game but salmon, and dried stuff, and any berries in season. The child did not ask about this. It made sense to her. She was going to ask Coyote why she slept at night and waked in the day like humans, instead of the other way round like coyotes, but when she framed the question in her mind she saw at once that night is when you sleep and day when you're awake; that made sense too. But one question she did ask, one hot day when they were lying around slapping fleas.

"I don't understand why you all look like people," she said.

"We are people."

"I mean, people like me, humans."

"Resemblance is in the eye," Coyote said. "How is that lousy eye, by the way?"

"It's fine. But—like you wear clothes—and live in houses—with fires and stuff—"

"That's what you think . . . If that loudmouth Jay hadn't horned in, I could have done a really good job."

The child was quite used to Coyote's disinclination to stick to any one subject, and to her boasting. Coyote was like a lot of kids she knew, in some respects. Not in others.

"You mean what I'm seeing isn't true? Isn't real—like on TV, or something?"

"No," Coyote said. "Hey, that's a tick on your collar." She reached over, flicked the tick off, picked it up on one finger, bit it, and spat out the bits.

"Yecch!" the child said. "So?"

"So, to me you're basically greyish yellow and run on four legs. To that lot—" she waved disdainfully at the warren of little houses next down the hill—"you hop around twitching your nose all the time. To Hawk, you're an egg, or maybe getting pinfeathers. See? It just depends on how you look at things. There are only two kinds of people."

"Humans and animals?"

"No. The kind of people who say, 'There are two kinds of people' and the kind of people who don't." Coyote cracked up, pounding her thigh and yelling with delight at her joke. The child didn't get it, and waited.

"OK," Coyote said. "There's the first people, and then the others. That's the two kinds."

"The first people are—?"

"Us, the animals . . . and things. All the old ones. You know. And you pups, kids, fledglings. All first people."

"And the—others?"

"Them," Coyote said. "You know. The others. The new people. The ones who came." Her fine, hard face had gone serious, rather formidable. She glanced directly, as she seldom did, at the child, a brief gold sharpness. "We were here," she said. "We were always here. We are always here. Where we are is here. But it's their country now. They're running it . . . Shit, even I did better!"

The child pondered and offered a word she used to hear a good deal: "They're illegal immigrants."

"Illegal!" Coyote said, mocking, sneering. "Illegal is a sick bird. What the fuck's illegal mean? You want a code of justice from a coyote? Grow up, kid!''

"I don't want to.''

"You don't want to grow up?''

"I'll be the other kind if I do.''

"Yeah. So,'' Coyote said, and shrugged. "That's life.'' She got up and went around the house, and the child heard her pissing in the back yard.

A lot of things were hard to take about Coyote as a mother. When her boyfriends came to visit, the child learned to go stay with Chipmunk or the Rabbits for the night, because Coyote and her friend wouldn't even wait to get on the bed but would start doing that right on the floor or even out in the yard. A couple of times Coyote came back late from hunting with a friend, and the child had to lie up against the wall in the same bed and hear and feel them doing that right next to her. It was something like fighting and something like dancing, with a beat to it, and she didn't mind too much except that it made it hard to stay asleep.

Once she woke up and one of Coyote's friends was stroking her stomach in a creepy way. She didn't know what to do, but coyote woke up and realized what he was doing, bit him hard, and kicked him out of bed. He spent the night on the floor, and apologized next morning—"Aw, hell, Ki, I forgot the kid was there, I thought it was you—''

Coyote, unappeased, yelled, "You think I don't got any standards? You think I'd let some coyote rape a kid in my bed?'' She kicked him out of the house, and grumbled about him all day. But a while later he spent the night again, and he and Coyote did that three or four times.

Another thing that was embarrassing was the way Coyote peed anywhere, taking her pants down in public. But most people here didn't seem to care. The thing that worried the child most, maybe, was when Coyote did number two anywhere and then turned around and talked to it. That seemed so awful. As if Coyote was—the way she often seemed, but really wasn't—crazy.

The child gathered up all the old dry turds from around the house one day while Coyte was having a nap, and buried them in a sandy place near where she and Bobcat and some of the other people generally went and did and buried their number twos.

Coyote woke up, came lounging out of Bide-A-Wee, rubbing her hands through her thick, fair, greyish hair and yawning, looked all around once with those narrow eyes, and said, "Hey! Where are they?" Then she shouted, "Where are you? Where are you?"

And a faint, muffled chorus came from over in the sandy draw, "Mommy! Mommy! We're here!"

Coyote trotted over, squatted down, raked out every turd, and talked with them for a long time. When she came back she said nothing, but the child, redfaced and heart pounding, said, "I'm sorry I did that."

"It's just easier when they're all around close by," Coyote said, washing her hands (despite the filth of her house, she kept herself quite clean, in her own fashion.)

"I kept stepping on them," the child said, trying to justify her deed.

"Poor little shits," said Coyote, practicing dance-steps.

"Coyote," the child said timidly. "Did you ever have any children? I mean real pups?"

"Did I? Did I have children? Litters! That one that tried feeling you up, you know? that was my son. Pick of the litter . . . Listen, Gal. Have daughters. When you have anything, have daughters. At least they clear out."

III

The child thought of herself as Gal, but also sometimes as Myra. So far as she knew, she was the only person in town who had two names. She had to think about that, and about what Coyote had said about the two kinds of people; she had to think about where she belonged. Some persons in town made it clear that as far as they were concerned she didn't and never would belong there. Hawk's furious stare burned through her; the Skunk children made audible remarks about what she smelled like. And though Whitefoot and Chipmunk and their families were kind, it was the generosity of big families, where one more or less simply doesn't count. If one of them, or

Cottontail, or Jackrabbit, had come up on her in the desert lying lost and half-blind, would they have stayed with her, like Coyote? That was Coyote's craziness, what they called her craziness. She wasn't afraid. She went between the two kinds of people, she crossed over. Buck and Doe and their beautiful children weren't really afraid, because they lived so constantly in danger. The rattler wasn't afraid, because he was so dangerous. And yet maybe he was afraid of her, for he never spoke, and never came close to her. None of them treated her the way Coyote did. Even among the children, her only constant playmate was one younger than herself, a preposterous and fearless little boy called Horned Toad Child. They dug and built together, out among the sagebrush, and played at hunting and gathering and keeping house and holding dances, all the great games. A pale, squatty child with fringed eyebrows, he was a self-contained but loyal friend; and he knew a good deal for his age.

"There isn't anybody else like me here," she said, as they sat by the pool in the morning sunlight.

"There isn't anybody much like me anywhere," said Horned Toad Child.

"Well, you know what I mean."

"Yeah . . . There used to be people like you around, I guess."

"What were they called?"

"Oh—people. Like everybody . . ."

"But where do my people live? They have towns. I used to live in one. I don't know where they are, is all. I ought to find out. I don't know where my mother is now, but my daddy's in Canyonville. I was going there when."

"Ask Horse," said Horned Toad Child, sagaciously. He had moved away from the water, which he did not like and never drank, and was plaiting rushes.

"I don't know Horse."

"He hangs around the butte down there a lot of the time. He's waiting till his uncle gets old and he can kick him out and be the big honcho. The old man and the women don't want him around till then. Horses are weird. Anyway, he's the one to ask. He gets around a lot. And his people came here with the new people, that's what they say, anyhow."

Illegal immigrants, the girl thought. She took Horned Toad's advice, and one long day when Coyote was gone on one of her unannounced and unexplained trips, she took a pouchful of dried salmon and salmonberries and went off alone to the flat-topped butte miles away in the southwest.

There was a beautiful spring at the foot of the butte, and a trail to it with a lot of footprints on it. She waited there under willows by the clear pool, and after a while Horse came running, splendid, with copper-red skin and long, strong legs, deep chest, dark eyes, his black hair whipping his back as he ran. He stopped, not at all winded, and gave a snort as he looked at her. "Who are you?"

Nobody in town asked that—ever. She saw it was true: Horse had come here with her people, people who had to ask each other who they were.

"I live with Coyote," she said, cautiously.

"Oh, sure, I heard about you," Horse said. He knelt to drink from the pool, long deep drafts, his hands plunged in the cool water. When he had drunk he wiped his mouth, sat back on his heels, and announced, "I'm going to be king."

"King of the Horses?"

"Right! Pretty soon now. I could lick the old man already, but I can wait. Let him have his day," said Horse, vain-glorious, magnanimous. The child gazed at him, in love already, forever.

"I can comb you hair, if you like," she said.

"Great!" said Horse, and sat still while she stood behind him, tugging her pocket comb through his coarse, black, shin-ing, yard-long hair. It took a long time to get it smooth. She tied it in a massive ponytail with willowbark when she was done. Horse bént over the pool to admire himself. "That's great," he said. "That's really beautiful!"

"Do you ever go . . . where the other people are?" she asked in a low voice.

He did not reply for long enough that she thought he wasn't going to; then he said, "You mean the metal places, the glass places? The holes? I go around them. There are all the walls now. There didn't used to be so many. Grandmother said there didn't used to be any walls. Do you know Grandmother?" he asked naively, looking at her with his great, dark eyes.

"Your grandmother?"

"Well, yes—Grandmother—You know. Who makes the web. Well, anyhow. I know there's some of my people, horses, there. I've seen them across the walls. They act really crazy. You know, we brought the new people here. They couldn't have got here without us, they only have two legs, and they have those metal shells. I can tell you that whole story. The King has to know the stories."

"I like stories a lot."

"It takes three nights to tell it. What do you want to know about them?"

"I was thinking that maybe I ought to go there. Where they are."

"It's dangerous. Really dangerous. You can't go through— they'd catch you."

"I'd just like to know the way."

"I know the way," Horse said, sounding for the first time entirely adult and reliable; she knew he did know the way. "It's a long run for a colt." He looked at her again. "I've got a cousin with different-color eyes," he said, looking from her right to her left eye. "One brown and one blue. But she's an Appaloosa."

"Bluejay made the yellow one," the child explained. "I lost my own one. In the . . . when . . . You don't think I could get to those places?"

"Why do you want to?"

"I sort of feel like I have to."

Horse nodded. He got up. She stood still.

"I could take you, I guess," he said.

"Would you? When?"

"Oh, now, I guess. Once I'm King I won't be able to leave, you know. Have to protect the women. And I sure wouldn't let my people get anywhere near those places!" A shudder ran right down his magnificent body, yet he said, with a toss of his head, "They couldn't catch me, of course, but the others can't run like I do . . ."

"How long would it take us?"

Horse thought a while. "Well, the nearest place like that is over by the red rocks. If we left now we'd be back here around tomorrow noon. It's just a little hole."

She did not know what he meant by "a hole," but did not ask.

"You want to go?" Horse said, flipping back his ponytail.

"OK," the girl said, feeling the ground go out from under her.

"Can you run?"

She shook her head. "I walked here, though."

Horse laughed, a large, cheerful laugh. "Come on," he said, and knelt and held his hands backturned like stirrups for her to mount to his shoulders. "What do they call you?" he teased, rising easily, setting right off at a jogtrot. "Gnat? Fly? Flea?"

"Tick, because I stick!" the child cried, gripping the willowbark tie of the black mane, laughing with delight at being suddenly eight feet tall and travelling across the desert without even trying, like a tumbleweed, as fast as the wind.

Moon, a night past full, rose to light the plains for them. Horse jogged easily on and on. Somewhere deep in the night they stopped at a Pygmy Owl camp, ate a little, and rested. Most of the owls were out hunting, but an old lady entertained them at her campfire, telling them tales about the ghost of a cricket, about the great invisible people, tales that the child heard interwoven with her own dreams as she dozed and half-woke and dozed again. Then Horse put her up on his shoulders and on they went at a tireless slow lope. Moon went down behind them, and before them the sky paled into rose and gold. The soft nightwind was gone; the air was sharp, cold, still. On it, in it, there was a faint, sour smell of burning. The child felt Horse's gait change, grow tighter, uneasy.

"Hey, Prince!"

A small, slightly scolding voice: the child knew it, and placed it as soon as she saw the person sitting by a juniper tree, neatly dressed, wearing an old black cap.

"Hey, Chickadee!" Horse said, coming round and stopping. The child had observed, back in Coyote's town, that everybody treated Chickadee with respect. She didn't see why. Chickadee seemed an ordinary person, busy and talkative like most of the small birds, nothing like so endearing as Quail or so impressive as Hawk or Great Owl.

"You're going on that way?" Chickadee asked Horse.

"The little one wants to see if her people are living there," Horse said, surprising the child. Was that what she wanted?

Chickadee looked disapproving, as she often did. She whistled a few notes thoughtfully, another of her habits, and then got up. "I'll come along."

"That's great," Horse said, thankfully.

"I'll scout," Chickadee said, and off she went, surprisingly fast, ahead of them, while Horse took up his steady long lope.

The sour smell was stronger in the air.

Chickadee halted, way ahead of them on a slight rise, and stood still. Horse dropped to a walk, and then stopped. "There," he said in a low voice.

The child stared. In the strange light and slight mist before sunrise she could not see clearly, and when she strained and peered she felt as if her left eye were not seeing at all. "What is it?" she whispered.

"One of the holes. Across the wall—see?"

It did seem there was a line, a straight, jerky line drawn across the sagebrush plain, and on the far side of it—nothing? Was it mist? Something moved there—"It's cattle!" she said. Horse stood silent, uneasy. Chickadee was coming back towards them.

"It's a ranch," the child said. "That's a fence. There's a lot of Herefords." The words tasted like iron, like salt in her mouth. The things she named wavered in her sight and faded, leaving nothing—a hole in the world, a burned place like a cigarette burn. "Go closer!" she urged Horse. "I want to see."

And as if he owed her obedience, he went forward, tense but unquestioning.

Chickadee came up to them. "Nobody around," she said in her small, dry voice, "but there's one of those fast turtle things coming."

Horse nodded, but kept going forward.

Gripping his broad shoulders, the child stared into the blank, and as if Chickadee's words had focused her eyes, she saw again: the scattered whitefaces, a few of them looking up with bluish, rolling eyes—the fences—over the rise a chimneyed house-roof and a high barn—and then in the distance something moving fast, too fast, burning across the ground straight at them at terrible speed. "Run!" she yelled to Horse, "run away! Run!" As if released from bonds he wheeled and ran, flat out, in great reaching strides, away from sunrise, the fiery burning chariot, the smell of acid, iron, death. And Chickadee flew before them like a cinder on the air of dawn.

IV

"Horse?" Coyote said. "That prick? Catfood!"

Coyote had been there when the child got home to Bide-A-Wee, but she clearly hadn't been worrying about where Gal was, and maybe hadn't even noticed she was gone. She was in a vile mood, and took it all wrong when the child tried to tell her where she had been.

"If you're going to do damn fool things, next time do 'em with me, at least I'm an expert," she said, morose, and slouched out the door. The child saw her squatting down, poking an old, white turd with a stick, trying to get it to answer some question she kept asking it. The turd lay obstinately silent. Later in the day the child saw two coyote men, a young one and a mangy-looking older one, loitering around near the spring, looking over at Bide-A-Wee. She decided it would be a good night to spend somewhere else.

The thought of the crowded rooms of Chipmunk's house was not attractive. It was going to be a warm night again tonight, and moonlit. Maybe she would sleep outside. If she could feel sure some people wouldn't come around, like the Rattler . . . She was standing indecisive halfway through town when a dry voice said, "Hey, Gal."

"Hey, Chickadee.'

The trim, black-capped woman was standing on her doorstep shaking out a rug. She kept her house neat, trim like herself. Having come back across the desert with her the child now knew, though she still could not have said, why Chickadee was a respected person.

"I thought maybe I'd sleep out tonight," the child said, tentative.

"Unhealthy," said Chickadee. "What are nests for?"

"Mom's kind of busy," the child said.

"Tsk!" went Chickadee, and snapped the rug with disapproving vigor. "What about your little friend? At least they're decent people."

"Horny-toad? His parents are so shy . . ."

"Well. Come in and have something to eat, anyhow," said Chickadee.

The child helped her cook dinner. She knew now why there were rocks in the mush pot.

"Chickadee," she said, "I still don't understand, can I ask you? Mom said it depends who's seeing it, but still, I mean if I see you wearing clothes and everything like humans, then how come you cook this way, in baskets, you know, and there aren't any—any of the things like they have—there where we were with Horse this morning?"

"I don't know," Chickadee said. Her voice indoors was quite soft and pleasant. "I guess we do things the way they always were done. When your people and my people lived together, you know. And together with everything else here. The rocks, you know. The plants and everything." She looked at the basket of willowbark, fernroot, and pitch, at the blackened rocks that were heating in the fire. "You see how it all goes together . . . ?

"But you have fire—That's different—"

"Ah!" said Chickadee, impatient, "you people! Do you think you invented the sun?"

She took up the wooden tongs, plopped the heated rocks into the water-filled basket with a terrific hiss and steam and loud bubblings. The child sprinkled in the pounded seeds, and stirred.

Chickadee brought out a basket of fine blackberries. They sat on the newly-shaken-out rug, and ate. The child's two-finger scoop technique with mush was now highly refined.

"Maybe I didn't cause the world," Chickadee said, "but I'm a better cook than Coyote."

The child nodded, stuffing.

"I don't know why I made Horse go there," she said, after she had stuffed. "I got just as scared as him when I saw it. But now I feel again like I have to go back there. But I want to stay here. With my, with Coyote. I don't understand."

"When we lived together it was all one place," Chickadee

said in her slow, soft home-voice. "But now the others, the new people, they live apart. And their places are so heavy. They weigh down on our place, they press on it, draw it, suck it, eat it, eat holes in it, crowd it out . . . Maybe after a while longer there'll only be one place again, their place. And none of us here. I knew Bison, out over the mountains. I knew Antelope right here. I knew Grizzly and Greywolf, up west there. Gone. All gone. And the salmon you eat at Coyote's house, those are the dream salmon, those are the true food; but in the rivers, how many salmon now? The rivers that were red with them in spring? Who dances, now, when the First Salmon offers himself? Who dances by the river? Oh, you should ask Coyote about all this. She knows more than I do! But she forgets . . . She's hopeless, worse than Raven, she has to piss on every post, she's a terrible housekeeper . . ." Chickadee's voice had sharpened. She whistled a note or two, and said no more.

After a while the child asked very softly, "Who is Grandmother?"

"Grandmother," Chickadee said. She looked at the child, and ate several blackberries thoughtfully. She stroked the rug they sat on.

"If I built the fire on the rug, it would burn a hole in it," she said. "Right? So we build the fire on sand, on dirt . . . Things are woven together. So we call the weaver the Grandmother." She whistled four notes, looking up the smokehole. "After all," she added, "maybe all this place, the other places too, maybe they're all only one side of the weaving. I don't know. I can only look with one eye at a time, how can I tell how deep it goes?"

Lying that night rolled up in a blanket in Chickadee's back yard, the child heard the wind soughing and storming in the cottonwoods down in the draw, and then slept deeply, weary from the long night before. Just at sunrise she woke. The eastern mountains were a cloudy dark red as if the level light shone through them as through a hand held before the fire. In the tobacco patch—the only farming anybody in this town did was to raise a little wild tobacco—Lizard and Beetle were singing some kind of growing song or blessing song, soft and desultory, huh-huh-huh-huh, huh-huh-huh-huh, and as she lay warm-curled on the ground the song made her feel rooted in the ground, cradled on it and in it, so where her fingers ended and the dirt began she did not know, as if she were dead, but she was wholly alive, she was the earth's life. She got up dancing, left the blanket folded neatly on Chickadee's neat and already empty bed, and danced up the hill to Bide-A-Wee. At the half-open door she sang,

"Danced with a gal with a hole in her stocking
And her knees kept a-knocking
    and her toes kept a-rocking,
Danced with a gal with a hole in her stocking,
Danced by the light of the moon!"

Coyote emerged, tousled and lurching, and eyed her narrowly. "Sheeeoot," she said. She sucked her teeth and then went to splash water all over her head from the gourd by the door. She shook her head and the water-drops flew. "Let's get out of here," she said. "I have had it. I don't know what got into me. If I'm pregnant again, at my age, oh, shit. Let's get out of town. I need a change of air."

In the foggy dark of the house, the child could see at least two coyote men sprawled snoring away on the bed and floor. Coyote walked over to the old white turd and kicked it. "Why didn't you stop me?" she shouted.

"I *told* you," the turd muttered sulkily.

"Dumb shit," Coyote said. "Come on, Gal. Let's go. Where to?" She didn't wait for an answer. "I know. Come on!"

And she set off through town at that lazy-looking rangy walk that was so hard to keep up with. But the child was full of pep, and came dancing, so that Coyote began dancing too, skipping and pirouetting and fooling around all the way down the long slope to the level plains. There she slanted their way off north-eastward. Horse Butte was at their backs, getting smaller in the distance.

Along near noon the child said, "I didn't bring anything to eat."

"Something will turn up," Coyote said, "sure to." And

pretty soon she turned aside, going straight to a tiny grey shack hidden by a couple of half-dead junipers and a stand of rabbit-brush. The place smelled terrible. A sign of the door said: FOX. PRIVATE. NO TRESPASSING!—but Coyote pushed it open, and trotted right back out with half a small smoked salmon. "Nobody home but us chickens," she said, grinning sweetly.

"Isn't that stealing?" the child asked, worried.

"Yes," Coyote answered, trotting on.

They ate the fox-scented salmon by a dried-up creek, slept a while, and went on.

Before long the child smelled the sour burning smell, and stopped. It was as if a huge, heavy hand had begun pushing her chest, pushing her away, and yet at the same time as if she had stepped into a strong current that drew her forward, helpless.

"Hey, getting close!" Coyote said, and stopped to piss by a juniper stump.

"Close to what?"

"Their town. See?" She pointed to a pair of sage-spotted hills. Between them was an area of greyish blank.

"I don't want to go there."

"We won't go all the way in. No way! We'll just get a little closer and look. It's fun," Coyote said, putting her head on one side, coaxing. "They do all these weird things in the air."

The child hung back.

Coyote became business-like, responsible. "We're going to be very careful," she announced. "And look out for big dogs, OK? Little dogs I can handle. Make a good lunch. Big dogs, it goes the other way. Right? Let's go, then."

Seemingly as casual and lounging as ever, but with a tense alertness in the carriage of her head and the yellow glance of her eyes, Coyote led off again, not looking back; and the child followed.

All around them the pressures increased. It was as if the air itself was pressing on them, as if time was going too fast, too hard, not flowing but pounding, pounding, pounding, faster and harder till it buzzed like Rattler's rattle. Hurry, you have to hurry! everything said, there isn't time! everything said. Things rushed past screaming and shuddering. Things turned, flashed, roared, stank, vanished. There was a boy—he came into focus all at once, but not on the ground: he was going along a couple of inches above the ground, moving very fast, bending his legs from side to side in a kind of frenzied swaying dance, and was gone. Twenty children sat in rows in the air all singing shrilly and then the walls closed over them. A basket no a pot no a can, a garbage can, full of salmon smelling wonderful no full of stinking deerhides and rotten cabbage stalks, keep out of it, Coyote! Where was she?

"Mom!" the child called. "Mother!"—standing a moment at the end of an ordinary small-town street near the gas station, and the next moment in a terror of blanknesses, invisible walls, terrible smells and pressures and the overwhelming rush of Time straight forward rolling her helpless as a twig in the race above a waterfall. She clung, held on trying not to fall— "Mother!"

Coyote was over by the big basket of salmon, approaching it, wary, but out in the open, in the full sunlight, in the full current. And a boy and a man borne by the same current were coming down the long, sage-spotted hill behind the gas station, each with a gun, red hats, hunters, it was killing season. "Hell, will you look at that damn coyote in broad daylight big as my wife's ass," the man said, and cocked aimed shot all as Myra screamed and ran against the enormous drowning torrent. Coyote fled past her yelling, "Get out of here!" She turned and was borne away.

Far out of sight of that place, in a little draw among low hills, they sat and breathed air in searing gasps until after a long time it came easy again.

"Mom, that was *stupid*," the child said furiously.

"Sure was," Coyote said. "But did you see all that food!"

"I'm not hungry," the child said sullenly. "Not till we get all the way away from here."

"But they're your folks," Coyote said. "All yours. Your kith and kin and cousins and kind. Bang! Pow! There's Coyote! Bang! There's my wife's ass! Pow! There's anything— BOOOOM! Blow it away, man! BOOOOOOM!"

"I want to go home," the child said.

"Not yet," said Coyote. "I got to take a shit." She did so,

then turned to the fresh turd, leaning over it. "It says I have to stay," she reported, smiling.

"It didn't say anything! I was listening!"

"You know how to understand? You hear everything, Miss Big Ears? Hears all—Sees all with her crummy gummy eye—"

"You have pine-pitch eyes too! You told me so!"

"That's a story," Coyote snarled. "You don't even know a story when you hear one! Look, do what you like, it's a free country. I'm hanging around here tonight. I like the action." She sat down and began patting her hands on the dirt in a soft four-four rhythm and singing under her breath, one of the endless tuneless songs that kept time from running too fast, that wove the roots of trees and bushes and ferns and grass in the web that held the stream in the streambed and the rock in the rock's place and the earth together. And the child lay listening.

"I love you," she said.

Coyote went on singing.

Sun went down the last slope of the west and left a pale green clarity over the desert hills.

Coyote had stopped singing. She sniffed. "Hey," she said. "Dinner." She got up and moseyed along the little draw. "Yeah," she called back softly. "Come on!"

Stiffly, for the fear-crystals had not yet melted out of her joints, the child got up and went to Coyote. Off to one side along the hill was one of the lines, a fence. She didn't look at it. It was OK. They were outside it.

"Look at that!"

A smoked salmon, a whole chinook, lay on a little cedarbark mat. "An offering! Well, I'll be darned!" Coyote was so impressed she didn't even swear. "I haven't seen one of these for years! I thought they'd forgotten!"

"Offering to who?"

"Me! Who else? Boy, *look* at that!"

The child looked dubiously at the salmon.

"It smells funny."

"How funny?"

"Like burned."

"It's smoked, stupid! Come on."

"I'm not hungry."

"OK. It's not your salmon anyhow. It's mine. My offering, for me. Hey, you people! You people over there! Coyote thanks you! Keep it up like this and maybe I'll do some good things for you too!''

"Don't, don't yell, Mom! They're not that far away—"

"They're all my people," said Coyote with a great gesture, and then sat down cross-legged, broke off a big piece of salmon, and ate.

Evening Star burned like a deep, bright pool of water in the clear sky. Down over the twin hills was a dim suffusion of light, like a fog. The child looked away from it, back at the star.

"Oh," Coyote said. "Oh, shit."

"What's wrong?"

"That wasn't so smart, eating that," Coyote said, and then held herself and began to shiver, to scream, to choke—her eyes rolled up, her long arms and legs flew out jerking and dancing, foam spurted out between her clenched teeth. Her body arched tremendously backwards, and the child, trying to hold her, was thrown violently off by the spasms of her limbs. The child scrambled back and held the body as it spasmed again, twitched, quivered, went still.

By moonrise Coyote was cold. Till then there had been so much warmth under the tawny coat that the child kept thinking maybe she was alive, maybe if she just kept holding her, keeping her warm, she would recover, she would be all right. She held her close, not looking at the black lips drawn back from the teeth, the white balls of the eyes. But when the cold came through the fur as the presence of death, the child let the slight, stiff corpse lie down on the dirt.

She went nearby and dug a hole in the stony sand of the draw, a shallow pit. Coyote's people did not bury their dead, she knew that. But her people did. She carried the small corpse to the pit, laid it down, and covered it with her blue and white bandanna. It was not large enough; the four stiff paws stuck out. The child heaped the body over with sand and rocks and a scurf of sagebrush and tumbleweed held down with more rocks. She also went to where the salmon had lain on the cedar mat, and finding the carcass of a lamb heaped dirt and rocks over the poisoned thing. Then she stood up and walked away without looking back.

At the top of the hill she stood and looked across the draw toward the misty glow of the lights of the town lying in the pass between the twin hills.

"I hope you all die in pain," she said aloud. She turned away and walked down into the desert.

V

It was Chickadee who met her, on the second evening, north of Horse Butte.

"I didn't cry," the child said.

"None of us do," said Chickadee. "Come with me this way now. Come into Grandmother's house."

It was underground, but very large, dark and large, and the Grandmother was there at the center, at her loom. She was making a rug or blanket of the hills and the black rain and the white rain, weaving in the lightning. As they spoke she wove.

"Hello, Chickadee. Hello, New Person."

"Grandmother," Chickadee greeted her.

The child said, "I'm not one of them."

Grandmother's eyes were small and dim. She smiled and wove. The shuttle thrummed through the warp.

"Old person, then," said Grandmother. "You'd better go back there now, Granddaughter. That's where you live."

"I lived with Coyote. She's dead. They killed her."

"Oh, don't worry about Coyote!" Grandmother said, with a little huff of laughter. "She gets killed all the time."

The child stood still. She saw the endless weaving.

"Then I—Could I go back home—to her house—?"

"I don't think it would work," Grandmother said. "Do you, Chickadee?"

Chickadee shook her head once, silent.

"It would be dark there now, and empty, and fleas . . . You got outside your people's time, into our place; but I think that Coyote was taking you back, see. Her way. If you go back now, you can still live with them. Isn't your father there?"

The child nodded.

"They've been looking for you."

"They have?"

"Oh, yes, ever since you fell out of the sky. The man was dead, but you weren't there—they kept looking."

"Serves him right. Serves them all right," the child said. She put her hands up over her face and began to cry terribly, without tears.

"Go on, little one. Granddaughter," Spider said. "Don't be afraid. You can live well there. I'll be there too, you know. In your dreams, in your ideas, in dark corners in the basement. Don't kill me, or I'll make it rain . . ."

"I'll come around," Chickadee said. "Make gardens for me."

The child held her breath and clenched her hands until her sobs stopped and let her speak.

"Will I ever see Coyote?"

"I don't know," the Grandmother replied.

The child accepted this. She said, after another silence, "Can I keep my eye?"

"Yes. You can keep your eye."

"Thank you, Grandmother," the child said. She turned away then and started up the night slope towards the next day. Ahead of her in the air of dawn for a long way a little bird flew, black-capped, light-winged.

All My Darling Daughters
by Connie Willis

Introduction

Connie Willis holds the record for delivering the funniest Nebula Award presentation speech in history. She has also delighted many readers with her screwball comedies—has anyone else won a Nebula for a farce?—and it's quite possible, meeting her, to come away with the impression that Willis is the most good-natured and kind-hearted, the wittiest writer ever to wear a Peter Pan collar at a convention.

And that impression is true—as far as it goes. The danger comes when you start to think that Willis is nothing more than that. Such a delusion can easily set you up for an experience rather akin to reaching out to pet a frisky cocker spaniel and getting your fingers bitten off by a snarling pit bull.

Connie Willis, you see, is more than what she seems in polite company. The razor-sharp vision that expresses itself as gentle barbs in her comedy can also come out as plain old razor blades. You never know what will happen to you when you put yourself in Willis's hands—but you always know that the ride will be memorable, even if the scars take a while to heal.

"All My Darling Daughters" appeared in her first story collection, the only original story among reprints. Like many of *her works, it is artistically challenging; it is also unbearably painful. Indeed, some might think I have chosen the least typical of Willis's stories to represent her in this collection. But I chose this story, rather than some of her tamer, funnier, or more sentimental works, precisely because, like a rent in the side of a volcano, "All My Darling Daughters" reveals most clearly the hot magma out of which all her cooler stories are composed.*

Willis knows that I disagree violently with the worldview that I think this story expresses. I said so once in print, at some length. What is often overlooked is the fact that I also admire this story, and stand in awe of the ability and the integrity that allowed her to create it.

Connie Willis, like most of the leading science fiction writers, broke into print in the magazines. I remember very clearly when her first story, "Daisy, in the Sun," made quite a splash when it was published in an early issue of Charlie Ryan's Galileo back in the seventies. In fact, it was partly because Galileo was publishing her work that it so quickly became a prominent magazine in the field. Magazines are never better than the authors they publish—and new magazines need terrific new authors in order to survive.

What? You haven't seen Galileo on the stands lately? That's because after a very strong start as a subscription-only magazine published by Avenue Victor Hugo Bookstore in Boston, Galileo died ingloriously in the attempt to break into the big time as a newsstand magazine—taking the bookstore down with it. Charlie Ryan is back, though, as editor of Aboriginal SF, which started in 1986 as the first science fiction tabloid, and which seems to be going strong. As before, Ryan is open to new writers, which means that there are voices being heard in Aboriginal that have never been heard before.

A lot of science fiction magazines have come and gone over the years; only a few have had real staying power.

The long-timers?

Astounding, which first achieved greatness under the editorship of John W. Campbell, Jr., and which continues—as Analog—to be the largest-circulation fiction magazine in the field. The magazine broadened under Ben Bova to publish stories

*that Campbell would never have bought—my own first stories
included. Under current editor Stanley Schmidt, however, Analog has focused on a fairly narrow range of fiction—primarily
techno-fiction, in which hardware is the protagonist, and idea
stories, in which the author uses characters primarily as tools
to explain or "discover" a scientific or satirical idea.*

The Magazine of Fantasy & Science Fiction, *affectionately
known as* F&SF, *with Edward L. Ferman as owner and editor.
Long the bellwether of the field,* F&SF *is still noted for publishing some of the best and most original writers.* F&SF *is
also noted for its nonfiction: Isaac Asimov has had a compulsively readable science column in* F&SF *since the deluge; Algis
Budrys re-earns his reputation as the field's foremost critic
every month in his column; and for several years now, the
pages have sizzled with Harlan Ellison's science fiction film
reviews. (Recently I was permitted to join that distinguished
company with a column of short book reviews.)*

Amazing Stories, *the first science fiction magazine, founded
by Hugo Gernsback, for whom the Hugo Award is named. It
has been more than five decades since* Amazing *has been a
significant influence in the field; for many years the magazine
hovered on the brink of extinction, never quite going over the
edge. After years of incompetent management and marginal
editing,* Amazing *was bought by TSR, the Dungeons and Drag-
ons® people, where—first under George Scithers, now
under Patrick Price—it stays alive—and lively—despite minus-
cule circulation.*

*Some new magazines have come along, two of them moving
immediately into leadership roles in the field.* Isaac Asimov's
Science Fiction Magazine *was founded by Davis Publications
in the seventies in the hope of echoing the success of* Alfred
Hitchcock's Mystery Magazine *by following the famous-name
formula. Asimov's name certainly helped, as do his best-in-the-
field editorials. Under founding editor George Scithers,* Asimov's *almost immediately became the largest-circulation fiction
magazine. The lead didn't last, and in years since then, as
editors Shawna McCarthy and, later, Gardner Dozois brought
the magazine into literary dominance, circulation has remained in second place behind* Analog. *(A few years ago, when
Conde Nast was cleaning house, they sold* Analog *to Davis*

publications, so that today the editors of the two leading fiction magazines work only a few doors away from each other in the same building in Manhattan.)

Omni, *founded by* Penthouse *publisher Bob Guccione, has another kind of dominance in the field. Though* Omni *is a science magazine, one of the most beautifully-designed popular publications in the world, Guccione's longtime love for science fiction led him to insist on including sf stories in* Omni *from the beginning, even though the fiction is almost irrelevant to the magazine's wide circulation and financial success. Ben Bova,* Omni*'s first fiction editor, brought the same wide-ranging vision that he had shown at* Analog, *but later fiction editors have allowed the magazine's sf to drift. It hardly matters—because* Omni *pays thousands of dollars for stories instead of the hundreds offered by the other magazines, most writers send all their short fiction to* Omni *first, so that even if you picked stories randomly from the* Omni *slushpile you'd end up publishing some of the finest short stories in the field. Yet despite the quality of the submissions,* Omni*'s fiction remains disappointingly uneven.*

Omni *and* Asimov's *were launched by major publishers, with the financial resources to eat huge losses at the beginning of the venture. Other magazines have started much smaller—and the science fiction field is vital enough to keep some of them alive, too. Besides Charlie Ryan's already-mentioned* Aboriginal, *the strongest small-circulation periodical is Jim Baen's paperback "bookazine"* New Destinies, *in all its incarnations. Baen came up with the concept of publishing a magazine in paperback book form when he was an editor at Ace Books; the result was the quarterly anthology* Destinies, *complete with editorials, book reviews, and other features usually reserved for magazines. When Baen left* Destinies, *the magazine died; later, when Baen founded his own book publishing company, he revived the concept with* Far Frontiers, *co-edited by Jerry Pournelle. When Pournelle withdrew after a couple of years, Baen changed the name to* New Destinies. *Dominated by libertarian and militaristic stories and Baen's pronounced political views, the magazine is thriving, but has little influence on the rest of the field.*

Other magazines have been launched—or at least rumored.

David Hartwell's Cosmos *lasted only a few issues. Bridge Publications talked about starting a new magazine, and still may. Many amateur magazine publishers have dreamed of cracking the professional market. Some may make it.*

Ever since the demise of the pulps after World War II, people have been foretelling the death of the science fiction magazine. It's about time we just told those people to shut up. You can point to the downward trend in circulation for Asimov's *and* F&SF; *but you can also point to the fact that they are publishing fiction that's as good as ever. Sometimes the audience loses track of the magazines. Eventually, though, they come back— or a new generation discovers them.*

Science fiction's vitality depends on that. Ryan's Galileo *discovered Connie Willis. George Scithers's* Asimov's *discovered John M. Ford and Somtow Sucharitkul—and many others. Stan Schmidt's* Analog *discovered Jack McDevitt—and many others. Patrick Price's* Amazing *discovered Rebecca Ore—and many others. That is what editors take the most pride in—the authors they discover. And even though Charlie Ryan would not dream of taking credit for Connie Willis's triumphant career, he is justified in murmuring, as she wins another Nebula or receives another glowing review, "I found her on the slushpile. I was the first to recognize what she could do." That's what editors are: the front line in our search for new, true visions.*

Barrett: I'll have her dog . . . Octavius.
Octavius: Sir?
Barrett: Her dog must be destroyed. At once.
Octavius: I really d-don't see what the p-poor little beast
            has d-done to . . .

                                    —The Barretts of Wimpole Street

THE FIRST THING MY NEW ROOMMATE DID WAS TELL ME HER life story. Then she tossed up all over my bunk. Welcome to

Hell. I know, I know. It was my own fucked fault that I was stuck with the stupid little scut in the first place. Daddy's darling had let her grades slip till she was back in the freshman dorm and she would stay there until the admin reported she was being a good little girl again. But he didn't have to put me in the charity ward, with all the little scholarship freshmen from the front colonies—frightened virgies one and all. The richies had usually had their share of jig-jig in boarding school, even if they were mostly edge. And they were willing to learn.

Not this one. She wouldn't know a bone from a vaj, and wouldn't know what went into which either. Ugly, too. Her hair was chopped off in an old-fashioned bob I thought nobody, not even front kids, wore anymore. Her name was Zibet and she was from some godspit colony called Marylebone Weep and her mother was dead and she had three sisters and her father hadn't wanted her to come. She told me all this in a rush of what she probably thought was friendliness before she tossed her supper all over me and my nice new slickspin sheets.

The sheets were the sum total of good things about the vacation Daddy Dear had sent me on over summer break. Being stranded in a forest of slimy slicksa trees and noble natives was supposed to build my character and teach me the hazards of bad grades. But the noble natives were good at more than weaving their precious product with its near frictionless surface. Jig-jig on slickspin is something entirely different, and I was close to being an expert on the subject. I'd bet even Brown didn't know about this one. I'd be more than glad to teach him.

"I'm so *sorry*," she kept saying in a kind of hiccup while her face turned red and then white and then red again like a fucked alert bell, and big tears seeped down her face and dripped on the mess. "I guess I got a little sick on the shuttle."

"I guess. Don't bawl, for jig's sake, it's no big deal. Don't they have laundries in Mary Boning It?"

"Marylebone Weep. It's a natural spring."

"So are you, kid. So are you." I scooped up the wad, with the muck inside. "No big deal. The dorm mother will take care of it."

She was in no shape to take the sheets down herself, and I figured Mumsy would take one look at those big fat tears and assign me a new roommate. This one was not exactly perfect.

I could see right now I couldn't expect her to do her homework
and not bawl giant tears while Brown and I jig-jigged on the
new sheets. But she didn't have leprosy, she didn't weigh eight
hundred pounds, and she hadn't gone for my vaj when I bent
over to pick up the sheets. I could do a lot worse.

I could also be doing some better. Seeing Mumsy on my
first day back was not my idea of a good start. But I trotted
downstairs with the scutty wad and knocked on the dorm mother's door.

She is no dumb lady. You have to stand in a little box of an
entryway waiting for her to answer your knock. The box works
on the same principle as a rat cage, except that she's added her
own little touch. Three big mirrors that probably cost her a
year's salary to cart up from earth. Never mind—as a weapon,
they were a real bargain. Because, Jesus Jiggin' Mary, you
stand there and sweat and the mirrors tell you your skirt isn't
straight and you hair looks scutty and that bead of sweat on
your upper lip is going to give it away immediately that you
are scared scutless. By the time she answers the door—five
minutes if she's feeling kindly—you're either edge or you're
not there. No dumb lady.

I was not on the defensive, and my skirts are never straight,
so the mirrors didn't have any effect on me, but the five minutes took their toll. That box didn't have any ventilation and I
was way too close to those sheets. But I had my speech all
ready. No need to remind her who I was. The admin had probably filled her in but good. And I'd get nowhere telling her
they were my sheets. Let her think they were the virgie's.

When she opened the door I gave her a brilliant smile and
said, ''My roommate's had a little problem. She's a new freshman, and I think she got a little excited coming up on the
shuttle and—''

I expected her to launch into the ''supplies are precious,
everything must be recycled, cleanliness is next to godliness''
speech you get for everything you do on this godspit campus.
Instead she said, ''What did you do to her?''

''What did I—look, she's the one who tossed up. What do
you think I did, stuck my fingers down her throat?''

''Did you give her something? Samurai? Float? Alcohol?''

"Jiggin' Jesus, she just got here. She walked in, she said she was from Mary's Prick or something, she tossed up."

"And?"

"And what? I may look depraved, but I don't think freshmen vomit at the sight of me."

From her expression, I figured Mumsy might, I stuck the smelly wad of sheets at her. "Look," I said, "I don't care what you do. It's not my problem. The kid needs clean sheets."

Her expression for the mucky mess was kinder than the one she had for me. "Recycling is not until Wednesday. She will have to sleep on her mattress until then."

Mary Masting, she could knit a sheet by Wednesday, especially with all the cotton flying around this fucked campus. I grabbed the sheets back.

"Jig you, scut," I said.

I got two months' dorm restricks and a date with the admin.

I went down to the third level and did the sheets myself. It cost a fortune. They want you to have an *awareness* of the harm you are doing the delicate environment by failing to abide, etc. Total scut. The environment's about as delicate as a senior's vaj. When Old Man Moulton bought this thirdhand Hell-Five, he had some edge dream of turning it into the college he went to as a boy. Whatever possessed him to even buy the old castoff is something nobody's ever figured out. There must have been a Lagrangian point on the top of his head.

The realtor must have talked hard and fast to make him think Hell could ever look like Ames, Iowa. At least there'd been some technical advances since it was first built or we'd all be *floating* around the godspit place. But he couldn't stop at simply gravitizing the place, fixing the plumbing, and hiring a few good teachers. Oh, no, he had to build a sandstone campus, put in a football field, and plant *trees*! This all cost a fortune, of course, which put it out of the reach of everybody but richies and trust kids, except for Moulton's charity scholarship cases. But you couldn't jig-jig in a plastic bag to fulfill your fatherly instincts back then, so Moulton had to build himself a college. And here we sit, stuck out in space with a bunch of fucked cottonwood trees that are trying to take over.

Jesus Bonin' Mary, cottonwoods! I mean, so what if we're

a hundred years out of date. I can take the freshman beanies and the pep rallies. Dorm curfews didn't stop anybody a hundred years ago either. And face it, pleated skirts and cardigans make for easy access. But those godspit trees!

At first they tried the nature-dupe stuff. Freeze your vaj in winter, suffocate in summer, just like good old Iowa. The trees were at least bearable then. Everybody choked in cotton for a month, they baled the stuff up like Mississippi slaves and shipped it down to earth and that was it. But finally something was too expensive even for Daddy Moulton and we went on even-climate like all the other Hell-Fives. Nobody bothered to tell the trees, of course, so now they just spit and drop leaves whenever they feel like it, which is all the time. You can hardly make it to class without choking to death.

The trees do their dirty work down under, too, rooting happily away through the plumbing and the buried cables so that nothing works. Ever. I think the whole outer shell could blow away and nobody would ever know. The fucked root system would hold us together. And the admin wonders why we call it Hell. I'd like to upset their delicate balance once and for all.

I ran the sheets through on disinfect and put them in the spin. While I was sitting there, thinking evil thoughts about freshman and figuring how to get off restricks, Arabel came wandering in.

"Tavvy, hi! When did you get back?" She is always too sweet for words. We played lezzies as freshmen, and sometimes I think she's sorry it's over. "There's a great party," she said.

"I'm on restricks," I said. Arabel's not the world's greatest authority on parties. I mean, herself and a plastic bone would be a great party. "Where is it?"

"My room. Brown's there," she said languidly. This was calculated to make me rush out of my pants and up the stairs, no doubt. I watched my sheets spin.

"So what are you doing down here?" I said.

"I came down for some float. Our machine's out. Why don't you come on over? Restricks never stopped you before."

"I've been to your parties, Arabel. Washing my sheets might be more exciting."

"You're right," she said, "it might." She fiddled with the machine. This was not like her at all.

"What's up?"

"Nothing's up." She sounded puzzled. "It's samurai-party time without the samurai. Not a bone in sight and no hope of any. That's why I came down here."

"Brown, too?" I asked. He was into a lot of edge stuff, but I couldn't quite imagine celibacy.

"Brown, too. They all just sit there."

"They're on something, then. Something new they brought back from vacation." I couldn't see what she was so upset about.

"No," she said. "They're not on anything. This is different. Come see. Please."

Well, maybe this was all a trick to get me to one of Arabel's scutty parties and maybe not. But I didn't want Mumsy to think she'd hurt my feelings by putting me on restricks. I threw the lock on the spin so nobody'd steal the sheets and went with her.

For once Arabel hadn't exaggerated. It was a godspit party, even by her low standards. You could tell that the minute you walked in. The girls looked unhappy, the boys looked uninterested. It couldn't be all bad, though. At least Brown was back. I walked over to where he was standing.

"Tavvy," he said, smiling, "how was your summer? Learn anything new from the natives?"

"More than my fucked father intended." I smiled back at him.

"I'm sure he had your best interests at heart," he said. I started to say something clever to that, then realized he wasn't kidding. Brown was just like I was. He had to be kidding. Only he wasn't. He wasn't smiling anymore either.

"He just wanted to protect you, for your own good."

Jiggin' Jesus, he had to be on something. "I don't need any protecting," I said. "As you well know."

"Yeah," he said, sounding disappointed. "Yeah." He moved away.

What in the scut was going on? Brown leaned against the wall, watching Sept and Arabel. She had her sweater off and was shimmying out of her skirt, which I have seen before, sometimes even helped with. What I had never seen before was the look of absolute desperation on her face. Something was very wrong. Sept stripped, and his bone was as big as Arabel could have wanted, but the look on her face didn't change. Sept shook his head almost disapprovingly at Brown and went down on Arabel.

"I haven't had any straight-up all summer," Brown said from behind me, his hand on my vaj. "Let's get out of here."

Gladly. "We can't go to my room," I said. "I've got a virgie for a roommate. How about yours?"

"No!" he said, and then more quietly, "I've got the same problem. New guy. Just off the shuttle. I want to break him in gently."

You're lying, Brown, I thought. And you're about to back out of this, too. "I know a place," I said, and practically raced him to the laundry room so he wouldn't have time to change his mind.

I spread one of the dried slickspin sheets on the floor and went down as fast as I could get out of my clothes. Brown was in no hurry, and the frictionless sheet seemed to relax him. He smoothed his hands the full length of my body. "Tavvy," he said, brushing his lips along the line from my hips to my neck, "your skin's so soft. I'd almost forgotten." He was talking to himself.

Forgotten what, for fucked's sake, he couldn't have been without any jig-jig all summer or he'd be showing it now, and he acted like he had all the time in the world.

"Almost forgotten . . . nothing like . . ."

Like what? I thought furiously. Just what have you got in that room? And what has it got that I haven't? I spread my legs and forced him down between them. He raised his head a little, frowning, then he started that long, slow, torturing passage down my skin again. Jiggin' Jesus, how long did he think I could wait?

"Come on," I whispered, trying to maneuver him with my hips. "Put it in, Brown. I want to jig-jig. Please."

He stood up in a motion so abrupt that my head smacked against the laundry-room floor. He pulled on his clothes, looking . . . what? Guilty? Angry?

I sat up. "What in the holy scut do you think you're doing?"

"You wouldn't understand. I just keep thinking about your father."

"My *father*? What in the scut are you talking about?"

"Look. I can't explain it. I just can't . . ." And left. Like that. With me ready to go off any minute and what do I get? A cracked head.

"I don't have a father, you scutty godfucker!" I shouted after him.

I yanked my clothes on and started pulling the other sheet out of the spin with a viciousness I would have liked to have spent on Brown. Arabel was back, watching from the laundry-room door. Her face still had that strained look.

"Did you see that last charming scene?" I asked her, snagging the sheet on the spin handle and ripping a hole in one corner.

"I didn't have to. I can imagine it went pretty much the way mine did." She leaned unhappily against the door. "I think they've all gone bent over the summer."

"Maybe." I wadded the sheets together into a ball. I didn't think that was it, though. Brown wouldn't have lied about a new boy in his room in that case. And he wouldn't have kept talking about my father in that edge way. I walked past Arabel. "Don't worry, Arabel, if we have to go lezzy again, you know you're my first choice."

She didn't even look particularly happy about that.

My idiot roommate was awake, sitting bolt upright on the bunk where I'd left her. The poor brainless thing had probably been sitting there the whole time I'd been gone. I made up the bunk, stripped off my clothes for the second time tonight, and crawled in. "You can turn out the light any time," I said.

She hopped over to the wall plate, swathed in a night-gown that dated as far back as Old Man Moulton's college days, or farther. "Did you get in trouble?" she asked, her eyes wide.

"Of course not, I wasn't the one who tossed up. If anybody's in trouble, it's you," I added maliciously.

She seemed to sag against the flat wallplate as if she were clinging to it for support. "My father—will they tell my father?" Her face was flashing red and white again.

And where would the vomit land this time? That would teach me to take out my frustrations on my roommate. "Your father? Of course not. Nobody's in trouble. It was a couple of fucked sheets, that's all."

She didn't seem to hear me. "He said he'd come and get me if I got in trouble. He said he'd make me go home."

I sat up in the bunk. I'd never seen a freshman yet that wasn't dying to go home, at least not one like Zibet, with a whole loving family waiting for her instead of a trust and a couple of snotty lawyers. But Zibet here was scared scutless at the idea. Maybe the whole campus was going edge. "You didn't get in trouble," I repeated. "There's nothing to worry about."

She was still hanging onto that wallplate for dear life.

"Come on"—Mary Masting, she was probably having an attack of some kind, and I'd get blamed for that, too. "You're safe here. Your father doesn't even know about it."

She seemed to relax a little. "Thank you for not getting me in trouble," she said and crawled back into her own bunk. She didn't turn the light off.

Jiggin' Jesus, it wasn't worth it. I got out of bed and turned the fucked light off myself.

"You're a good person, you know that," she said softly into the darkness. Definitely edge. I settled down under the covers, planning to masty myself to sleep, since I couldn't get anything any other way, but very quietly. I didn't want any more hysterics.

A hearty voice suddenly exploded into the room. "To the young men of Moulton College, to all my strong sons, I say—"

"What's that?" Zibet whispered.

"First night in Hell," I said, and got out of bed for the thirtieth time.

"May all your noble endeavors be crowned with success," Old Man Moulton said.

I slapped my palm against the wallplate and then fumbled through my still-unpacked shuttle bag for a nail file. I stepped up on Zibet's bunk with it and started to unscrew the intercom.

"To the young women of Moulton College," he boomed again, "to all my darling daughters." He stopped. I tossed the screws and file back in the bag, smacked the plate, and flung myself back in bed.

"Who was that?" Zibet whispered.

"Our founding father," I said, and then remembering the effect the word "father" seemed to be having on everyone in this edge place, I added hastily, "That's the last time you'll have to hear him. I'll put some plast in the works tomorrow and put the screws back in so the dorm mother won't figure it out. We will live in blessed silence for the rest of the semester."

She didn't answer. She was already asleep, gently snoring. Which meant so far I had misguessed every single thing today. Great start to the semester.

The admin knew all about the party. "You *do* know the meaning of the word restricks, I presume?" he said.

He was an old scut, probably forty-five. Dear Daddy's age. He was fairly good-looking, probably exercising like edge to keep the old belly in for the freshman girls. He was liable to get a hernia. He probably jig-jigged into a plastic bag, too, just like Daddy, to carry on the family name. Jiggin' Jesus, there oughta be a law.

"You're a trust student, Octavia?"

"That's right." You think I'd be stuck with a fucked name like Octavia if I wasn't?

"Neither parent?"

"No. Paid mother-surr. Trust name till twenty-one." I watched his face to see what effect that had on him. I'd seen a lot of scared faces that way.

"There's no one to write to, then, except your lawyers. No way to expel you. And restricks don't seem to have any appreciable effect on you. I don't quite know what would."

I'll bet you don't. I kept watching him, and he kept watching me, maybe wondering if I was his darling daughter, if that expensive jism in the plastic bag had turned out to be what he was boning after right now.

"What exactly was it you called your dorm mother?"

"Scut," I said.

"I've longed to call her that myself a time or two."

The sympathetic buildup. I waited, pretty sure of what was coming.

"About this party. I've heard the boys have something new going. What is it?"

The question wasn't what I expected. "I don't know," I said and then realized I'd let my guard down. "Do you think I'd tell you if I knew?"

"No, of course not. I admire that. You're quite a young woman, you know. Outspoken, loyal, very pretty, too, if I may say so."

Um-hmm. And you just happen to have a job for me, don't you?

"My secretary's quit. She likes younger men, she says, although if what I hear is true, maybe she's better off with me. It's a good job. Lots of extras. Unless, of course, you're like my secretary and prefer boys to men."

Well, and here was the way out. No more virgie freshman, no more restricks. Very tempting. Only he was at least forty-five, and somehow I couldn't quite stomach the idea of jig-jig with my own father. Sorry, sir.

"If it's the trust problem that's bothering you, I assure you there are ways to check."

Liar. Nobody knows who their kids are. That's why we've got these storybook trust names, so we can't show up on Daddy's doorstep: Hi, I'm your darling daughter. The trust protects them against scenes like that. Only sometimes with a scut like the admin here, you wonder just who's being protected from whom.

"Do you remember what I told my dorm mother?" I said.

"Yes."

"Double to you."

Restricks for the rest of the year and a godspit alert band welded onto my wrist.

"I know what they've got," Arabel whispered to me in class. It was the only time I ever saw her. The godspit alert band went off if I even mastied without permission.

"What?" I asked, pretty much without caring.

"Tell you after."

I met her outside, in a blizzard of flying leaves and cotton.

The circulation system had gone edge again. "Animals," she said.

"Animals?"

"Little repulsive things about as long as your arm. Tessels, they're called. Repulsive little brown animals."

"I don't believe it," I said. "It's got to be more than beasties. That's elementary school stuff. Are they bio-enhanced?"

"You mean pheromones or something?" She frowned. "I don't know. I sure didn't see anything attractive about them, but the boys—Brown brought his to a party, carrying it around on his arm, calling it Daughter Ann. They all swarmed around it, petting it, saying things like 'Come to Daddy.' It was really edge."

I shrugged. "Well, if you're right, we don't have anything to worry about. Even if they're bio-enhanced, how long can beasties hold their attention? It'll all be over by midterms."

"Can't you come over? I never see you." She sounded like she was ready to go lezzy.

I held up the banded wrist. "Can't. Listen, Arabel, I'll be late to my next class," I said, and hurried off through the flailing yellow and white. I didn't have a next class. I went back to the dorm and took some float.

When I came out of it, Zibet was there, sitting on her bunk with her knees hunched up, writing busily in a notebook. She looked much better than the first time I saw her. Her hair had grown out some and showed enough curl at the ends to pick up on her features. She didn't look strained. In fact she looked almost happy.

"What are you doing?" I hoped I said. The first couple of sentences out of float it's anybody's guess what's going to come out.

"Recopying my notes," she said. Jiggin', the things that make some people happy. I wondered if she'd found a boyfriend and that was what had given her that pretty pink color. If she had, she was doing better than Arabel. Or me.

"For who?"

"What?" She looked blank.

"What boy are you copying your notes for?"

"Boy?" Now there was an edge to her voice. She looked frightened.

I said carefully, "I figure you've got to have a boyfriend."
And watched her go edge again. Mary doing Jesus, that must
not have come out right at all. I wondered what I'd really said
to send her off like that.

She backed up against the bunk wall like I was after her with
something and held her notebook flat against her chest. "Why
do you think that?"

Think what? Holy scut, I should have told her about float
before I went off on it. I'd have to answer her now like it was
still a real conversation instead of a caged rat being poked with
a stick, and hope I could explain later. "I don't know why I
think that. You just looked—"

"It's true, then," she said, and the strain was right back,
blinking red and white.

"What is?" I said, still wondering what it was the float had
garbled my innocent comment into.

"I had braids like you before I came here. You probably
wondered about that." Holy scut, I'd said something mean
about her choppy hair.

"My father . . ."—she clutched the notebook like she had
clutched the wallplate that night, hanging on for dear life. "My
father cut them off." She was admitting some awful thing to
me and I had no idea what.

"Why did he do that?"

"He said I tempted . . . men with it. He said I was a—that
I made men think wicked thoughts about me. He said it was
my fault that it happened. He cut off all my hair."

It was coming to me finally that I had asked her just what I
thought I had: whether she had a boyfriend.

"Do you think I—do that?" she asked me pleadingly.

Are you kidding? She couldn't have tempted Brown in one
of his bone-a-virgin moods. I couldn't say that to her, though,
and on the other hand, I knew if I said yes it was going to be
toss-up time in dormland again. I felt sorry for her, poor kid,
her braids chopped off and her scut of a father scaring the hell
out of her with a bunch of lies. No wonder she'd been so edge
when she first got here.

"Do you?" she persisted.

"You want to know what I think," I said, standing up a
little unsteadily. "I think fathers are a pile of scut." I thought

of Arabel's story. Little brown animals as long as your arm and Brown saying, "Your father only wants to protect you."

"Worse than a pile of scut," I said, "All of them."

She looked at me, backed up against the wall, as if she would like to believe me.

"You want to know what my father did to me?" I said. "He didn't cut my braids off. Oh, no, this is lots better. You know about trust kids?"

She shook her head.

"Okay. My father wants to carry on his precious name and his precious jig-juice, but he doesn't want any of the trouble. So he sets up a trust. He pays a lot of money, he goes jig-jig in a plastic bag, and presto, he's a father, and the lawyers are left with all the dirty work. Like taking care of me and sending me someplace for summer break and paying my tuition at this godspit school. Like putting one of these on me." I held up my wrist with the ugly alert band on it. "He never even saw me. He doesn't even know who I am. Trust me. I know about scutty fathers."

"I wish . . ." Zibet said. She opened her book and started copying her notes again. I eased down onto my bunk, starting to feel the post-float headache. When I looked at her again, she was dripping tears all over her precious notes. Jiggin' Jesus, everything I said was wrong. The most I could hope for in this edge place was that the boys would be done playing beasties by midterms and I could get my grades up.

By midterms the circulation system had broken down completely. The campus was knee-deep in leaves and cotton. You could hardly walk. I trudged through the leaves to class, head down. I didn't even see Brown until it was too late.

He had the animal on his arm. "This is Daughter Ann." Brown said. "Daughter Ann, meet Tavvy."

"Go jig yourself," I said, brushing by him.

He grabbed my wrist, holding on hard and pressing his fingers against the alert band until it hurt. "That's not polite, Tavvy. Daughter Ann wants to meet you. Don't you, sweetheart?" He held the animal out to me. Arabel had been right. Hideous little things. I had never gotten a close look at one before. It had a sharp little brown face, with dull eyes and a tiny pink mouth. Its fur was coarse and brown, and its body hung limply off Brown's arm. He had put a ribbon around its neck.

"Just your type," I said. "Ugly as mud and a hole big enough for even you to find."

His grip tightened. "You can't talk that way to my . . ."

"Hi," Zibet said behind me. I whirled around. This was all I needed.

"Hi," I said, and yanked my wrist free. "Brown, this is my roommate. My *freshman* roommate. Zibet, Brown."

"And this is Daughter Ann," he said, holding the animal up so that its tender pink mouth gaped stupidly at us. Its tail was up. I could see tender pink at the other end, too. And Arabel wonders what the attraction is?

"Nice to meet you, freshman roommate," Brown muttered and pulled the animal back close to him. "Come to Papa," he said, and stalked off through the leaves.

I rubbed my poor wrist. Please, please let her not ask me what a tessel's for? I have had about all I can take for one day. I'm not about to explain Brown's nasty habits to a virgie.

I had underestimated. her. She shuddered a little and pulled her notebooks against her chest. "Poor little beast," she said.

"What do you know about sin?" she asked me suddenly that night. At least she had turned off the light. That was some improvement.

"A lot," I said. "How do you think I got this charming bracelet?"

"I mean really doing something wrong. To somebody else. To save yourself." She stopped. I didn't answer her, and she didn't say anything more for a long time. "I know about the admin," she said finally.

I couldn't have been more surprised if Old Scut Moulton had suddenly shouted, "Bless you, my daughter," over the intercom.

"You're a good person. I can tell that." There was a dreamy quality to her voice. If it had been anybody but her I'd have thought she was masting. "There are things you wouldn't do, not even to save yourself."

"And you're a hardened criminal, I suppose?"

"There are things you wouldn't do," she repeated sleepily, and then said quite clearly and irrelevantly, "My sister's coming for Christmas."

Jiggin', she was full of surprises tonight. "I thought you were going home for Christmas," I said.

"I'm never going home," she said.

"Tavvy!" Arabel shouted halfway across campus. "Hello!"

The boys are over it, I thought, and how in the scut am I going to get rid of this alert band? I felt so relieved I could have cried.

"Tavvy," she said again. "I haven't seen you in weeks!"

"What's going on?" I asked her, wondering why she didn't just blurt it out about the boys in her usual break-neck fashion.

"What do you mean?" she said, wide-eyed, and I knew it wasn't the boys. They still had the tessels, Brown and Sept and all the rest of them. They still had the tessels. It's only beasties, I told myself fiercely, it's only beasties and why are you so edge about it? Your father has your best interests at heart. Come to Daddy.

"The admin's secretary quit," Arabel said. "I got put on restricks for a samurai party in my room." She shrugged. "It was the best offer I'd had all fall."

Oh, but you're trust, Arabel. You're trust. He could be your father. Come to Papa.

"You look terrible," Arabel said. "Are you doing too much float?"

I shook my head. "Do you know wnat it is the boys do with them?"

"Tavvy, sweetheart, if you can't figure out what that big pink hole is for—"

"My roommate's father cut her hair off," I said, "She's a virgie. She's never done anything. He cut off all her hair."

"Hey," Arabel said, "you are really edging it. Listen, how long have you been without jig-jig? I can set you up, younger guys than the admin, nothing to worry about. Guaranteed no trusters. I could set you up."

I shook my head. "I don't want any."

"Listen, I'm worried about you. I don't want you to go edge on me. Let me ask the admin about your alert band at least."

"No," I said clearly. 'I'm all right, Arabel. I've got to get to class."

"Don't let this tessel thing get to you, Tavvy. It's only beasties."

"Yeah." I walked steadily away from her across the spitting, leaf-littered campus. As soon as I was out of her line of sight, I slumped against one of the giant cottonwoods and hung on to it like Zibet had clung to that wallplate. For dear life.

Zibet didn't say another thing about her sister until right before Christmas break. Her hair, which I had thought was growing out, looked choppier than ever. The old look of strain was back and getting worse every day. She looked like a radiation victim.

I wasn't looking that good myself. I couldn't sleep, and float gave me headaches that lasted a week. The alert band started a rash that had worked its way halfway up my arm. And Arabel was right. I was going edge. I couldn't get the tessels off my mind. If you'd asked me last summer what I thought of beasties, I'd have said it was great fun for everyone, especially the animals. Now the thought of Brown with that hideous little brown and pink thing on his arm was enough to make me toss up. I keep thinking about your father. If it's the trust thing you're worried about, I can find out for you. He has your best interests at heart. Come to Papa.

My lawyers hadn't succeeded in convincing the admin to let me go to Aspen for Christmas, or anywhere else. They'd managed to wangle full privileges as soon as everybody was gone, but not to get the alert band off. I figured if the dorm mother got a good look at what it was doing to my arm, though, she'd let me have it off for a few days and give it a chance to heal. The circulation system was working again, blowing winds of hurricane force all across Hell. Merry Christmas, everybody.

On the last day of class, I walked into our dark room, hit the wallplate, and froze. There sat Zibet in the dark. On my bed. With a tessel in her lap.

"Where did you get that?" I whispered.

"I stole it," she said.

I locked the door behind me and pushed one of the desk chairs against it. "How?"

"They were all at a party in somebody else's room."

"You went in the boys' dorm?"

She didn't answer.

"You're a freshman. They could send you home for that," I said, disbelieving. This was the girl who had gone quite literally up the wall over the sheets, who had said, "I'm never going home again."

"Nobody saw me," she said calmly. "They were all at a party."

"You're edge," I said. "Whose is it, do you know?"

"It's Daughter Ann."

I grabbed the top sheet off my bunk and started lining my shuttle bag with it. Holy scut, this would be the first place Brown would look. I rifled through my desk drawer for a pair of scissors to cut some air slits with. Zibet still sat petting the horrid thing.

"We've got to hide it," I said. "This time I'm not kidding. You really are in trouble."

She didn't hear me. "My sister Henra's pretty. She has long braids like you. She's good like you, too," and then in an almost pleading voice, "she's only fifteen."

Brown demanded and got a room check that started, you guessed it, with our room. The tessel wasn't there. I'd put it in the shuttle bag and hidden it in one of the spins down in the laundry room. I'd wadded the other slickspin sheet in front of it, which I felt was fitting irony for Brown, only he was too enraged to see it.

"I want another check," he said after the dorm mother had given him the grand tour. "I know it's here." He turned to me. "I know you've got it."

"The last shuttle's in ten minutes," the dorm mother said. "There isn't time for another check."

"She's got it. I can tell by the look on her face. She's hidden it somewhere. Somewhere in this dorm."

The dorm mother looked like she'd like to have him in her Skinner box for about an hour. She shook her head.

"You lose, Brown," I said, "You stay and you'll miss your shuttle and be stuck in Hell over Christmas. You leave and you lose your darling Daughter Ann. You lose either way, Brown."

He grabbed my wrist. The rash was almost unbearable under the band. My wrist had started to swell, puffing out purplish-red over the metal. I tried to free myself with my other hand, but his grip was as hard and vengeful as his face. "Octavia here was at a samurai party in the boys' dorm last week," he said to the dorm mother.

"That's not true," I said. I could hardly talk. The pain from his grip was making me so nauseated I felt faint.

"I find that difficult to believe," the dorm mother said, "since she is confined by an alert band."

"This?" Brown said, and yanked my arm up. I cried out. "This thing?" He twisted it around my wrist. "She can take it off any time she wants. Didn't you know that?" He dropped my wrist and looked at me contemptuously. "Tavvy's too smart to let a little thing like an alert band stop her, aren't you, Tavvy?"

I cradled my throbbing wrist against my body and tried not to black out. It isn't beasties, I thought frantically. He would never do this to me just for beasties. It's something worse. Worse. He must never, never get it back.

"There's the call for the shuttle," the dorm mother said. "Octavia, your break privileges are canceled."

Brown shot a triumphant glance at me and followed her out. It took every bit of strength I had to wait till the last shuttle was gone before I went to get the tessel. I carried it back to the room with my good hand. The restricks hardly mattered. There was no place to go anyway. And the tessel was safe. "Everything will be all right," I said to the tessel.

Only everything wasn't all right. Henra, the pretty sister, wasn't pretty. Her hair had been cut off, as short as scissors could make it. She was flushed bright red and crying. Zibet's face had gone stony white and stayed that way. I didn't think from the looks of her that she'd ever cry again. Isn't it wonderful what a semester of college can do for you?

Restricks or no, I had to get out of there. I took my books and camped down in the laundry room. I wrote two term papers, read three textbooks, and, like Zibet, recopied all my notes. He cut off my hair. He said I tempted men and that was why it happened. Your father was only trying to protect you.

Come to Papa. I turned on all the spins at once so I couldn't hear myself think and typed the term papers.

I made it to the last day of break, gritting my teeth to keep from thinking about Brown, about tessels, about everything. Zibet and her sister came down to the laundry room to tell me Henra was going back on the first shuttle. I said goodbye. "I hope you can come back," I said, knowing I sounded stupid, knowing there was nothing in the world that could make me go back to Marylebone Weep if I were Henra.

"I am coming back. As soon as I graduate."

"It's only two years," Zibet said. Two years ago Zibet had the same sweet face as her sister. Two years from now, Henra too would look like death warmed over. What fun to grow up in Marylebone Weep, where you're a wreck at seventeen.

"Come back with me, Zibet," Henra said.

"I can't."

Toss-up time. I went back to the room, propped myself on my bunk with a stack of books, and started reading. The tessel had been asleep on the foot of the bunk, its gaping pink vaj sticking up. It crawled onto my lap and lay there. I picked it up. It didn't resist. Even with it living in the room I'd never really looked at it closely. I saw now that it couldn't resist if it tried. It had tiny little paws with soft pink underpads and no claws. It had no teeth, either, just the soft little rosebud mouth, only a quarter of the size of the opening at the other end. If it had been enhanced with pheromones, I sure couldn't tell it. Maybe its attraction was simply that it had no defenses, that it couldn't fight even if it wanted to.

I laid it over my lap and stuck an exploratory finger a little way into the vaj. I'd done enough lezzing when I was a freshman to know what a good vaj should feel like. I eased the finger farther in.

It screamed.

I yanked the hand free, balled it into a fist, and crammed it against my mouth hard to keep from screaming myself. Horrible, awful, pitiful sound. Helpless. Hopeless. The sound a woman must make when she's being raped. No. Worse. The sound a child must make, I thought, I have never heard a sound like that in my whole life, and at the same instant, this is the sound I have been hearing all semester. Pheromones. Oh, no, a far greater attraction than some chemical. Or is fear a chemical, too?

I put the poor little beast onto the bed, went into the bathroom, and washed my hands for about an hour. I thought Zibet hadn't known what the tessels were for, that she hadn't had more than the vaguest idea what the boys were doing to them. But she had known. Known and tried to keep it from me. Known and gone into the boys' dorm all by herself to steal one. We should have stolen them all, all of them, gotten them away from those scutting god-fucking . . . I had thought of a lot of names for my father over the years. None of them was bad enough for this. Scutting Jesus-jiggers. Fucking piles of scut.

Zibet was standing in the door of the bathroom.

"Oh, Zibet," I said, and stopped.

"My sister's going home this afternoon," she said.

"No," I said, "Oh, no," and ran past her out of the room.

I guess I had kind of a little breakdown. Anyway, I can't account very well for the time. Which is edge, because the thing I remember most vividly is the feeling that I needed to hurry, that something awful would happen if I didn't hurry.

I know I broke restricks because I remember sitting out under the cottonwoods and thinking what a wonderful sense of humor Old Man Moulton had. He sent up Christmas lights for the bare cottonwoods, and the cotton and the brittle yellow leaves blew against them and caught fire. The smell of burning was everywhere. I remember thinking clearly, smokes and fires, how appropriate for Christmas in Hell.

But when I tried to think about the tessels, about what to do, the thoughts got all muddy and confused, like I'd taken too much float. Sometimes it was Zibet Brown wanted and not Daughter Ann at all, and I would say, "You cut off her hair. I'll never give her back to you. Never." And she would struggle and struggle against him. But she had no claws, no teeth. Sometimes it was the admin, and he would say, "If it's the trust thing you're worried about, I can find out for you," and I would say, "You only want the tessels for yourself." And sometimes Zibet's father said, "I am only trying to protect you. Come to Papa." And I would climb up on the bunk to unscrew the intercom but I couldn't shut him up. "I don't need protecting," I would say to him. Zibet would struggle and struggle.

A dangling bit of cotton had stuck to one of the Christmas lights. It caught fire and dropped into the brown broken leaves. The smell of smoke was everywhere. Somebody should report that. Hell could burn down, or was it burn up, with nobody here over Christmas break. I should tell somebody. That was it, I had to tell somebody. But there was nobody to tell. I wanted my father. And he wasn't there. He had never been there. He had paid his money, spilled his juice, and thrown me to the wolves. But at least he wasn't one of them. He wasn't one of them.

There was nobody to tell. "What did you do to it?" Arabel said. "Did you give it something? Samurai? Float? Alcohol?"

"I didn't . . ."

"Consider yourself on restricks."

"It isn't beasties," I said. "They call them Baby Dear and Daughter Ann. And they're the fathers. They're the fathers. But the tessels don't have any claws. They don't have any teeth. They don't even know what jig-jig is."

"He has her best interests at heart," Arabel said.

"What are you talking about? He cut off all her hair. You should have seen her, hanging onto the wallplate for dear life! She struggled and struggled, but it didn't do any good. She doesn't have any claws. She doesn't have any teeth. She's only fifteen. We have to hurry."

"It'll all be over by midterms," Arabel said. "I can fix you up. Guaranteed no trusters."

I was standing in the dorm mother's Skinner box, pounding on her door. I did not know how I had gotten there. My face looked back at me from the dorm mother's mirrors. Arabel's face: strained and desperate. Flashing red and white and red again like an alert band: my roommate's face. She would not believe me. She would put me on restricks. She would have me expelled. It didn't matter. When she answered the door, I could not run. I had to tell somebody before the whole place caught on fire.

"Oh, my dear," she said, and put her arms around me.

* * *

I knew before I opened the door that Zibet was sitting on my bunk in the dark. I pressed the wallplate and kept my bandaged hand on it, as if I might need it for support. "Zibet," I said. "Everything's going to be all right. The dorm mother's going to confiscate the tessels. They're going to outlaw animals on campus. Everything will be all right."

She looked up at me. "I sent it home with her," she said.

"What?" I said blankly.

"He won't . . . leave us alone. He—I sent Daughter Ann home with her."

No. Oh, no.

"Henra's good like you. She won't save herself. She'll never last the two years." She looked steadily at me. "I have two other sisters. The youngest is only ten."

"You sent the tessel home?" I said. "To your *father*?"

"Yes."

"It can't protect itself," I said. "It doesn't have any claws. It can't protect itself."

"I told you you didn't know anything about sin," she said, and turned away.

I never asked the dorm mother what they did with the tessels they took away from the boys. I hope, for their own sakes, that somebody put them out of their misery.

In the Realm of the Heart, In the World of the Knife

by Wayne Wightman

Introduction

Wayne Wightman was first discovered when he published sto-ries in Elinor Mavor's Amazing. *Since that magazine was barely clinging to life at the time, his work was barely noticed, and there followed several years when he published nothing in the field of science fiction.*

When he was rediscovered by Ed Ferman, and his stories started appearing in F&SF *in the mid-eighties, he had made a quantum leap forward. In fact, it was his fiction that brought me back to reading short stories. I had burned out after a couple of years of writing my short-fiction review column for Richard E. Geis's* Science Fiction Review *at the turn of the decade. Months of reading every story published had finally brought me to a point where I couldn't bear to pick up a mag-azine. It felt too much like work. I was no longer a fit audience for the stories these writers had to tell.*

In fact, for several years I stopped reading science fiction altogether. I was working on graduate degrees in literature—I had enough of Milton, Spenser, Joyce, and Thackeray to read that there was no time for contemporary literature, short or long. Until in the middle of a business trip, far from home, I found myself with nothing to read. *This is an unbearable situation. The only store nearby was an all-night grocery, and it happened that there was a lone copy of* Fantasy & Science Fiction *on the magazine rack. Perhaps it had been enough years that I had lost my aversion to the magazines; or perhaps it was simply the fact that the other magazines were things like* Road and Track *and* Biker *and* Professional Wrestling. *Anyway, I bought it, took it to the lonely guest room, and opened it to Wayne Wightman's first story in F&SF.*

It was powerful. It was fresh. It made me realize that I had been missing something during the years I had ignored current sf. And when, in later years, more and more of his stories appeared, his became one of the names I learned to look for. He has yet to disappoint me.

Wightman is a junior-college English teacher. He is also a romantic whose stories confess his belief that individuals can be larger than life, that their decisions can change the world around them. "In the Realm of the Heart" *is perhaps his simplest, plainest tale. Superficially, it's a thriller in an almost timeless milieu. But I don't put stories in this book for superficial reasons.*

OBESE AND SWEATING, ERRIT STATTOR STROLLED SMILING through his outer office, reviewing those who served him. He tried to be humble. The archaic incandescent lighting made his aides look paper-yellow, hollow-eyed, and slack. When he entered those immense and weirdly anachronistic stained-glass doors, all voices ceased, all movement stopped, and in a single motion, everyone stood. They bowed, and as he passed by them, he smiled and nodded.

"Please," he said, "please sit—these formalities . . ."

But they remained standing and bowing. Stattor sighed. "Your devotion impresses me," he said, "but . . . please . . ."

No one sat, and he was impressed, but today, as he reviewed them, smiling, the fat of his cheeks pushed up in tight sweat-sheened balls beneath his eyes, he had more reason to appear pleased than they could know. Today, at 11:00 A.M., Usko Imani was going to be brought to him. She was the last woman who had voluntarily made love to him, and he had not seen her in twenty years, as of today. Seeing her, speaking to her, was to be a sort of anniversary gift to both of them. It was one of the several loose ends in his life that remained to be tied up.

As Stattor crossed through his office, sweat ran in crooked streams out of his scalp, and he smelled of deceased generations of sweat-loving bacteria. It was unfortunate, he knew; he did what he could about it, but nothing helped much. No one mentioned it.

With the yellow light hazing the air, Stattor's two dozen aides remained standing beside their desks, bowed and dead-faced, waiting for him to complete his passage among them.

Supervisor Stattor surveyed the nerve center of his domain, the place where he could order any action on any of twenty thousand worlds, and today he felt not only a peculiar sense of serenity beyond that which he normally experienced, but he also felt one of those increasingly frequent twinges of immortality. It seemed as though something grandly mysterious was about to happen to him. He suspected that it would not happen to him today—but then, it *would* happen, and it *would* be a surprise. . . . And it would be strange and wonderful, and this entire branch of humanity would know of it, because he was Errit Stattor, Supervisor of United Tarassis, and he had opened to mankind the treasures of alien technologies, and he was admired and respected on more worlds than he could comprehend. Without him, they knew and he knew that they would have become backward, a slave race, trashlife.

"Please," he said, "be comfortable. Treat me as anyone else."

No one moved, and Stattor appreciated their devotion.

He nodded and smiled at his personnel and left them in the yellow-aired room. The crystalline door of his private office sensed his presence, opened, and he passed grandly through it.

Alone, he folded forward and clasped his distended guts in his arms. His intestines felt like a tangle of fire, and waves of pain flowed up his legs and pooled in his thighs, reservoirs of agony. Being chain-whipped, he thought, would probably not hurt more. After so many organ replacements, so much reconstructive surgery, and with fifteen or twenty biomechs floating somewhere beneath his tides of fat, with all this, he could not walk far, or sleep well, or think as sharply as he once could. But he no longer needed to.

From a dozen light-years above the hub of the galaxy, in this space station that housed over fourteen thousand workers, he directed the ebb and flow of wealth and workers from world to world, eliminating obstacles and annoyances as this part of humanity moved in a swarming tide across the galaxy.

Stattor forced himself erect. The sight of his office usually soothed him. Standing just inside the doorway, on the carpeted area, where those who came to see him would stand, he relished the awesomeness of his design. The entry area was carpeted with the textured skin of some alien beast or other, but this was just a small part of his vast office, which was inside a transparent blister on one of the non-rotating rings of the station. To approach Stattor's gleaming desk, one had to step onto the thermoplast floor where underfoot, looking close enough to touch, stars and gasses defiled the purity of the void.

When one came to do business with Stattor, to ask his aid or intercession, one felt suspended in space, and Stattor would sit at his shining black desk, smiling, saying, "Please, allow me to help you. Ask what you need." And behind him, through the transparency, the frozen hub of the galaxy was smeared across half the sky. Just above his head and to the right was a globular cluster that looked too perfect to be real. Sitting there, like that, listening and smiling, Stattor listened and judged.

But now he hobbled to his specially designed chair, sank into it, and felt it adjust to him, caress him, comfort and hold him.

He rummaged through one of the desk drawers, pawing over his pharmaceuticals for help with his legs. They had been tingling since he had awakened. His right shoulder felt bruised for some unknown reason, and for three days now, his hands had trembled. There were so many things in the drawer that he knocked it shut and leaned back and tried to breathe deeply. Phlegm rattled in his throat.

He thought of food. Sometimes that helped. He so loved to

eat, to chew, and churn his tongue through the flavors and then to feel them slide down his throat and enter his body. . . .

He had eaten with Usko Imani many times, long ago, in other days. Her fingers were long, delicate, and had wrapped like flower vines around . . .

He thought of food. He knew it was a weakness. Aside from opening up a new world of technology, Stattor loved nothing more than feeling thick sweet creams slicking the insides of his cheeks—or the oily spiciness of rare meat flooding across his tongue and through his mouth. In the privacy of his opulent living quarters, he would sometimes hold in his hand a cluster of some exotic fruit and slowly crush it and drink the cool juices from the cup of his palm. He adored these moments.

His stomach rumbled and burned. He wondered if Usko Imani was as close to death as he was. She had been imprisoned for seventeen years now at a labor camp. Most inmates lived only half that long. Something tickled in Stattor's throat. As he coughed it up and reswallowed it, needles of pain arced from his chest down to his arms. From his tunic he took a beta-blocker and swallowed it dry. When the pain subsided, he reached, without looking, to touch the call button on the autovox. He wanted to call Zallon, his chief aide, to ask about Usko, but his fingers missed the call button completely and fell through empty air.

The autovox had been moved.

Zallon had rearranged the position of the autovox without asking him.

Stattor remembered mentioning two days previously that it sometimes hurt his arm to reach across the desk to it. So Zallon had taken it upon himself to move it to the corner of the desk nearest Stattor's right hand. And he hadn't asked. And, Stattor noticed, in its current position, it blocked his view through the curved plastic bubble of a particularly attractive nebula, the Stattor Nebula. From the comfort of his chair, he could only see the upper right corner of it.

What had Zallon been thinking?

Stattor fumbled his numbed fingers over the face of the autovox and depressed the call button. "Zallon," he said, "come to me."

The door to the outer office instantly irised open and the

chief of staff entered, his flat eyes shrouded in the shadows of
his eye-ridges. His eyelids were very thick, as though he had
some exotic disease. "Yes sir?"

"The autovox . . ." Stattor said, raising his eyebrows and
putting an apologetic smile on his face. "I reached for it, and
. . . it had been moved. I know you must have gone to some
trouble." He imagined that he looked like anyone's uncle.

Zallon's throat convulsed as he swallowed. "If it caused you
any inconvenience, Supervisor, I deeply regret—"

"Is Usko Imani going to be here by eleven?"

"Yes, Supervisor." His shrouded eyes glittered with fear.
"She's on the station now. They're cleaning her up."

"Fine." Stattor smiled pleasantly at Zallon. "Bring me the
dispersal list. I'll look at that before she gets here."

"Yes, Supervisor." Zallon nodded and quickly departed.
The crystalline door irised shut behind him.

Again, Stattor glanced at the repositioned autovox. It completely blocked the lower left corner of his nebula. He deeply
regretted that, and something would have to be done. There
were few pleasures left in his life, and the view from his desk
was one of them. Zallon should have consulted him. Something
should be done.

He leaned back in his chair and it adjusted to him. Lately
he had felt more comfortable alone, much unlike the old days.
In his thoughts he saw the face of Usko Imani, twenty years
ago, when he had last seen her, several years before he had
ordered her arrest and imprisonment at an outer world mining
camp where alien lowlife and criminal humans worked side by
side, clawing chromium ore out of subterranean dirt. Now,
today, he would see her again and have the chat he had planned
for two decades.

Ghostly silent, Zallon returned and moved across the carpeted entryway onto the transparent floor. He laid the list precisely in front of Stattor.

"If my actions have displeased you, Supervisor—"

At the slightest motion of Stattor's head, Zallon left the office, silent as air, the door closing behind him.

Usko Imani had been beautiful. Once they had made love,
and he remembered those moments more clearly than he remembered the day he made himself Supervisor of United Tar-

assis. He remembered her hands and her lips—he remembered the way she laughed and the way, that one time, her hands had touched him.

He fingered the dispersal list, not looking at it, and let his thoughts drift over the early years when she and Stattor and a handful of others had struggled in the corporate courts, suing for the right to borrow technology from alien cultures, and then maneuvering to set up United Tarassis. She had been undeviating in her loyalty and purpose and as idealistic as she had been beautiful. And, in the end, after the tired degenerate government had granted their petition, United Tarassis moved on hundreds of alien worlds, taking what was useful and selling the rest. Finally, United Tarassis had become the government.

He remembered the day of the court's final decision in their favor . . . they had celebrated, he and Usko alone, and without expecting it or knowing what it would lead to, they had made love—for the first and only time. He had been different then. The world had been new and wide and various, and in the unknown he saw beauty and richness and joy.

His eyes stopped on the repositioned autovox. He wondered what other action Zallon might be capable of without telling him.

He gazed at the list lying on the desk before him . . . the dispersal list . . . it consisted of the names of those who no longer functioned effectively in the workings of the corporation. It was a grim task, looking over the names—but he did it, sparing some nameless underling the guilt of passing the names on to the Action Committee. But Stattor was used to it. These were the names of the unreliable and the potentially unreliable who would be sedated and shot into the core of the space station where their component molecules would separate and give up their energies to power the station's lights for several evenings, provide heat and comfort and enable the work of probing distant worlds to go on. Here, nothing was wasted.

He usually gave the lists only a cursory glance and then forwarded them to the Action Committee. It was his prerogative, of course, to put a checkmark beside the name of any person he decided to exempt from execution.

Most of the manes were unfamiliar. Blisson, E., . . . Lanyon, R., . . . Blodian, A.

Aros Blodian was on the list? Stattor remembered him from twenty or more years ago. He and Usko and a dozen others had worked for the same goals, for the advancement of humankind through the use of alien resources. But then . . . Stattor vaguely remembered ordering Blodian to be confined for some reason or other—but the recollection was unclear. And now one of the Division heads was asking for Blodian's dispersal.

Stattor turned his chair to face the galaxy-smeared void. Those old days always seemed warm and fragrant when Stattor thought of them, and for a few moments, the constriction in his chest loosened and he could breathe easier. Blodian had been one of the inner members of the movement until . . . until what?

Stattor gazed above the glow of the galaxy's hub into the emptiness and remembered one evening in particular, sitting with Aros beside a rippled lake, the purple sky paling to a cream color over the rounded mountains. They had been discussing the construction of probe stations like the one in which Stattor now sat and meditated on the loose ends of his life.

He and Aros were on a planet that had evolved only vegetation, and there, amid the tree-ferns and thick-leafed shrubs, beside the warm water of the lake, they had felt comfortable to sit without much talking and to listen to the water lap at the pebbled shore. The air had been rich with the smells of earth, and for the moment, everything was beauty, quiet, and pleasure.

And Usko had been there, he remembered suddenly. Yes, Usko had been there, and he remembered her laughing—she had come up from the shore, laughing and carrying a thick bouquet of colorful weeds. How strange that he should remember such details now, from so long ago and so far away, from such an ancient evening.

Stattor took up a pen and started to place a checkmark next to Blodian's name. For old times' sake. He had been a friend. And now he was probably old and gnarled and with none of the fire he had had in former days when he would take on the most dangerous of schemes, and through courage alone, force them to success.

The autovox chirped.

Stattor reached for it, without looking, and his hand dropped through the air, touching nothing. He glared at the machine.

"What," he said, barely parting his teeth when he spoke.

Zallon's voice was restrained. "Usko Imani has arrived, Supervisor."

Stattor inhaled deeply. His stomach rumbled and his back ached. What would she think of him? Would she recoil at his fatness? He wanted her to like him. Would she be gray and old and unrecognizable?

Stattor tried to calm himself by gazing again into space.

The churning hub of the galaxy lay frozen before him. It seemed as though it had paused for the period of his lifetime so he could look upon it, become familiar with it, and use it for humankind. Years ago, he could stare at those trailing billows of stars for hours, but, now, in truth, the part he most liked to look upon was the area above the galaxy, beyond the sprinkle of globular clusters, higher up, where there was darkness, emptiness, and only the occasional blemish of a distant smear of stars. The smoothness of the black, the absence of matter, of life, those were the things that now appealed to him. Something grand approached.

Stattor turned his chair back to face the door from the waiting room, positioned his feet beneath his weight, braced his hands on his desk, and stood.

In the instant before he spoke to the autovox, he thought of her lips and hands, of how once she had looked at him and how once she had touched him. . . .

"Send her in," he said.

In the several seconds before the door irised open, he started to feel oppressed by the heaviness of his body, and he felt the rolls of fat pressing against each other around his neck and around his stomach. A dozen pains sparkled in his ankles, and it was no wonder, he thought, that his body was trying so desperately to die.

The door opened.

Usko Imani had been a square-shouldered, strong-bodied woman with long, tight-curled blond hair, a woman whose footing on the earth had been as solid as her belief in Stattor and the blending of alien and human technologies. As long as Stattor had known her, all those years, he had never suspected that she ever felt any doubt about what she was doing or her purpose in the world. When it came to her belief in utilizing alien ways, she never hesitated, whatever it cost her.

But now she hesitated. She stood in the doorway, stooped and gray-skinned, her hair a thinning shag of frizz across parts of her scalp. Inside the person who stood on the carpeted entryway, staring at the transparent floor before her, Stattor could detect only the faintest ghost of who she had been.

She glanced to either side of the doorway, then across to Stattor, and then behind him at the shimmering hub of the galaxy.

"Come in," he said, gesturing at one of the chairs. "Please."

Tentatively, she moved into the room, placing her feet on the transparent floor, as though she might disturb the universe with her passage. She sat down very slowly, her black prison garb pulling tight at her bony joints. She allowed her gaze to meet his.

Stattor smiled. "It's been a long time," he said. "How many years?"

"Twenty, I guess," she said unsurely. Her voice was gravelly and low and the right side of her mouth drooped when she spoke. She folded her knobby hands on her lap. "A long time."

Stattor lowered his mass into his chair. The pain in his ankles was replaced by a tight compressed feeling in his spine. "A long time," he repeated. "Twenty years, exactly, as of today."

"I didn't know that," she said. "I didn't think I'd see you again."

"Life is mysterious, isn't it? I've been feeling the need to tie up some loose ends," he said. He paused and nodded his head backward at the stars. "Up here, apart from any world, it's easy to forget one's past. By the way, do you remember Aros Blodian? I was thinking of him today."

Her old face looked vaguely surprised. "Of course I remember him. Where is he? Is he here?"

"I was thinking of a time when the three of us were at a lake, it was evening, and you were coming up from the shore. You were laughing. It's kind of a mental snapshot."

She looked at him blankly. "I can't remember."

Stattor shifted in his chair. His stomach burned a little on one side. His hands ached again too. "You probably wonder why I sent you to prison. You hadn't done anything disloyal to United Tarassis."

She nodded. "I wondered," she said slowly, the one side of her mouth dead and unmoving, "but I always understood."

"You understood?"

"Sometimes things have to be done that seem unfair. The individual sometimes has to sacrifice himself in that way, for the benefit of others."

"You never grew bitter? You never cursed me for your years in prison?"

She glanced at the floor, seemed uncomfortable, and moved in her chair with a tired nervousness. "It's because of you that our race has advanced to its position. You led us in the exploration of alien cultures. If my imprisonment helped humankind—and it did, or you wouldn't have put me there—then I have lived my life just as I always wanted."

With one finger, Stattor wiped the sweat out of the fold of skin beside his mouth. "I had forgotten how devoted you were. Tell me what life in prison was like."

"In camp, we got news every week," she said, "so I know what you've accomplished in all these years." She cleared her throat and ran the back of one hand across her temple, as though she were pushing back her short bristly hair. "I was in a support camp on Perda, 37th Sector. It's a cold place." She held out her left hand for him to see the missing fingertips. "We had aliens working in the chromium mines nearby. In my camp, we sewed shirts and pants for them, and in the last six years, we made shoes once every two months. Since we got heaters in a year ago, I could cut out ninety-six pairs of soles a day." She reversed her folded hands. "I have friends there. . . . I haven't been lonely. But it is cold. The ground is frozen most of the year." Her face brightened momentarily. "There're birds there." She shook her head as though chastising herself. "They were insects, but they were so big we thought of them as birds. Two weeks a year, in the warm season, they migrate south, and they sing." She looked weakened, haggard and old, but she did not look unhappy. "In ways

I don't understand, my imprisonment served the higher destiny of mankind. I'm not bitter.''

"You suffered," Stattor said.

"Everyone suffers.''

"Have I suffered?" Stattor said, spreading his arms at the stars.

"You guided us." Her voice was firm. "Without you, we would still be in our provincial human backwater, weak and struggling for any step of progress.''

Stattor leaned forward on his desk. He was smiling. The desk creaked under his weight. "You no longer have to suffer, Usko. I've set up a physical rehabilitation program for you, and when you've recovered, you'll be given living quarters on the world of your choosing, transportation privileges wherever you want to go, and an allotment of 500,000 credits a year.''

She stared at him, and it seemed that for a full half minute she did not register what he had said.

"How much did they pay you on Perda?" he asked.

She swallowed heavily, her chin dipping as she did so. "They put 200 a year into an account for each of us.''

"And how much have you earned so far?"

She shook her head helplessly. "I can't figure like that anymore.''

"You may not know," Stattor said, "there's a severance tax of 28 percent. A prisoner who completes his sentence is required to pay for the food he has eaten." He smiled. "The severance tax was my idea.''

"If it hadn't been necessary for our cause, you wouldn't have done it.''

Stattor shook his head. This was the Usko Imani of his memories. When he had doubts, he had only to speak to her; her vision was intensely single-minded, sincere, and idealistic. She was unique. In part, that was why he had sent her to Perda.

"Would you like a drink?" Stattor asked suddenly.

"I haven't had a drink in—''

He pressed the call button and said to Zallon. "Bring Ms. Imani a gin and lemon." Stattor turned back to Usko and said. "That was your favorite drink. I remember. Perhaps you'll still have a taste for it." He leaned back in his chair. "No one was ever more dedicated to our cause than you. I admired you. I envied you for that. I remember a justice named Kudensa, a skinny, reactionary low-grade. . . . Do you remember him?''

She shook her head.

"You volunteered to bed him, to get information, although we knew what he would put you through."

Still, she was shaking her head.

"I remember it took eight weeks for you to recover."

She looked blank. "Did I get the information?"

Stattor nodded. "You did." He thought he saw her face start to relax.

Zallon entered with a tray, from which he took the cloudy yellow drink and placed it in Usko's hands with a linen napkin. Without a sound, the aide left the office.

"It was very loyal of you to do that," Stattor said.

"I don't remember it. It couldn't have hurt me badly. The good of humankind is important. I've served that."

"You're the only person who could say that that I would believe. That's why I put you in prison."

She had her drink halfway to her lips—her gnarled hands stopped there.

"Because of your idealism," Stattor explained. "That's why you spent twenty years in prison."

"I don't understand."

Stattor shrugged and sipped his drink. "Let's talk about the old days for a minute. Do you remember the Setback? When we lost nearly all of our secret council?"

Her face went suddenly grim. "I remember. On Perda, every year, we have half a day off to remember and study the works of those we lost. And to read the story of Kenda Dean, the informer."

"You knew Kenda well, didn't you?"

"I never suspected he could do such a thing—or that the government had been paying him the whole time. I accept it now, but I never understood it."

"You never understood it because he didn't do it. *I* did it. *I* informed."

She looked at him as though he were still speaking. Then, suddenly, she laughed, and he remembered how, long ago, she had laughed. He remembered her lips as she had come up from the lakeside. He remembered her hands and he remembered the morning they had awakened in each other's arms.

"It's true," he said. "I informed on them all."

"You didn't. You couldn't have."

"The government police had been paying me for almost a year prior to that. I used the police to eliminate opposition to my chairmanship of the movement."

"You couldn't—"

"I did it for myself. I have always done everything for myself."

"This is some kind of test," she said. "You're testing me in some clever way. You could never do such a thing. You've led the human race to dominance in the galaxy. You've devoted your life to—"

"To the acquisition of power," he said. "I did it for myself."

"I won't believe this."

"Believe it. I did it because I wanted everything, and everything is mine now." He grinned. "Everything. You're mine."

"That isn't true, It's a lie, a test."

"It isn't wise, Usko, to tell Supervisor Stattor that he is lying. Normally, those who accuse me of lying are thrown into the core of the station. He smiled a bit more fiercely. "Then we can turn our thermostats up a few degrees."

"You couldn't have done that."

"If you don't tell me that you believe me, Usko, you'll be back cutting out your ninety-six pieces of shoe leather before the day is over. You'll do it till you die." He paused. "By the way, do you know where your 'leather' comes from?"

"Animals," she said tentatively.

"If you think your supervisor is incapable of betrayal and cruelty, I'll tell you where your shoe leather comes from." He waited for her response, but she said nothing. He leaned forward and the desk creaked under his weight. "Do you believe me?"

"Whatever you did, you did for the advancement of knowledge and for the security of the human race."

"I did it because I don't like competition, either from humans or trashlife. I had your friends butchered because they were in my way."

"You can't make me believe this," she said firmly. She sat up straighter and reached forward to put her drink on the edge of his desk. "We all sacrificed for our people, not for ourselves. I knew you well."

"You never knew me," he said. He leaned back and laced his fingers over his rolled stomach. For a moment, he seemed to be chewing something. "You're overburdened with misinformation. Let me clarify your situation. You have a choice. You can tell me that you believe me—that I informed on your friends and as a result they were sliced. Then you can walk out of here, have a warm place to live, and 500,000 credits a year. Or you can believe that this is a test, that Supervisor Stattor is lying to you, and *that*, Usko, is treason. For treason, you will spend the rest of your life dying on Perda, cutting shoe soles out of 'leather'."

Whatever small thing Stattor had sucked out of his teeth, he swallowed.

"Well?" he asked.

Her age, her fear, and her dread pushed her deeper into her chair. She had lowered her head and Stattor could see the dry frizzy hair that grew there in erratic patches.

She looked up. Above the mouth that was twisted by paralysis, her eyes sparkled as though they were filled with chips of silver. "You brought me here to offer me comfort and disgrace or a slow death for a wasted life. Why?"

"I'm an insecure man. I sleep better when I know that others operate from self-interest. Your idealism makes me . . . uneasy." Stattor smiled. "When you accept my offer of generosity, you'll be as corrupt as the rest of us. There's no reason for you to go back to prison now, because the ideal you sacrificed for was an illusion."

"You're taking the one thing . . ."

Stattor smiled even harder. "And we used to think human nature was so damned mysterious." He pressed the call button on the autovox and Zallon entered immediately. "See that Ms. Imani has priority transportation to the rehabilitation center. Her welfare is of special importance to me."

"I understand."

"That's gratifying," Stattor said.

As Zallon helped her out of her chair, she said, "If I were strong enough to use these hands—"

"We mustn't let our lives be spoiled with regrets," Stattor said pleasantly.

As Zallon helped Usko through the door, she looked back once, it was just a glimpse, and Stattor was reminded of the other reason he had sent her to prison. It happened so many years ago, when they had awakened in each other's arms. She had slept so beautifully, her smooth, translucent eyelids closed over her quiet eyes—and then she had awakened and her eyes had opened suddenly and she had looked at him. There, wrapped in the sheets, with the morning sun streaming across the room, she had looked at him with that same expression— a kind of horrified surprise.

The door irised shut behind them, and Stattor nodded to himself. Yes, it was probably at that moment, with the sun filling the room—and he remembered there was a bowl of or-anges on a table, radiant with sunlight—it was at that moment that he decided that some way, somehow, he would do this to her, and not long after that he began giving information to the government police.

So now it had all worked out. The loose end was tied to everything else.

He swept his hand across the lower part of his stomach. He did not feel so bad now. Neither his arms nor his legs ached, and his stomach did not seem filled with bile.

Stattor turned in his chair and gazed out the transparent bub-ble at the churning hub of the galaxy and then at his globular cluster. But beyond those stars, in the textureless black, there was what drew his eyes. When he looked into it, he almost felt his soul drawn out of his bloated and diseased body and sent into a place where there was neither light nor matter nor decay nor care.

The autovox chirped.

"Supervisor," Zallon's voice said gently, "there is the mat-ter of the dispersal list."

Stattor grunted and spun his chair to face the desk again. The list lay there, face up, awaiting his final decision whether or not to exempt any of the condemned. He thought of Aros waiting in some detention cell, old, haggard, half dead, and then he thought of himself and Usko, there beside the lake, so long ago. She had brought a bouquet of colored weeds up from the shoreline, and Aros had stood up, laughing, his arms wide to receive her—

His eyes stopped on the autovox.

Zallon had overstepped his limits. Stattor could barely see the green blossom of his nebula behind it. His emotionless aide, that sunken-eyed reptile, never revealed his feelings about anything, so how could he be trusted? He was an unknown.

Excepting no one from execution, Stattor pushed the list away from him. He had never liked Aros. Nor Zallon. With his fatted hand, Stattor retrieved the list and entered Zallon's name at the bottom. One way or another, so many people tried to stand in his way, to annoy him, or to prevent the grand and mysterious thing that was about to happen to him. It was very close. He could feel it come nearer every hour.

For a moment, his stomach did not burn and the beta-blocker made his life easier. He leaned back in his chair and again turned to face the absorbing blackness beyond the galaxy, and he was content to know that soon, so very soon, his flesh would turn to myth.

Rat

by James Patrick Kelly

Introduction

You wouldn't know it from this story, but James Patrick Kelly is a gentle man. I met him at the first Sycamore Hill Writers Workshop, and one of the reasons I look forward to returning each year is that I will see him again. We have not become friends in the social sense, but in the emotionally charged community that forms around that workshop table, Kelly is the ground, the place where all the sparks are gathered in and brought to earth. There are no fools at Sycamore Hill; Kelly is not the only wise critic in the group. His gift is to understand what the author is trying to do, and see where, in the structure of the story, the author has kept himself from succeeding. His criticism is frank, but never brutal. Even as he tells you how desperately this draft of your story has failed, Kelly also implicitly assures you that success is possible; the tale is worth telling; and if you only follow up this abandoned thread, drop this digression, show this scene and summarize that one, the tale will work. At the end, you never feel like a victim. Instead you're full of hope, eager to discover what the new draft will be.

Kelly does all this without posture or importunity. Nothing's more obnoxious at a workshop than a participant—usually the least gifted critic, alas—who attempts to summarize what everyone else has said and offer the final word on what the author ought to do. And nothing's more tempting, as a critic, than to try to argue forcefully for your point of view, as if you had a stake in how the author finally decides to revise his work. I've never seen Kelly do either. And yet, when he's through, you often feel as if he has reached to the crux of the story, the fulcrum on which all else will balance easily; and even though he speaks mildly, not attempting to bully you into seeing things his way, his vision of your story is always so clear that you are invariably persuaded.

In fact, if Kelly didn't have such an outstanding career as a writer, he could easily make a living as a story doctor, coming to the rescue when some other author is baffled by his story's failure. That's how George S. Kaufman got his name on half the best American comedies of the 1930s—it's too bad for us that most of us authors aren't humble enough to know when it's time to cry out for help!

I believe, though, that Kelly's gifts as a critic are founded, not in his intellect or talent or experience, but rather in his soul. He is intelligent, but so are many others; he is talented, but talent is cheap; he has experience, but so does everyone whoever wrote a Sweet Valley Twins installment. Kelly is a fundamentally charitable man, in the best and highest sense of that word. He approaches other people with unstinting love, hoping to receive their best, eager to understand their intent, ready to help them along the path. It is that attitude toward other people that gives him the ability to see to the heart of their stories—for authors, wittingly or not, put their souls into every tale they tell. I feel, whenever Kelly reads and responds to a manuscript I lay on the workshop table, that he has found my most secret self within those pages; that he has found me, not monstrous, but acceptable; that if I will only trust him, he can lead me out of the labyrinth of my own confusion and doubt.

Does my language sound, perhaps, overemotional? A good writers workshop is a time of heightened emotion, and Sycamore Hill is the best I've heard of, the best I've seen. I have shouted and been shouted at; I have slashed and been attacked in turn; tears are shed at that table, and some of them have been mine. When we leave after a week of such intensity, the mem-

*ory fades, our relationships calm down and assume normal
proportions. But during that week, we are stripped of our bark
like trees awaiting a graft. Many a public façade is stripped
away; latent paranoia blossoms; some wounds inflicted there
are so deep they never seem to heal. Under such circumstances, Jim Kelly is invariably revealed to be even kinder,
even more perceptive, even wiser than he seemed before.*

*One of the delights of writing this introduction is that every-
thing I've said, while true, leaves you absolutely unprepared
for the story you're about to read. "Rat," if filmed, would
make* Miami Vice *seem languid; would make* Bladerunner's
*city seem to be a kinder, gentler place. There are other stories
that I might have chosen, stories that would clearly show you
the James Patrick Kelly I have just described. But that would
be playing fair.*

Rᴀᴛ ʜᴀᴅ sᴛᴀsʜᴇᴅ ᴛʜᴇ ᴅᴜsᴛ ɪɴ ꜰᴏᴜʀ ᴘʟᴀsᴛɪᴄ ᴄᴀᴘsᴜʟᴇs ᴀɴᴅ
then swallowed them. From the stinging at the base of his ribs,
he guessed they were now squeezing into his duodenum. Still
plenty of time. The bullet train had been shooting though the
vacuum of the TransAtlantic tunnel for almost two hours now;
they would arrive at Port Authority/Koch soon. Customs had
already been fixed, according to the maréchal. All Rat had to
do was to get back to his nest, lock the smart door behind him,
and put the word out on his protected nets. He had enough
Algerian Yellow to dust at least half the cerebrums on the East
Side. If he could turn this deal, he would be rich enough to
bathe in Dom Perignon and dry himself with Gromaire tapes-
tries. Another pang shot down his left flank. Instinctively his
hind leg came off the seat and scratched at air.

There was only one problem; Rat had decided to cut the
maréchal out. That meant he had to lose the old man's spook
before he got home.

The spook had attached herself to him at Marseilles. She
braided her blonde hair in pigtails. She had freckles, wore
braces on her teeth. Tiny breasts nudged a modest silk turtle-

neck. She looked to be between twelve and fourteen. Cute. She had probably looked that way for twenty years, would stay the same another twenty if she did not stop a slug first or get cut in half by some automated security laser that tracked only heat and could not read—or be troubled by—cuteness. Their passports said they were Mr. Sterling Jaynes and daughter Jessalynn, of Forest Hills, New York. She was typing in her notebook, chubby fingers curled over the keys. Homework? A letter to a boyfriend? More likely she was operating on some corporate database with scalpel code of her own devising.

"Ne fais pas semblant d'étudier, ma petite," Rat said, *"Que fais-tu?"*

"Oh, Daddy," she said, pouting, "can't we go back to plain old English? After all, we're almost home." She tilted her notebook so that he could see the display. It read: "Two rows back, second seat from aisle. Fed. If he knew you were carrying, he'd cut the dust out of you and wipe his ass with your pelt." She tapped the Return key, and the message disappeared.

"All right, dear." He arched his back, fighting a surge of adrenaline that made his incisors click. "You know, all of a sudden I feel hungry. Should we do something here on the train or wait until we get to New York?" Only the spook saw him gesture back toward the fed.

"Why don't we wait for the station? More choice there."

"As you wish dear." He wanted her to take the fed out *now*, but there was nothing more he dared say. He licked his hands nervously and groomed the fur behind his short, thick ears to pass the time.

The International Arrivals Hall at Koch Terminal was unusually quiet for a Thursday night. It smelled to Rat like a setup. The passengers from the bullet shuffled through the echoing marble vastness toward the row of customs stations. Rat was unarmed; if they were going to put up a fight, the spook would have to provide the firepower. But Rat was not a fighter, he was a runner. Their instructions were to pass through Station Number Four. As they waited in line, Rat spotted the federally appointed vigilante behind them. The classic invisible man: neither handsome nor ugly, five-ten, about one-seventy, brown hair, dark suit, white shirt. He looked bored.

"Do you have anything to declare?" The customs agent looked bored, too. Everybody looked bored except Rat, who had two million new dollars' worth of illegal drugs in his gut and a fed ready to carve them out of him.

"We hold these truths to be self-evident," said Rat, "that all men are created equal." He managed a feeble grin—as if this were a witticism and not the password.

"Daddy, please!" The spook feigned embarrassment. "I'm sorry, ma'am; it's his idea of a joke. It's the Declaration of Independence, you know."

The customs agent smiled as she tousled the spook's hair. "I know that, dear. Please put your luggage on the conveyor." She gave a perfunctory glance at her monitor as their suitcases passed through the scanner, and then nodded at Rat. "Thank you, sir, and have a pleasant . . ." The insincere thought died on her lips as she noticed the fed pushing through the line toward them. Rat saw her spin toward the exit at the same moment that the spook thrust her notebook computer into the scanner. The notebook stretched a blue finger of point discharge toward the magnetic lens just before the overhead lights novaed and went dark. The emergency backup failed as well. Rat's snout filled with the acrid smell of electrical fire. Through the darkness came shouts and screams, thumps and cracks—the crazed pounding of a stampede gathering momentum.

He dropped to all fours and skittered across the floor. Koch Terminal was his territory. He had crisscrossed its many levels with scent trails. Even in total darkness he could find his way. But in his haste he cracked his head against a pair of stockinged knees, and a squawking weight fell across him, crushing the breath from his lungs. He felt an icy stab on his hindquarters and scrabbled at it with his hind leg. His toes came away wet and he squealed. There was an answering scream, and the point of a shoe drove into him, propelling him across the floor. He rolled left and came up running. Up a dead escalator, down a carpeted hall. He stood upright and stretched to his full twenty-six inches, hands scratching until they found the emergency bar across the fire door. He hurled himself at it, a siren shrieked, and with a whoosh the door opened, dumping him into an alley. He lay there for a moment, gasping, half in and half out of Koch Terminal. With the certain knowledge that he was bleeding to death, he touched the coldness on his back. A sticky purple substance; he sniffed, then tasted it. Ice cream.

Rat threw back his head and laughed. The high squeaky sound echoed in the deserted alley.

But there was no time to waste. He could already hear the buzz of police hovers swooping down from the night sky. The blackout might keep them busy for a while; Rat was more worried about the fed. And the spook. They would be out soon enough, looking for him. Rat scurried down the alley toward the street. He glanced quickly at the terminal, now a black hole in the galaxy of bright holographic sleaze that was Forty-second Street. A few cops with flashlights were trying to fight against the flow of panicky travelers pouring from its open doors. Rat smoothed his ruffled fur and turned away from the disaster, walking crosstown. His instincts said to run, but Rat forced himself to dawdle like a hick shopping for big-city excitement. He grinned at the pimps and windowshopped the hardware stores. He paused in front of a pair of mirror-image sex stops—GIRLS! LIVE! GIRLS! and LIVE! GIRLS! LIVE!—to sniff the pheromone-scented sweat pouring off an androgynous robot shill that was working the sidewalk. The robot obligingly put its hand to Rat's crotch, but he pushed it away with a hiss and continued on. At last, sure that he was not being followed, he powered up his wallet and tapped into the transnet to summon a hovercab. The wallet informed him that the city had cordoned off midtown airspace to facilitate rescue operations at Koch Terminal. It advised trying the subway or a taxi. Since he had no intention of sticking an ID chip—even a false one!—into a subway turnstile, he stepped to the curb and began watching the traffic.

The rebuilt Checker that rattled to a stop beside him was a patchwork of orange ABS and stainless-steel armor. "No we leave Manhattan," said a speaker on the roof light. "No we north of a hundred and ten." Rat nodded and the door locks popped. The passenger compartment smelled of chlorobenzyl-malononitrile and urine.

"First Avenue Bunker," said Rat, sniffing. "Christ, it stinks back here. Who was your last fare—the circus?"

"Troubleman." The speaker connections were loose, giving a scratchy edge to the cabbie's voice. The locks reengaged as the Checker pulled away from the curb. "Ha-has get a fulls-noot of tear gas in this hack."

Rat had already spotted the pressure vents in the floor. He peered through the gloom at the registration. A slogan had been lased in over it—probably by one of the new Mitsubishi penlights. "Free the dead." Rat smiled: the dead were his customers. People who had chosen the dust road. Twelve to eighteen months of glorious addiction: synthetic orgasms, recursive hallucinations leading to a total sensory overload and an ecstatic death experience. One dose was all it took to start down the dust road. The feds were trying to cut off the supply—with dire consequences for the dead. They could live a few months longer without dust, but their joyride down the dusty road was transformed into a grueling marathon of withdrawal pangs and madness. Either way, they were dead. Rat settled back onto the seat. The penlight graffito was a good omen. He reached into his pocket and pulled out a leather strip that had been soaked with a private blend of fat-soluble amphetamines and began to gnaw at it.

From time to time he could hear the cabbie monitoring NYPD net for flameouts or wildcat tolls set up by street gangs. They had to detour to heavily guarded Park Avenue all the way uptown to Fifty-ninth before doubling back toward the bunker. Originally built to protect U.N. diplomats from terrorists, the bunker had gone condo after the dissolution of the United Nations. Its hype was that it was the "safest address in the city." Rat knew better, which is why he had had a state-of-the-art smart door installed. Its rep was that most of the owners' association were candidates either for a mindwipe or an extended vacation on a fed punkfarm.

"Hey, Fare," said the cabbie, "Net says the dead be rioting front of your door. Crash through or roll away?"

The fur along Rat's backbone went erect. "Cops?"

"Letting them play for now."

"You've got armor for a crash?"

"Shit, yes. Park this hack to ground zero for the right fare." The cabbie's laugh was static. "Don't worry, bunkerman. Give those deadboys a shot of old CS gas and they be too busy scratching they eyes out to bother us much."

Rat tried to smooth his fur. He could crash the riot and get stuck. But if he waited, either the spook or the fed would be stepping on his tail before long. Rat had no doubt that both had managed to plant locator bugs on him.

" 'Course, riot crashing don't come cheap," said the cabbie.

"Triple the meter." The fare was already over two hundred dollars for the fifteen-minute ride. "Shoot for Bay Two—the one with the yellow door." He pulled out his wallet and started tapping its luminescent keys. "I'm sending recognition code now."

He heard the cabbie notify the cops that they were coming through. Rat could feel the Checker accelerate as they passed the cordon, and he had a glimpse of strobing lights, cops in blue body armor, a tank studded with water cannons. Suddenly the cabbie braked, and Rat pitched forward against his shoulder harness. The Checker's solid rubber tires squealed, and there was the thump of something bouncing off the hood. They had slowed to a crawl, and the dead closed around them.

Rat could not see out the front because the cabbie was protected from his passengers by steel plate. But the side windows filled with faces streaming with sweat and tears and blood. Twisted faces, screaming faces, faces etched by the agonies of withdrawal. The soundproofing muffled their howls. Fear and exhilaration filled Rat as he watched them pass. If only they knew how close they were to dust, he thought. He imagined the dead faces gnawing through the cab's armor in a frenzy, pausing only to spit out broken teeth. It was wonderful. The riot was proof that the dust market was still white-hot. The dead must be desperate to attack the bunker like this looking for a flash. He decided to bump the price of his dust another ten percent.

Rat heard a clatter on the roof; then someone began to jump up and down. It was like being inside a kettledrum. Rat sank claws into the seat and arched his back. "What are you waiting for? Gas them, damn it!"

"Hey, Fare. Stuff ain't cheap. We be fine—almost there."

A woman with bloody red hair matted to her head pressed her mouth against the window and screamed. Rat reared up on his hind legs and made biting feints at her. Then he saw the penlight in her hand. At the last moment Rat threw himself backward. The penlight flared, and the passenger compartment filled with the stench of melting plastic. A needle of coherent light singed the fur on Rat's left flank; he squealed and flopped onto the floor, twitching.

The cabbie opened the external gas vents, and abruptly the faces dropped away from the windows. The cab accelerated, bouncing as it ran over the fallen dead. There was a dazzling transition from the darkness of the violent night to the floodlit calm of Bay Number Two. Rat scrambled back onto the seat and looked out the back window in time to see the hydraulic doors of the outer lock swing shut. Something was caught between them—something that popped and spattered. The inner door rolled down on its track like a curtain coming down on a bloody final act.

Rat was almost home. Two security guards in armor approached. The door locks popped, and Rat climbed out of the cab. One of the guards leveled a burster at his head; the other wordlessly offered him a printreader. He thumbed it, and bunker's computer verified him immediately.

"Good evening, sir," said one of the guards. "Little rough out there tonight. Did you have luggage?"

The front door of the cab opened, and Rat heard the low whine of electric motors as a mechanical arm lowered the cabbie's wheelchair onto the floor of the bay. She was a gray-haired woman with a rheumy stare who looked like she belonged in a rest home in New Jersey. A knitted shawl covered her withered legs. "You said triple." The cab's hoist clicked and released the chair; she rolled toward him. "Six hundred and sixty-nine dollars."

"No luggage, no." Now that he was safe inside the bunker, Rat regretted his panic-stricken generosity. A credit transfer from one of his own accounts was out of the question. He slipped his last thousand-dollar bubble chip into his wallet's card reader, dumped $331 from it into a Bahamian laundry loop, and then dropped the chip into her outstretched hand. She accepted it dubiously: for a minute he expected her to bite into it like they did sometimes on fossil TV. Old people made him nervous. Instead she inserted the chip into her own card reader and frowned at him.

"How about a tip?"

Rat sniffed. "Don't pick up strangers."

One of the guards guffawed obligingly. The other pointed, but Rat saw the skunk port in the wheelchair a millisecond too late. With a wet *plot* the chair emitted a gaseous stinkball that bloomed like an evil flower beneath Rat's whiskers. One guard tried to grab at the rear of the chair, but the old cabbie backed suddenly over his foot. The other guard aimed his burster.

The cabbie smiled like a grandmother from hell. "Under the pollution index. No law against sharing a little scent, boys. And you wouldn't want to hurt me anyway. The hack monitors my EEG. I go flat and it goes berserk."

The guard with the bad foot stopped hopping. The guard with the gun shrugged. "It's up to you, sir."

Rat batted the side of his head several times and then buried his snout beneath his armpit. All he could smell was rancid burger topped with sulphur sauce. "Forget it. I haven't got time."

"You know," said the cabbie. "I never get out of the hack, but I just wanted to see what kind of person would live in a place like this." The lifts whined as the arm fitted its fingers into the chair. "And now I know." She cackled as the arm gathered her back into the cab. "I'll park it by the door. The cops say they're ready to sweep the street."

The guards led Rat to the bank of elevators. He entered the one with the open door, thumbed the print-reader, and spoke his access code.

"Good evening, sir," said the elevator. "Will you be going straight to your rooms?"

"Yes."

"Very good, sir. Would you like a list of the communal facilities currently open to serve you?"

There was no shutting the sales pitch off, so Rat ignored it and began to lick the stink from his fur.

"The pool is open for lap swimmers only," said the elevator as the doors closed. "All environments except for the weightless room are currently in use. The sensory deprivation tanks will be occupied until eleven. The surrogatorium is temporarily out of female chassis; we apologize for any inconvenience . . ."

The cab moved down two and a half floors and then stopped just above the subbasement. Rat glanced up and saw a dark gap opening in the array of light diffuser panels. The spook dropped through it.

". . . the holo therapist is off-line until eight tomorrow

morning, but the interactive sex booths will stay open until midnight. The drug dispensary . . .''

She looked as if she had been water-skiing through the sewer. Her blonde hair was wet and smeared with dirt; she had lost the ribbons from her pigtails. Her jeans were torn at the knees, and there was an ugly scrape on the side of her face. The silk turtleneck clung wetly to her. Yet despite her dishevelment, the hand that held the penlight was as steady as a jewel cutter's.

"There seems to be a minor problem," said the elevator in a soothing voice. "There is no cause for alarm. This unit is temporarily nonfunctional. Maintenance has been notified and is now working to correct the problem. In case of emergency, please contact Security. We regret this temporary inconvenience."

The spook fired a burst of light at the floor selector panel; it spat fire at them and went dark. "Where the hell were you?" said the spook. "You said the McDonald's in Time Square if we got separated."

"Where were *you*?" Rat rose up on his hind legs. "When I got there the place was swarming with cops."

He froze as the tip of the penlight flared. The spook traced a rough outline of Rat on the stainless-steel door behind him. "Fuck your lies," she said. The beam came so close that Rat could smell his fur curling away from it. "I want the dust."

"Trespass alert!" screeched the wounded elevator. A note of urgency had crept into its artificial voice. "Security reports unauthorized persons within the complex. Residents are urged to return immediately to their apartments and engage all personal security devices. Do not be alarmed. We regret this temporary inconvenience."

The scales on Rat's tail fluffed. "We have a deal. The maréchal needs my networks to move his product. So let's get out of here before . . ."

"The dust."

Rat sprang at her with a squeal of hatred. His claws caught on her turtleneck and he struck repeatedly at her open collar, gashing her neck with his long red incisors. Taken aback by the swiftness and ferocity of his attack, she dropped the penlight and tried to fling him against the wall. He held fast, worrying at her and chittering rabidly. When she stumbled under the open emergency exit in the ceiling, he leaped again. He cleared the suspended ceiling, caught himself on the inductor, and scrabbled up onto the hoist cables. Light was pouring into the shaft from above; armored guards had forced the door open and were climbing down toward the stalled car. Rat jumped from the cables across five feet of open space to the counterweight and huddled there, trying to use its bulk to shield himself from the spook's fire. Her stand was short and inglorious. She threw a dazzler out of the hatch, hoping to blind the guards, then tried to pull herself through. Rat could hear the shriek of burster fire. He waited until he could smell the aroma of broiling meat and scorched plastic before he emerged from the shadows and signaled to the security team.

A squad of apologetic guards rode the service elevator with Rat down to the storage subbasement where he lived. When he had first looked at the bunker, the broker had been reluctant to rent him the abandoned rooms, insisting that he live aboveground with the other residents. But all of the suites they showed him were unacceptably open, clean, and uncluttered. Rat much preferred his musty dungeon, where odors lingered in the still air. He liked to fall asleep to the booming of the ventilation system on the level above him, and slept easier knowing that he was as far away from the stink of other people as he could get in the city.

The guards escorted him to the gleaming brass smart door and looked discreetly as he entered his passcode on the keypad. He had ordered it custom-built from Mosler so that it would recognize high-frequency squeals well beyond the range of human hearing. He called to it and then pressed trembling fingers onto the printreader. His bowels had loosened in terror during the firefight, and the capsules had begun to sting terribly. It was all he could do to keep from defecating right there in the hallway. The door sensed the guards and beeped to warn him of their presence. He punched in the override sequence impatiently, and the seals broke with a sigh.

"Have a pleasant evening, sir," said one of the guards as he scurried inside. "And don't worry ab—" The door cut him off as it swung shut.

Against all odds, Rat had made it. For a moment he stood, tail switching against the inside of the door, and let the magnificent chaos of his apartment soothe his jangled nerves. He had earned his reward—the dust was all his now. No one could take it away from him. He saw himself in a shard of mirror propped up against an empty THC aerosol and wriggled in self-congratulation. He was the richest rat on the East Side, perhaps in the entire city.

He picked his way through a maze formed by a jumble of overburdened steel shelving left behind years, perhaps decades, ago. The managers of the bunker had offered to remove them and their contents before he moved in; Rat had insisted that they stay. When the fire inspector had come to approve his newly installed sprinkler system, she had been horrified at the clutter on the shelves and had threatened to condemn the place. It had cost him plenty to buy her off, but it had been worth it. Since then Rat's trove of junk had at least doubled in size. For years no one had seen it but Rat and the occasional cockroach.

Relaxing at last, Rat stopped to pull a mildewed wing tip down from the huge collection of shoes; he loved the bouquet of fine old leather and gnawed and gnawed it whenever he could. Next to the shoes was a heap of books: his private library. One of Rat's favorite delicacies was the first edition of *Leaves of Grass* that he had pilfered from the rare book collection at the New York Public Library. To celebrate his safe arrival, he ripped out page 43 for a snack and stuffed it into the wing tip. He dragged the shoe over a pile of broken sheetrock and past shelves filled with scrap electronics: shattered monitors and dead typewriters, microwaves and robot vacuums. He had almost reached his nest when the fed stepped from behind a dirty Hungarian flag that hung from a broken fluorescent light fixture.

Startled, Rat instinctively hurled himself at the crack in the wall where he had built his nest. But the fed was too quick. Rat did not recognize the weapon; all he knew was that when it hissed, Rat lost all feeling in his hindquarters. He landed in a heap but continued to crawl, slowly, painfully.

"You have something I want." The fed kicked him. Rat skidded across the concrete floor toward the crack, leaving a thin gruel of excrement in his wake. Rat continued to crawl until the fed stepped on his tail, pinning him.

"Where's the dust?"

"I . . . I don't . . ."

The fed stepped again; Rat's left fibula snapped like cheap plastic. He felt no pain.

"The dust." The fed's voice quavered strangely.

"Not here. Too dangerous."

"Where?" The fed released him. "Where?"

Rat was surprised to see that the fed's gun hand was shaking. For the first time he looked up at the man's eyes and recognized the telltale yellow tint. Rat realized then how badly he had misinterpreted the fed's expression back at Koch. Not bored. *Empty.* For an instant he could not believe his extraordinary good fortune. Bargain for time, he told himself. There's still a chance. Even though he was cornered, he knew his instinct to fight was wrong.

"I can get it for you fast if you let me go," said Rat. "Ten minutes, fifteen. You look like you need it."

"What are you talking about?" The fed's bravado started to crumble, and Rat knew he had the man. The fed wanted the dust for himself. He was one of the dead.

"Don't make it hard on yourself," said Rat. "There's a terminal in my nest. By the crack. Ten minutes." He started to pull himself toward the nest. He knew the fed would not dare stop him; the man was already deep into withdrawal. "Only ten minutes and you can have all the dust you want." The poor fool could not hope to fight the flood of neuroregulators pumping crazily across his synapses. He might break any minute, let his weapon slip from trembling hands. Rat reached the crack and scrambled through into comforting darkness.

The nest was built around a century-old shopping cart and a stripped subway bench. Rat had filled the gaps in with pieces of synthetic rubber, a hubcap, plastic greeting cards, barbed wire, disk casings, Baggies, a No Parking sign, and an assortment of bones. Rat climbed in and lowered himself onto the soft bed of shredded thousand-dollar bills. The profits of six years of deals and betrayals, a few dozen murders, and several thousand dusty deaths.

The fed sniffled as Rat powered up his terminal to notify Security. "Someone set me up some vicious bastard slipped it to me I don't know when I think it was Barcelona . . . it would kill Sarah to see . . ." He began to weep. "I wanted to turn myself in . . . they keep working on new treatments you know but it's not fair damn it! The success rate is less than . . . I made my first buy two weeks only two God it seems . . . killed a man to get some lousy dust . . . but they're right it's, it's, I can't begin to describe what it's like . . ."

Rat's fingers flew over the glowing keyboard, describing his situation, the layout of the rooms, a strategy for the assault. He had overridden the smart door's recognition sequence. It would be tricky, but Security could take the fed out if they were quick and careful. Better risk a surprise attack than to dicker with an armed and unraveling dead man.

"I really ought to kill myself . . . would be best but it's not only me . . . I've seen ten-year olds . . . what kind of animal sells dust to kids . . . I should kill myself and you." Something changed in the fed's voice as Rat signed off. "And you." He stooped and reached through the crack.

"It's coming," said Rat quickly. "By messenger. Ten doses. By the time you get to the door, it should be here." He could see the fed's hand and burrowed into the rotting pile of money. "You wait by the door, you hear? It's coming any minute."

"I don't want it." The hand was so large it blocked the light. Rat's fur went erect and he arched his spine. "Keep your fucking dust."

Rat could hear the guards fighting their way through the clutter. Shelves crashed. So clumsy, these men.

"It's you I want." The hand sifted through the shredded bills, searching for Rat. He had no doubt that the fed could crush the life from him—the hand was huge now. In the darkness he could count the lines on the palm, follow the whorls on the fingertips. They seemed to spin in Rat's brain—he was losing control. He realized then that one of the capsules must have broken, spilling a megadose of first-quality Algerian Yellow dust into his gut. With a hallucinatory clarity, he imagined sparks streaming through his blood, igniting neurons like tinder. Suddenly the guards did not matter. Nothing mattered except that he was cornered. When he could no longer fight the instinct to strike, the fed's hand closed around him. The man was stronger than Rat could have imagined. As the fed hauled him—clawing and biting—back into the light, Rat's only thought was of how terrifyingly large a man was. So much larger than a rat.

Vestibular Man
by Felix C. Gotschalk

Introduction

One of the diseases that the academic–literary establishment has brought to American storytelling is elitism. Young writers-to-be rise up through English classes in high school and on to literature courses in college, where they are invariably taught that the truly great literature can only be understood when it has been properly explained by an academic. Thus the young student labors through Moby-Dick and As I Lay Dying years before he is mature enough to understand them—years before he is ready to become part of their natural audience. He learns the obvious lesson that truly great literature is hard to read; that one must work to receive it properly; and because he is too young to grasp the story well enough to respond with strong, immediate emotion, he learns that the proper response of the reader is to admire.

So far, this is simply the accidental by-product of a natural tendency in all teachers—the desire to teach the "best stuff" to students who aren't ready for it. Historians do it, trying to discuss fine points of historiography with undergraduates who don't yet know the difference between the Thirty and the Hundred Years Wars. Mathematicians did it on a national basis

*when the New Math stole basic arithmetic skills from a gener-
ation of baffled American children, who are now terrific at sets
and lousy at deficits.*

*Where the academic–literary establishment becomes perni-
ciously elitist is in their rejection of stories that are* not *difficult.
I have often declared to English teachers my firm belief that*
Gone with the Wind *is the great American novel of the twen-
tieth century, as* Huckleberry Finn *was the great American
novel of the nineteenth. Most ignore me; some get angry; a few,
though, candidly admit that, on my evidence, I might be right.
The story has shown its staying power and its universality; it
deals with themes of poverty, slavery, exploitation, and power
with great honesty and sophistication. Yet these professors invariably say the same thing. "You're right—*Gone with the
Wind *is a very important book. But I can't teach it because I
have nothing to say about it."*

*There it is—the reason for elitism. Professors can only
"teach" the stories that need mediation—the stories that can't
be understood without training. Therefore, only the stories that
need mediation will be taught at the university. But this is never
explained to the students. No, the students are left with the
clear implication—and, often, the explicit statement—that the
stories taught at the university are the only ones* worth *teaching, and therefore the only ones worth* reading; *and, for those
students who have ambitions to become writers themselves, the
only kind of story worth emulating.*

*If in fact the universities and their step-children, the high
schools, taught all the classics, all the stories with staying
power, all the stories that matter, then their position as arbiters
of American literary value might be defensible. But the truth is
just the opposite. Many of the greatest works of American literature, the stories that spoke most deeply and enduringly to
the American soul, are still in print even though they are almost
never required reading for any class. They are read solely by
volunteers. Louisa May Alcott's* Little Women *and* Little Men;
Margaret Mitchell's Gone with the Wind; *Lew Wallace's* Ben-
Hur; *Edgar Rice Burrough's* Tarzan of the Apes; *until recently,
Lloyd Douglas's* The Robe. *Many of these are now dismissed
as "category fiction"—*Ben-Hur *and* The Robe *as religious fiction;* Tarzan *and Alcott's works as children's literature;* Gone

with the Wind *as a "bodice-ripper" or, more politely, a "women's historical romance." Yet all these works have had far more influence on the American mind and soul than anything by Faulkner or Melville, not only because of the sheer numbers of readers—Harold Robbins has probably had more— but also because of the great importance these books have in the memories of their readers.* Little Women *and* Tarzan *and* Gone with the Wind *are thrust into the hands of young readers because their parents or grandparents or librarians or friends have read them and treasured them. These are stories designed, not to be admired, but rather to be experienced and then held in memory forever.*

And so skillful was the artistry of these authors that even after the passage of several generations, the stories can still be received without mediation. In that sense they are still subversive—if these stories were recognized as literature, then we would discover that we did not need professors of literature to teach us how to read. In fact, we would begin to wonder if some of the unreadable books were really so great after all. We might even suspect that the real lesson of Faulkner's and Joyce's experimental fiction is that their experiments did not work, *that after writers of great ability did their best, such stories remained inaccessible, thus proving that these techniques were not viable tools for future storytellers.*

Yet today's academic–literary establishment teaches young writers that the goal of fiction writing is to be admired, not just by anybody, but by critics and professors of the establishment; that great fiction must be written in such a way as to require decoding; that stories that can be immediately apprehended by the reader are inferior—mere "popular literature," beneath the dignity of serious *writers; that good writing must be daring and experimental—but only so long as the experiments fall into time-honored categories, and only so long as the writer does not dare to speak to an audience that has not been properly indoctrinated by the establishment.*

Thus the establishment is able to enroll many talented writers and convince them that their slavish conformity is "revolutionary," that their stylistic self-indulgence is "art," and that the absence of any worthwhile story in their work is a sign that they refuse to pander to the masses. When someone like me accuses such deliberately obscurantist, omphaloskeptic writers of being elitist, however, they immediately howl that I'm trying to make them "conform to one way of writing," when in fact I'm trying to liberate them from their blind, self-destructive conformity and open up the possibility of dialogue with a real live audience of volunteers who might actually read their stories with passion instead of calculation.

But does this mean that every writer who attracts a wide audience is therefore virtuous, and every writer whose audience is small must be elitist? No indeed. What I'm saying is that a good storyteller will never make his story unnecessarily difficult; that a good storyteller will never deform his story by pandering to anyone, be it the mass audience or the academic-literary establishment.

It is inevitable that some of our finest storytellers will have such original vision, such painful or surprising stories to tell, that even when the tale is told with perfect clarity, in exactly the way it must be told, only a few people will be capable of receiving it. Moby-Dick is, in fact, as good as the professors say it is—but it is a book that must be discovered, not forced. When a reader is ready for it, it will be a delight; until then Moby-Dick is difficult, and its rewards often invisible.

Felix Gotschalk can be a difficult writer. This is not because he sets out to be, or because he has been taught that obscurity is a virtue. His stories aren't difficult because he puts barriers in the reader's way, or because he spends all his time on symbolism or style, ignoring the tale itself. On the contrary, he focuses his attention exclusively on the tale, and his style reflects the attitude and voice of the point-of-view character in such a way that story and character are inseparable. Above all, Gotschalk writes with almost supernatural clarity. But Gotschalk's angle of vision is so quirky and strange that it is often hard for the reader to understand what he's seeing—like those super-close-up photographs of common household objects that you can't for the life of you recognize until at last somebody says, "It's a can opener!" or "It's the base of a lightbulb!" Then, of course, you see clearly what it is; you laugh in delight and say, "I never saw it that way before."

I promise you that you have never seen anything the way that Gotschalk sees it. But after reading this story of a man who takes pride in the very fleshiness of his flesh and despises those who have machine parts, you will look at your own body and say, "I never saw it that way before." This is fiction that will change you, if you're ready to receive it.

DEREK CARLSON GREW UP IN THE SUBTROPICAL MARSHLANDS of the deep southern U.S. He had never seen anything more mountainous than a fire-ant mound until he went on a class trip to Old Orleans Park with his group of pubescent age-peers one typical steamy day in late spring of the year 2800. There the boys marveled at the simulated hill, some thirty feet high, constructed in the 1930s, for the half-serious and half-whimsical purpose of letting young children see what a real hill looked like. The Old Orleans area was below sea level, flat and green and mossy as the top of a billiard table, and soggy-springy-resilient, so that digging down as little as a foot or two in the richly impacted loam invariably yielded sulfurous *water*.

For Derek, visual horizons seemed always to be at eye level and higher, a linearity to defer to, to look up at; and for him to stand just below the grassy crest of the levee when the great river was at flood stage was to see threateningly high aquatic horizons, as if the entire earth were awash. It was very much like being at sea.

Derek's vestibular organs were set snugly inboard of his slightly flared ear-funnels, the well protected semicircular canals giving him the comfortable signals of equilibratory quiescence, as well as the infinitely varied topological cues of his precise relationship to his flat spongy home at the bottom of the continent. With low barometric pressure, high heat and humidity, and minimal changes in elevation, Derek's vestibular system had fed him mostly tranquil cues for years. Then puberty school was over, and he was marshaled into warrior training at a camp set high in the Brevard Mountains, a jagged range of new topographic ridges along the famous fault line that had been dormant until the great earthquake of the year 2714. This part of the country was so topographically different from any other part that it triggered an alien sense of fear in Derek, though he had never been there. Now it was to be home for him, at least for a while.

The speeding landskimmer was filled with forty fresh warrior plebes, each young man encapsulated in an impact-neutralizer amniotic sack, and there was a babble of talk as the wedge-shaped skimmer rode on its silicon foils, angled deep down into the energy trough that was now called Azimuth 95, and had been the ancient U.S. Highway 11 that ran from the southwest corner of Virginius all the way to the collapsed Huey Long Bridge in Old Orleans.

"Hey, my ears just popped," a dark-skinned plebe said.

"Swallow hard," said his rack-mate, "it's just the air pressure at these higher levels." Derek swallowed and felt the pops in his own ears. The sensation was faintly pleasurable, but then also ominous. He looked out at the leavening, swollen, whitish cliffsides looming up from a slate-colored Alabamus River, and realized with exhilarating perceptual clarity that he *was actually looking down on the broad mantle of the land*, something new in his experience. It gave him a sense of power and pleasure to look out and down on the smooth hills, pine forests, ghost towns, ICBM concrete plains, meandering rivers, filigreed agricultural plots, and geodesic domes. In some areas the kudzu carpet was ten feet deep, like a latticed lava flow of thick vines and leaves.

The skimmer sped straight up the face of the earth, ever nearer to the true, absolute horizontality of the North Pole, accruing latitudinal increments as it swept along; and yet, visually, the generic flatness of the land still cued comfortable and new signals into Derek's perceptual matrices, safe signals that the land was still basically flat, and that he was looking down at it.

"It's like climbing up out of a bowl," Derek said to his rack-mate.

"We're about a thousand feet above sea level already," another plebe said. "That's the same as hanging a thousand feet straight up in the air over the Superdome."

"Denver is five thousand feet above the sea," another said, "and some parts of Mexicalus are nine thousand feet up."

'Wonder how high up the warrior camp is," Derek said.

"About three thousand feet, I hear," a plebe put in.

"God, the top of the world!" yet another voice came through the audio.

"Don't forget the Himalayan chain," a quietly assertive voice came in. "That's thirty thousand." A silence fell over the group, and then the return of the generalized babble, small talk, predictions, jocular rumors, expectations—all the young bull-psyching-up for the manhood rituals and trials that were to come, the programmed experiences codified for all the young men of the area.

Now the skimmer shot along the straight chute at the base of Lookout Mountain, Tennessee Territory, clipped through the northwest corner of Georgia, and began to arc and bend through the gentle mountain domes at the lower end of the old Appalachian Mountains. The air was pure and clear, and far off in the eastern sky, Derek could already see the sawtooth peaks of the Brevard chain, cutting bold purple points up into the vista. These were very new mountains, geologically agonized up out of the earth, rocky extrusions of slate and quartz and granite. Ragged though they looked from this great distance, they were actually soft and treacherous to move upon, terrestrially neophytic, brash sharp embryos among Methuselaic counterparts. Derek wondered why a warrior camp was built in so precarious and isolated a spot, but then knew that some archetypal castles and monasteries were built high in the Swiss Alps and in the Himalayas.

Derek closed his eyes for a few seconds, angled his head just slightly, right and left, and felt the reassuring vestibular fluid level activate the cilia higher up in his semicircular canals, and the corresponding exposure of cilia where the fluid lowered. It continued to fascinate him that this system of closed buds and fluids could make him aware, almost to the exact degree, of the angled position of his head and body. Somesthetic-proprioceptive gravity awareness was very important to him. It articulated his relationship to the graviton matrix, kept him at a proper ninety-degree angle to the flat earth, and defined such factors as gait patterns, postures, setting and hunkering and squatting, slumping or stiffening; the vulnerability of supine sleep, the security of the dextral-fetal curl, or the mashed-face ventrality of prone slumber. To do side-straddle hops in calisthenics class was to splash the vestibular tincture about, like shaking heavy dregs in yellow tea, and this fed back diffuse and disturbing somesthetic cues. To do sit-ups or touch-the-toes was overly pressurizing to the canals, and it was only when the body was at rest that, like heavy oil in sealed beakers, the vestibular fluids sought their gravity-mediated basal quietude of horizontal rest.

Derek bio-fed the faintest microcosmic ripples into his vestibular caverns and felt in command, secure, then suddenly patriotic, even jingoistic. He was going to be a warrior, and that was a thing of honor. The human body was a marvel of osteal keels, spars, ribs, gussets, fillets, and bulkheads. There were fulcrum-pivots of great power in the coccygeal nest, the lifting lever of the spinal cord, the tibial-femoral extensor, and the flexor pattern of the elbow and wrist joints. To utilize the osteal and muscular kinesthesias of the body in combat was the ultimate paradigm of personal power: to overcome an opponent in unarmed combat, to dominate, to control, to conquer, to triumph. Combat was an ancient practice, perhaps homologous to mock fighting in animals, though animals rarely if ever fought to the death. It remained for man to use his cognition to upset the evolutionary adaptiveness of mock fighting by inventing ritual killings and codes of conduct—in dueling, for example—that carried an insult, minor or egregious, into capstans of encounters that routinely resulted in death or serous injury.

Warfare, too, perhaps singularly, was justified—even glorified—through its sanctioned institutional status, as when hysterical patriotic fervor gripped nations. And though war was condemned on all sides, it was also practiced with sporadic ferocity on all sides. Justification through condemnation, Derek thought. It was oddly invented reasoning somehow; but, once caught up in the mob hysteria, any recourse to sober reasoning drew rage response from the mob. The power of networked outrage in human groups was remarkably like feeding frenzies in sharks, the waterfall rush of lemmings over an arctic precipice, the thunder of a cattle stampede, or indeed, the networked sputter of reticular outrages in epileptic seizure. Once launched, there was no turning back.

Derek slept for an hour or so, a light, pleasing nap, when

the jarring stop of the skimmer awakened him. They had arrived at the camp. He stepped from the skimmer, saw the Brevard heights close up, now partially misted over, and before both his feet were yet solidly on the quay, a tomato-faced instructor was nose to nose with him, shouting, flicking plosive microbubbles of spittle on his face. Derek surged in autonomic anger. His was an eighteen-inch world; no person came closer than this, and if so, was repulsed. The private life-space of any citizen included a foot and a half of buffer zone encasing the body. The instructor recognized Derek's response; it was his job to evoke it. Now he shouted in Derek's ear, and in instant reflex, Derek elbowed the man in the ribs. It was a hard, efficient, satisfying blow, and Derek felt the spare rib cave in with a soft, sluicing pop. The instructor let out an odd, airy groan and backed off. Derek dropped into a gunfighter stance, ready for anything, momentarily fueled by hypothalamic fire, and then he had a cognitive flash, wondering if his striking the man had already washed him out of the training program.

"Stand at attention," the instructor said, his voice at neutral command level. "I am bionic. I could kill you easily. Do you read me? *Do you read me, Plebe?*" The instructor grasped Derek's elbow and squeezed it. Derek gasped and almost fainted at the pain. He stood at attention and steeled himself for a retaliatory blow, but it did not come. He riveted his eyes on the low white barracks across the quad and felt tears of pain well up. Then the instructor strode off, down the gathering line of young men, his bulging triceps clearly visible beneath his beige-colored bodysuit. Three other instructors were moving about, pushing the plebes, shouting at them, insulting them in nose-to-nose postures. Derek closed his eyes and began to sway. At the far end of the line, a portly plebe was shouting back at an instructor in a curiously loud, yet timorous, grating voice.

"Yes, sir!"

"I can't hear you!"

"Yes, sir!"

"Sing it out, you baby plebe!"

"Yo! Affirm! Yessir!" The vocal feeling tones of the instructors came through like jabs to the body and face: dartlike, quick, immobilizing, inexorable. The intensity of the stimulus disarrayed normal response repertories, so that Derek and his peer-plebes were obliterated by the action. Even the strongest of these young men, the boldest, most secure, most dominant, offered no overt resistance. Physical strength was no recourse, no invariant kinesthetic force. Many of the young plebes were, at least temporarily, cataleptically weak and flaccid. Far down the rank, a thin boy's knees buckled, and he sank slowly to the ground, as if keeling to pray.

"Don't touch him!" the tomato-faced instructor bellowed. "Let him be!" He strode over to where the boy lay on his side, beginning to draw into a soft fetal curl. Without a word, he lifted the boy into a fireman's carry position, as easily as if the boy were a kitten or a blanket, or a light sack of flour. The instructor's body showed absolutely no sense of the burden, no visible allowance for the weight of the boy's 160 or so pounds as he made his effortless saunter across the quad. As if adjusting an epaulet, or simply shrugging, the instructor loosed the boy into a shallow stone fountain, and the boy fairly exploded into life with the shock of the cold water, which Derek later discovered to be kept at forty-two degrees Fahrenheit. It was July, and hot, but the waters of the fountain were kept chillingly cold. Two relatively unimpressive-looking bionic figures came out of the barracks and took the drenched but invigorated plebe inside.

"Who else needs a cold bath?" the tomato-faced warrior-instructor yelled, his authoritarian tone ringing down the lines of men like a single audible hand slapping every face. "Who wants to faint? Any thumbsuckers here? Any tantrum-pitchers?" He said these last words with such consummate articulatory clarity, such plosive consonance, that the inanity of the connotation fled in the face of the thrusting timbre of its deliverance. The words were flinty particles to duck away from, warning drums, snarls from a stone ledge above one's head, heavy rustling in saw grass, screams of pop-off valves, trumpetings at sacrificial rites. The voice is bionic, Derek concluded, like an air horn on a car, or a siren, or a ship's whistle. No human voice could produce such controlled explosions, such surges of power.

Now the voice modulated to quieter levels, but still very much command quality: "You men are barely dry behind the

ears. Fresh young cubs straight from the maternal breast. . . .''
Here Derek wondered at the word-choice; much cruder levels
of reference came to his mind. ''. . . little foxes just out of the
den, babies protected by parents. Up until now, perhaps until
this very day, you have been nurtured. People have been as-
signed to protect you. Society has been charged with your ad-
vocacy. It is the function of the warrior to *fight*, and by the
gods, you will be fighters, or you will return home to nurse at
the breast. To be a fighter is to know freedom from fear, to
forge your body into a combat machine that has but one destiny, and that is the vanquishment of an enemy. You will develop new spirits here, new cores of confidence, new
orientations. Some of you will become permanent members of
the warrior caste, and be greatly rewarded for your actions.
The expectation level is high, and will cull out the weaker
among you, separate the men from the boys, weed out the few
that we need for permanent service—Hey, where's the brash
kid that tried to cave in my ribs?''

Derek's stomach churned, and he felt a tinny ringing ger-
minate in his ears. He had been temporarily lulled by the intelligent turn of the instructor's talk. Now Derek fancied his
vestibular cochlear shells as cringing fetuses with watery pip-
ing systems.

''Hey, Samson! Hercules! Hey, boy hero, get your ass out
here so the rest of these boys can have a look-see at you!''

Derek stepped forward, hesitatingly, and the instructor
brusquely motioned him forward. He's going to stomp the shit
out of me, Derek thought, but he was strangely unafraid. I
could cower and slink, he thought, but I'm beyond that. I'll
take him any way I can. He's not going to kill me. Then Derek
felt the ordinary contempt reaction to bionic people, and saw
the instructor as a mere device to outwit, if not eventually
conquer. There was something about bio-humans that reduced
their generic credibility. One wanted always to test their bionic
mettle, to bushwhack them, to prod their limits; because, at
least in the full bionics and robots, no inappropriate retaliatory
response would be forthcoming, since biones and robots were
eminently *fair*, by law and precedent and construction. Once,
Derek had seen a tiny boy tease a sanitation robot unmerci-
fully, with no response from the bot. Finally, when the boy

tried to trip the bot, it gave the boy an eye-rattling electro-shock that dramatically validated the robot's dominance.

Derek decided to close with the instructor. "Come on, puppy," the instructor snarled, "come get your ass whipped." It was a desperation move on Derek's part. Bravery is a form of stupidity, he thought as he approached the man on the balls of his feet, still feeling no fear. He's stuffed full of Akai transistors, Derek thought, and aimed a haymaker at the man's mandibular joint, just forward of the ear and low on the jawline, hoping for a quick break of this vulnerable fulcrum. For a moment he forgot that this was no ordinary man, and sold short on the assurance that biones were a minority group (and thus scapegoatable). In the flash of a microsecond, the looming facial target was gone, and the inertia of Derek's swing spun him off balance. The instructor had ducked the punch with incredible agility and reflexive speed. Derek thought of tiger cubs teasing cobras, the reflexes of the cats all but guaranteeing their safety.

"Now see this!" the instructor trumpeted to the row of young men. "This is how tough I am." And he clamped a single bionic hand around Derek's elbow. Again Derek gasped, and wilted in the machinelike power of the grip. He cried out— a strangling, air-bellows, laryngeal moan—and hung, like a limp puppet, in the grip. It was as if every tendon in his body were soft as taffy strands. The pain panicked him, and his very lifesense flared in his elbow joint, as if giant pliers were crushing the frail osteal wing. His vestibular cues flared alarm, overload, critical mass, redline, in extremis, and he fainted.

He came awake, just seconds later, in an infusive shock of icy immersion, and knew, with immediate, blue-steel clarity, that he was in the waters of the stone fountain. His equilibratory centers gave him to know he was supine, and he rolled dextral, drew up his knees, and just barely fought off the urge to open his mouth, the icy waters inundating the base of the occipital lobe, keying in this often fatal reflex. His feet touched the bottom of the shallow pool, and he felt a new and temporarily commanding power over his lifespace. He sprang from the bottom of the shallow fountain and broke the surface like a breaching whale. He heard the cheers of the men, and then the two drone-level biones lifted him out and took him inside the barracks. He was something of a hero in the eyes of the other plebes.

The new plebes, the vestigial warriors, were lined up and marched to an ancient-looking tin-shed building called HY-GIENIC UNIT. Waves of heat shimmered in the air above the roof, and Derek thought the place to resemble the camp build-ings of Buchenwald or Auschwitz. Inside the men were told to strip naked and to put their clothing and possessions in heavy canvas bags. One plebe asked what to do with the $491 in barter-script he had brought with him, and was told to dump it with everything else, that he would get a receipt for it, and that he wouldn't need any script where he was going, that he was a nipplehead to carry that amount around with him, and finally, that the government was going to do all his worrying for him. Derek had traveled light: jockey shorts, cotton jeans, tennis shirt, socks, soft shoes, a handkerchief, a thin wallet, and a few coins. The filled canvas bags were fluxed shut, and as each man hefted his onto a corner, a bionic drone affixed an ID plate and gave the men a small receipt plate. The naked men were then lined up against the corrugated metal walls, twenty on one side of the room, and twenty on the other. Forty naked young men in one room, Derek realized, and the scene was without precedent in his experience. He could not help but appraise the bodies of the men, to compare the somatotypes with his own. There were a few plump ones, their bodies re-markably feminine, and Derek had a memory-trace of cabin boys and sodomy in the British navy in ancient times. Given an imprisoned sample of men, with no access to women, and the intromissive drives still sought culmination, and it was a matter of targeting in on female surrogates and alternative ap-ertures. There were thin, asthenic boys, with every muscle visible beneath thin skin; a few hairy mesomorphs; at least one heavily muscled bodybuilder stereotype—in all, a seemingly endless variation of body sizes, shapes, and proportions. And every penis hung flaccid and somesthetically numb. Into this thin metal cage of fish-belly white vulnerability strode the tomato-faced drill instructors, the "D.I."

"All right, you shitbirds," he bellowed, "this row, LEFT FACE! And over here—yeah, Plebe, face to the left—*you* baby plebes, RIGHT FACE!'' Some of the men knew nothing at all of close-order drill, but others performed the movements snappily. A door opened in the face of the corrugated tin wall, and Derek could see into a small room, the floor of which was covered with *hair*. It was, he realized, a makeshift barbershop, an absurd tonsorial palace, a hirsuite grooming station, an emasculation parlor, an evolutionary precursor of medical surgery. In places the hair was a foot deep on the floor. There were convoluted clumps of ebony wire, brown thatch, auburn swatches, kinky ebony plumage, coppery red wires, greasy duckback residuals, coiled swirls of blond locks—in all, a weird instant rug of freshly cut hair, from the heads of innumerable young men.

The haircut did not take very long: Derek sat in the smooth wooden chair, careful not to mash his soft scrotal walnuts, and the barber man made a few quick swaths across his head, with a heavy shaver that sounded loud enough to cut wire. Derek rubbed his hand across his head and felt the bony vulnerability of total baldness. Where there had been luxuriant hair, perhaps fifty thousand individual long hairs, there was now tight skin, keenly etched cranial fissures, osteal bumps he didn't know he had, piebald marks, excoriated pustules, stubble, epidermal oil, sebaceous dew, and most of all, the primal white skin. Derek had never felt more neutered in his life. He was a eunuch, a Samson shorn of his locks, a virility symbol suddenly rendered impotent, a grassy carpet clean cut from the earth, revealing the barest worn, hard, sterile dirt.

Quickly the forty men became cranially homogenized, their identities gone, individualities neutralized, charismatic covariances canceled. There seemed to be no pecking order now. A massively built, lantern-jawed boy was opposite Derek as the group lined up once more, and the boy looked innocuous, harmless, pathetic.

Derek's vestibular nests seemed like terminal message stations, relaying to him in the keenest wavelengths those routine graviton-matrix cues he took so much for granted. His richly sensitized footpads felt the individual cubes of grit on the curiously warm cement floor (deck, you shitbirds, it's a *deck*!), and he could feel the infinitesimal ebbings of cochlear fluid in his semicircular canals as his locus of balance shifted slowly from heel to ball, then up along the outboard calves, to the thighs; the staunchly underpinned pelvic girdle, the snakelike tubings of cradled viscera, the cautiously throbbing heart, the rib-box with its bladders of precious air, the pylon of the cervical post, and the bony crown of the skull with its cheesy gray furrows of brain mass.

"Move it!" the instructor bellowed, and Derek's column of men moved into a shower room, where the similarity to a Buchenwald gas-chamber was institutionally unmistakable. Would stinging sprays of water erupt from those grayish-green shower heads, Derek thought, or mists of poison gas? He discovered rapidly enough, and even felt triumphant, as he adjusted the water spray to warm. A few of the men turned the metal knobs to hot, and the room began to fill with steam. The soap was hard, brownish-colored, strong, and yielded a bare minimum of lather. The instructor left the men in the room, and there were careful chitterings of babble-talk, an occasional whoop, and an increasing din of moderate yips and whistles and plosive sputterings. The scene was Dantesque: wet white bodies, hairy chests, bare chests, circumsized phalluses, uncircumcized phalluses, bulging pectorals, bird-chests, tight bellies with well-defined muscles, flaccid paunches, varicose veins, drowned pubic sporrans, sagging varicoceles, scars, moles, prurient pustules, freckles, piebald filigrees—a bizarre, noncontextual amalgam of basic bipedal humanoid bodies, all humbled and homogenized by nakedness, wetness, waterproofed cleanliness, and shaved craniums. After ten minutes the D.I. bellowed for the men to get out. A muffin-faced ectomorph named Hovorka was trying to soap his phallus into tumescence, but with little success. As the men emerged from the shower room, they were issued a stack of four thick green towels, green dungaree pants, loose jackets, and soft-billed caps. The clothing was stiff and substantial, and Derek felt like a grubworm encased in a denim exoskeleton. With damp towels around their necks, thick socks and heavy brogan shoes on their feet, and hefting the canvas bags now stuffed with underwear, bedding, and toilet articles, the men were marched to the barracks. I don't feel like a warrior at all, Derek thought, looking at the drab, slumping, shuffling column of men in front of him. I feel like a convict, a conscript, a drone, a laborer, a mental patient in some ancient, snake-pit hospital, with confining pens and drain rooms.

The barracks room was like a cement vault some one hundred feet long and forty feet wide, with wooden floors (*deck*, you shitbird!), a great many windows, and lined with ancient iron double-decker bunks. Derek had been accustomed to sleeping on graviton chaises, in gelatinous coffins, or on filmy forcefield beds, and he wondered at the primitiveness of the olive drab bunks and their thin mattresses.

"Find a sack," the tomato-faced D.I. said, and the shuffling of the men toward the beds suggested a mass game of musical chairs. The pattern of instant response to command was already becoming obvious. When the bionic D.I. said shit, the instant response was to squat and strain.

How the hell did I get into this, Derek asked himself, stashing his gear on the wooden locker box beneath the bunk, and easing down onto the mattress. A curious, disproportionate sense of security accrued from the simple feel of the moderately resilient mattress. Why do young men fight the wars started by old men? he wondered; how is it that patriotism is so exploited, why should I be a warrior, anyway?

"Chow in half an hour," the D.I. barked, and left, his stride rapid and powerful and sure, his body a deadly strong device. Derek watched the disappearing figure with a mixture of admiration and scorn. No mere human could control men so totally, he thought. Half bones and flesh, blood and tendons, half circuit-paks and nuclear cubes. He almost said it aloud: Suppose one of his circuits failed? Would he be like a puppet with cut strings? Derek lay supine on the bunk and closed his eyes, relishing the absence of visual cues. He felt the keel of his spinal cord settle into the mattress; the arches of his ribbed bone-box became the crests of hills, his extremities were peninsulas, his genital stalk a detumescent sprig, and his head a quiescent cognition terminal. Deep inside his vestibular nests, the eternal equilibratory fluid now lay ninety degrees from verticality, and it gave him to know both the comfort as well as the ventral vulnerability of supinity. Across the squad bay, a thick Bronx accent curled out its street-smart denotations, and was answered by a whanging, colloquial Southern drawl. A mulatto-looking Italian boy was reviving the 1860s U.S. Civil

War with a jingle-jawed Kentucky plowboy. A wrist-wrestling match formed up, and the Kentuckian took the Bronxite easily, the plowboy's small biceps belying the strength of his wrists and hands. He allowed that milking cows was what had made him so strong. The lunch was a rush of lines, rattling metal trays, steak and potatoes and milk and cake, and what every young man came to believe in for the rest of his life: something called saltpeter, put in all the food, to keep you from getting penile erections. Derek's first day in warrior training passed in a frantic blur of diffuse and, for him, aimless actions.

Next morning the reveille bugle blew at 5:45 A.M., and the men bounded from their beds. Most wore towels around their waists (nudity was not explicitly disallowed, but turned out to be rare among the young warrior-striplings) as they shuffled to the shower room, and then stood before the line of mirrors to shave and brush their teeth. A radio blared syrupy commercials and unobtrusive music, and Derek thought how soft and easy the deejay's life must be. Up and down the line of men, there were ancient shaving mugs and brushes, pressurized foam in cans, fat white worms of cream in tubes, the raucous buzzing of electric shavers, tooth brushing sounds, hawking, spitting, snorting, a conglomerate of mass toilet sounds, all amplified in the resonant concrete room. Then back to the squad bay to pull on the stiff denim uniforms, and out into the early sunrise to muster into ragged ranks.

The bionic D.I. strode from his billet across from the barracks. He was dressed in light-colored khaki, soft-looking, an often-laundered look, a "salty" look that was the mark of his tenure. Bionic shit, Derek thought, mannequin, waxwood figurine, plastic monster, breeding fault, curiosity; and yet the charismatic force the D.I. exuded was ineluctable. The voice barked and rolled, and the men came to attention in a kind of reversed collapsing movement, like old movies played backward. The platoon of men shuffled off toward the mess hall, where they were again rushed past the sullen-angry messboys, who filled their trays with scrambled eggs, thick bacon, grits, fried potatoes, bread, and butter. On the tables were metal jars of milk and coffee. The men set about the business of eating with vigor and speed, fueling their young bodies, swelling their intestines, inducing rhythmic peristalsis, elevating blood-sugar levels; and the feeling of satiety was good and right and best and natural. The mess hall was filled with several hundred men, and the sounds were metallic and clicking, sloshing and swishing, babbling and murmuring, and yet serious and subdued.

At least we are not harassed when we eat, Derek thought, and then he saw the D.I. patrolling the aisles. I wonder if he eats, he thought, and the thought was a mental smirk. I bet he puts fuel-paks in his gut instead. I bet he eats iron and zinc and lithium and silicon grease. That means he doesn't shit, either. He probably has some kind of exhaust port, some spring-loaded valve he had to take out and clean with an air hose every month. The D.I. moved close to Derek, and there was the all but imperceptible whir of tungsten helices in ambergris fulcra-paks. *Machine*, Derek thought.

"How's the chow, hero boy?" the D.I. asked Derek, the voice interrogatory and cruel, yet with a sliver of sincerity coming through. Derek swallowed a piece of thick bacon. It tasted full and salty and complex, a genuine blastula of compressed fat.

"Good," he answered, looking up at the aminoplast mouth, the absolute symmetry of the nasal ports, the steady look of the steely bright visual agates.

"You don't have a worry in the world, boy," the D.I. said, beginning to walk away, "the government's going to feed you like a king."

It was the man's bionic status that *offended* him, Derek realized. I am organic, he said to himself, I am colloidal, humanoid, *alive*, vestibular, *aware aware aware*, and he is machinated, quasi-organic, para-android, a windup tin soldier. Derek could not escape the now diffuse strategems of how he might set about dysfunctioning the D.I.

A long, hot, compacted month passed. The men learned close-order drill, the manual of arms, the saber manual, the anatomy and physiology of weapons, dirty fighting, ancient bayonet combat, judo, karate, and even medieval Scottish wrestling. They marched; they ran obstacle courses; climbed hemp ropes thick as billy clubs, dove through blind holes in walls (there was a mudhole on the other side of the wall); they crawfished, supine, beneath barbed-wire screens while machine-gun bullets whistled just above them; jumped from platforms into water topped by blazing oil; boxed each other with gloves and with padded staff; they feinted and dodged, crouched and sprang, struck and parried, rolled and lunged, galloped and stalked; crawled, inched, skewered, and insinuated their young bodies in so many ways that Derek felt he knew every way to fight a man hand to hand. He knew the trick of breaking a jaw, crushing a windpipe, eye gouging, testicle ramming, and hitting always below the belt. He knew how to bite and spit and twist and wrench, and began to wonder if being a warrior meant anything other than hand-to-hand combat. Then came the introduction to the history of weapons.

The men fired the ancient .22–caliber rifle, the 1906 rifle, the World War II Garand; the carbine; Browning automatic rifle; air-cooled and water-jacketed machine guns; the heavy, bucking, inaccurate .45–caliber pistol; and the infamous, torquing Thompson submachine gun. Then came the M–12 series, the M–16, M–18, and M–24, each one deadlier in the sense of the number of projectiles it could spit per unit of time. They fired the recoilless rifle, the mercilessly recoiling grenade launcher, the stovepipe bazooka, and the fat stovepipe mortars. They were getting into the laser weapons now, and the D.I. had harassed Derek more than the other men. Derek did not have bad blood feelings for the D.I., but he came increasingly to see him as a personal challenge. Here was a smart machine to outwit.

One fiercely baking August day, Derek saw a rheostat knob flush on the D.I.'s belly, as the instructor led the platoon in a grueling calisthenics session. Ah, there's his switch, Derek thought, there's his power knob. I wonder if he turned it off at night. I wonder if he has to plug into a recharger while he sleeps—*if* he sleeps. Men are the masters of their machines, he thought, and the thought of dysfunctioning the D.I. grew stronger in him. Again, it wasn't out of hate, it was rather to show that humans outrank bionics. Machines work for people, he concluded immediately, they may not oppress us, they respond *to* us. They pump and they churn, they reciprocate their pistons and turbine-spin their fluted blades, and at our specific whims. It is the routine option of the man to control his machine.

That night Derek did a reckless thing. He crept from his bunk in the dark, circled the barracks to avoid the sentry placed on fire-watch duty, and climbed an asbestos-wrapped pipe to peer into the D.I.'s quarters. The room looked like a machine shop and a spare-parts storehouse for electronic hardware. The D.I. was stripped. Derek had never seen him naked before. He clung to the large, warm pipe outside the window, his bare feet hurting, thrust against a thick plastic collar that held the pipe to the wall. The D.I.'s back was to him, a broad back, but one sectioned like the thorax of an insect. Exoskeletal dung beetle, Derek thought; roach, scarab, segmented lobster. The D.I.'s deltoids shone like geodesic epaulets, the trapezius muscles were like gussets on an aircraft fuselage, and the lats like retracted wings on ancient delta-shaped jet planes. A plasticized corset encircled the waist, and the pelvic girdle was that of a store-window mannequin. Polystyrene training pants, Derek thought, Pampers for a machine. A complex network of external tendon-prostheses connected the waistline to the rear of the knees. He's a damned puppet, Derek said softly, and the D.I.'s torso began to swivel, like a turntable in an antique railroad roundhouse.

It was so rare a sight that Derek's breathing stopped. The torso swiveled ninety degrees starboard, and the D.I.'s arm moved to lubricate two grease nipples on the pelvic edge, exposed like drainage nodules in a garbage-disposal sump. A small square of epithelium had been removed from the side of his face, and where teeth and jawbone should have been showing through, there was microcircuitry. One muscular arm hung slack, like a girder being lifted into place by its end, and the other seemed curiously alive, the movements rapid, certain, perfectly synchronized. The calves were crosshatched with bindings that appeared to be embedded in the mass of the leg.

Derek saw the room as alien. It had no prettifiers in it; no furniture, no plants, no pictures, no books, no stereo, records, rugs, ashtrays, dishes, no signs of food, no papers, pencils, pets, or lamps. He lives in a spare-parts room, Derek thought; he has to stay garaged in a maintenance shack. No toilet or sink, no tub or shower, no stove or refrigerator, no bread, grapes, wine, peanuts, or molasses. He began to feel sorry for the D.I. The torso swiveled back to its normal position, and the other flaccid arm came alive, reaching for a snaking conduit that led along the gritty floor and into the shadows. The D.I.'s head had not moved at all, and his feet remained in place, like those of a statue on its base.

Then the head turned, smoothly, like a signal-seeking radar dish, and the pair of faceted eyes looked up, directly at Derek. The facial expression was curiously slack, like a person who has had a stroke, and then it turned very human and leering. The aminoplast mouth moved, and Derek heard a voice inside his head, as if a microcassette had been implanted in his inner ear. The voice said, GET IN HERE, HERO BOY.

It was all Derek could do to prevent his body from going to jelly. He clung to the pipe and forced his body to respond, descending carefully, his breath now coming in dysrhythmic snorts. The tone of the voice had been commanding, and yet matter-of-fact, a quiet, casual order. There was no anger or indignation in it, neither was it colorlessly robotic. Derek imagined he had heard a fleeting nuance of camaraderie in the command, as if he was now privy to some secret. He felt the spongy turf beneath his bare feet, and the grass whispered there, quickly dampening the completely vascular podiatric pads, so sensitively keyed into his vestibular pods. The only sound he heard was the soft hiss of the wrapped steam lines, and then the call of a bobwhite, far off.

"What are you, some kind of fucking *voyeur*?" the D.I. said, as Derek entered the room and closed the door. The word sounded too soft, an affectedly onomatopoetic sound. For that matter, the word *fucking* was too fleshy a sound for a nonflesh bionic D.I. to use.

"I was damnably curious about you, I'll have to admit," Derek said. "I'll take whatever's coming to me." He did not feel fearful. Certain kinds of men can induce fear, but no bione could. The D.I. quickly replaced the missing part of his face, and dressed quickly in pants and shirt. He doesn't have to put on his clothes, Derek thought, but then the uniform presented an authoritarian set.

"We can't have plebes climbing up steam pipes and doing Peeping Tom numbers," the D.I. said, moving toward him.

"Stand at attention." Derek liked to snap his heels together in this stance, the valid impact-clack of thick leather shoes, but now the movement felt silly and hurt his bare heels. Beneath his feet, the floor (*deck*, shithead!) felt like a gritty hatch on a rusting Lebanese freighter. The strange metallic room sang soft electronic soprano songs, and somewhere along one wall (*bulkhead*, you shithead!), a relay closed and opened in rhythmic tickings. The D.I. walked behind Derek. "Eyes front," he said, again softly authoritarian. "You're a fair strapping young buck." The voice came from behind, the umbilical conduit moving to compensate for the change in position, and then the D.I. moved back to face Derek. "You figure you can whip my ass?" The voice was not nearly so baiting in its effect as it would have been coming from another man.

"No, *sir*," Derek said, his voice too loud in the resonant room. A hollow steel pole support column nearby rang with the volume of his reply.

"What kind of trouble are you looking for, sneaking around like a second-story man in the middle of the night? Stand at ease."

"I'm curious about you. I never saw a superhuman person before." The flexible conduit was attached to the D.I.'s umbilical plug, like a high-pressure fuel line. He's getting recharged, Derek thought to himself.

"You looking for some way to get at me?"

"I don't see any way, sir. If you can't beat 'em, join 'em."

"You resent biones?"

"I guess I resent your invincibility."

"That's what makes me a D.I., Plebe. My job is to make you invincible. You buy that?"

"I guess any man wants to be invincible."

"You volunteer or get conscripted?"

"Conscripted."

"Where you from, hero boy?"

"Old Orleans."

"You got any bionics in you?"

"Some plastic knee cartilage."

"How much of a bione you figure I am?"

"You look like a 90–percenter to me."

"Ninety-seven," the D.I. said. "You have your original memory banks? You had any erasures?"

"No, sir."

"Then listen good. I was hit by a commuter cab when I was ten tiers old. The impact jellied my brain. My guardians bartered my body to the Gladiator Service in exchange for lifelong pensions. I got a modified George Patton persona implant, and a set of kinesthetic paks that make me strong as a gorilla. I can squat with 2,000 pounds, bench-press 1,000, reverse-curl 250, and do the hundred-yard dash in five flat. I can fire offhand bull's-eyes at 1,000 yards."

"Christ," Derek muttered, unbelieving.

"I can field-strip an '06 in forty-seven seconds, and categorize tactical philosophies from Genghis Khan through Rommel and Rickover and Haig. My data banks recapitulate the history of warfare."

"Why are you telling me this?" Derek asked, with some growing feeling of empathy. "Why not just discipline me and get on with it?"

"I am validating my dominance," the D.I. said. "If you have any doubts about it, put them aside. As for discipline, you don't know the half of it, hero boy. You've got too much self-actualization in you to make much of a gladiator. What you need is a good shot of hypothalamic amperage." The D.I. moved toward a cabinet, and Derek had an old memory-trace of a dentist reaching into the sterile tray for the huge Novocaine syringe. His first instinct was to run, and then he saw the hatchet. It was rusty and lay on a lathe-bed, as if unused for tiers. The conduit that connected the D.I.'s umbilicus to the recesses beneath the metal credenza lay like a fat snake sleeping in the sun. The conduit rotated easily in the abdominal socket as the D.I. reached into the cabinet. He palmed a small phaser and turned toward Derek.

No machine is going to zap me, Derek thought, and in one fluid motion, born of reflex-level survival instinct, he snatched the hatchet from the lathe and swung it in both hands at the fat snake-conduit on the metal floor (*deck*, shithead!). The old blade bit into resilient rubber, fiber, polyester web, and then into the bright pure metallic strands carrying the recharging current. The floor rang with the impact of the blow, and a burst of blue sparks spat up in Derek's face, taking away half his eyebrow. A shock electrified his body, rattling every rib. The dry wooden handle of the hatchet had saved him from a serious shock. The shock served as a reflex-arc stimulus for repeated blows, and he screamed ancient karate cries as the fourth blow severed the conduit. The sparks flashed orange and amber, then died in an acrid little plume of smoke. The D.I. stood, like a Colossus of Rhodes statue, as if his feet were bolted to the floor. His head began to turn very slowly, and it rotated a full 180 degrees, and looked at Derek. The face looked out at him, and the shoulder blade surrogates were where the pectorals should have been. The sight of the dorsol torso and the ventral head horrified Derek. Very slowly, the D.I. began to sink to his knees, like a massive steel puppet being lowered by taut cables.

"A stupid move, hero boy." the voice was pitched lower, the cadence slowed. "Destruction of government property, umbilical assault, trespass, military maladaptive behaviors. Your organic ass is going straight to the brig." The D.I.'s arms began to draw up, so that the forearms were extraordinarily parallel to the upper arms, far more so than possible in humans. Across the room a bank of oscillographic screens flashed bright red bars, and the bell-shaped Gaussian tracings there decremented to gentle excurvatures, and then flattened into horizontal lines.

"I'm going on nonverbal." The voice was even lower, slower, and softer. "Your vestibular ass is mud, hero boy." The D.I.'s calves drew up behind his thighs, again in the bizarre mechanical sense of absolute parallelism, and Derek marveled and disbelieved what he saw: the torso was sinking to the floor, and the thighs retracting into it. The torso cylinder was encasing the extremity-pistons. Then came the supreme horror. The head itself began to lower down into the thoracic cavity. At the cervical base, annealed stitch-patterns parted and closed, like flexible sliding doors, like irising ports, and the head disappeared into the thorax.

"Christ," Derek said aloud, "he's retracted himself." He spun on the metal floor and felt the grit abrade his feet. He walked quickly to the door, drew it open rapidly, slipped out into the humid darkness, and closed the door. He loped slowly through the grass, and the dew immediately watered his feet in familiar, cold, total immersion. The fire-watch sentry was at the far end of the barracks, his dimly luminous helmet glowing, and Derek's feet left damply fading prints as he made for his bunk. He crept silently into the metal-framed bed, breathing louder than he wanted to, and drew the light blanket up over him. From the bunk above came the slow chittering purr of a man snoring. Derek held his breath as the fire-watch sentry padded by. The distant echo-call of the bobwhite sounded, and Derek felt a kinship with the bird. I am one of God's most vulnerable creatures, he thought, and so is the bird. The D.I. is a faulty block of machinery. He felt triumphant, despite his fear of both immediate and ultimate discovery, and he slept well, dreaming of high-speed, low-altitude flights over complexly bristling megalopitan vistas.

Word of the incident spread rapidly. The fire-watch reported to the D.I.'s quarters at 5:30 A.M., got no response, entered, and saw the overtly squared torso on the floor. He alerted the assistant D.I. (a 32–percent bione), who called the post commander (a 12–percenter). The fire-watch was a scrawny, sociosyntonic, bird-faced boy from West Virginius, who delighted in telling what he saw. "By God, his belly-button string was cut plumb in two. His head was By God down in his chest, and his arms and legs were folded up like broken branches. He was By God on the floor like an old packing crate By God."

After breakfast, the men were confined to their barracks and instructed to field-strip their archaic Garands until further notice. At the noon mess call formation, the post commander himself addressed the entire battalion, the twelve platoons ranked up six abreast and two deep. The post commander was short, thick, muscular, with a salt-and-pepper-colored handlebar mustache, and his chest was embroidered with four equal rows of campaign bars. The silver eagles of his rank lay supine on his khaki epaulets and vertical on his pisscutter cap. The men were hungry and restive, but intent on his words.

"Sergeant S–5 Alpha 430 was maliciously deactivated sometime between 10 P.M. last night and 5:30 A.M. this morning by person or persons unknown. Sergeant Alpha 430 is a gladiatorial bione of the highest order. He represents a government investment in the range of 8 million preferred barter-script units. It is our assumption that one or more of you men committed this action, but we have no suspects as yet. If any one man jack of you here has information about this, you are ordered to report it at once. The Bionics Guild has already authorized a twenty-five-thousand-unit reward for information leading to the arrest and conviction of the perpetrators. This is no matter of simple personal assault. A valuable item of government property has been damaged—quite extensively, I might add—and the person responsible must be apprehended. That is all. Platoon leaders, carry on!''

Oh, shit, Derek thought, as the men trooped into the resonant mess hall, I will be suspected. But I will lie, and if they break me, I will claim self-defense. That D.I. box of transistorized pneumoplast was going to zap me with a phaser.

A large number of the plebes had witnessed Derek's two encounters with the D.I., and so when Derek was summoned to the post commander's quarters the next day, he was not surprised, nor did he suspect any particular informant. With a quickly posted reward of twenty-five thousand units, he even thought there might have been a torrent of early informants. Derek ran through his plan again: he was to deny the incident, plead self-defense if clearly discovered, and give as his base of defense that fact that the D.I. had violated the ancient and honorable robotic code by pointing a phaser at him. He was not accustomed to lying, but felt this a justifiable first line of defense. After all, he was merely protecting himself from a malfunctioning machine. One need not have a code of honor when dealing with a machine. His denial would be strategic, the confession objective, and the circumstances extenuating. But Derek did not reckon on the cruel sophistication of the interrogation process, nor did he expect it to begin with such startling suddenness.

He entered the commandant's office and was immediately phaser-stunned by an MP standing behind the door. He was dragged into a small room adjacent to the commandant's office. He later remembered that he had just begun his salute when the phaser hit him. Now he was set upright in a square chaise, his arms and legs and head quickly bound, and various monitoring devices were connected to his body. Psychogalvanometers were set up, the thin, snaking leads attached to the tops of his hands by exquisitely small, sharp needles. An electroencephalographic skullcap was lowered down over his head, and an eye photography scanner fitted over his face. Videotape cameras telescoped out from the walls, like Cyclopean howitzer barrels capped with a single glowing eye-lens.

He tensed for a sigmoidal probe and was grateful that it did not come. Through the slightly anesthetic haze the phaser-stun had produced, Derek saw something comparable to the move the D.I. had made with the phaser: a medic moving toward him, an injection pistol in his hand. He tried to move, to surge, to burst his bonds, but was totally flaccid and powerless. The medic blatted in Pentothal and Demerol synthetes in both Derek's arms and groin, and Derek felt a pleasurable ballooning, as if his essence were filling the entire room. He felt primally secure, and yet light and airy, swimming effortlessly in warm gelatin, his skeleton glowing, his organs itching deliciously, but not needing to be scratched, his muscles perfectly striated slabs of tensile colloid, the color-coded wires of his neural filigrees alive and singing with rapidly somersaulting ions, like tiny prickly spheres of radiating thorns, parading through the myelin-sheathed tubes. His skull, his cranial world, felt huge, a wonderously burgeoning resonant grotto of osteal integrity; his visual agates soft rubbery insets; and his vestibular channels the purest springs of nectar in their cilial nests, twin fleshy mediators of his total somesthetic comfort.

"I am vestibular man," he found himself saying, and it was a proudly echoing pronouncement, as if quadraphonic speakers were sounding in a great stone hall.

"What was that he said?" the commandant asked the medic.

"Didn't catch it," the medic said. "Something like 'vestibule.'"

"Is he ready for interrogation?"

"Yessir."

"Gladiatorial creep," Derek said. "Immature militant soldier boy. Spuriously programmed ramrod, obscene nest of transistors—"

"Silence, Plebe," the commandant hissed. "State your name, rank, and serial number."

"Go suck a swagger stick," Derek said, his voice permeated

by confidence. He felt like a man kneeling by a pool of liquid gold, and the gold was cool and thick, like mercury, and it was beautiful to see and touch and drink. He saw the pool as his id-level psychic energy, his generic fuel cell, his power source, his organismic distillate, his holistic tincture.

"What the hell did you shoot this boy with?" the commandant asked the medic.

"Routine blats of Pentothal and Demerol. It should clear away his inhibitions."

"Name, rank, and serial number," the commandant tried again.

"Bionic D.I.'s eat silicon shit," Derek said. "All gladiators hop their pneumoplastic grannies. They have grease-pit asses—"

"Whatever you shot him with has broken something loose," the commandant said to the medic. "Shoot him with something else."

"Give it a little more time."

"You gave him too much. He's talking crazy."

Derek looked out at the short man with the eagles on his shoulders and the water buffalo horned mustache, and saw him as a windup toy soldier. The 2,000 cc's of chemical filled his bloostream with gently pressuring tranquility, and he felt omnipotent and at the center of the world. He stood in the grotto of his skull and watched the capillary pumpings, the crackling of synaptic junctures, the tumescent arc of the vestibular cilia, and the placid horzontality of the inner-ear fluid. He smelled wet leather, lemon rinds, mushroom cellars, and ambergris. He felt infused with slowly metabolizing anthracite briquettes, nodules of mercury, cubes of congealed honey, crystalline amber ellipses, and the soft inner seedpods of apricots and mangoes. A fat orange candle simmered in his thorax, and the flame was painless and nourishing and energizing. The oxygen level in his inhibitory cortices was low, and his life-space felt gaseous. I am a thick mist, he thought to himself, and yet I am a sodden giant, a black hole in space, a thick-skinned balloon full of liquified Stilton, a fleshy embryo with eight extremities, a plump fetus, a star with wet tendons.

"How come you got silver birdies on your shoulders, boy?" Derek asked the commandant. The man's body stiffened, but his face sagged imperceptibly, and the medic barely held back a smile.

"I am your commanding officer," the man replied, affecting a marginally effective authoritarian retort. Derek's face remained flaccidly confident.

"You're a tin-box soldier boy, you mean. You pin metal sparrows on your shoulders, besides. And you wear water buffalo horned hairs under your bulb-nose. You lack authoritarian presence also."

"Name, rank, and serial number," the colonel persisted.

"You know me. You know me. You sure as hell know me."

"Did you attack Sergeant Alpha 430 last night?"

"Didn't know that clanking can of tin and plastic had a name. He's got some sort of serial number, some metal tag stapled to his ass."

"Did you attack him?"

"Don't use personal pronouns for that *device*."

"Did you sever his umbilical conduit?"

"He damn well needed to be unplugged."

"Then you did attack him?"

"I disconnected a faulty machine. When you get a burnout, you pull the plug, you shut down. You shoot horses, don't you?"

"Why did you sever the conduit?"

"That hive of cheap circuitry pulled a phaser on me."

"That is within the scope of his duties."

"Robots don't point phasers at humans. Robots have their robotic roles. This bag of bolts blew his pop-off valve. He was going bonkers. He flipped out. He blew a fuse."

"You admit the cutting of the conduit?"

"Well, hell, yes. I performed a good deed. I shut off a crazy machine."

"Do you understand the consequences of your action?"

"Yeah, and I want a robotic cluster on my basic hero medal."

"Jesus H. Christ on a styrofoam crutch," the commandant said, "am I hearing this plebe right?"

"The tapes are getting it," the medic replied. "It beats anything I ever heard."

"Do you admit to trespass, assault, and maladaptive actions?" the commandant continued to Derek.

"I admit to unplugging a malfunctioning machine. And I admit to the stupidity of gladiatorial pursuits. And I admit to the emotional immaturity of military types. Furthermore, I admit that fire is the most potent extension of man, that career gladiators have frustrated dependency needs, disproportionately large hypothalamuses, dull normal cranial amperage, and poor body image."

"Heavy. Weird," the medic said.

"How did this boy ever get accepted into war school?" The commandant turned to the medic again. "How's his personality profile?"

"Centile fifty, across the boards," the medic said, producing Derek's readouts quickly. "A garden variety normal."

"Wonder how he'd respond detoxed."

"We'll have to wait and see."

"Stash him in the brig—no, stash him in the infirmary. Flush all the tranquilizers out of him. Get him detoxed. We'll have another go at him later."

Derek was hospitalized for several days and recovered rapidly from the massive sedation effects. He was brought again to the commandant's office on yet another bright steaming afternoon, and the silent air-conditioned room was a welcome change from the outside heat. This time the commandant was flanked by two majors, one a judge advocate, and the other a psychonomist.

"You are charged with malicious assault, destruction of government property, and military maladaptive behaviors. How do you plead?" It was the surprisingly robotic-sounding voice of the judge advocate.

"I do not *plead* in any context," Derek answered, his voice boldly inflected, for now he was convinced that the judge advocate himself was a bione.

"Did you sever the conduit attached to Sergeant Alpha 430 on the night of 22 July last?"

"I did."

"And why did you do this?"

"That plastic bag of ropes and pulleys pointed a phaser at me."

"Are you anti-bionic? Do you hate biones?"

"No more than I'd hate an antique parking meter, or a robot copter pilot, or a stripped Phillips-head screw. I'd have to be mechanophobic to hate a *machine*."

"You then plead self-defense?"

"I *plead* nothing. A machine malfunctioned, and I cut off the machine."

"It is within the scope of a drill instructor's power to use his phaser on his troops," the judge advocate said in his dull robotic voice.

"A robot may not harm a humanoid, sir. I'm sure you are aware of this six-hundred-year-old statute."

"Sergeant Alpha 430 is not a robot."

"He is a 97–percenter," Derek shot back, "and he broke one of the prime laws of robotics."

"I repeat, he is not a robot."

"No hive of Akai-Sony transistor paks points a phaser at me."

"You've got a good record here," the commandant said. "What could have motivated you to take these actions?"

"Self-preservation, sir, defense against unreasonable force, an instinct for survival."

"You have no malicious motives, then?"

"None, sir."

"How do you know Sergeant Alpha 430 to be 97–percent bionic?"

"He told me so, himself."

"How do we know he truly pulled a phaser on you?"

"It was in his hand when I chopped the cable."

The judge advocate closed a dossier—rather noisily, Derek thought. "That's it, gentlemen," he said, "this man is telling the truth. The phaser was indeed found in the retracted hand of the sergeant. Since 66–percent biones come under the purview of the robotic code, I must conclude that this man acted appropriately. The rebuilding of Sergeant Alpha will doubtless reveal the cause of the malfunction."

"The sergeant is covered by the robotic code, then?" Derek questioned the judge advocate.

"He is." Derek heard a relay click in the man's body as he spoke.

"May I ask, sir, your own bionic percentage?"

"Seventy-two percent," the judge advocate answered Derek, and there was another click, this time clearly from the thorax area.

"And yours?" he asked the silent psychonomist.

"Eighty-nine," the very deep voice replied, and it was obvious that the man had had a laryngeal implant. God, I'm talking to another bunch of machines, Derek thought. He looked at the faces of the two majors and felt disdain for them. Then a sliver of mechanomorphic empathy stirred in him.

"Dismissed," the 12–percent bionic commandant barked.

Derek Carlson, Plebe I, Eastern Continental Gladiatorial Service, was discharged on Christmas Eve of the year 2800. The discharge cube read that he was constitutionally unsuited for gladiator training. It was later revealed that the bionic drill instructor, Sergeant Alpha 430, had been abused as a fledgling bione, and that his programming had not extirpated his residual hostility against humans. It was further determined that Sergeant Alpha had been, in effect, abusing himself with nonstandard, hedonistically reinforcing recharging regimens. He had become hooked on his own nuclear-pak rechargers, and, over the years, this had come to dilute the inhibitory mechanisms of his cortical matrices. He was indeed a machine gone bad, his cognition scornful of his ersatz personality and identity; and deep in his bionic matrices, a kind of primitive-instinctual death wish had developed—a computerized Thanatos drive. Sergeant Alpha's computer-repressed destiny had been to die as a biohuman kamikaze bomb. He fantasized being in single combat with large numbers of enemy, and to die as a hero atomized by a thoracic nuclear device. Now his George Patton personatype was being carefully replaced by an Eisenhower, and the plans were to make him a captain at the war college.

After this incident the gladiator service promptly switched its major bione contracts from IBM Akai to AT&T Mitsubishi. The Bionics Guild filed a class action suit against the gladiator service, and in a central Georgia pasture, the ancient KKK burned an archetypal robot effigy. In the Vatican exile island of Scorpio, the 27–percent bionic pope was summoned by the College of Cardinals for a review of his infallibility parameters, and there was a brief backlash of commuters teasing robot policemen on the major traffic quay of Chicago City.

Aboard the Amtrak terrafoil van back to Old Orleans, Derek looked up into the multifaceted visual agates of the 92-percent bionic conductor and demanded the full itinerary of the route-manifest. Later he ventured a gluteal pat on the 78-percent bionic stewardess, who flashed a coy smile at him, warned him of her stunbolt implant, and then introduced him to an 87-percent copulatress. While the terrafoil shot over the mountains and valleys of the Tennessee Territory, the copulatress fitted Derek with a pubococcygeal probe, and performed a panaperture sexual regimen on him that yielded his orgasm at centile 99. The barter-unit price was high, and the girl kept breathing, "To the victor belongs the spoils." For a few pinacular seconds, Derek felt oceanically penile, and decidedly nonvestibular.

Home again, the horizons of the Old Orleans marshlands once more rode high in his visual field, and he felt the familiar infusion of subtropical heat and muggy humidity and low barometric pressure. Once again he wriggled his bare toes deep into the mats of dewy Saint Augustine grass on the lawns around his home. He saw the snakes, fat as fire hoses, sleeping on the bayou flats, caught a hundred-pound gar, ate a bucket of crawfish, and took his pirogue deep into the swamps at dawn, where a huge owl flew low past him in the most profoundly feathered silence. Somewhere, a thousand miles up on the face of the globe, and three thousand feet higher above the sea, lay the memories of his brief and exciting gladiatorial exploits. I am organic with this place, he thought as he looked down into the black waters of the bayou, and it is here I will stay. I am atomic, yes. I am molecular, organic, tendinous, muscular, bipedal, kinesthetic, somesthetic, vestibular, and *human*. And there is a wholeness, a natural integrity in being human that I must cleave to. There are the men and there are the machines, and I am a man.

Green Days in Brunei
by Bruce Sterling

Introduction

Most people try to understand the world, and then adapt to it. A few people try to understand the world and, dissatisfied with what they find, change the world to fit their vision of what it ought to be.

Bruce Sterling is out to change the world. Not necessarily by reaching for power directly—that is the path followed by Fidel, Ho, Lenin, Mao, Robespierre, Caesar, and William the Conqueror. Sterling knows that the common people are usually unaffected by the change of leadership—and when the change really is revolutionary, there's usually a lot more egg-breaking than omelet-making, and the bills are always paid by the common people. Revolution is rarely an altruistic business.

Sterling has followed, so far, the other path—not revolution but transformation. Sterling, so far, is a storyteller, not a guerrilla. A storyteller changes the world by teaching people to see the world differently, by changing the meanings of common events; when readers come to believe in the world as the storyteller presents it to them, their behavior changes to reflect their new understanding of How Things Work. Sterling seems to be following the path toward transformation used by Rousseau, Marx, Locke, Hobbes, Jesus, Buddha, and Mohammed.

Sterling was drawn to tell his transformative stories through science fiction at least in part because science fiction alone of the literary genres allows an author to create a realistic changed world. But in order to use science fiction, Sterling first had to wake up the field to its own possibilities.

Sterling came to a genre that for many years had suffered from a serious lack of intelligent invention. The best young writers—the ones who should be re-envisioning the future—tended to treat future worlds and alien worlds as mere devices. Cardboard worlds were slapped together, with all the credibility and staying power of huts in a São Paulo favela. Then these writers devoted all their effort to character studies and literary experimentation. And the writers who were not the best seemed to be in love with technology and completely ignorant of the forces that actually tear and build in the real world of human beings.

In short, few science fiction writers seemed to understand the power and responsibility that could be theirs if they would only use it. Worse yet, the audience had become quite content with science fiction that had no connection with the real world. The audience was unprepared to receive pointed satires and realistic extrapolations, stories that called for and warned of proximate social change. Science fiction was the tool that Sterling had to use, and yet it was a tool whose intellectual edge was so blunted by misuse and dulled by neglect that he first had to do some grinding within the field in order to do any transforming outside it. He had to create a fit audience for his own stories, and to do that he had to enlist other writers, willing or not, in his camp.

He began with a writers workshop and a magazine. The Turkey City Writers Workshop in Austin, Texas, gathered many talented and some brilliant writers, and because he had such clear vision and powerful expression, Sterling quickly had them examining each other's stories not only for literary shortcomings, but also for failures of extrapolation. It was not enough to show a few changes in the future. All changes lead to more changes—Sterling demanded that writers think through the consequences of change in their fictional futures, and find the *consequences of consequences, many layers deep. Sterling also found a writer with the talent and intelligence and sheer force of will to match his—Lew Shiner—and through mutual abrasion they sharpened each other, then, together, turned their shining blades on the science fiction world outside.*

The magazine was Cheap Truth. *Sterling mailed it to a few regulars, but since it would do him no good to preach to the choir, he also mailed it to many people who he believed ought to receive it—in other words, the very people he was criticizing, the very people whom he most wanted to change. He also encouraged people to copy and reprint the magazine freely, so it received a much wider circulation than he could have paid for.*

I'm not sure why Sterling chose to keep most of it pseudonymous, concealing the identities of the contributors, but it was a correct and effective choice. Science fiction is such a clubby genre that few critics dare to speak bluntly, and those that do are often beaten down. Furthermore, writers tend to take the words of "big names" seriously and ignore comments by "nobodies"—regardless of the relative intelligence or truth of the things they say. When Sterling and Shiner started out, they were, in terms of fame, nobody. But when Sterling wrote as Vincent Omniaveritas and Lew Shiner as Sue Denim, they weren't nobody, they were Nobody, and therefore Somebody. The personas they created took on lives of their own; I think it's fair to say that for a period of several years, two nonexistent persons were the most influential and exasperating critics in science fiction. Their ideas were listened to; *prominent writers felt obliged to answer them. I believe that if the same words had been published under the names Sterling and Shiner, their motives and careers would have been attacked and their ideas largely ignored.*

They were not *ignored. Sterling continued to correspond with William Gibson, who had already begun on his own to create stories in an unusually well-extrapolated future, and they influenced each other greatly through collaborations and mutual criticism. Some writers came aboard the Movement as the natural culmination of long personal struggles—for instance, John Shirley, Rudy Rucker, Michael Swanwick. Others, unfortunately, caught on that this was Something Important, but were never able to muster the intelligence to accomplish in their fiction what Sterling called for; even they were useful, though, as they joined the cheering section and helped call attention to the Movement.*

Some of the writers who were attacked took it very personally and have yet to forgive Sterling and Shiner for the cruelty of their rhetoric; Sterling is a man of conscience, and this may be part of the reason why he recently shed the Vincent Omniaveritas persona with obvious relief. However, many of the gifted young writers who were under attack had the wisdom and humility to recognize that there was truth in what Cheap Truth said. They did not join Sterling's movement, but they allowed their fiction to respond to Sterling's concerns, not because they feared attack, but because they themselves had come to share some of those concerns. You can see that at least some stories of John Kessel, Kim Stanley Robinson, James Patrick Kelly, and many others have a greater rigor in world-creation, an increased socio-political awareness; they do not necessarily wish to change the world in the ways Sterling wants to, but they have acquired from Sterling some of the tools with which to change it.

Now, gradually, the audience is changing. The movement is not "Cyberpunk" anymore—it is much broader than that, while the name "Cyberpunk" has been co-opted to become the latest fad among the shallowest of artists in many fields who always seize on novelty, having long since given up on truth. Within science fiction, however, Sterling himself has said that by the time everyone heard of "Cyberpunk," the movement—as a discrete group within the field—was already over. Much of Sterling's ideology has already become a part of what "everyone knows" is necessary in "good science fiction." An ideology that everyone believes had stopped belonging to the person who first uttered it.

But the Movement was something Sterling did, not who Sterling was or is. For even as he publicly demanded greater rigor in one area of sf writing, he privately took himself through a literary course of studies that would daunt most of us. No two of his published short stories were alike. Rather than work repeatedly within one literary tradition, as Gibson did, Sterling wrote stories in every tradition, stories that at once mastered and subverted all the requirements of that tradition. His "Little Magic Shop," for instance, is a wonderful magic-shop story. It also ridicules all magic shop stories, revolts against traditional expectations, and brings in completely unrelated techniques so that the audience is dizzy by the end. By now there is hardly a tradition he hasn't explored.

At the same time, Sterling was also learning how to tell stories well. Contrary to a common impression, Sterling wasn't born knowing everything. He only knows everything today because he has read and studied everything. Perhaps you doubt me—this only shows you have not conversed with him. Sterling's first novels, while they were fine examples of world-creation, were extremely weak as stories. A lesser writer, noticing that Schismatrix *remained inaccessible or uninteresting to most readers, might have said, "Well, then, to hell with them!" But Sterling, you'll remember, is out to change the world. You can't change the world if you can't get the world to listen.*

Sterling's most recent novel, Islands in the Net, *shows a nearly perfect mastery of every aspect of storytelling. Even if a reader cares nothing about serious extrapolation,* Islands *is a wonderful read. It's a love story, a political thriller, a quest; it's a hero-tale that is truthful to the core. None of this is cynically added on—Sterling is not a hack, trying to discover the formula for financial success. Indeed,* Islands *is still so intellectually and emotionally demanding that I doubt it will sell to an audience of Ludlumesque proportions. What* Islands *does, though, is speak powerfully to the best audience. The audience that is willing to think, willing to feel, willing to let a story change them. And, given what I have seen of Sterling already, I expect that future books will be even better, by every standard of measure. For unlike many who have the wish to remake the world in their own image, Sterling also is willing to remake himself in order to fit his ideals, instead of deforming his ideals to fit his own weaknesses. If you disagree with Sterling, you must recognize that this is what makes him most dangerous. He will not allow even himself to stand in the way of what he wants to accomplish.*

I met Sterling at Sycamore Hill. (The fact that John Kessel and Mark Van Name invited him and the fact that he came make it clear that the conflict between them, though real, was not personal; these are men of passion and ideals and ideas, and they respect others who have the same fire inside.) We did not become intimates; nor did we convert each other. We are both too committed to distinct ideological programs for that. But we did share several brief conversations and one long one. By my own choice I mostly questioned and listened (an assertion that some will doubt, but it's true). I had long since given up on finding any writer—in or out of science fiction—who had a firm grasp of history, of the interplay of peoples and nations and individuals in the real world. Writers who attempted to deal with historical issues usually embarrassed themselves. Never mind nations—I even despaired of finding many writers who understood how families worked.

But Sterling clearly understood. Sterling saw the whole picture. More, he saw things from angles that had never been available to me. The more he spoke, the more I realized that he had the firmest grasp on large-scale reality of any person I've ever met, including me. We live in the same conceived world, I realized; we recognize many of the same diseases afflicting it. And even though we sometimes disagree strongly on the treatment and the cure, the world we want to end up living in is profoundly similar. In short, if Sterling succeeds in changing the world as he wants to, I'll be glad of it.

The story you are about to read is the first of his published works to demonstrate Sterling's full powers—as extrapolator, satirist, and storyteller. ''Green Days in Brunei'' is so full of details of world-creation that lesser writers could make careers out of writing Analog stories based on ideas that Sterling tosses away. Yet the detail never interferes with the story. After all that I've said about ideology and transformation, you can read ''Green Days'' for the sheer fun of it; or you can read it for excitement; or you can read it for its deeply plausible future; or you can read it for the political philosophy; or you can read it for its evocation of a non-western society trying to adapt to the technological world without being consumed by it; or you can read it for the discovery of character; or you can read it for the crystalline language that enhances the story without ever distracting from it.

If, instead of having several volumes, I could show you the

*1980s through the work of only one writer, the writer I would
point to would be Bruce Sterling. More than any other writer
since Robert Heinlein, Sterling has reinvented science fiction in
his own time and set it on a new course for the future.*

Two MEN WERE FISHING FROM THE CORRODED EDGE OF AN
offshore oil rig. After years of decrepitude, the rig's concrete
pillars were thick with barnacles and waving fronds of sea-
weed. The air smelled of rust and brine.

"Sorry to disturb your plans," the minister said. "But we
can't just chat up the Yankees every time you hit a little con-
tretemps." The minister reeled in and revealed a bare hook.
He cursed mildly in his native Malay. "Hand me another bait,
there's a good fellow."

Turner Choi reached into the wooden bait bucket and gave
the minister a large dead prawn. "But I need that phone link,"
Turner said. "Just for a few hours. Just long enough to access
the net in America and download some better documentation."

"What ghastly jargon," said the minister, who was formally
known as the Yang Teramat Pehin Orang Kaya Amar Diraja
Dato Seri Paduka Abdul Kahar. He was minister of industrial
policy for the Sultanate of Brunei Darussalam, a tiny nation
on the northern shore of the island of Borneo. The titles of
Brunei's aristocracy were in inverse proportion to the country's
size.

"It'd save us a lot of time, Tuan Minister," Turner said.
"Those robots are programmed in an obsolete language, forty
years old. Strictly Neanderthal."

The minister deftly baited his hook and flicked it out in a
long spinning cast. "You knew before you came here how the
sultanate feels about the world information order. You shall
just have to puzzle out this conundrum on your own."

"But you're making weeks, months maybe, out of a three-
hour job!" Turner said.

"My dear fellow, this is Borneo," the minister said benignly. "Stop looking at your watch and pay some attention to catching us dinner."

Turner sighed and reeled in his line. Behind them, the rig's squatter population of Dayak fisherfolk clustered on the old helicopter pad, mending nets and chewing betel-nut.

It was another slow Friday in Brunei Darussalam. Across the shallow bay, Brunei Town rose in tropical sunlight, its soaring high rises festooned with makeshift solar roofs, windmills, and bulging greenhouse balconies. The golden-domed mosque on the waterfront was surrounded by the towering legacy of the twentieth-century oil boom: boxlike office blocks, now bizarrely transmuted into urban farms.

Brunei Town, the sultanate's capital, had a hundred thousand citizens: Malays, Chinese, Ibans, Dayaks, and a sprinkling of Europeans. But it was a city under a hush. No cars. No airport. No television. From a distance it reminded Turner of an old Western fairy tale: Sleeping Beauty, the jury-rigged high-rises with their cascading greenery like a hundred castles shrouded in thorns. The Bruneians seemed like sleepwalkers, marooned from the world, wrapped in the enchantment of their ideology.

Turner baited his hook again, restive at being away from the production line. The minister seemed more interested in converting him than in letting him work. To the Bruneians, the robots were just another useless memento of their long-dead romance with the West. The old robot assembly line hadn't been used in twenty years, since the turn of the century.

And yet the royal government had decided to retrofit the robot line for a new project. For technical help, they had applied to Kyocera, a Japanese multinational corporation. Kyocera had sent Turner Choi, one of their new recruits, a twenty-six-year-old Chinese–Canadian CAD-CAM engineer from Vancouver.

It wasn't much of a job—a kind of industrial archeology whose main tools were chicken-wire and a ball-peen hammer—but it was Turner's first and he meant to succeed. The Bruneians were relaxed to the point of coma, but Turner Choi had his future ahead of him with Kyocera. In the long run, it was Kyocera who would judge his work here. And Turner was running out of time.

The minister, whooping in triumph, hauled hard on his line.

A fat, spotted fish broke the surface, flopping on the hook. Turner decided to break the rules and to hell with it.

The local neighborhood organization, the *kampong*, was showing a free movie in the little park fourteen stories below Turner's window. Bright images crawled against the bleak white Bauhaus wall of a neighboring high-rise.

Turner peered down through the blinds. He had been watching the flick all night as he finished his illegal tinkering.

The Bruneians, like Malays everywhere, adored ghost stories. The film's protagonist, or chief horror (Turner wasn't sure which) was an acrobatic monkey-demon with razor-sharp forearms. It had burst into a depraved speakeasy and was slaughtering drunkards with a tremendous windmilling flurry of punches, kicks, and screeches. Vast meaty sounds of combat, like colliding freight trains packed with beef, drifted faintly upward.

Turner sat before his bootleg keyboard, and sighed. He'd known it would come to this ever since the Bruneians had confiscated his phone at the customs. For five months he'd politely tried to work his way around it. Now he had only three months left. He was out of time and out of patience.

The robots were okay, under caked layers of yellowing grease. They'd been roped down under tarps for years. But the software manuals were a tattered ruin.

Just thinking about it gave Turner a cold sinking feeling. It was a special, private terror that had dogged him since childhood. It was the fear he felt when he had to confront his grandfather.

He thought of his grandfather's icy and pitiless eyes, fixed on him with that "Hong Kong Bad Cop" look. In the 1970s, Turner's grandfather had been one of the infamous "millionaire sergeants" of the Hong Kong police, skimming the cream of the Burmese heroin trade. He'd emigrated in the Triad bribery scandals of 1973.

After forty-seven years of silk suits and first-class flights between his mansion in Taipei and Vancouver, Grandfather Choi still had that cold eye and that grim shakedown look. It was an evil memory for Turner, of being weighed and found wanting.

The documentation was hopeless, crumbling and mildewed, alive with silverfish. The innocent Bruneians hadn't realized that the information it held was the linchpin of the whole enterprise. The sultanate had bought the factory long ago, with the last gush of Brunei's oil money, as a stylish, doomed gesture in Western industrial chic. Somehow, robots had never really caught on in Borneo.

But Turner had to seize this chance. He had to prove that he could make it on his own, without Grandfather Choi and the stifling weight of his money.

For days, Turner had snooped around down on the waterfront, with its cubbyholed rows of Chinese junkshops. It was Turner's favorite part of Brunei Town, a white-elephant's graveyard of dead tech. The wooden and bamboo shops were lined with dead, blackened televisions like decaying teeth.

There, he'd set about assembling a bootleg modern phone. He'd rescued a water-stained keyboard and screen from one of the shops. His modem and recorder came from work. On the waterfront he'd found a Panamanian freighter whose captain would illegally time-share on his satellite navigation dish.

Brunei Town was full of phone booths that no one ever seemed to use, grimy old glass-and-plastic units labeled in Malay, English, and Mandarin. A typical payphone stood on the street outside Turner's high-rise. It was an old twentieth-century job with a coin-feed and a rotary dial, and no video screen.

In the dead of night he'd crept down there to install a radio link to his apartment on the fourteenth floor. Someone might trace his illegal call back to the phone booth, but no farther. With the radio link, his own apartment would stay safe.

But when he'd punch-jacked the payphone's console off, he'd found that it already had a bootleg link hooked up. It was in fine working order, too. He'd seen then that he wasn't alone, and that Brunei, despite all its rhetoric about the Neo-Colonial World Information Order, was not entirely free of the global communications net. Brunei was wired too, just like the West, but the net had gone underground.

All those abandoned payphones had taken on a new and mildly sinister significance for him since that discovery, but he wasn't going to kick. All his plans were riding on his chance to get through.

Now he was ready. He re-checked the satellite guide in the back of his ASME Handbook. Arabsat 7 was up, in its leisurely low-orbit ramble over the tropics. Turner dialed from his apartment down through the payphone outside, then patched in through the Panamanian dish. Through Arabsat he looked up to an American geosynchronous sat and down into the American ground net. From there he direct-dialed his brother's house.

Georgie Choi was at breakfast in Vancouver, dressed in a French-cuffed pinstripe shirt and varsity sweater. Behind him, Turner's sleek sister-in-law, Marjorie, presided over a table crowded with crisp linen napkins and silver cutlery. Turner's two young nieces decorously spread jam on triangles of toast.

"Is it you, Turner?" Georgie said. "I'm not getting any video."

"I couldn't get a camera," Turner said. "I'm in Brunei—phone quarantine, remember? I had to bootleg it just to get sound."

A monsoon breeze blew up outside Turner's window. The windpower generators bolted to the high-rise walls whirred into life, and threw broad bars of raw static across the screen. Georgie's smooth brow wrinkled gracefully. "This reception is terrible! You're not even in stereo." He smiled uncertainly. "No matter, we'll make do. We haven't heard from you in ages. Things all right?"

"They will be," Turner said. "How's Grandfather?"

"He's flown in from Taipei for dialysis and his blood change," Georgie said. "He hates hospitals, but I had good news for him." He hesitated. "We have a new great-grandchild on the way."

Marjorie glanced up and bestowed one of her glittering wifely smiles on the camera. "That's fine," Turner said reflexively. Children were a touchy subject with Turner. He had not yet married, despite his family's endless prodding and nagging.

He thought guiltily that he should have spent more time with Georgie's children. Georgie was already in some upscale never-neverland, all leather-bound law and municipal politics, but it wasn't his kids' fault. Kids were innocent. "Hi, kids," he said in Mandarin. "I'll bring you something you'll like."

The younger girl looked up, her elegant child's mouth crusted with strawberry jam. "I want a shrunken head," she said in English.

"You see?" Georgie said with false joviality. "This is what comes of running off to Borneo."

"I need some modem software," Turner said, avoiding the issue. Grandfather hadn't approved of Borneo. "Could you get it off the old Hayes in my room?"

"If you don't have a modem protocol, how can I send you a program?" Georgie said.

"Print it out and hold it up to the screen," Turner explained patiently. "I'll record it and type it in later by hand."

"That's clever," Georgie said. "You engineers."

He left to set it up. Turner talked guardedly to Marjorie. He had never been able to figure the woman out. Turner would have liked to know how Marjorie really felt about cold-eyed Bad Cop Grandfather and his eight million dollars in Triad heroin money.

But Marjorie was so coolly elegant, so brilliantly designed, that Turner had never been able to bring himself to probe her real feelings. It would have been like popping open some factory-sealed peripheral that was still under warranty, just so you could sneak a look at the circuit boards.

Even he and Georgie never talked frankly any more. Not since Grandfather's health had turned shaky. The prospect of finally inheriting that money had left a white hush over his family like fifteen feet of Canadian snow.

The horrible old man relished the competition for his favor. He insisted on it. Grandfather had a second household in Taipei; Turner's uncle and cousins. If Grandfather chose them over his Canadian brood, Georgie's perfect life would go to pieces.

A childhood memory brushed Turner: Georgie's toys, brightly painted little Hong Kong wind-ups held together with folded tin flaps. As a child, Turner had spent many happy, covert hours dexterously prying Georgie's toys apart.

Marjorie chatted about Turner's mother, a neurotic widow who ran an antique store in Atlanta. Behind her, a Chinese maid began clearing the table, glancing up at the camera with the spooked eyes of an immigrant fresh off the boat.

Turner was used to phone cameras, and though he didn't have one he kept a fixed smile through habit. But he could feel himself souring, his face knotting up in that inherited Bad Cop glare. Turner had his Grandfather's face, with hollow cheeks, and sunken eyes under heavy, impressive brows.

But Canada, Turner's birthplace, had left its mark on him. Years of steak and Wonder Bread had given him a six-foot frame and the build of a linebacker.

Georgie came back with the printout. Turner said goodbye and cut the link.

He pulled up the blinds for the climax of the movie downstairs. The monkey-demon massacred a small army of Moslem extremists in the corroded remnants of a Shell refinery. Moslem fanatics had been stock villains in Brunei since the failure of their coup of '98.

The last of the reel flickered loose. Turner unpinned a banana-leaf wrapping and dug his chopsticks into a midnight snack of rice fried with green pineapple. He leaned on the open window, propping one booted foot on the massive windowbox with its dense ranks of onions and pepper plants.

The call to Vancouver had sent a shiver of culture shock through him. He saw his apartment with new eyes. It was decorated with housewarming gifts from other members of his *kampong*. A flat leather shadowpuppet, all perforations and curlicues. A gold-framed photo of the sultan shaking hands with the King of England. A hand-painted glass ant farm full of inch-long Borneo ants, torpid on molasses. And a young banyan bonsai tree from the *kampong* headman.

The headman, an elderly Malay, was a political wardheeler for Brunei's ruling party, the Greens, or "Partai Ekolojasi." In the West, the Greens had long ago been co-opted into larger parties. But Brunei's Partai Ekolojasi had twenty years of deep roots.

The banyan tree came with five pages of meticulous instructions on care and feeding, but despite Turner's best efforts the midget tree was yellowing and shedding leaves. The tree was not just a gift, it was a test, and Turner knew it. The *kampong* smiled, but they had their ways of testing, and they watched.

Turner glanced reflexively at his deadbolt on the door. The locks were not exactly forbidden, but they were frowned on.

The Greens had converted Brunei's old office building into huge multilayered village longhouses. Western notions of privacy were unpopular.

But Turner needed the lock for his work. He had to be discreet. Brunei might seem loose and informal, but it was still a one-party state under autocratic rule.

Twenty years earlier, when the oil crash had hit, the monarchy had seemed doomed. The Muslim insurgents had tried to murder them outright. Even the Greens had had bigger dreams then. Turner had seen their peeling, forgotten wall posters, their global logo of the Whole Earth half-buried under layered years of want-ads and soccer schedules.

The Royal Family had won through, a symbol of tradition and stability. They'd weathered the storm of the Muslim insurgence, and stifled the Green's first wild ambitions. After five months in Brunei, Turner, like the Royals, had grasped Brunei's hidden dynamics. It was *adat*, Malay custom, that ruled. And the first law of *adat* was that you didn't embarrass your neighbors.

Turner unpinned his favorite movie poster, a big promotional foursheet for a Brunei historical epic. In garish four-color printing, a boatload of heroic Malay pirates gallantly advanced on a sinister Portuguese galleon. Turner had carved a hideout in the sheetrock wall behind the poster. He stowed his phone gear.

Somebody tried the door, hit the deadbolt, and knocked softly. Turner hastily smoothed the poster and pinned it up.

He opened the door. It was his Australian neighbor, McGinty, a retired newscaster from Melbourne. McGinty loved Brunei for its utter lack of televisions. It was one of the last places on the planet in which one could truly get away from it all.

McGinty glanced up and down the hall, stepped inside, and reached into his loose cotton blouse. He produced a cold quart can of Foster's Lager. "Have a beer, chum?"

"Fantastic!" Turner said. "Where'd you get it?"

McGinty smiled evasively. "The bloody fridge is on the blink, and I thought you'd fancy one while they're still cold."

"Right," Turner said, popping the top. "I'll have a look at your fridge as soon as I destroy this evidence." The *Kampong* ran on a web of barter and mutual obligation. Turner's skills were part of it. It was tiresome, but a Foster's Lager was good pay. It was a big improvement over the liquid brain damage from the illegal stills down on Floor 4.

They went to McGinty's place. McGinty lived next door with his aged parents; four of them, for his father and mother had divorced and both remarried. The ancient Australians thrived in Brunei's somnolent atmosphere, pottering about the *kampong* gardens in pith helmets, gurkha shorts, and khaki bush vests. McGinty, like many of his generation, had never had children. Now in retirement he seemed content to shepherd these older folk, plying them with megavitamins and morning Tai Chi exercises.

Turner stripped the refrigerator. "It's your compressor," he said. "I'll track you down one on the waterfront. I can jury-rig something. You know me. Always tinkering."

McGinty looked uncomfortable, since he was now in Turner's debt. Suddenly he brightened. "There's a party at the privy councilor's tomorrow night. Jimmy Brooke. You know him?"

"Heard of him," Turner said. He'd heard rumors about Brooke: hints of corruption, some long-buried scandal. "He was a big man when the Partai got started, right? Minister of something."

"Communications."

Turner laughed. "That's not much of a job around here."

"Well, he still knows a lot of movie people." McGinty lowered his voice. "And he has a private bar. He's chummy with the Royal Family. They make allowances for him."

"Yeah?" Turner didn't relish mingling with McGinty's social circle of wealthy retirees, but it might be smart, politically. A word with the old com minister might solve a lot of his problems. "Okay," he said. "Sounds like fun."

The privy councilor, Yang Amat Mulia Pengiran Indera Negara Pengiran Jimmy Brooke, was one of Brunei's odder relics. He was a British tax exile, a naturalized Bruneian, who had shown up in the late '90s after the oil crash. His wealth had helped cushion the blow and had won him a place in the government.

Larger and better-organized governments might have thought twice about co-opting this deaf, white-haired eccentric, a washed-up pop idol with a parasitic retinue of balding bohemians. But the aging rock star, with his decaying glamor, fit in easily with the comic-opera glitter of Brunei's tiny aristocracy. He owned the old Bank of Singapore office block, a *kampong* of remarkable looseness where peccadillos flourished under Brooke's noblesse oblige.

Monsoon rain pelted the city. Brooke's henchmen, paunchy bodyguards in bulging denim, had shut the glass doors of the penthouse and turned on the air conditioning. The party had close to a hundred people, mostly retired Westerners from Europe and Australia. They had the stifling clubbiness of exiles who have all known each other too long. A handful of refugee Americans, still powdered and rouged with their habitual video makeup, munched imported beer nuts by the long mahogany bar.

The Bruneian actress Dewi Serrudin was holding court on a rattan couch, surrounded by admirers. Cinema was a lost art in the West, finally murdered and buried by video; but Brunei's odd policies had given it a last toe-hold. Turner, who had a mild, long-distance crush on the actress, edged up between two hopeful *émigrés*: a portly Madrasi producer in dhoti and jubbah, and a Hong Kong chop-socky director in a black frogged cotton shirt.

Miss Serrudin, in a gold lamé blouse and a skirt of antique ultrasuede, was playing the role to the hilt, chattering brightly and chain-burning imported Rothmans in a jade holder. She had the ritual concentration of a Balinese dancer evoking postures handed down through the centuries. And she was older than he'd thought she was.

Turner finished his whiskey sour and handed it to one of Brooke's balding gofers. He felt depressed and lonely. He wandered away from the crowd, and turned down a hall at random. The walls were hung with gold albums and old, yellowing pub-shots of Brooke and his band, all rhinestones and platform heels, their flying hair lavishly backlit with klieg lights.

Turner passed a library, and a billiards room where two wrinkled, turbaned Sikhs were racking up a game of snooker. Further down the hall, he glanced through an archway, into a

sunken conversation pit lavishly carpeted with ancient, inde-
structible synthetic plush.

A bony young Malay woman in black jeans and a satin jacket
sat alone in the room, reading a month-old issue of *New Musical Express*. It was headlined "Leningrad Pop Cuts Loose!"
Her sandaled feet were propped on a coffee table next to a
beaten silver platter with a pitcher and an ice-bucket on it. Her
bright red, shoulder-length hair showed two long inches of
black roots.

She looked up at him in blank surprise. Turner hesitated at
the archway, then stepped into the room. "Hi," he said.

"Hello. What's your *kampong*?"

"Citibank Building," Turner said. He was used to the question by now. "I'm with the industrial ministry, consulting engineer. I'm a Canadian. Turner Choi."

She folded the newspaper and smiled, "Ah, you're the bloke
who's working on the robots."

"Word gets around," Turner said, pleased.

She watched him narrowly. "Seria Bolkiah Mu'izzaddin
Waddaulah."

"Sorry, I don't speak Malay."

"That's my name," she said.

Turner laughed. "Oh Lord. Look, I'm just a no-neck Ca-
nuck with hay in my hair. Make allowances, okay?"

"You're a Western technician," she said. "How exotic. How
is your work progressing?"

"It's a strange assignment," Turner said. He sat on the couch
at a polite distance, marveling at her bizarre accent. "You've
spent some time in Britain?"

"I went to school there." She studied his face. "You look
rather like a Chinese Keith Richards."

"Sorry, don't know him."

"The guitarist of the Rolling Stones."

"I don't keep up with the bands," Turner said. "A little
Russian pop, maybe." He felt a peculiar tension in the situation. Turner glanced quickly at the woman's hands. No wed-
ding ring, so that wasn't it.

"Would you like a drink?" the woman said. "It's grape
juice."

"Sure," Turner said. "Thanks." She poured gracefully; innocent grape juice over ice. She was a Moslem, Turner thought, despite her dyed hair. Maybe that was why she was oddly standoffish.

He would have to bend the rules again. She was not conventionally pretty, but she had the kind of neurotic intensity that Turner had always found fatally attractive. And his love life had suffered in Brunei; the *kampongs* with their prying eyes and village gossip had cramped his style.

He wondered how he could arrange to see her. It wasn't a question of just asking her out to dinner—it all depended on her *kampong*. Some were stricter than others. He might end up with half-a-dozen veiled Muslim chaperones—or maybe a gang of muscular cousins and brothers with a bad attitude about Western lechers.

"When do you plan to start production, Mr. Choi?"

Turner said, "We've built a few fishing skiffs already, just minor stuff. We have bigger plans once the robots are up."

"A real factory," she said. "Like the old days."

Turner smiled, seeing his chance. "Maybe you'd like a tour of the plant?"

"It sounds romantic," she said. "Those robots are free labor. They were supposed to take the place of our free oil when it ran out. Brunei used to be rich, you know. Oil paid for everything. The Shellfare state, they used to call us." She smiled wistfully.

"How about Monday?" Turner said.

She looked at him, surprised, and suddenly blushed. "I'm afraid not."

Turner caught her eye. It's not me, he thought. It was something in the way—*adat* or something. "It's all right," he said gently. "I'd like to see you, is that so bad? Bring your whole *kampong* if you want."

"My *kampong* is the Palace," she said.

"Uh-oh." Suddenly he had that cold feeling again.

"You didn't know," she said triumphantly. "You thought I was some rock groupie."

"Who are you, then?"

"I'm the Duli Yank Maha Mulia Diranee . . . Well, I'm the princess. Princess Seria." She smiled.

"Good lord." He had been sitting and flirting with the royal princess of Brunei. It was bizarre. He half expected a troupe of bronzed enuchs to burst in, armed with scimitars. "You're the sultan's daughter?"

"You mustn't think too much of it," she said. "Our country is only two thousand square miles. It's so small that it's a family business, that's all. The mayor of your Vancouver rules more people than my family does."

Turner sipped his grape juice to cover his confusion. Brunei was a Commonwealth country, after all, with a British-educated aristocracy. The sultan had polo ponies and cricket pitches. But still, a princess . . .

"I never said I was from Vancouver," he told her. "You knew who I was all along."

"Brunei doesn't have many tall Chinese in lumberjack shirts." She smiled wickedly. "And those boots."

Turner glanced down. His legs were armored in knee-high engineering boots, a mass of shiny leather and buckles. His mother had bought them for him, convinced that they would save his life from snakebite in savage Borneo. "I promised I'd wear them," he said. "Family obligation."

She looked sour. "You, too? That sounds all too familiar, Mr. Choi." Now that the spell of anonymity was broken, she seemed flustered. Their quick rapport was grinding to a halt. She lifted the music paper with a rustle of pages. He saw that her nails were gnawed down to the quick.

For some perverse reason this put Turner's libido jarringly back into gear. She had the edgy flyaway look that spelled trouble with a capital "T." Ironically, she was just his type.

"I know the mayor's daughter in Vancouver," he said deliberately. "I like the local version a lot better."

She met his eyes. "It's really too bad about family obligations . . ."

The privy councilor appeared suddenly in the archway. The wizened rock star wore a cream-colored seersucker suit with ruby cufflinks. He was a cadaverous old buzzard with rheumy eyes and a wattled neck. A frizzed mass of snow-white hair puffed from his head like cotton from an aspirin bottle.

"Highness," he said loudly. "We need a fourth at bridge."

Princess Seria stood up with an air of martyrdom. "I'll be right with you," she shouted.

"And who's the young man?" said Brooke, revealing his dentures in an uneasy smile.

Turner stepped nearer. "Turner Choi, Tuan Privy Councilor," he said loudly. "A privilege to meet you, sir."

"What's your *kampong*, Mr. Chong?"

"Mr. Choi is working on the robot shipyard!" the princess said.

"The what? The shipyard? Oh, splendid." Brooke seemed relieved.

"I'd like a word with you, sir," Turner said. "About communications."

"About what?" Brooke cupped one hand to his ear.

"The phone net, sir! A line out!"

The princess looked startled. But Brooke, still not understanding, nodded blankly. "Ah yes. Very interesting . . . My entourage and I will bop by some day when you have the line up! I love the sound of good machines at work!"

"Sure," Turner said, recognizing defeat. "That would be, uh, groovy."

"Brunei is counting on you, Mr. Chong," Brooke said, his wrinkled eyes gleaming with bogus sincerity. "Good to see you here. Enjoy yourself." He shook Turner's hand, pressing something into his palm. He winked at Turner and escorted the Princess out into the hall.

Turner looked at his hand. The old man had given him a marijuana cigarette. Turner shook himself, laughed, and threw it away.

Another slow Monday in Brunei Town. Turner's work crew meandered in around midmorning. They were Bruneian Chinese, toting wicker baskets stuffed with garden-fresh produce, and little lacquered lunchboxes with *satay* shishkabobs and hot shrimp paste. They started the morning's food barter, chatting languidly in Malay-accented Mandarin.

Turner had very little power over them. They were hired by the Industrial Ministry, and paid little or nothing. Their labor was part of the invisible household economy of the *kampongs*. They worked for *kampong* perks, like chickens or movie tickets.

The shipyard was a cavernous barn with overhead pulley

tracks and an oil-stained concrete floor. The front section, with its bare launching rails sloping down to deep water, had once been a Dayak *kampong*. The Dayaks had spraybombed the concrete-block walls with giant neon-bright murals of banshees dead in childbirth, and leaping cricket-spirits with evil dayglo eyes.

The back part was two-story, with the robots' machine shop at ground level and a glass-fronted office upstairs that looked down over the yard.

Inside, the office was decorated in crass '80s High-Tech Moderne, with round-cornered computer desks between sleek modular partitions, all tubular chrome and grainy beige plastic. The plastic had aged hideously in forty years, absorbing a gray miasma of fingerprints and soot.

Turner worked alone in the neck-high maze of curved partitions, where a conspiracy of imported clerks and programmers had once efficiently sopped up the last of Brunei's oil money. He was typing up the bootlegged modem software on the IBM, determined to call America and get the production line out of the Stone Age.

The yard reeked of hot epoxy as the crew got to work. The robots were one-armed hydraulic jobs, essentially glorified tea-trolleys with single, swivel-jointed manipulators. Turner had managed to get them up to a certain crude level of donkey-work: slicing wood, stirring glue, hauling heavy bundles of lumber.

But, so far, the crew handled all the craft-work. They laminated the long strips of shaved lumber into sturdy panels of epoxied plywood. They bent the wet panels into hull and deck shapes, steam-sealing them over curved molds. They lapped and veneered the seams, and painted good-luck eye-symbols on the bows.

So far, the plant had produced nothing larger than a twenty-foot skiff. But on the drawing boards was a series of freighter-sized floating *kampongs*, massive sail-powered trimarans for the deep ocean, with glassed-in greenhouse decks.

The ships would be cheap and slow, like most things in Brunei, but pleasant enough, Turner supposed. Lots of slow golden afternoons on the tropical seas, with plenty of fresh fruit. The whole effort seemed rather pointless, but at least it would break Brunei's isolation from the world, and give them a crude merchant fleet.

The foreman, a spry old Chinese named Leng, shouted for Turner from the yard. Turner saved his program, got up, and looked down through the office glass. The minister of industrial policy had arrived, tying up an ancient fiberglass speedboat retrofitted with ribbed lateen sails.

Turner hurried down, groaning to himself, expecting to be invited off for another avuncular lecture. But the minister's zen-like languor had been broken. He came almost directly to the point, pausing only to genially accept some milk from the foreman.

"It's His Highness the Sultan," the minister said. "Someone's put a bee in his bonnet about these robots. Now he wants to tour the plant."

"When?" Turner said.

"Two weeks," said the minister. "Or maybe three."

Turner thought it over, and smiled. He sensed the princess's hand in this and felt deeply flattered.

"I say," the minister said. "You seem awfully pleased for a fellow who was predicting disaster just last Friday."

"I found another section of the manual," Turner lied glibly. "I hope to have real improvements in short order."

"Splendid," said the minister. "You remember the prototype we were discussing?"

"The quarter-scale model?" Turner said. "Tuan Minister, even in miniature, that's still a fifty-foot trimaran."

"Righto. How about it? Do you think you could scatter the blueprints about, have the robots whir by looking busy, plenty of sawdust and glue?"

Politics, Turner thought. He gave the minister his Bad Cop look. "You mean some kind of Potemkin village. Don't you want the ship built?"

"I fail to see what pumpkins have to do with it," said the minister, wounded. "This is a state occasion. We shall have the newsreel cameras in. Of course build the ship. I simply want it impressive, that's all."

Impressive, Turner thought. Sure. If Seria was watching, why not?

* * *

Luckily the Panamanian freighter was still in port, not leaving till Wednesday. Armed with his new software, Turner tried another bootleg raid at ten P.M. He caught a Brazilian comsat and tied into Detroit.

Reception was bad, and Doris had already moved twice. But he found her finally in a seedy condominium in the Renaissance Center historical district.

"Where's your video, man?"

"It's out," Turner lied, not wanting to burden his old girlfriend with two years of past history. He and Doris had lived together in Toronto for two semesters, while he studied CAD–CAM. Doris was an automotive designer, a rust-belt refugee from Detroit's collapse.

For Turner, school was a blissful chance to live in the same pair of jeans for days on end, but times were tough in the Rust Belt and Doris had lived close to the bone. He'd ended up footing the bills, which hadn't bothered him (Bad Cop money), but it had preyed on Doris's mind. Months passed, and she spent more each week. He picked up her bills without a word, and she quietly went over the edge. She ended up puking drunk on her new satin sheets, unable to go downstairs for the mail without a line of coke.

But then word had come of his father's death. His father's antique Maserati had slammed head-on into an automated semi-trailer rig. Turner and his brother had attended the cremation in a drizzling Vancouver rain. They put the ashes on the family altar and knelt before little gray ribbons of incense smoke. Nobody said much. They didn't talk about Dad's drinking. Grandfather wouldn't have liked it.

When he'd gone back to Toronto, he found that Doris had packed up and left.

"I'm with Kyocera now," he told her. "The consulting engineers."

"You got a job, Turner?" she said, brushing back a frizzed tangle of blonde hair. "It figures. Poor people are standing in line for a chance to do dishes." She frowned. "What kind of hours you keeping, man? It's seven A.M. You caught me without my vid makeup."

She turned the camera away and walked out of sight. Turner studied her apartment: concrete blocks and packing crates, vinyl beanbag chairs, peeling walls festooned with printout. She was still on the Net, all right. Real Net-heads resented every penny not spent on information.

"I need some help, Doris. I need you to find me someone who can system-crack an old IBM robotics language called AML."

"Yeah?" She called out. "Ten percent agent's fee?"

"Sure. And this is on the hush, okay? Not Kyocera's business, just mine."

He heard her shouting from the condo's cramped bathroom. "I haven't heard from you in two years! You're not mad that I split, huh?"

"No."

"It wasn't that you were Chinese, okay? I mean, you're about as Chinese as maple syrup, right? It's just, the high life was making my sinuses bleed."

Turner scowled. "Look, it's okay. It was a temporary thing."

"I was crazy then. But I've been hooked up to a good shrink program, it's done wonders for me, really." She came back to the screen; she'd put on rouge and powder. She smiled and touched her cheek. "Good stuff, huh? The kind the President uses."

"You look fine."

"My shrink makes me jog every day. So, how you doin', man? Seeing anybody?"

"Not really." He smiled. "Except a princess of Borneo."

She laughed. "I thought you'd settle down by now, man. With some uptown family girl, right? Like your brother and what's-her-face."

"Didn't work out that way."

"You like crazy women, Turner, that's your problem. Remember the time your mom dropped by? She's a fruitcake, that's why."

"Aw, Jesus Christ, Doris," Turner said. "If I need a shrink, I can download one."

"Okay," she said, hurt. She touched a remote control. A television in the corner of the room flashed into life with a crackle of video music. Doris didn't bother to watch it. She'd turned it on by reflex, settling into the piped flow of cable like a hot bath. "Look, I'll see what I can scare you up on the Net. AML language, right? I think I know a—"

BREAK

The screen went blank. Alphanumerics flared up: ENTERING (C)HAT MODE

The line zipped up the screen. The words spelled out in 80-column, glowing bright green. WHAT ARE YOU DOING ON THIS LINE?

SORRY, Turner typed.

ENTER YOUR PASSWORD:

Turner thought fast. He had blundered into the Brunei underground net. He'd known it was possible, since he was using the pre-rigged payphone downstairs. MAPLE SYRUP, he typed at random.

CHECKING. . . . THAT IS NOT A VALID PASSWORD.

SIGNING OFF, Turner typed.

WAIT, said the screen. WE DON'T TAKE LURKERS LIGHTLY HERE. WE HAVE BEEN WATCHING YOU. THIS IS THE SECOND TIME YOU HAVE ACCESSED A SATELLITE. WHAT ARE YOU DOING IN OUR NET??

Turner rested one finger on the off switch.

More words spilled out. WE KNOW WHO YOU ARE, "MAPLE SYRUP." YOU ARE TURNER CHONG.

"Turner *Choi*," Turner said aloud. Then he remembered the man who had made that mistake. He felt a sudden surge of glee. He typed: OKAY, YOU'VE GOT ME—TUAN COUNCILOR JIMMY BROOKE!

There was a long blank space. Then: CLEVER, Brooke typed. SERIA TOLD YOU. SERIA, ARE YOU ON THIS LINE??

I WANT HER NUMBER!! Turner typed at once.

THEN LEAVE A (M)ESSAGE FOR "GAMELAN ROCKER," Brooke typed. I AM "NET HEADHUNTER."

THANKS, Turner typed.

I'LL LOG YOU ON, MAPLE SYRUP, SINCE YOU'RE ALREADY IN, YOU'D BETTER BE IN ON OUR TERMS. BUT JUST REMEMBER: THIS IS OUR ELECTRONIC KAMPONG. SO YOU LIVE BY OUR RULES, OUR "ADAT," OKAY?"

I'LL REMEMBER, SIR.

AND NO MORE BOOTLEG SATELLITE LINKS, YOU'RE SCREWING UP OUR GROUND LINES.

OKAY, Turner typed.

YOU CAN RENT TIME ON OUR OWN DISHES. NEXT TIME CALL 85-1515 DIRECTLY. OUR GAMES SECTION COULD USE SOME UPLOADS, BY THE WAY.

The words flashed off, replaced by the neatly ranked commands of a computer bulletin board. Turner accessed the message section, but then sat sweating and indecisive. In his mind, his quick message to Seria was rapidly ramifying into a particularly touchy and tentative love letter.

This was good, but it wasn't how he'd planned it. He was getting in over his head. He'd have to think it through.

He logged off the board. Doris's face appeared at once. "Where the hell have you been, man?"

"Sorry," Turner said.

"I've found you some old geezer out in Yorktown Heights," she said. "He says he used to work with Big Blue back in prehistory."

"It's always some old geezer," Turner said in resignation.

Doris shrugged. "Whaddya expect, man? Birth control got everybody else."

Down in the yard, the Sultan of Brunei chatted with his minister as technicians in sarongs and rubber sandals struggled with their huge, ancient cameras. The sultan wore his full regalia, a high-collared red military jacket with gold-braided shoulderboards, heavy with medals and pins. He was an elderly Malay with a neatly clipped white mustache and sad, wise eyes.

His son, the crown prince, had a silk ascot and an air force pilot's jacket. Turner had heard that the prince was nuts about helicopters. Seria's formal wear looked like a jazzed-up Girl Guide's outfit, with a prim creased skirt and a medal-clustered shoulder-sash.

Turner was alone in the programming room, double-checking one of the canned routines he'd downloaded from America. They'd done wonders for the plant already; the robots had completed one hull of the trimaran. The human crew was handling the delicate work: the glassed-in greenhouse. Braced sections of glass now hung from ceiling pulleys, gleaming photogenically in geodesic wooden frames.

Turner studied his screen.

```
IF QMONITOR(FMONS(2)) EQ O THEN RETURN ('TOO SMALL')
TOGO = GRIPPER-OPENING + MIN-OFS-QPOSITION (GRIPPER)
DMOVE(XYZ# < GRIPPER > , (-TOGO/2*HANDFRAME) (2,2))
< TOGO > ,FMONS(2));
```

This was more like it! Despite its low-powered crudity, AML was becoming obsessive with him, its rhythms sticking like poetry. He picked up his coffee-cup, thinking: REACH-GRASP-TOGO ‡ (MOUTH) + SIP; RETURN.

The sluggishness of Brunei had vanished overnight once he'd hooked to the Net. The screen had eaten up his life. A month had passed since his first bootleg run. All day he worked on AML; at night he went home to trade electronic mail with Seria.

Their romance had grown through the Net; not through modern video, but through the ancient bulletin board's anonymous green text. Day by day it became more intense, for it was all kept in a private section of memory, and nothing could be taken back. There were over a hundred messages on their secret disks, starting coolly and teasingly, and working slowly up through real passion to a kind of mutual panic.

They hadn't planned it to happen like this. It was part of the dynamic of the Net. For Seria, it had been a rare chance to escape her role and talk to an interesting stranger. Turner was only looking for the kind of casual feminine solace that had never been hard to find. The Net had tricked them.

Because they couldn't see each other. Turner realized now that no woman had ever known and understood him as Seria did, for the simple reason that he had never had to talk to one so much. If things had gone as they were meant to in the West, he thought, they would have chased their attraction into bed and killed it there. Their two worlds would have collided bruisingly, and they would have smiled over orange juice the next morning and mumbled tactful goodbyes.

But that wasn't how it had happened. Over the weeks, it had all come pouring out between them: his family, her family, their resentment, his loneliness, her petty constraints, all those irritants that ulcerate a single person, but are soothed by two. Bizarrely, they had more in common than he could have ever expected. Real things, things that mattered.

The painfully simple local Net filtered human relations down to a single channel of printed words, leaving only a high-flown Platonic essence. Their relationship had grown into a classic, bloodless, spiritual romance in its most intense and dangerous sense. Human beings weren't meant to live such roles. It was the stuff of high drama because it could very easily drive you crazy.

He had waited on tenterhooks for her visit to the shipyard. It had taken a month instead of two weeks, but he'd expected as much. That was the way of Brunei.

"Hello, Maple Syrup."

Turner started violently and stood up. "Seria!"

She threw herself into his arms with a hard thump. He staggered back, hugging her. "No kissing," she said hastily. "Ugh, it's nasty."

He glanced down at the shipyard and hauled her quickly out of sight of the window. "How'd you get up here?"

"I sneaked up the stairs. They're not looking. I had to see you. The real you, not just words on a screen."

"This is crazy." He lifted her off the ground, squeezing her hard. "God, you feel wonderful."

"So do you. Ouch, my medals, be careful."

He set her back down. "We've got to do better than this. Look, where can I see you?"

She gripped his hands feverishly. "Finish the boat, Turner. Brooke wants it, his new toy. Maybe we can arrange something." She pulled his shirt tail out and ran her hands over his midriff. Turner felt a rush of arousal so intense that his ears rang. He reached down and ran his hand up the back of her thigh. "Don't wrinkle my skirt!" she said, trembling. "I have to go on camera!"

Turner said, "This place is nowhere. It isn't right for you, you need fast cars and daiquiris and television and jet trips to the goddamn Bahamas."

"So romantic," she whispered hotly. "Like rock stars, Turner. Huge stacks of amps and mobs at the airport. Turner, if you could see what I'm wearing under this, you'd go crazy."

She turned her face away. "Stop trying to kiss me! You Westerners are weird. Mouths are for eating."

"You've got to get used to Western things, precious."

"You can't take me away, Turner. My people wouldn't let you."

"We'll think of something. Maybe Brooke can help."

"Even Brooke can't leave," she said. "All his money's here. If he tried, they would freeze his funds. He'd be penniless."

"Then I'll stay here," he said recklessly. "Sooner or later we'll have our chance."

"And give up all your money, Turner?"

He shrugged. "You know I don't want it."

She smiled sadly. "You tell me that now, but wait till you see your real world again."

"No, listen—"

Lights flashed on in the yard.

"I have to go, they'll miss me. Let go, let go." She pulled free of him with vast, tearing reluctance. Then she turned and ran.

In the days that followed, Turner worked obsessively, linking subroutines like data tinkertoys, learning as he went along, adding each day's progress to the master program. Once it was all done, and he had weeded out the redundancy, it would be self-sustaining. The robots would take over, transforming information into boats. He would be through. And his slow days in Brunei would be history.

After his job, he'd vaguely planned to go to Tokyo, for a sentimental visit to Kyocera corporate headquarters. He'd been recruited through the Net; he'd never actually seen anyone from Kyocera in the flesh.

That was standard practice. Kyocera's true existence was as data, not as real estate. A modern multinational company was not its buildings or its stock. Its real essence was its ability to pop up on a screen, and to funnel that special information known as money through the global limbo of electronic banking.

He'd never given this a second thought. It was old hat. But filtering both work and love-life through the screen had left him feeling Netburned. He took to long morning walks through Brunei Town after marathon sessions at the screen, stretching cramped muscles and placing his feet with a daze AML deliberation: TOGO = DMOVE<KNEE> + - QPOSITION(FOOT).

He felt ghostlike in the abandoned streets; Brunei had no nightlife to speak of, and a similar lack of muggers and predators. Everybody was in everyone else's lap, doing each other's laundry, up at dawn to the shrieks of *kampong* roosters. People gossiped about you if you were a mugger. Pretty soon you'd have nightsoil duty and have to eat bruised mangos.

When the rain caught him, as it often did in the early morning, he would take shelter in the corner bus stations. The bus stops were built of tall glass tubes, aquaculture cylinders, murky green soups full of algae and fat, sluggish carp.

He would think about staying then, sheltered in Brunei forever, like a carp behind warm glass. Like one of those little bonsai trees in its cramped and cosy little pot, with people always watching over you, trimming you to fit. That was Brunei for you: the whole East, really: wonderful community, but people always underfoot and in your face. . . .

But was the West any better? Old people locked away in bursting retirement homes . . . Soaring unemployment, with no one knowing when some robot or expert system would make him obsolete . . . People talking over televisions when they didn't know the face of the man next door. . . .

Could he really give up the West, he wondered, abandon his family, ruin his career? It was the craziest sort of romantic gesture, he thought, because even if he was brave or stupid enough to break all the rules, she wouldn't. Seria would never escape her *adat*. Being royalty was worse than Triad.

A maze of plans spun though his head like an error-trapping loop, always coming up empty. He would sit dazedly and watch the fish circle in murky water, feeling like a derelict, and wondering if he was losing his mind.

Privy Councilor Brooke bought the boat. He showed up suddenly at the shipyard one afternoon, with his claque of followers. They'd brought a truckload of saplings in tubs of dirt. They began at once to load them aboard the greenhouse, clumping up and down the stepladders to the varnished deck.

Brooke oversaw the loading for a while, checking a deck

plan from the pocket of his white silk jacket. Then he jerked his thumb at the glassed-in front of the data center. "Let's go upstairs for a little talk, Turner."

Mercifully, Brooke had brought his hearing aid. They sat in two of the creaking, musty swivel-chairs. "It's a good ship," Brooke said.

"Thanks."

"I knew it would be. It was my idea, you know."

Turner poured coffee. "It figures," he said.

Brooke cackled. "You think it's a crazy notion, don't you? Using robots to build tubs of cheap glue and scrubwood. But your head's on backwards, boy. You engineers are all mystics. Always goosing God with some new Tower of Babel. Masters of nature, masters of space and time. Aim at the stars, and hit London."

Turner scowled. "Look, Tuan Councilor, I did my job. Nothing in the contract says I have to share your politics."

"No," Brooke said. "But the sultanate could use a man like you. You're a *bricoleur*, Chong. You can make do. You can retrofit. That's what *bricolage* is—it's using the clutter and rubble to make something worth having. Brunei's too poor now to start over with fresh clean plans. We've got nothing but the junk the West conned us into buying, every last bloody Coke can and two-car garage. And now we have to live in the rubble, and make it a community. It's a tough job, *bricolage*. It takes a special kind of man, a special eye, to make the ruins bloom."

"Not me," Turner said. He was in one of his tough-minded moods. Something about Brooke made him leery. Brooke had a peculiar covert sleaziness about him. It probably came from a lifetime of evading drug laws.

And Turner had been expecting this final push; people in his *kampong* had been dropping hints for weeks. They didn't want him to leave; they were always dropping by with pathetic little gifts. "This place is one big hothouse," he said. "Your litte *kampongs* are like orchids, they can only grow under glass. Brunei's already riddled with the Net. Someday it'll break open your glass bubble, and let the rest of the world in. Then a hard rain's gonna fall."

Brooke stared. "You like Bob Dylan?"

"Who?" Turner said, puzzled.

Brooke, confused, sipped his coffee, and grimaced. "You've been drinking this stuff? Jesus, no wonder you never sleep."

Turner glowered at him. Nobody in Brunei could mind their own business. Eyes were everywhere, with tongues to match. "You already know my real trouble."

"Sure." Brooke smiled with a yellowed gleam of dentures. "I have this notion that I'll sail upriver, lad. A little shake-down cruise for a couple of days. I could use a technical adviser, if you can mind your manners around royalty."

Turner's heart leapt. He smiled shakily. "Then I'm your man, Councilor."

They bashed a bottle of nonalcoholic grape juice across the center bow and christened the ship the *Mambo Sun*. Turner's work crew launched her down the rails and stepped the masts. She was crewed by a family of Dayaks from one of the offshore rigs, an old woman with four sons. They were the dark, beautiful descendants of headhunting pirates, dressed in hand-dyed sarongs and ancient plastic baseball caps. Their language was utterly incomprehensible.

The *Mambo Sun* rode high in the water, settling down into her new element with weird drumlike creaks from the hollow hulls. They put out to sea in a stiff offshore breeze.

Brooke stood with spry insouciance under the towering jib sail, snorting at the sea air. "She'll do twelve knots," he said with satisfaction. "Lord, Turner, it's great to be out of the penthouse and away from that crowd of flacks."

"Why do you put up with them?"

"It comes with the money, lad. You should know that."

Turner said nothing. Brooke grinned at him knowingly. "Money's power, my boy. Power doesn't go away. If you don't use it yourself, someone else will use you to get it."

"I hear they've trapped you here with that money," Turner said. "They'll freeze your funds if you try to leave."

"I let them trap me," Brooke said. "That's how I won their trust." He took Turner's arm. "But you let me know if you have money troubles here. Don't let the local Islamic Bank fast-talk you into anything. Come see me first."

Turner shrugged him off. "What good has it done you? You're surrounded with yes-men."

"I've had my crew for forty years." Brooke sighed nostalgically. "Besides, you should have seen them in '98, when the streets were full of Moslem fanatics screaming for blood. Molotovs burning everywhere, pitched battles with the blessed Chinese, the sultan held hostage. . . . My crew didn't turn a hair. Held the mob off like a crowd of teenyboppers when they tried to rush my building. They had grit, those lads."

An ancient American helicopter buzzed overhead, its orange seafloats almost brushing the mast. Brooke yelled to the crew in their odd language; they furled the sails and set anchor, half a mile offshore. The chopper wheeled expertly and settled down in a shimmering circle of wind-flattened water. One of the Dayaks threw them a weighted line.

They hauled in. "Permission to come aboard, sir!" said the crown prince. He and Seria wore crisp nautical whites. They clambered from the float up a rope ladder and onto the deck. The third passenger, a pilot, took the controls. The crew hauled anchor and set sail again; the chopper lifted off.

The prince shook Turner's hand. "You know my sister, I believe."

"We met at the filming," Turner said.

"Ah yes. Good footage, that."

Brooke, with miraculous tact, lured the prince into the greenhouse. Seria immediately flung herself into Turner's arms. "You haven't written in two days," she hissed.

"I know." Turner said. He looked around, quickly to make sure the Dayaks were occupied. "I keep thinking about Vancouver. How I'll feel when I'm back there."

"How you left your Sleeping Beauty behind in the castle of thorns? You're such a romantic, Turner."

"Don't talk like that. It hurts."

She smiled. "I can't help being cheerful. We have two days together, and Omar gets seasick."

The river flowed beneath their hulls like thin gray grease. Jungle leaned in from the banks; thick, clotted green mats of foliage over skinny, light-starved trunks, rank with creepers. It was snake country, leech country, a primeval reek stewing in deadly humidity, with air so thick that the raucous shrieks of birds seemed to cut it like ripsaws. Bugs whirled in dense mating swarms over rafts of slime. Suspicious, sodden logs loomed in the gray mud. Some logs had scales and eyes.

The valley was as crooked as an artery, snaking between tall hills smothered in poisonous green. Sluggish wads of mist wreathed their tops. Where the trees failed, sheer cliffs were shrouded in thick ripples of ivy. The sky was gray, the sun a muddy glow behind tons of haze.

The wind died, and Brooke fired up the ship's tiny alcohol engine. Turner stood on the central bow as they sputtered upstream. He felt glazed and dreamy. Culture shock had seized him; none of it seemed real. It felt like a television. Reflexively, he kept thinking of Vancouver, sailboat trips out to clean pine islands.

Seria and the prince joined him on the bow. "Lovely isn't it?" said the prince. "We've made it a game preserve. Someday there will be tigers again."

"Good thinking, Your Highness," Turner said.

"The city feeds itself, you know. A lot of the old paddies and terraces have gone back to jungle." The prince smiled with deep satisfaction.

With evening, they tied up at a dock by the ruins of a riverine city. Decades earlier, a flood had devastated the town, leaving shattered walls, where vines snaked up trellises of rusting reinforcement rods. A former tourist hotel was now a ranger station.

They all went ashore to review the troops: Royal Malay Rangers in jungle camo, and a visiting crew of Swedish ecologists from the World Wildlife Fund. The two aristocrats were gung-ho for a bracing hike through the jungle. They chatted amiably with the Swedes as they soaked themselves with gnat and leech repellent. Brooke pleaded his age, and Turner managed to excuse himself.

Behind the city rose a soaring radio aerial and the rain-blotched white domes of satellite dishes.

"Jamming equipment," said Brooke with a wink. "The sultanate set it up years ago. Islamic, Malaysian, Japanese—you'd be surprised how violently people insist on being listened to."

"Freedom of speech," Turner said.

"How free is it when only rich nations can afford to talk? The Net's expensive, Turner. To you it's a way of life, but for

us it's just a giant megaphone for Coca-Cola. We built this to
block the shouting of the outside world. It seemed best to set
the equipment here in the ruins, out of harm's way. This is a
good place to hide secrets." Brooke sighed. "You know how
the corruption spreads. Anyone who touches it is tempted. We
use these dishes as the nerve center of our own little Net. You
can get a line out here—a real one, with video. Come along,
Turner. I'll stand Maple Syrup a free call to civilization, if you
like."

They walked through leaf-littered streets, where pigs and
lean, lizard-eyed chickens scattered from underfoot. Turner saw
a tattooed face, framed in headphones, at a shattered second-
story window. "The local Murut tribe," Brooke said, glancing
up. "They're a bit shy."

The central control room was a small white concrete blockhouse surrounded by sturdy solar-panel racks. Brooke opened
a tarnished padlock with a pocket key, and shot the bolt. Inside, the windowless blockhouse was faintly lit by the tiny
green and yellow power-lights of antique disk drives and personal computers. Brooke flicked on a desk lamp and sat on a
chair cushioned with moldy foam rubber. "All automated, you
see? The government hasn't had to pay an official visit in years.
It keeps everyone out of trouble."

"Except for your insiders," Turner said.

"We *are* trouble," said Brooke. "Besides, this was my idea
in the first place." He opened a musty wicker chest and pulled
a video camera from a padded wrapping of cotton batik. He
popped it open, sprayed its insides with silicone lubricant, and
propped it on a tripod. "All the comforts of home." He left
the blockhouse.

Turner hesitated. He'd finally realized what had bothered
him about Brooke. Brooke was *hip*. He had that classic hip
attitude of being in on things denied to the uncool. It was
amazing how sleazy and suspicious it looked on someone who
was *really old*.

Turner dialed his brother's house. The screen remained dark.
"Who is it?" Georgie said.

"Turner."

"Oh." A long moment passed; the screen flashed on to
show Georgie in a maroon silk houserobe, his hair still flat-

tened from the pillow. "That's a relief. We've been having some trouble with phone flashers."

"How are things?"

"He's dying, Turner."

Turner stared. "Good God."

"I'm glad you called." Georgie smoothed his hair shakily. "How soon can you get here?"

"I've got a job here, Georgie."

Georgie frowned. "Look, I don't blame you for running. You wanted to live your own life; okay, that's fine. But this is *family business*, not some two-bit job in the middle of nowhere."

"Goddammit," Turner said, pleading. "I *like* it here, Georgie."

"I know how much you hate the old bastard. But he's just a dying old man now. Look, we hold his hands for a couple of weeks, and it's all ours, understand? The Riviera, man."

"It won't work, Georgie," Turner said, clutching at straws. "He's going to screw us."

"That's why I need you here. We've got to double-team him, understand?" Georgie glared from the screen. "Think of my kids, Turner. We're your family, you owe us."

Turner felt growing despair. "Georgie, there's a woman here . . ."

"Christ, Turner."

"She's not like the others. Really."

"Great. So you're going to marry this girl, right? Raise kids."

"Well . . ."

"Then what are you wasting my time for?"

"Okay," Turner said, his shoulders slumping. "I gotta make arrangements. I'll call you back."

The Dayaks had gone ashore. The prince blithely invited the Swedish ecologists on board. They spent the evening chastely sipping orange juice and discussing Krakatoa and the swamp rhinoceros.

After the party broke up, Turner waited a painful hour and crept into the deserted greenhouse.

Seria was waiting in the sweaty green heat, sitting cross-legged, in watery moonlight crosshatched by geodesics, brushing her hair. Turner joined her on the mat. She wore an erotic red synthetic nightie (some groupie's heirloom from the legion of Brooke's women), crisp with age. She was drenched in perfume.

Turner touched her fingers to the small lump on his forearm, where a contraceptive implant showed beneath his skin. He kicked his jeans off.

They began in caution and silence, and ended, two hours later, in the primeval intimacy of each other's musk and sweat. Turner lay on his back, with her head pillowed on his bare arm, feeling a sizzling effervescence of deep, cellular pleasure.

It had been mystical. He felt as if some primal feminine energy had poured off her body and washed through him, to the bone. Everything seemed different now. He had discovered a new world, the kind of world a man could spend a lifetime in. It was worth ten years of a man's life just to lie here and smell her skin.

The thought of having her out of arm's reach, even for a moment, filled him with a primal anxiety close to pain. There must be a million ways to make love, he thought languidly. As many as there are to talk or think. With passion. With devotion. Playfully, tenderly, frantically, soothingly. Because you want to, because you need to.

He felt an instinctive urge to retreat to some snug den—anywhere with a bed and a roof—and spend the next solid week exploring the first twenty or thirty ways in that million.

But then the insistent pressure of reality sent a trickle of reason into him. He drifted out of reverie with a stabbing conviction of the perversity of life. Here was all he wanted—all he asked was to pull her over him like a blanket and shut out life's pointless complications. And it wasn't going to happen.

He listened to her peaceful breathing and sank into black depression. This was the kind of situation that called for wild romantic gestures, the kind that neither of them were going to make. They weren't allowed to make them. They weren't in his program, they weren't in her *adat*, they weren't in the plans.

Once he'd returned to Vancouver, none of this would seem real. Jungle moonlight and erotic sweat didn't mix with cool piny fogs over the mountains and the family mansion in Churchill Street. Culture shock would rip his memories away, snapping the million invisible threads that bind lovers.

As he drifted toward sleep, he had a sudden lucid flash of precognition: himself, sitting in the back seat of his brother's Mercedes, letting the machine drive him randomly around the city. Looking past his reflection in the window at the clotted snow in Queen Elizabeth Park, and thinking: *I'll never see her again.*

It seemed only an instant later that she was shaking him awake. "Shh!"

"What?" he mumbled.

"You were talking in your sleep." She nuzzled his ear, whispering. "What does 'Set-position Q-move' mean?"

"Jesus," he whispered back. "I was dreaming in AML." He felt the last fading trail of nightmare then, some unspeakable horror of cold iron and helpless repetition. "My family," he said. "They were all robots."

She giggled.

"I was trying to repair my grandfather."

"Go back to sleep, darling."

"No." He was wide awake now. "We'd better get back."

"I hate that cabin. I'll come to your tent on deck."

"No, they'll find out. You'll get hurt, Seria." He stepped back into his jeans.

"I don't care. This is the only time we'll have." She struggled fretfully into the red tissue of her nightie.

"I want to be with you," he said. "If you could be mine, I'd say to hell with my job and my family."

She smiled bitterly. "You'll think better of it, later. You can't throw away your life for the sake of some affair. You'll find some other woman in Vancouver. I wish I could kill her."

Every word rang true, but he still felt hurt. She shouldn't have doubted his willingness to totally destroy his life. "You'll marry too, someday. For reasons of state."

"I'll never marry," she said aloofly. "Someday I'll run away from all this. My grand romantic gesture."

She would never do it, he thought with a kind of aching pity. She'll grow old under glass in this place. "One grand gesture was enough," he said. "At least we had this much."

She watched him gloomily. "Don't be sorry you're leaving,

darling. It would be wrong of me to let you stay. You don't know all the truth about this place. Or about my family.''

"All families have secrets. Yours can't be any worse than mine.''

"My family is different.'' She looked away. "Malay royalty are sacred, Turner. Sacred and unclean. We are aristocrats, shields for the innocent . . . Dirt and ugliness strikes the shield, not our people. We take corruption on ourselves. Any crimes the State commits are our crimes, understand? They belong to our family.''

Turner blinked. "Well, what? Tell me, then. Don't let it come between us.''

"You're better off not knowing. We came here for a reason, Turner. It's a plan of Brooke's.''

"That old fraud?'' Turner said, smiling. "You're too romantic about Westerners, Seria. He looks like hot stuff to you, but he's just a burnt-out crackpot.''

She shook her head. "You don't understand. It's different in your West.'' She hugged her slim legs and rested her chin on her knee. "Someday I will get out.''

"No,'' Turner said, "it's *here* that it's different. In the West families disintegrate, money pries into everything. People don't belong to each other there, they belong to money and their institutions . . . Here at least people really care and watch over each other. . . .''

She gritted her teeth. "Watching. Yes, always. You're right, I have to go.''

He crept back through the mosquito netting of his tent on deck, and sat in the darkness for hours, savoring his misery. Tomorrow the prince's helicopter would arrive to take the prince and his sister back to the city. Soon Turner would return as well, and finish the last details, and leave. He played out a fantasy: cruising back from Vanc with a fat cashier's check. Tea with the sultan. *Er, look, Your Highness, my granddad made it big in the heroin trade, so here's two mill. Just pack the girl up in excelsior, she'll love it as an engineer's wife, believe me. . . .*

He heard the faint shuffle of footsteps against the deck. He peered through the tentflap, saw the shine of a flashlight. It was Brooke. He was carrying a valise.

The old man looked around surreptitiously and crept down over the side, to the dock. Weakened by hours of brooding, Turner was instantly inflamed by Brooke's deviousness. Turner sat still for a moment, while curiosity and misplaced fury rapidly devoured his common sense. Common sense said Brunei's secrets were none of his business, but common sense was making his life hell. Anything was better than staying awake all night wondering. He struggled quickly into shirt and jeans and boots.

He crept over the side, spotted Brooke's white suit in a patch of moonlight, and followed him. Brooke skirted the edge of the ruins, and took a trail into the jungle, full of ominous vines and the promise of snakes. Beneath a spongy litter of leaves and moss, the trail was asphalt. It had been a highway, once.

Turner shadowed Brooke closely, realizing gratefully that the deaf old man couldn't hear the crunching of his boots. The trail led uphill, into the interior. Brooke cursed goodnaturedly as a group of grunting hogs burst across the trail. Half a mile later he rested for ten long minutes in the rusting hulk of a Land Rover, while vicious gnats feasted on Turner's exposed neck and hands.

They rounded a hill and came across an encampment. Faint moonlight glittered off twelve-foot barbed wire and four dark watchtowers. The undergrowth had been burned back for yards around. There were barracks inside.

Brooke walked nonchalantly to the gate. The place looked dead. Turner crept near, sheltered by the darkness.

The gate opened. Turner crawled forward between two bushes, craning his neck.

A watchtower spotlight cacked on and framed him in dazzling light from forty yards away. Someone shouted at him through a bullhorn, in Malay. Turner lurched to his feet, blinded, and put his hands high. "Don't shoot!" he yelled, his voice cracking. "Hold your fire!"

The light flickered out. Turner stood blinking in darkness and watched four little red fireflies crawling across his chest. He realized what they were and reached higher, his spine icy. Those little red fireflies were laser sights for automatic rifles.

The guards were on him before his eyesight cleared. Dim forms in jungle camo. He saw the wicked angular magazines

in their rifles, leveled at his chest. Their heads were bulky:
they wore night-sight goggles.

They handcuffed him and hustled him forward toward the
camp. "You guys speak English?" Turner said. No answer.
"I'm a Canadian, okay?"

Brooke waited, startled, beyond the gate. "Oh," he said.
"It's you. What sort of dumbshit idea was this, Turner?"

"A really bad one," Turner said sincerely.

Brooke spoke to the guards in Malay. They lowered their
guns; one freed his hands. They stalked off unerringly back
into the darkness.

"What *is* this place?" Turner said.

Brooke turned his flashlight on Turner's face. "What does
it look like, jerk? It's a political prison." His voice was so cold
from behind the glare that Turner saw, in his mind's eye, the
sudden flash of a telegram. DEAR MADAM CHOI, REGRET TO
INFORM YOU THAT YOUR SON STEPPED ON A VIPER IN THE JUN-
GLES OF BORNEO AND YOUR BOOTS DIDN'T SAVE HIM. . . .

Brooke spoke quietly. "Did you think Brunei was all sweetness and light? It's a nation, damn it, not your toy train set.
All right, stick by me and keep your mouth shut."

Brooke waved his flashlight. A guard emerged from the
darkness and led them around the corner of the wooden barracks, which was set above the damp ground on concrete
blocks. They walked up a short flight of steps. The guard
flicked an exterior switch and the cell inside flashed into harsh
light. The guard peered through close-set bars in the heavy
ironbound door, then unlocked it with a creak of hinges.

Brooke murmured thanks and carefully shook the guard's
hand. The guard smiled below the ugly goggles and slipped
his hand inside his camo jacket.

"Come on," Brooke said. They stepped into the cell. The
door clanked shut behind them.

A dark-skinned old man was blinking wearily in the sudden
light. He sat up in his iron cot and brushed aside yellowed
mosquito netting, reaching for a pair of wire-rimmed spectacles on the floor. He wore gray-striped prison canvas: draw-
string trousers and a rough, buttoned blouse. He slipped the
spectacles carefully over his ears and looked up. "Ah," he
said. "Jimmy."

It was a bare cell: wooden floor, a chamberpot, a battered aluminum pitcher and basin. Two wire shelves above the bed held books in English and a curlicued alphabet Turner didn't recognize.

"This is Dr. Vikram Moratuwa," Brooke said. "The founder of the Partai Ekolojasi. This is Turner Choi, a prying young idiot."

"Ah," said Moratuwa. "Are we to be cellmates, young man?"

"He's not under arrest," Brooke said. "Yet." He opened his valise. "I brought you the books."

"Excellent," said Moratuwa, yawning. He had lost most of his teeth. "Ah, Mumford, Florman, and Lévi-Strauss. Thank you, Jimmy."

"I think it's okay," Brooke said, noticing Turner's stricken look. "The sultan winks at these little charity visits, if I'm discreet. I think I can talk you out of trouble, even though you put your foot in it."

"Jimmy is my oldest friend in Brunei," said Moratuwa. "There is no harm in two old men talking."

"Don't you believe it," Brooke said. "This man is a dangerous radical. He wanted to dissolve the monarchy. And him a privy councilor, too."

"Jimmy, we did not come here to be aristocrats. That is not Right Action."

Turner recognized the term. "You're a Buddhist?"

"Yes. I was with Sarvodaya Shramadana, the Buddhist technological movement. Jimmy and I met in Sri Lanka, where the Sarvodaya was born."

"Sri Lanka's a nice place to do videos," Brooke said. "I was still in the rock biz then, doing production work. Finance. But it was getting stale. Then I dropped in on a Sarvodaya rally, heard him speak. It was damned exciting!" Brooke grinned at the memory. "He was in trouble there, too. Even thirty years ago, his preaching was a little too pure for anyone's comfort."

"We were not put on this earth to make things comfortable for ourselves," Moratuwa chided. He glanced at Turner. "Brunei flourishes now, young man. We have the techniques, the expertise, the experience. It is time to fling open the doors and let Right Action spread to the whole earth! Brunei was our greenhouse, but the fields are the greater world outside.''

Brooke smiled. "Choi is building the boats.''

"Our Ocean Arks?'' said Moratuwa. "Ah, splendid.''

"I sailed here today on the first model.''

"What joyful news. You have done us a great service, Mr. Choi.''

"I don't understand,'' Turner said. "They're just sailboats.''

Brooke smiled. "To you, maybe. But imagine you're a Malaysian dock worker living on fish meal, and single-cell protein. What're you gonna think of a ship that costs nothing to build, nothing to run, and gives away free food?''

"Oh,'' said Turner slowly.

"Your sailboats will carry our Green message around the globe,'' Moratuwa said. "We teachers have a saying: 'I hear and I forget; I see and I remember; I do and I understand.' Mere preaching is only words. When people see our floating *kampongs* tied up at docks around the world, then they can touch and smell and live our life aboard those ships, then they will truly understand our Way.''

"You really think that'll work?'' Turner said.

"That is how we started here,'' Moratuwa said. "We had textbooks on the urban farm, textbooks developed in your own West, simple technologies anyone can use. Jimmy's building was our first Green *kampong*, our demonstration model. We found many to help us. Unemployment was severe, as it still is throughout the world. But idle hands can put in skylights, haul nightsoil, build simple windmills. It is not elegant, but it is food and community and pride.''

"It was a close thing between our Partai and the Moslem extremists,'' Brooke said. "They wanted to burn every trace of the West—we wanted to retrofit. We won. People could see and touch the future we offered. Food tastes better than preaching.''

"Yes, those poor Moslem fellows,'' said Moratuwa. "Still here after so many years. You must talk to the sultan about an amnesty, Jimmy.''

"They shot his brother in front of his family,'' Brooke said. "Seria saw it happen. She was only a child.''

Turner felt a spasm of pain for her. She had never told him.

But Moratuwa shook his head. "The royals went too far in protecting their power. They tried to bottle up our Way, to control it with their royal *adat*. But they cannot lock out the world forever, and lock up those who want fresh air. They only imprison themselves. Ask your Seria." He smiled. "Buddha was a prince also, but he left his palace when the world called out."

Brooke laughed sourly. "Old troublemakers are stubborn." He looked at Turner. "This man's still loyal to our old dream, all that wild-eyed stuff that's buried under twenty years. He could be out of here with a word, if he promised to be cool and follow the *adat*. It's a crime to keep him in here. But the royal family aren't saints, they're politicians. They can't afford the luxury of innocence."

Turner thought it through, sadly. He realized now that he had found the ghost behind those huge old Green Party wall-posters, those peeling Whole Earth sermons buried under sport ads and Malay movie stars. This was the man who had saved Seria's family—and this was where they had put him. "The sultan's not very grateful," Turner said.

"That's not the problem. You see, my friend here doesn't really give a damn about Brunei. He wants to break the green-house doors off, and never mind the trouble to the locals. He's not satisfied to save one little postage-stamp country. He's got the world on his conscience."

Moratuwa smiled indulgently. "And my friend Jimmy has the world in his computer terminal. He is a wicked Westerner. He has kept the simple natives pure, while he is drenched in whiskey and the Net."

Brooke winced. "Yeah. Neither one of us really belongs here. We're both goddamn outside agitators, is all. We came here together. His words, my money—we thought we could change things everywhere. Brunei was going to be our laboratory. Brunei was just small enough, and desperate enough, to listen to a couple of crackpots." He tugged at his hearing aid and glared at Turner's smile. "You're no prize either, Choi. Y'know, I was wrong about you. I'm glad you're leaving."

"Why?" Turner said, hurt.

"You're too straight, and you're too much trouble. I checked

you out through the Net a long time ago—I know all about
your granddad the smack merchant and all that Triad shit. I
thought you'd be cool. Instead you had to be the knight in
shining armor—bloody robot, that's what you are.''

Turner clenched his fist. ''Sorry I didn't follow your program, you old bastard.''

''She's like a daughter to me,'' Brooke said. ''A quick bump-
and-grind okay, we all need it, but you had to come on like
Prince Charming. Well, you're getting on that chopper tomorrow, and it's back to Babylon for you, kid.''

''Yeah?'' Turner said defiantly. ''Or else, huh? You'd put me
in this place?''

Brooke shook his head. ''I won't have to. Think it over, Mr.
Choi. You know damn well where you belong.''

It was a grim trip back. Seria caught his mood at once.
When she saw his bad cop scowl, her morning-after smile died
like a moth in a killing bottle. She knew it was over. They
didn't say much. The roar of the copter blades would have
drowned it anyway.

The shipyard was crammed with the framework of a massive
Ocean Ark. It had been simple to scale the process up with the
programs he'd downloaded. The work crew was overjoyed, but
Turner's long-expected triumph had turned to ashes for him.
He printed out a letter of resignation and took it to the minister
of industry.

The minister's *kampong* was still expanding. They had
webbed off a whole city block under great tent-like sheets of
translucent plastic, which hung from the walls of tall buildings
like giant dew-soaked spiderwebs. Women and children were
casually ripping up the streets with picks and hoes, revealing
long-smothered topsoil. The sewers had been grubbed up and
diverted into long troughs choked with watercress.

The minister lived in a long flimsy tent of cotton batik. He
was catching an afternoon snooze in a woven hammock anchored to a highrise wall and strung to an old lamp post.

Turner woke him up.

''I see,'' the minister yawned, slipping on his sandals. ''Ill-
ness in the family, is it? You have my sympathies. When may
we expect you back?''

Turner shook his head. "The job's done. Those 'bots will be pasting up ships from now till doomsday."

"But you still have two months to run. You should oversee the line until we're sure we have the beetles out."

"Bugs," Turner said. "There aren't any." He knew it was true. Building ships that simple was monkey-work. Humans could have done it.

"There's plenty of other work here for a man of your talents."

"Hire someone else."

The minister frowned. "I shall have to complain to Kyocera."

"I'm quitting them, too."

"Quitting your multinational? At this early stage in your career? Is that wise?"

Turner closed his eyes and summoned his last dregs of patience. "Why should I care? Tuan Minister, I've never even *seen* them."

Turner cut a last deal with the bootleg boys down on Floor 4 and sneaked into his room with an old gas can full of rice beer. The little screen on the end of the nozzle was handy for filtering out the thickest dregs. He poured himself a long one and looked around the room. He had to start packing.

He began stripping the walls and tossing souvenirs onto his bed, pausing to knock back long shuddery glugs of warm rice beer. Packing was painfully easy. He hadn't brought much. The room looked pathetic. He had another beer.

His bonsai tree was dying. There was no doubt of it now. The cramping of its tiny pot was murderous. "You poor little bastard," Turner told it, his voice thick with self-pity. On impulse, he broke its pot with his boot. He carried the tree gently across the room, and buried its gnarled roots in the rich black dirt of the windowbox. "There," he said, wiping his hands on his jeans. "Now *grow*, dammit!"

It was Friday night again. They were showing another free movie down in the park. Turner ignored it and called Vancouver.

"No video again?" Georgie said.

"No."

"I'm glad you called, anyway. It's bad, Turner. The Paipei cousins are here. They're hovering around the old man like a pack of buzzards."

"They're in good company, then."

"Jesus, Turner! Don't say that kind of crap! Look, Honorable Grandfather's been asking about you every day. How soon can you get here?"

Turner looked in his notebook. "I've booked passage on a freighter to Labuan Island. That's Malaysian territory. I can get a plane there, a puddle-jumper to Manila. Then a Japan Air jet to Midway and another to Vanc. That puts me in at, uh, eight P.M. your time Monday."

"Three *days*?"

"There are no *planes* here, Georgie."

"All right, if that's the best you can do. It's too bad about this video. Look, I want you to call him at the hospital, okay? Tell him you're coming."

"Now?" said Turner, horrified.

Georgie exploded. "I'm sick of doing your explaining, man! Face up to your goddamn obligations, for once! The least you can do is call him and play good boy grandson! I'm gonna call-forward you from here."

"Okay, you're right," Turner said. "Sorry, Georgie, I know it's been a strain."

Georgie looked down and hit a key. White static blurred, a phone rang, and Turner was catapulted to his Grandfather's bedside.

The old man was necrotic. His cheekbones stuck out like wedges, and his lips were swollen and blue. Stacks of monitors blinked beside his bed. Turner spoke in halting Mandarin. "Hello, Grandfather. It's your grandson, Turner. How are you?"

The old man fixed his horrible eyes on the screen. "Where is your picture, boy?"

"This is Borneo, Grandfather. They don't have modern telephones."

"What kind of place is that? Have they no respect?"

"It's politics, Grandfather."

Grandfather Choi scowled. A chill of terror went through Turner. Good God, he thought, I'm going to look like that when I'm old. His grandfather said, ''I don't recall giving my permission for this.''

''It was just eight months, Grandfather.''

''You prefer these barbarians to your own family, is that it?''

Turner said nothing. The silence stretched painfully. ''They're not barbarians,'' he blurted at last.

''What's that, boy?''

Turner switched to English. ''They're British Commonwealth, like Hong Kong was. Half of them are Chinese.''

Grandfather sneered and followed him to English. ''Why they need you, then?''

''They need me,'' Turner said tightly, ''because I'm a trained engineer.''

His Grandfather peered at the blank screen. He looked feeble suddenly, confused. He spoke Chinese. ''Is this some sort of trick? My son's boy doesn't talk like that. What is that howling I hear?''

The movie was reaching a climax downstairs. Visceral crunches and screaming. It all came boiling up inside Turner then. ''What's it sound like, old man? A Triad gang war?''

His grandfather turned pale. ''That's it, boy. Is all over for you.''

''Great,'' Turner said, his heart racing. ''Maybe we can be honest, just this once.''

''My money bought you diapers, boy.''

''*Fang-pa*,'' Turner said. ''Dog's-fart. You made our lives hell with that money. You turned my dad into a drunk and my brother into an ass-kisser. That's blood money from junkies and I wouldn't take it if you begged me!''

''You talk big, boy, but you don't show the face,'' the old man said. He raised one shrunken fist, his bandaged forearm trailing tubes. ''If you were here I give you a good beating.''

Turner laughed giddily. He felt like a hero. ''You old fraud! Go on, give the money to Uncle's kids. They're gonna piss on your altar every day, you stupid old bastard.''

''They're good children, not like you.''

''They hate your guts, old man. Wise up.''

''Yes, they hate me,'' the old man admitted gloomily. The truth seemed to fill him with grim satisfaction. He nestled his head back into his pillow like a turtle into its shell. ''They all want more money, more, more, more. You want it, too, boy, don't lie to me.''

"Don't need it," Turner said airily. "They don't use money here."

"Barbarians," his grandfather said. "But you need it when you come home."

"I'm staying here," Turner said. "I *like* it here. I'm free here, understand? Free of the money and free of the family and free of you!"

"Wicked boy," his grandfather said. "I was like you once. I did bad things to be free." He sat up in bed, glowering. "But at least I helped my family."

"I could never be like you," Turner said.

"You wait till they come after you with their hands out," his grandfather said, stretching out one wrinkled palm. "The end of the world couldn't hide you from them."

"What do you mean?"

His grandfather chuckled with an awful satisfaction. "I leave you all the money, Mr. Big Freedom. You see what you do then when you're in my shoes."

"I don't want it!" Turner shouted. "I'll give it all to charity!"

"No you won't," his grandfather said. "You'll think of your duty to your family, like I had to. From now on *you* take care of them, Mr. Runaway, Mr. High and Mighty."

"I won't!" Turner said. "You can't!"

"I'll die happy now," his grandfather said, closing his eyes. He lay back on the pillow and grinned feebly. "It worth it just to see the look on their faces."

"You can't make me!" Turner yelled. "I'll never go back, understand? I'm staying—"

The line went dead.

Turner shut down his phone and stowed it away.

He had to talk to Brooke. Brooke would know what to do. Somehow, Turner would play off one old man against the other.

Turner still felt shocked by the turn of events, but beneath his confusion he felt a soaring confidence. At last he had faced down his grandfather. After that, Brooke would be easy. Brooke would find some loophole in the Bruneian government that would protect him from the old man's legacy. Turner would stay safe in Brunei. It was the best place in the world to frustrate the banks of the Global Net.

But Brooke was still on the river, on his boat.

Turner decided to meet Brooke the moment he docked in town. He couldn't wait to tell Brooke about his decision to stay in Brunei for good. He was feverish with excitement. He had wrenched his life out of the program now; everything was different. He saw everything from a fresh new angle, with a *bricoleur*'s eyes. His whole life was waiting for a retrofit.

He took the creaking elevator to the ground floor. In the park outside, the movie crowd was breaking up. Turner hitched a ride in the pedicab of some teenagers from a waterfront *kampong*. He took the first shift pedaling, and got off a block away from the dock Brooke used.

The cracked concrete quays were sheltered under a long, rambling roof of tin and geodesic bamboo. Half-a-dozen fishing smacks floated at the docks, beside an elderly harbor dredge. Brooke's first boat, a decrepit pleasure cruiser, was in permanent drydock with its diesel engine in pieces.

The headman of the dock *kampong* was a plump, motherly Malay grandmother. She and her friends were having a Friday night quilting bee, repairing canvas sails under the yellow light of an alcohol lamp.

Brooke was not expected back until morning. Turner was determined to wait him out. He had not asked permission to sleep out from his *kampong*, but after a long series of garbled translations he established that the locals would vouch for him later. He wandered away from the chatter of Malay gossip and found a dark corner.

He fell back on a floury pile of rice bags, watching from the darkness, unable to sleep. Whenever his eyes closed, his brain ran a loud interior monologue, rehearsals for his talk with Brooke.

The women worked on, wrapped in the lamp's mild glow. Innocently, they enjoyed themselves, secure in their usefulness. Yet Turner knew machines could have done the sewing faster and easier. Already, through reflex, as he watched, some corner of his mind pulled the task to computerized pieces, thinking: simplify, analyze, reduce.

But to what end? What was it really for, all that tech he'd learned? He'd become an engineer for reasons of his own. Because it offered a way out for him, because the gift for it had always been there in his brain and hands and eyes. . . . Because of the rewards it offered him. Freedom, independence, money, the rewards of the West.

But what control did he have? Rewards could be snatched away without warning. He'd seen others go to the wall when their specialties ran dry. Education and training were no defense. Not today, when a specialist's knowledge could be programmed into a computerized expert system.

Was he really any safer than these Bruneians? A thirty-minute phone call could render these women obsolete—but a society that could do their work with robots would have no use for their sails. Within their little greenhouse, their miniature world of gentle technologies, they had more control than he did.

People in the West talked about the "technical elite"—and Turner knew it was a damned lie. Technology roared on, running full-throttle on the world's last dregs of oil, but no one was at the wheel, not realy. Massive institutions, both governments and corporations, fumbled for control, but couldn't understand. They had no hands-on feel for tech and what it meant, for the solid feeling in a good design.

The "technical elite" were errand boys. They didn't decide how to study, what to work on, where they could be most useful, or to what end. Money decided that. Technicians were owned by the abstract ones and zeros in bankers' microchips, paid out by silk-suit hustlers who'd never touched a wrench. Knowledge wasn't power, not really, not for engineers. There were too many abstractions in the way.

But the gift was real—Brooke had told him so, and now Turner realized it was true. That was the reason for engineering. Not for money, because there was more money in shuffling paper. Not for power; that was in management. For the gift itself.

He leaned back in darkness, smelling tar and rice dust. For the first time, he truly felt he understood what he was doing. Now that he had defied his family and his past, he saw his work in a new light. It was something bigger than just his private escape hatch. It was a worthy pursuit on its own merits: a thing of dignity.

It all began to fall into place for him, then, bringing with it a warm sense of absolute rightness. He yawned, nestling his head into the burlap.

He would live here and help them. Brunei was a new world, a world built on a human scale, where people mattered. No it didn't have the flash of a hot CAD CAM establishment with its tons of goods and reams of printout; it didn't have that technical sweetness and heroic scale.

But it was still good work. A man wasn't a Luddite because he worked for people instead of abstractions. The green technologies demanded *more* intelligence, more reason, more of the engineer's true gift. Because they went against the blind momentum of a dead century, with all its rusting monuments of arrogance and waste. . . .

Turner squirmed drowsily into the scrunchy comfort of the rice bags, in the fading grip of his epiphany. Within him, some unspoken knot of division and tension eased, bringing a new and deep relief. As always, just before sleep, his thoughts turned to Seria. Somehow, he would deal with that too. He wasn't sure just how yet, but it could wait. It was different now that he was staying. Everything was working out. He was on a roll.

Just as he drifted off, he half-heard a thrashing scuffle as a *kampong* cat seized and tore a rat behind the bags.

A stevedore shook him awake the next morning. They needed the rice. Turner sat up, his mouth gummy with hangover. His T-shirt and jeans were caked with dust.

Brooke had arrived. They were loading provisions aboard his ship: bags of rice, dried fruit, compost fertilizer. Turner, smiling, hoisted a bag over his shoulder and swaggered up the ramp on board.

Brooke oversaw the loading from a canvas deck chair. He was unshaven, nervously picking at a gaudy acoustic guitar. He started violently when Turner dropped the bag at his feet.

"Thank God you're here!" he said. "Get out of sight!" He grabbed Turner's arm and hustled him across the deck into the greenhouse.

Turner stumbled along reluctantly. "What the hell? How'd you know I was coming here?"

Brooke shut the greenhouse door. He pointed through a dew-streaked pane at the dock. "See that little man with the black songkak hat?"

"Yeah?"

"He's from the Ministry of Islamic Banking. He just came from your. *kampong*, looking for you. Big news from the gnomes of Zurich. You're hot property now, kid."

Turner folded his arms defiantly. "I've made my decision, Tuan Councilor. I threw it over. Everything. My family, the West . . . I don't want that money. I'm turning it down! I'm staying."

Brooke ignored him, wiping a patch of glass with his sleeve. "If they get their hooks into your cash flow, you'll never get out of here." Brooke glanced at him, alarmed. "You didn't sign anything, did you?"

Turner scowled. "You haven't heard a word I've said, have you?"

Brooke tugged at his hearing aid. "What? These damn batteries . . . Look, I got spares in my cabin. We'll check it out, have a talk." He waved Turner back, opened the greenhouse door slightly, and shouted a series of orders to the crew in their Dayak dialect. "Come on," he told Turner.

They left by a second door, and sneaked across a patch of open deck, then down a flight of plywood steps into the center hull.

Brooke lifted the paisley bedspread of his cabin bunk and hauled out an ancient steamer chest. He pulled a jingling set of keys from his pocket and opened it. Beneath a litter of ruffled shirts, a shaving kit, and cans of hair spray, the trunk was packed to the gills with electronic contraband: coax cables, multiplexers, buffers and converters, shiny plug-in cards still in their heat-sealed baggies, multiplugged surge suppressors wrapped in tentacles of black extension cord. "Christ," Turner said. He heard a gentle thump as the ship came loose, followed by a rattle of rigging as the crew hoisted sail.

After a long search, Brooke found batteries in a cloisonné box. He popped them into place.

Turner said, "Admit it! You're surprised to see me, aren't you? Still think you were wrong about me?"

Brooke looked puzzled. "Surprised? Didn't you get Seria's message on the Net?"

"What? No. I slept on the docks last night."

"You missed the message?" Brooke said. He mulled it over. "Why are you here, then?"

"You said you could help me if I ever had money trouble," Turner said. "Well, now's the time. You gotta figure some way to get me out of this bank legacy. I know it doesn't look like it, but I've broken with my family for good. I'm gonna stay here, try to work things out with Seria?"

Brooke frowned. "I don't understand. You want to stay with Seria?"

"Yes, here in Brunei, with her!" Turner sat on the bunk and waved his arms passionately. "Look, I know I told you that Brunei was just a glass bubble, sealed off from the world, and all that. But I've changed now! I've thought it through, I understand things. Brunei's important! It's small, but it's the ideas that matter, not the scale. I can get along, I'll fit in—you said so yourself."

"What about Seria?"

"Okay, that's part of it," Turner admitted. "I know she'll never leave this place. I can defy my family and it's no big deal, but she's Royalty. She wouldn't leave here, any more than you'd leave all your money behind. So you're both trapped here. All right. I can accept that." Turner looked up, his face glowing with determination. "I know things won't be easy for Seria and me, but it's up to me to make the sacrifice. Someone has to make the grand gesture. Well, it might as well be me."

Brooke was silent for a moment, then thumped him on the shoulder. "This is a new Turner I'm seeing. So you faced down the old smack merchant, huh? You're quite the hero!"

Turner felt sheepish. "Come on, Brooke."

"And turning down all that nice money, too."

Turner brushed his hands together, dismissing the idea. "I'm sick of being manipulated by old geezers."

Brooke rubbed his unshaven jaw and grinned. "Kid, you've got a lot to learn." He walked to the door. "But that's okay, no harm done. Everything still works out. Let's go up on deck and make sure the coast is clear.''

Turner followed Brooke to his deck chair by the bamboo railing. The ship sailed rapidly down a channel between mud flats. Already they'd left the waterfront, paralleling a shoreline densely fringed with mangroves. Brooke sat down and opened a binocular case. He scanned the city behind them.

Turner felt a lightheaded sense of euphoria as the triple bows cut the water. He smiled as they passed the first offshore rig. It looked like a good place to get some fishing done.

"About this bank," Turner said. "We have to face them some time—what good is this doing us?"

Brooke smiled without looking up from his binoculars. "Kid, I've been planning this day a long time. I'm running it on a wing and a prayer. But, hey, I'm not proud, I can adapt. You've been a lot of trouble to me, stomping in where angels fear to tread, in those damn boots of yours. But I've finally found a way to fit you in. Turner, I'm going to retrofit your life.''

"Think so?" Turner said. He stepped closer, looming over Brooke. "What are you looking for, anyway?"

Brooke sighed. "Choppers. Patrol boats.''

Turner had a sudden terrifying flash of insight. "You're leaving Brunei. Defecting!'' He stared at Brooke. "You bastard! You kept me on board!'' He grabbed the rail, then began tearing at his heavy boots, ready to jump and swim for it.

"Don't be stupid!'' Brooke said. "You'll get her in a lot of trouble!'' He lowered the binoculars. "Oh Christ, here comes Omar.''

Turner followed his gaze and spotted a helicopter, rising gnatlike over the distant high-rises. "Where is Seria?''

"Try the bow.''

"You mean she's here? She's leaving too?'' He ran forward across the thudding deck.

Seria wore bell-bottomed sailor's jeans and a stained nylon windbreaker. With the help of two of the Dayak crew, she was installing a meshwork satellite dish in an anchored iron plate in the deck. She had cut away her long dyed hair; she looked up at him, and for a moment he saw a stranger. Then her face shifted, fell into a familiar focus. "I thought I'd never see you again, Turner. That's why I had to do it."

Turner smiled at her fondly, too overjoyed for her words to sink in. "Do what, angel?"

"Tap your phone, of course. I did it because I was jealous, at first. I had to be sure. You know. But then when I knew you were leaving, well, I had to hear your voice one last time. So I heard your talk with your Grandfather. Are you mad at me?"

"You tapped my phone? You heard all that?" Turner said.

"Yes, darling. You were wonderful. I never thought you'd do it."

"Well," Turner said, "I never thought you'd pull a stunt like this, either."

"Someone had to make a grand gesture," she said. "It was up to me, wasn't it? But I explained all that in my message."

"So you're defecting? Leaving your family?" Turner knelt beside her, dazed. As he struggled to fit it all together, his eyes focussed on a cross-threaded nut at the base of the dish. He absently picked up a socket wrench. "Let me give you a hand with that," he said through reflex.

Seria sucked on a barked knuckle. "You didn't get my last message, did you? You came here on your own!"

"Well, yeah," Turner said. "I decided to stay. You know. With you."

"And now we're abducting you!" She laughed. "How romantic!"

"You and Brooke were leaving together?"

"It's not just me, Turner. Look."

Brooke was walking toward them, and with him Dr. Moratuwa, newly outfitted in saffron-colored baggy shorts and T-shirt. They were the work clothes of a Buddhist technician. "Oh, no," Turner said. He dropped his wrench with a thud.

Seria said, "Now you see why I had to leave, don't you? My family locked him up. I had to break *adat* and help Brooke set him free. It was my obligation, my *dharma*!"

"I guess that makes sense," Turner said. "But it's gonna take me a while, that's all. Couldn't you have warned me?"

"I tried to! I wrote you on the Net!" She saw he was crestfallen, and squeezed his hand. "I guess the plans broke down. Well, we can improvise."

"Good day, Mr. Choi," said Moratuwa. "It was very brave of you to cast in your lot with us. It was a gallant gesture."

"Thanks," Turner said. He took a deep breath. So they were all leaving. It was a shock, but he could deal with it. He'd just have to start over and think it through from a different angle. At least Seria was coming along.

He felt a little better now. He was starting to get it under control.

Moratuwa sighed. "And I wish it could have worked."

"Your brother's coming," Brooke told Seria gloomily. "Remember this was all my fault."

They had a good headwind, but the crown prince's helicopter came on faster, its drone growing to a roar. A Gurkha palace guard crouched on the broad orange float outside the canopy, cradling a light machine gun. His gold-braided dress uniform flapped in the chopper's downwash.

The chopper circled the boat once. "We've had it," Brooke said. "Well, at least it's not a patrol boat with those damned Exocet missiles. It's family business with the princess on board. They'll hush it all up. You can always depend on *adat*." He patted Moratuwa's shoulder. "Looks like you get a cellmate after all, old man."

Seria ignored them. She was looking up anxiously. "Poor Omar," she said. She cupped her hands to her mouth. "Brother, be careful!" she shouted.

The Prince's copilot handed the guard a loudspeaker. The guard raised it and began to shout a challenge.

The tone of the chopper's engines suddenly changed. Plumes of brown smoke billowed from the chromed exhausts. The prince veered away suddenly, fighting the controls. The guard, caught off balance, tumbled headlong into the ocean. The Dayak crew, who had been waiting for the order to reef sails, began laughing wildly.

"What in hell?" Brooke said.

The chopper pancaked down heavily into the bay, rocking in the ship's wake. Spurting caramel-colored smoke, its engines died with a hideous grinding. The ship sailed on. They watched silently as the drenched guard swam up and clung to the chopper's float.

Brooke raised his eyes to heaven. "Lord Buddha, forgive my doubts. . . ."

"Sugar," Seria said sadly. "I put a bag of sugar in brother's fuel tank. I ruined his beautiful chopper. Poor Omar, he really loves that machine."

Brooke stared at her, then burst into cackling laughter. Regally, Seria ignored him. She stared at the dwindling shore, her eyes bright. "Good-bye, Brunei. You cannot hold us now."

"Where are we going?" Turner asked.

"To the West," said Moratuwa. "The Ocean Arks will spread for many years. I must set the example by carrying the word to the greatest global center of unsustainable industry."

Brooke grinned. "He means America, man."

"We shall start in Hawaii. It is also tropical and our expertise will find ready application there."

"Wait a minute," Turner said. "I turned my back on all that! Look, I turned down a fortune so I could stay in the East."

Seria took his arm, smiling radiantly. "You're such a dreamer, darling. What a wonderful gesture. I love you, Turner."

"Look," said Brooke, "I left behind my building, my title of nobility, and all my old mates. I'm older than you, so my romantic gestures come first."

"But," Turner said, "it was all decided. I was going to help you in Brunei. I had ideas, plans. Now none of it makes any sense."

Moratuwa smiled. "The world is not built from your blueprints, young man."

"Whose, then?" Turner demanded. "Yours?"

"Nobody's, really," Brooke said. "We all just have to do our best with whatever comes up. *Bricolage*, remember?" Brooke spread his hands. "But it's a geezer's world, kid. We got your number, and we got you outnumbered. Fast cars and future shock and that hot Western trip . . . that's another century. We like slow days in the sun. We like a place to belong and gentle things around us." He smiled. "Okay, you're a little wired now, but you'll calm down by the time we reach Hawaii. There's a lot of retrofit work there. You'll be one of us!'' He gestured at the satellite dish. ''We'll set this up and call your banks first thing.''

''It's a good world for us, Turner,'' Seria said urgently. ''Not quite East, not quite West—like us two. It was made for us, it's what we're best at.'' She embraced him.

''You escaped,'' Turner said. No one ever said much about what happened after Sleeping Beauty awoke.

''Yes, I broke free,'' she said, hugging him tighter. ''And I'm taking you with me.''

Turner stared over her shoulder at Brunei, sinking into hot green mangroves and warm mud. Slowly, he could feel the truth of it, sliding over him like some kind of ambiguous quicksand. He was going to fit right in. He could see his future laid out before him, clean and predestined, like fifty years of happy machine language.

''Maybe I wanted this,'' he said at last. ''But it sure as hell wasn't what I planned.''

Brooke laughed. ''Look, you're bound for Hawaii with a princess and eight million dollars. Somehow, you'll just have to make do.''